She looked again at the scrap of paper, at Wilmot's name scrawled at the bottom of the few lines. Did it look shaky, as if written with a trembling hand, the hand of a man tortured and sick? 'We've got to keep going,' she said desperately. 'We've got to look after the children and ourselves and make sure Wilmot's got a home to come back to.'

She'd known even then that she was fooling herself, trying desperately to keep up a pretence because she could not bear to think of Wilmot, her darling, cheeky-faced sailor husband, being tortured and beaten but, as the time dragged by, she'd have to face it. The stories were too many to be discounted . . .

Now, however, on this dull and drizzly August morning, it was over at last, and soon, surely, Wilmot would be coming back. To a home that wouldn't be just as he remembered it, but a home nevertheless. And even though the house had been damaged – and again she turned her memory away from the thought of that night – it still stood, and they'd even been able to keep the business running. With Wilmot home again, the plans would leap ahead. For Wilmot would surely come out of the Navy now, and settle down at last in civvy street. The war would be behind them.

Lilian Harry grew up close to Portsmouth Harbour, where her earliest memories are of nights spent in an air-raid shelter listening to the drone of enemy aircraft and the thunder of exploding bombs. But her memories are also those of a warm family life shared with two brothers and a sister in a tiny back-street house where hard work, love and laughter went hand in hand. Lilian Harry now lives on the edge of Dartmoor where she has two ginger cats to love and laugh at. She has a son and daughter and two grand-children and, as well as gardening, country dancing and church bellringing, she loves to walk on the moors and – whenever possible – to go skiing in the mountains of Europe. She has written a number of books under other names, including historical novels and contemporary romances.

By Lilian Harry

Love & Laughter

LILIAN HARRY

ORION

An Orion paperback
First published in Great Britain by Orion in 1998
This paperback edition published in 1999 by
Orion Books Ltd,
Orion House, 5 Upper St Martin's Lane,
London WC2H 9EA

Third impression 2001

A CIP catalogue record for this book
is available from the British Library.

ISBN: 0 75282 605 0

Typeset at The Spartan Press Ltd, Lymington
Printed and bound in Great Britain by
Clays Ltd, St Ives plc

To Lesley, with love

Chapter One

Geoff Pengelly burst in from the street, his red hair standing on end, school tie little more than a knot of coloured string around his neck, blue eyes ablaze. He tore into the narrow hallway, almost colliding with a guest on his way out, skidded on the multi-coloured rug his grandmother had spent so many evenings making out of old rags, and hurled himself through the kitchen door to where the rest of the family was finishing breakfast.

'It's *over*! The war's really over! They've given in – just like that – the Japs've *given in*!' He skidded to a halt by the kitchen table, almost knocking his mother over as she started to her feet. 'Mum, it's over, we've *won* – Dad'll be able to come home.'

Lucy Pengelly stared at her son. 'Where d'you hear that?'

Geoff jigged impatiently from one foot to the other. 'Everyone's talking about it. People are coming back from work already – they've all got two days off. We'd have heard it ourselves if we'd got the wireless on.'

'Us'd have had it on too, if you'd got that accumulator charged yesterday like I told you,' his grandmother said from the end of the table. 'Always putting things off till tomorrow, that's your trouble. Why, when I was a liddle maid—'

'Never mind that now, Mum.' Lucy sat down as suddenly as she'd jumped up. 'If it's true that the Japs have given in . . .' She looked at her son again. 'Why? I thought they'd never surrender. Said they couldn't lose face. What happened?'

1

'I dunno. It's those big bombs the Yanks dropped, I think. Couldn't take it.' Geoffrey spoke with a touch of scorn. 'They should see what it's like in Plymouth. We had *thousands* of bombs and we never gave in.'

'These were atom bombs, though, weren't they?' Arthur Pengelly said. 'They were bigger than anything that's ever been used before. Just one of 'em could do more damage than all the bombs we had during the whole of the Blitz.'

Lucy had a brief vision of a Japanese city, laid waste in a few minutes by just one huge bomb, as Plymouth and Portsmouth and other cities had been in weeks or months by thousands. She tried to visualise the kind of explosion it must have been, to wreak even more terrible damage than had happened during those flame-filled weeks of the blitz in 1941 and all the others that had followed. In one night . . . But her sudden, unexpected flash of compassion for the innocents who had burned in the Japanese pyre was swiftly overtaken by the realisation of what it meant to her, to the family, to the whole of Britain, to the world . . . The war was over. *Over.*

And Wilmot would be coming home.

It would be a curious celebration.

In a way, it had all been done already, when the news of Victory in Europe had come at the beginning of May. Then, there'd been some warning and everyone had known in those last few days that the announcement would surely come. Mr Churchill, whose rousing speeches had kept their hearts up through the darkest days of the Battle of Britain, Dunkirk and the Blitz, and who had brought them the great news of D-Day, seemed reluctant to speak too soon of victory. But at last at three o'clock in the afternoon, he had made his historic broadcast and then everyone had gone mad, waving flags, blowing whistles, climbing lamp-posts and dancing all down the streets. Every ship in Devonport and the Sound had let off their hooters, and every church that was still standing and had bells to ring chimed in to join the general cacophony. And Lucy's mother had written to tell her that it was just the same back in Pompey. Every ship in the harbour, every church bell, every whistle and every wooden rattle, every drum. And for those who had no instrument, every pair of saucepan lids.

The rejoicings seemed to have been going on ever since. Dancing in the streets had extended to organised street parties, and for every ship that came home there was a new parade with bands playing and crowds to greet the returning heroes. And heroes they were, Arthur Pengelly said, every one of them. He'd served in the Great War – the one they were now calling the First World War – and he knew.

However, for all the gladness, there were still some hearts that ached: for the men who would not come home, and for those who were still caught up in the conflict. The war in the Far East had not yet ended and there was still the fear that many would die in action. And still many thousands held prisoner, in conditions that Lucy hardly dared think about.

'He says they're being treated well,' she'd said to her mother-in-law in the early days, holding the scrap of paper that was all Wilmot could send. 'He *says* so.'

'And what else could he say?' Maud Pengelly demanded, mopping her eyes. 'They're not going to let anyone tell the truth, are they? If it's all true what people say about the way they're torturing our boys and making them slave—'

'Mum, don't,' Lucy begged. 'It doesn't help to torment ourselves. We don't know that it's true. And it might not be all the camps, anyway – just one or two.' She looked again at the scrap of paper, at Wilmot's name scrawled at the bottom of the few lines. Did it look shaky, as if written with a trembling hand, the hand of a man tortured and sick? 'We've got to keep going,' she said desperately. 'We've got

3

to look after the children and ourselves and make sure Wilmot's got a home to come back to.'

She'd known even then that she was fooling herself, trying desperately to keep up a pretence because she could not bear to think of Wilmot, her darling, cheeky-faced sailor husband, being tortured and beaten but, as the time dragged by, she'd had to face it. The stories were too many to be discounted; and she came to understand that it would be wrong to go on pretending. If only I could share it with him, she'd thought then, if only I could help him bear it . . .

Now, however, on this dull and drizzly August morning, it was over at last, and soon, surely, Wilmot would be coming back. To a home that wouldn't be just as he remembered it, but a home nevertheless. And even though the house had been damaged – and again she turned her memory away from the thought of that night – it still stood, and they'd even been able to keep the business running. It was still a hotel – or more properly a guest house – of sorts. And already she'd begun to make plans to rebuild, to improve, to look forward.

With Wilmot home again, the plans would leap ahead. For Wilmot would surely come out of the Navy now, and settle down at last in civvy street. He would be at home all the time, a husband who shared her bed every night instead of occasionally, a father who could help bring up his children. And he would be filled with enthusiasm for this new life, full of plans for the future. The war would be behind them and, as the songs all said, there would be love and laughter, and peace ever after.

Tomorrow – when the world was free.

Lucy had been just eighteen when she first met Wilmot Pengelly. It had always been on the cards, of course, that she would marry a sailor. There were so many of them in Portsmouth, stationed on HMS *Vernon*, or over at Gosport

4

on the submarine base, HMS *Dolphin*, or serving aboard the many ships that were based in 'Pompey'. All the same, the Travers family weren't best pleased that it looked like being a Plymouth chap.

'I can't see why she had to pick a Devon boy,' Emily Travers said to her husband when Lucy went out to the front door to say goodnight to Wilmot, the first time she brought him home. 'Aren't there good enough ones in Portsmouth? I don't want her moving down to Devonshire.'

'You're being a bit previous, aren't you, girl? She's only known the bloke a week. Anyway, he'll be off back to sea before they can get too serious about each other, and his ship probably won't come to Pompey again.'

Lucy, too, dismissed her mother's fears. 'Don't be daft, Mum. You won't lose track of me. Even if I did move to Devon – and I'm not saying I ever would, mind – I'd still come back and see you. And it's a smashing place for a holiday.'

Emily sniffed. She and Joe hadn't had a holiday since they'd been on their honeymoon, back in 1908, and that had just been a weekend spent with her mother's cousin in London. Holidays were for people who could afford such luxuries, not for the likes of the Travers family. 'Plain, ordinary folk, that's what we are,' she said. 'It's all we can do to keep a home for you youngsters, with food on the table and clothes on your backs, never mind gallivanting round the countryside on holidays. But I suppose that chap knows all about such things, what with his mum and dad running a hotel in Plymouth.'

'I don't think it's a very big place,' Lucy said. 'Nothing really grand. It's just a sort of guest house, for commercial travellers and people wanting a bit of a holiday.'

However, any sort of hotel seemed grand to Emily. 'Don't you let it go to your head, that's all. I don't want you getting serious about a chap you're hardly ever going to see.'

'Serious!' Lucy said, and laughed. 'Wilmot's not the serious sort. He's always laughing and joking – that's what I like about him.'

'That doesn't mean he can't be serious about a girl,' Emily said, and she repeated her fears to Joe later on, as they got ready for bed. The rest of the family were all asleep – Lucy and her sisters in the back bedroom, the two boys in the front room downstairs. 'There was a look in his eye – he's proper sweet on her, you can tell he is. It's not that I don't like him, Joe – if you want the truth, I think he's the best of all the boys she's brought home yet – I just wish he was a Pompey chap.'

'Well, he'll be going off to sea soon.' Joe had been working on Wilmot's ship, doing repairs as it lay moored against the jetty in the dockyard, and he knew that the job would be over in a few days. 'I daresay they'll forget about each other in a couple of weeks. You know what our Lucy's like. She likes a bit of life – she's not the sort to stay indoors mooning after a chap.'

Wilmot did go away soon. His ship continued on its journey to Scotland and Scandinavia, and Lucy continued her life as before, setting out each morning to work at the naval outfitters where she was an apprentice, and going to the pictures with her sisters or out to walk along Southsea front with her friends. She didn't seem bothered about getting a new boyfriend, so when Emily opened the door one evening to find Wilmot standing on the step, a battered kitbag beside him, she wasn't altogether surprised.

'Wilmot! What on earth are you doing here?'

His cheeky face, ruddy from weeks at sea, looked anxious. 'I came to see Lucy, Mrs Travers. Is it all right? Is she in?'

'But where've you come from? I thought your ship was on its way to Scotland.'

'It is. I mean, it's there now, but I got a leave pass.' His eyes went past her, trying to see into the narrow passageway. 'I've only got tonight – it took me two days to hitch-hike here and I'm due back on Monday morning.'

'Well, you'd better come in.' Emily felt disturbed but knew better than to try to resist the inevitable. She looked at his kitbag. 'I don't know that we can offer you a bed.'

'Oh, that's all right, Mrs Travers. I wouldn't ask you. I can stop at Aggie Weston's or somewhere. If I can just put it in the passage –' He lifted the bag and humped it into the house, following her through to the back room. 'Is Lucy in? I didn't have a chance to let her know –'

Only Lucy's father and brothers were in the room when Wilmot entered it. Joe was sitting in his armchair by the fire, and Vic and Kenny were at the dining-table doing their homework. They looked up, bright eyed, and Joe laid his newspaper on his knees.

'Well, you're a surprise.'

'I just came to see Lucy,' Wilmot repeated, as if he'd walked round from the next street.

'Oh, she's not here,' Vic said immediately, nudging his brother. 'She's out with her new chap. Got a smashing car, he has – they're out in it all the time, aren't they, Ken? Something high up in the Navy, isn't he?'

'Admiral,' Kenny confirmed. He was eleven, only a year younger than his brother and almost as like him as a twin, with the same curly, reddish hair and freckles. Wilmot had found it difficult to tell them apart until he noticed that one of Vic's front teeth was chipped. It had happened in a fight, Lucy had told him. You'd never get Kenny in a fight, he took everything as a big joke.

'It's true,' Vic nodded, grinning at Wilmot's dismayed glance at Emily. 'Getting married in the cathedral, they are – Kenny and me're going to be bridesmaids!'

'Get off with you,' Emily told them severely. 'Don't you take any notice of them, Wilmot, they're just being silly like boys their age always are.' She turned as they heard footsteps coming down the stairs and Kitty appeared at the door. She had just washed her hair and it was screwed into paper curlers, only a few strands of dark auburn showing. All the Travers family had inherited their colouring from their mother, from the blazing carrot of Vic and Kenny's tousled curls to the rich auburn waves that shone and rippled like a winter sunset around Lucy's head. Kitty's and Alice's came somewhere in between – golden red for Kitty, and the fawny ginger of a biscuit for Alice.

'Go and tell your sister Wilmot's here. They're upstairs, the girls are, doing a bit of sewing. There's not room down here with the boys' homework spread out all over the table. As for you two –' she addressed her sons again – 'you can pack that lot away and go and help your dad out in the garden. There's plenty of potatoes to pick up, so he told me.'

'Dad's not out in the garden. He's here reading the paper—' but Emily gave Joe such a glance that he rose immediately and laid his paper on the arm of his chair, and all three went out, the boys giving Wilmot a wink as they departed.

'Here she is,' Emily said as they heard a light patter of footsteps on the stairs, and in the next moment Lucy stood at the door, her face flushed, violet eyes brilliant. She took a step towards him.

'*Wilmot* –'

Emily slipped through the door to the kitchen and closed it behind her. Wilmot and Lucy stared at each other for a moment, and then with a swift, stumbling movement were in each other's arms. Wilmot held her close and she felt the rough blue serge of his tunic against her cheek before she lifted her face for his kiss.

'Wilmot – oh, *Wilmot* – I've missed you so much.'

'I've missed you too, Lucy. I've hated being away from you.'

'It's been like having a huge hole inside me – part of me's been taken away.'

8

'I know. I know. It's like that for me too.'

They stood for a few minutes wrapped in each other's arms, breathing in each other's warmth. In the tiny kitchen on the other side of the door, they could hear Emily filling the kettle and getting out cups and saucers. They couldn't keep the family out for long. In a few moments the door would open again. Alice and Kitty would be wanting to come downstairs, Joe and the boys back in from the garden.

'We'll go for a walk,' Lucy said. 'As soon as you've had some tea. You must be starving.'

'I don't know. I don't care. I just wanted to see you again – I wanted to make sure –'

'Make sure of what? Didn't you get my letters? I've told you, over and over again.'

'I know,' he said, kissing her. 'I just wanted to make sure I wasn't imagining it all. I wanted to make sure you were real.'

They didn't get engaged that weekend – not officially, anyway. Joe would never have allowed it. But before Wilmot set out on the long journey back to Scotland, they had promised to stay faithful to each other and considered themselves as engaged as if Lucy wore a ring on her finger. And to mark their promise, Wilmot bought her a tiny brooch which formed his own initial.

'You don't need to wear it so everyone can see it,' he said. 'Just so long as you've got it, that's all I want.'

'Oh, I'll wear it.' She pinned it on her blouse. 'I don't mind people knowing that you're my boy. I *want* them to know.'

Wilmot went back to sea. After that, the Travers family became accustomed to finding him on their doorstep, sometimes expected, often unannounced, his kitbag beside him. It became quite apparent that it was only a matter of time before the engagement was made official, and Lucy was just twenty-one when, with Wilmot's tiny diamond sparkling on her finger, she walked up the aisle of St Mary's church, Portsea, to join him at the altar.

'It's a shame there aren't more people on the groom's side,' Emily murmured to her husband when he stepped back from giving the bride away. There was quite a crowd behind them – Vic and Kenny now growing youths of fourteen and fifteen, and all Joe and Emily's own brothers and sisters and their families from all over Portsmouth and even 'over the water' in Gosport. On Wilmot's side, however, there were only his parents, Arthur and Maud Pengelly, and an uncle and aunt from Torpoint – a place nobody else had ever heard of. 'He's an only child and there's nothing to be done about that, but I'm surprised there aren't any other relatives. Mr Pengelly's got another brother, from what I remember.'

'It's a long way to come from Devon for a wedding,' Joe muttered back. 'And they couldn't close the hotel – had to leave someone in charge of things.'

Wilmot was wearing his naval uniform, the square collar pressed till there wasn't even the tiniest of creases, and his lanyards shining white. His brown hair, usually tousled and hard to keep tidy, was brushed flat and shone with hair cream, and his fresh, ruddy complexion looked as if it had been polished as hard as the black shoes that gleamed on his feet. He laid his round, white-topped cap down on the seat as he stepped forward to wait for his bride, and when he turned to watch her walk up the aisle nobody could doubt the love that shone from his face. His blue eyes glittered brightly and he looked, Emily thought with sudden tenderness, almost ready to cry.

Lucy stood beside her bridegroom, tall and slender in the billowing white wedding dress she'd made herself. Her hair rippled down her back like a lion's mane, glowing through the white lace of her veil. She had wanted to draw it up at the back of her neck and pile it on top of her head in a mass of curls, but it had made her look taller than ever and when she'd tried on her head-dress the little white diamante coronet had been almost lost amongst the rich auburn, and the veil had hung awkwardly. So she had brushed it out instead and it added a splash of warm, shimmering colour to the cool white of her bridal gown.

Alice and Kitty waited behind her, each in robin's egg blue. It had seemed to Joe and the boys sometimes that the whole house had been a froth of shimmering fabrics, spreading everywhere so that there was barely room to have a bit of dinner, let alone sit down and read the paper or for Vic and Kenny to do a bit of Meccano. And then there'd been the wedding presents, arriving daily: saucepans, cups and saucers, tablecloths, bedlinen – you name it, those two seemed to be getting it. More than he and Emily had ever got at their wedding, Joe was sure. But it took a lot to set up home, and even though they were starting off in two nice furnished rooms down in Plymouth they needed some of their own stuff.

Still, it would seem empty after they'd gone. For the last few months the whole household had revolved around this wedding, and in a few hours they'd be gone and it would be all over bar the shouting, as the saying went. He listened to Lucy's voice, soft but firm as she made her vows, and was surprised to feel a sudden ache in his throat and a sting of moisture in his eye. He rubbed it surreptitiously with his finger and hoped nobody had noticed.

The neighbours had turned out to see Lucy leave the house, and they were there again when she came back on the arm of her new husband, followed by the guests.

As well as needlework there had been cooking and cleaning going on for the past week, and the two downstairs rooms had been made ready for the reception, with a table borrowed from next door and chairs all around the walls. Even then, it would have been a squash if the weather hadn't been fine and most of the guests able to spill out on to the pavement or in the back garden.

They were still there when Lucy and Wilmot left to catch their train to Plymouth, and it looked as if they were settled in for the evening when probably someone would drag a piano out into the street and everyone, neighbours and all, join in the party. Wilmot's parents and his uncle and aunt were catching the same train at the town station. Lucy giggled, feeling slightly embarrassed, as Wilmot hustled her into an empty compartment, making sure it was a no-corridor carriage. It seemed rude to be so pointedly making it clear they wanted to be on their own, but Wilmot ignored her protests, tossed his cap on to the seat and kissed her soundly.

'I've been waiting for this moment. Just getting you to myself – that's the trouble with weddings, there's too many people about. I shan't have another one.'

Lucy gave a little squeal. 'I should hope not! What a thing to say to your wife on her wedding day.'

'It's my wedding day as well.' He tilted his head back to look at her more seriously. 'Well, Mrs Pengelly, how does it feel to be a married woman?'

'How does it feel to be a married man?' she parried, and he gave her a wicked wink.

'Tell you that later. Or maybe –' He glanced out of the window. They were trundling along beside the top of the harbour, with the shimmering expanse of water on their left and Portsdown Hill on their right. 'I was thinking we might have time to do something about it now.' He cuddled her close against him and nuzzled her neck.

Lucy gave a little cry of alarm. 'Wilmot! Don't be so daft – we'll be in Fareham any minute. And someone might get in.'

'They won't dare. I'll do my famous imitation of Frankenstein's monster.' He pulled a terrifying face and then laughed. 'It's all right, maid – I can wait. I've waited long enough already. I want it to be special, tonight. As special as I can make it.'

Lucy blushed. Such things weren't a topic of conversation in the Travers household, but Wilmot had a breezily frank approach. It came of being a sailor, he told her, and it was why all the nice girls loved them.

'Go on. I'm the only nice girl you know.'

'You're the nicest, I'll say that.' But she knew that he was as innocent as she. Whatever his mates got up to when they were in port, Wilmot had saved himself for her. She had no fear at all that he would ever be unfaithful, any more than she would.

Feeling inexplicably and rather pleasantly older, secure in the knowledge of their love, she settled back into her husband's arms and gazed contentedly out of the window. This was the start of their new life together, and it was going to be good.

The sun beamed down from an almost cloudless sky, but as the train rumbled on into the west, a tiny cloud appeared as if from nowhere. It travelled slowly across the sky, small and dark, with no more than a rim of white. And when it passed across the sun, it cast a chill shadow on Lucy's face.

But, by that time, suddenly exhausted by the excitement of the day, she was sound asleep in the arms of the man she had vowed to love, honour and obey until parted by death.

Chapter Two

Lucy settled in quickly enough to being a sailor's wife. She liked Plymouth, though it seemed odd not to be able to see the ships in the harbour, like you could at Portsmouth; you felt more a part of things there, she thought. But she liked going up on the Hoe and looking out at Plymouth Sound. You could see the ships coming in and out, and it was lovely on the wide expanse where Drake had played bowls and even today people walked and played games and had picnics.

Below, the cliff fell away in terraces of white rock, and there were little bathing pools cut into the stone, and diving boards perched over the sea. There was a big swimming-pool, too, that had only just been built, and it was full of people at weekends and during the holidays. Lucy and Wilmot went down there quite a lot in the first few weeks of their marriage. Lucy had always enjoyed swimming and the whole family had spent a lot of time on the beach at Southsea, going there every fine Sunday during the summer. She was surprised to find that Wilmot wasn't so keen, but with her encouragement his awkward splashing turned into a passable crawl and they raced each other across the semicircular pool.

'I thought all sailors'd be able to swim,' she said as they climbed out and sat drying themselves in the sun. 'What would you do if the ship sank?'

'Since we'd probably be about a thousand miles from land, I don't think being able to swim would be much help,' he said. 'Anyway, why should we sink?'

'They said that about the *Titanic*,' said Lucy, who had

been two years old when that disaster had happened, so couldn't remember it but had heard enough about it since. 'I'd feel funny, going to sea if I couldn't swim.'

'Well, I can now,' Wilmot said, getting bored with the subject. 'So if ever the ship does go down, you'll know it's because of you that I don't drown.' Lucy shuddered and begged him not to talk like that.

Their carefree days didn't last for long, however. Very soon after that, Lucy began to feel sick in the mornings and it wasn't long before her doctor confirmed that she was expecting a baby. Geoffrey Edward was born exactly eleven months after their wedding, weighing eight and half pounds despite the fact that Lucy had been sick almost continuously throughout the pregnancy. Wilmot wasn't there to welcome his son into the world, though: his ship went to sea the day before Geoffrey was born, and didn't come back for a year.

They had better luck with the second baby, Patricia Ann. This time, Wilmot's ship was in refit in Devonport for the last three months of the pregnancy and he didn't go away until Patsy was three months old. This time, he could wonder with Lucy at the tiny fingernails and the first smile, but he missed the first tooth and the day when she began to crawl. However, he was back again for her first birthday and he was there two months later when she let go of the armchair she was standing beside and took her first unsteady steps across the room. By this time, Geoffrey was just over two years old and starting to put sentences together, and when Wilmot went back to sea he told Lucy it had never been so hard to leave.

'They're both so interesting now,' he said. 'I mean, you can almost hold a conversation with Geoff, and Patsy's not going to be so long before she's chattering away like a magpie. By the time I come home again they're going to be different all over again.'

'I know.' Lucy leant her head on his shoulder. 'Sometimes, I wish you could come out of the Navy, Wilmot. I know I went into it with my eyes open – I knew you'd be away a lot – but I didn't realise just how bad it would be and how lonely I'd feel without you. And it does seem so hard, the little ones growing up without you. They need their daddy.'

'Well, I've signed on till I'm thirty. There's nothing I can do about that. I reckon we'll think about it then, eh? I know Mum and Dad have always hoped I'd go into the hotel with them. It's only another five years.'

Five years. That made it 1940. It seemed a lifetime. Geoffrey would be eight and Patsy six. But it was something to look forward to.

'Would you mind coming out? You love the Navy, and going to sea.'

'I did when I was single. I don't love it so much now, I can tell you.' He grinned wryly. 'I reckon that's why they make us sign on, because they know blokes will all want to come out the minute they get wed.' He gave her a kiss. 'Anyway, maid, it's not so bad this time – I'll be back in six months' time. We'll have Christmas together.'

They had agreed they would like to have three or four children. Wilmot envied Lucy her family life and said he didn't want his nippers to be 'only' children, as he had been. It was all right in some ways, but children needed company.

'We'll just give ourselves this break,' Lucy said, 'and then we'll have another one. It won't be too far behind the others, and if it is, we'll just have to have two, for company.'

'Twins'd be nice, if you could arrange it,' Wilmot said.

But it wasn't twins. Instead, when Patsy was three and Geoffrey just starting at infants' school, Zannah came along.

They didn't call her Zannah at first. Susannah was her name, too long by half, Maud Pengelly said critically, and if they were going to shorten it to Susie or Sue, why not call her Susan in the first place? But Lucy stood firm. She liked the name Susannah and the child could shorten it herself when she got old enough, if she wanted to. None of them had thought of 'Zannah' – that was the baby's own idea, when she first began to speak and try to say her name. 'Zannah,' she said firmly, splaying a starfish hand over her chest. 'I Zannah.' And so Zannah she became.

'It's pretty,' Lucy said. 'And unusual too. But then you're a pretty and unusual little girl, aren't you, my love?'

Zannah enchanted everyone. She was like a miniature version of her mother, with the same deep red-gold hair and porcelain skin, and eyes of an even deeper hue of violet, almost purple, fringed by long, thick lashes. Her soft lips were always curved in a smile that lit her whole face, and she had a fascination for names. As well as her own, she would adapt and alter other people's in order to be able to say them, and the names had a magic of their own, so that people enjoyed hearing them and often others began to use them too.

'Grammy,' she said, climbing on Maud's knee, and 'Grampy,' when playing with her grandfather's fingers and bending her head sideways to listen to the ticking of his watch. And Grammy and Grampy they became, even to Patsy and Geoff.

As she grew, she was full of questions, listening gravely to the answers. Family relationships interested her deeply and she spent hours trying to work out what an uncle was, or a cousin. Going to Portsmouth was like a voyage of discovery with all the family there – uncles who turned out to be her mother's brothers yet not her father's, one auntie who was married to an uncle who for some reason wasn't Mummy's brother, another auntie who didn't have an 'uncle' of her own . . . It was all very confusing and needed constant explanation.

'She's a real little livewire, that one,' Lucy's father said when Lucy had put her to bed one night and sunk exhausted into a chair. 'Keeps you on your toes, doesn't she?'

17

'Oh, I know. And it's no good telling her she'll understand when she grows up – she wants to understand *now*. We've learnt to be very careful what we say in front of her, otherwise there's a real inquisition.'

'Kiddies that age are all the same,' Emily said. 'She's a sweetheart.'

There was a short pause. Then Lucy said, 'What do you think about all this talk of Hitler, Dad?'

Adolf Hitler had been coming into the news more and more. He'd started by getting into the German government, even though he was really an Austrian, and he'd seemed like a good thing for Germany, which was suffering deeply in the Depression that had overtaken the whole world. He'd got the country back on its feet and he'd organised the youth into an enthusiastic movement, dedicated to keeping fit and turning Germany into a nation of pure Aryans. Lucy had seen him at the pictures, on the Pathé Pictorial newsreels, and you could tell the people thought the world of him. He'd opened the Olympic Games in Berlin and then he'd held a big rally in Nuremberg, with thousands of people crowding to hear him and cheering their heads off as they lifted their arms in his special salute.

Joe shook his head. 'I don't take to the feller meself. All that shouting and waving his arms – not like our statesmen. There's no dignity in it. And he don't look like a proper leader, neither – he just looks commonplace, with that silly moustache and all.'

'He frightens me,' Emily said. 'The way he yells – I get the feeling people are scared to cross him. And he seems to want to take over other countries. I mean, Germany's joined up with Austria and now he's talking about Czechoslovakia. Suppose they don't want to be part of Germany? I don't know that it's a good thing to let Germany get too big anyway – look what happened before.'

'The war to end all wars,' Joe said. 'I don't believe it.

There'll always be wars, and it's people like this Hitler who cause them.'

Lucy went back to Plymouth feeling disturbed. Wilmot was on a new ship now, HMS *Exeter*, a big cruiser with eight-inch guns. She was suddenly aware that it was a fighting ship and Wilmot was part of a fighting Service. Until now, she'd thought of the Navy merely as a part of the ordinary structure of life, a job for men who liked ships. But those guns were meant for shooting. For killing.

'I don't want to think of you having to go to sea in a war,' she said. 'I'm glad you'll be coming out soon.'

Wilmot looked at her gravely. 'Don't bank on it, maid. They won't be letting men come out if there's a war. They'll be getting more in – conscripting them.'

She stared at him. 'But if you've served your time—'

'That doesn't count. Not if there's a war.'

She was relieved when Mr Chamberlain went to Munich and came back waving his 'piece of paper' and declaring that this meant there would be 'peace in our time'. Peace. She felt as if she had been holding her breath for months and could only now let it go in a great sigh of thankfulness. She cuddled her three children close, feeling the hot tears in her eyes as she realised how anxious she had been.

'Why are you crying, Mummy?' Zannah asked, twisting her head sideways to look up into Lucy's face.

'Because I'm happy, sweetheart. Because I'm very, very happy.'

'*I* don't cry when I happy.'

'That,' Lucy said, 'is because you've never been as happy as I am at this very moment.' And she held Zannah extra tightly, knowing now that she had been carrying within her a deep fear for these children, a fear that she hadn't realised until now. I'd fight to the last breath for them, she thought, but thank God I won't have to.

The relief was short lived, however, and all too soon the

talk of war began again. Politicians turned against Mr Chamberlain, saying that his policy had been one of appeasement, and that Hitler wouldn't be stopped in his drive to take over all of Europe. Already he had broken his agreement to leave Czechoslovakia alone, and now he was turning his attention to Poland. If he marched upon Poland, Britain and France would be united in declaring war upon him. The fears began again, looming all the blacker because of the relief that had been felt, and the government began to take positive precautions.

'It's been nothing but leaflets coming through the door,' Emily said on Lucy's next visit to Portsmouth. 'Rationing this, that and the other – we're all going to have to have books full of little squares and the grocer'll have to cut them off every time we buy something. Can't you just see the time it'll take? And the queues of people, all getting more and more fed up waiting while he does it. I mean, it's never going to work, people won't put up with it. And then there's the blackout.' She gestured at the pile of coarse black cotton material draped over Joe's armchair. 'Curtains I've got to make with that lot, and Joe's got to put them all on frames so we can fix them up to the windows every night and lift 'em down in the morning. It's either that or have the horrible stuff hanging there all the time like a funeral parlour. Well, half the people just aren't going to bother, are they? It stands to reason they won't.'

'They'll be in trouble if they don't,' Joe said, coming in. He was carrying a basket of soft fruit, grown on the allotment. 'There's going to be wardens going round all night to see if there's a light showing. It'll be a punishable offence.'

'You mean they'll put people in prison? Old women who can't manage it for themselves and got no one to help them?' Emily drew down the corners of her mouth and sniffed. 'If it's going to be like that living in a free country, we might as well let Hitler invade and get it over with.'

'Mum! Don't say that.' Lucy looked at the heap of black fabric. 'It's horrible, I know, but they say the Germans will send planes over to bomb the cities, and they can see even the smallest glimmer from up there. You wouldn't want to be responsible for Pompey getting bombed.'

Emily sighed and shook her head. ''Course I wouldn't. Sorry, love. It's just getting me on edge, that's all. We're getting the air-raid shelters next week, did I tell you that? Andersons, they're called – like little tiny Nissen huts, only half buried in the ground. Your dad's got to dig a great big hole in the garden, just as if he didn't have enough to do. And then they'll sound a kind of siren to tell us when the planes are coming, night or day, and we've all got to go and crouch down like rabbits in a burrow. I don't know what the world's coming to, I'm sure I don't.'

'And what about the boys?' Lucy asked quietly. 'Will they have to go in the Forces?'

Emily turned sharply away, and Lucy knew that this was the cause of her ill temper. Vic was twenty-four years old now, and Kenny twenty-three. They'd both served apprenticeships and had good jobs: Vic worked as a mechanic in a big garage, and Kenny was a Post Office engineer out at Telephone House, in Southsea. Vic had a steady girlfriend, Eileen Foster, and they were planning to get engaged soon and then married in a couple more years, but the talk of war could change all that.

'All young chaps will get called up,' Joe said heavily, 'unless they're in a reserved occupation or got some other reason why they shouldn't go. Our Vic and Kenny are just the sort they'll be looking for.' He moved across to his wife and patted her awkwardly on the shoulder. 'It's not necessarily going to come to it, love. There's still a chance—'

'A *chance*!' Emily rounded on him. She had always had the quick temper that went with red hair, although it was generally over almost as soon as it had begun. 'I thought we

21

had a chance last October when Mr Chamberlain came back waving that piece of paper, and look where we are now. Peace in our time! Barely nine months ago, that was, and here we are digging holes in the garden and making blackout curtains. There's going to be a war, you can't tell me otherwise, and our boys are going to get caught up in the thick of it. You were in the last lot, Joe. You know what it's going to be like. And they say it'll be worse this time.'

Joe sat down on the blackout curtains, ignoring his wife's bitten-off cry of exasperation. Lucy, watching them both, thought that her father looked suddenly old. Tired and worried, as if he'd seen enough and didn't want any more. He was nearly sixty, he'd been through a world war and survived it – survived too the flu epidemic that had followed it, killing both his parents and his brother Jim's son Fred. Apart from when he was in the Army, he'd worked hard all his life in the dockyard and brought up a family of five children, and it was time he had a rest. He shouldn't be worrying about a war.

Nor should her mother. And nor should I, Lucy thought with a sudden pang of terror for her own husband and children.

'What about you?' Emily asked her. 'I suppose they're doing all the same things in Plymouth – building shelters and all that. You'll be evacuated, won't you? You won't want to stop there in the front line.'

Lucy stared at her. 'Evacuated?'

'Yes, of course.' Her mother was impatient again. 'They haven't talked of nothing else here, when they haven't been going on about ration books and blackout and Andersons. All the kids have practised at school. They'll be took off by train the minute it starts and we won't know where they've gone till they've got there, and they'll just live with strangers till it's all over. But it'll be all right for you, you'll be able to go with them being as Zannah's still little and your hubby's in the Services and away all the time.'

Away fighting in the war, Lucy thought. She shook her head. 'They haven't said anything about evacuation in Plymouth.'

'What d'you mean, not said anything about it? They must have.'

'No. Plymouth's a neutral evacuation zone. They don't think we'll be in any danger.'

Her mother stared at her, 'Not in any *danger*? But that's daft. Of course Plymouth'll be in danger, same as Pompey will be. It's a naval base, isn't it? There's a big dockyard there. What makes them think the Germans won't bomb it?'

Lucy shrugged. 'How do I know? I just hope they're right.'

'I can't see the reason.' Emily turned to her husband. 'Can you, Joe? Can you see the reason? I mean, Plymouth's as important as Pompey, far as the Navy goes. It don't make any sense.'

'Your mother's right. You didn't ought to stay in Plymouth if there's a war. It's not safe for the kiddies.'

Lucy felt trapped. 'Well, what else can I do? I can't come back here. And if there's no evacuation programme I can't go anywhere else. I'd have to pay it all, and how can I do that and keep a home going in Plymouth for Wilmot to come back to? No, I reckon I'll just have to face it out.'

'Well, you've got to get a decent shelter, then. Has that hotel got a cellar? You'll have to get down there if anything happens. I don't reckon it's any good getting under the stairs, like they say – if a bomb hits your house, a few wooden stairs aren't going to stop it. You get down in that cellar.'

'But the hotel's two streets away.'

'You'd better go and live there, then.' Emily wasn't going to be put off. 'Got plenty of bedrooms, hasn't it? And there won't be many people going to Devonshire on their holidays, I can tell you that now.' She glanced at the clock. 'You'd better be going if you're taking the children over to Gosport to see your Uncle Percy and Auntie Daph. You know what she's like, tea'll be on the table at five o'clock sharp and woe betide anyone who's late.'

Lucy lined the three children up and inspected their hair and faces and hands. Geoff had managed to lose a garter as usual, so that one grey sock had concertina'd round his ankle, and his dark red hair stood up in a tuft that no amount of smoothing would force to lie down. She found a bit of elastic and put a couple of quick stitches in it to make a new garter and gave up on his hair. Zannah was, as always, as clean as if she'd just stepped out of the bath, her clothes tidy and her golden-red hair shining like fireglow around her face. Patsy, although tidy enough, still managed somehow to look as if she needed a good brushing, but there was never anything to be done about that.

They went out and walked through to Commercial Road. The Guildhall lions lay watching over the big square and Lucy led the children past the memorial to the soldiers who had died in the Great War, and into the park. They always enjoyed walking this way down to the ferry which would take them across the harbour to Gosport, but today Lucy looked at the figure of the soldier, crouching over his machine-gun, and felt a sick shiver of fear.

The harbour seemed different too. There were a lot of ships in, a lot of coming and going. The masts and rigging of HMS *Victory*, Nelson's flagship, loomed behind the semaphore tower and she heard the thin notes of a bosun's whistle, sounded as a ship slowly passed, in recognition of Britain's most famous admiral.

The ferry-boat was small and stubby. It took about seven minutes to cross the harbour, and in that time Lucy looked about her at the scene she had known so well all through her life, and tried to imagine the city of

Portsmouth and the town of Gosport laid waste by enemy bombs.

And Plymouth too, for surely her mother was right. Surely the Germans wouldn't ignore one of the most important naval bases in the country. Surely there wouldn't, in the end, be anywhere at all they would ignore.

The shiver that had taken her as she passed the bronze replica of the soldier gripped her again, and her teeth chattered as wave after wave of cold shudders shook her body.

Mum's right, she thought. They wouldn't be making all these preparations if they didn't know it was going to happen. It's not a question of *if* – it's *when*.

And by all appearances, it's going to be soon . . .

Back in Plymouth, she looked around for signs of preparation. Just as in Portsmouth, Anderson shelters were being delivered and gas masks issued. It looked just as serious, but there was still no talk of evacuation.

'Our boys'll get the Germans long before they get this far,' Arthur Pengelly said staunchly. 'Look at it this way, my handsome. They've got to come all the way down the Channel. Coming *past* Portsmouth on their way. They're not going to bother coming down here, putting their own lives at risk – never mind the extra fuel, those planes use up a lot of petrol, it's not like taking the family jalopy out for a Sunday afternoon run – not when they could bomb Portsmouth to bits.'

Lucy had to admit it made sense, though the idea of her beloved Portsmouth being 'bombed to bits' sent a chill through her body. All the same, there was a niggling sense that it didn't really ring true. If that really was what would happen, wouldn't the Navy send its ships to Plymouth, where they'd be safe? And wouldn't the Germans follow them?

'Your mum's right, maid,' Maud said suddenly. 'You belong here with us. Down in the cellar of a night – if there are any raids at all. You and the little 'uns could have those attic rooms to sleep in. You'm round here half the time as it is, helping out.'

Lucy smiled. It was true that she spent a lot of time at the hotel, helping her mother-in-law make beds or sweep the rooms, and helping Arthur with the books. Even though she had her hands full with the three children, it was still nice to share her days with the family and she enjoyed meeting the guests. Life as a naval wife could be very lonely.

'Thanks, Mum,' she said. 'I'll stop where I am for the time being, though. After all, we still don't know that there's definitely going to be a war, and I want to keep the home going for Wilmot to come back to. I don't want to give up the house if I can help it.'

Wilmot was away again. The *Exeter* had gone down to the South Atlantic, cruising round the Falkland Islands and South America. At least he'll be out of it, she thought, if there is a war. It'll never get that far. The thought of Wilmot being involved in a war at sea made her shiver. She remembered their laughing talk when she'd taught him to swim properly. *'If the ship goes down, I'll probably be a thousand miles away from land . . .'* No, she couldn't think about that.

But it was not long before Lucy discovered, as so many thousands of others were to discover, that when war came, you had to think the unthinkable.

Like the rest of the country, she listened with dread and horror to Mr Chamberlain's announcement on the radio on Sunday, 3 September. *'I have to tell you that no such undertaking has been received and that consequently this country is at war with Germany . . .'* Lucy, sitting at the kitchen table with Maud and Arthur, found that she had one hand covering her mouth while the other reached out blindly for comfort. '*You can imagine what a bitter blow this has been . . .*' Their hands met in the middle of the table, hers and Maud's and Arthur's, fingers clasping tightly. '*May God bless you all . . . I am certain that right will prevail . . .*'

'Let's hope he'm right,' Arthur said at last into the long silence that followed. 'Let's just hope he'm right.'

'Oh, Arthur,' Maud said, her voice shaking. 'Arthur, what be going to happen to us? And what about our Wilmot, out there at sea? What be going to happen to Wilmot?'

'He's all right,' Lucy said fiercely, as if saying so would make it true. 'He's nowhere near Germany. He'll be safe down there in the South Atlantic. The war won't get that far. Why should it?'

Arthur glanced at her as if about to say something, and then changed his mind. She knew what it was, though. He was going to ask her why she thought they'd let big, modern ships like the *Exeter* and the two other ships down there on patrol – the *Ajax* and the *Achilles* – stay there when they'd so obviously be needed somewhere else. But it would take them weeks to get back, she thought desperately, weeks, and by then it might all be over. Wasn't that what people were saying? All over by Christmas, that's what a lot of folk reckoned.

Lucy went home that afternoon, glancing anxiously up at the sky, wondering when the first raids would come. She knew that people had already started to leave some of the big cities. Children had been pouring out of Portsmouth and London, making for the country. There had still been no evacuation plans made for Plymouth, so she supposed that the authorities must think that there was no danger. She hoped they were right. She hoped, too, that she was right about Wilmot. He *must* be safe, down there in the South Atlantic.

To everyone's surprise, however, it was the South Atlantic and Wilmot's ship the *Exeter* which made some of the first news of the war.

Chapter Three

After the tension of the months before the war began, and the dread of that sad announcement that brought an end to 'peace in our time', nothing much seemed to happen.

People said that in some places the air-raid warnings had sounded as soon as Mr Chamberlain had finished speaking, as if the German planes had waited until that moment to make their appearance overhead. But there had been no enemy aircraft, no bombs, and for a long time, it seemed as if nobody knew quite what to do first. It was as if two boxers had come out of their corners at the sound of the bell and then stood facing each other, uncertain as to who was supposed to throw the first punch.

'People are already starting to come back from the country,' Emily wrote from Portsmouth. 'They reckon there's no need to be out there. And the way some of the kiddies are being treated, you wouldn't credit . . . Not all of them of course, it's just a big holiday to a lot of them, what with only having to go to school half days and all. But nobody seems to think it's going to be as bad as all that, after all.'

'They'm living in fool's paradise, then,' Arthur said when Lucy read the letter out. 'The Germans aren't playing party games. They'm just getting themselves ready. They'll hit us with all they've got, you see. And maybe if people didn't spend all their time staring at the sky they might see what's happening in other parts of the world.'

Lucy looked at him with a sudden rush of fear. 'What other parts of the world?'

Arthur screwed up the corners of his lips, as if annoyed with himself. 'Don't think about it, maid. I shouldn't have said nothing.'

'What, Dad?' Lucy's back tensed. 'What are you thinking of?'

'It's no good backing out of it now, Arthur,' Maud said. 'You'd better tell her what's on your mind.'

Arthur sighed. 'Well, you'll see it for yourself soon enough. It's this *Admiral Graf Spee*,' he said to Lucy. 'Pocket battleship, they call her. Been chasing our merchant ships all over the oceans, picking 'em off then zig-zagging off so no one can tell where her'll be next. Well, stands to reason us can't let 'em go on like that, so the whole of the Atlantic Fleet's been after her. And now—'

'The Atlantic Fleet?' Lucy repeated. Her voice sounded small, almost tiny. How, she wondered, could she have missed knowing all this? 'But – she's not gone south. She's not –'

'Her's gone all over the place,' Arthur said. 'It hasn't made all that much news yet and I was hoping – me and Maud was hoping – it'd all go quiet. But now they reckon her's going right down the South Atlantic, and those three ships are the ones that are there, and there's going to be –' He caught his wife's eye and chewed his lips again. 'Look at it this way, my pretty,' he said at last. 'There'll be a bit of a fight over it all. Bound to be.'

A bit of a fight. Before many days had passed, the *Graf Spee* was all you heard about on the wireless, all you saw in the papers. The Battle of the River Plate, they called it, and after it the *Graf Spee* had been forced into the port of Montevideo for repairs and sanctuary. While there, she was safe, but the moment she came outside the three-mile limit of neutrality, the ships awaiting her would pounce.

By this time, Lucy and the Pengellys were, like the rest of Plymouth, following the news avidly. Despair hit them when a false signal came through saying that the *Exeter* had been sunk with all hands, and until the rumour was scotched Lucy knew what it was to be a widow. Even when, just before Christmas, the *Graf Spee* was finally caught and scuttled, she could not be sure that Wilmot was safe. Sixty-one men aboard *Exeter* were reported dead, and there was no way of knowing if Wilmot were one of them. At last the *Evening Herald* published a list of all those killed, and she had to read it a dozen times before she could be convinced that Wilmot's name wasn't there.

'It might still be a mistake,' she said, almost as if she were unwilling to believe that he might be alive. 'They might have left his name off . . . Mum, I can't bear to think it's all right and then find out it's not.' She thought for a moment of those dark, cold nights when she'd believed herself a widow. 'I don't think I will be able to believe it till I see him walk in that door again.'

'I know, maid,' Maud said, 'but us've just got to put our trust in God and have faith, like the bishop says down St Andrew's. 'Tis all us can do.'

Lucy thought of all the men who had already been killed. No doubt many of them, and their wives and mothers too, had put their faith in God as well. And they were dead all the same. Her memories of the days and nights when she had thought herself bereaved were dark and cold, and she knew that only the warmth of Wilmot's arms about her would banish them.

She had to wait until February for that reassurance, but at last the *Exeter* and *Ajax* came home together, steaming up the Sound beneath bruised clouds still full of snow, with the Hoe crowded by people who had gathered to cheer their arrival. Lucy was tempted to take the children down to St Levan's Gate to meet Wilmot at the very first possible moment, but Arthur and Maud dissuaded her.

'You don't know what time he'll come ashore, and you don't even know he'll be coming out of St Levan's. You belong to be at home, with a fire lit and the kettle on. That's what he'll appreciate most.'

Reluctantly, Lucy agreed. She knew they were right, it was just that she had waited so long for Wilmot to come home that she felt she couldn't bear to wait a moment longer than necessary. And the time it took him to get from the dockyard to home was time they could be spending together, even if it was just on a tram . . .

She made fresh cutrounds and got hold of some clotted cream and put out a pot of home-made blackcurrant jam and the best teacups. She put clean sheets on the bed, washed the children and herself, brushed their hair a dozen times, brought in a bucket of coal so that no one would need to go outside again for the rest of the evening. She sat down with her knitting, got up again and peered out of the window. The afternoon was closing in already but there wasn't a light to be seen; people had already put up their blackout curtains and the streetlamps hadn't been lit for months.

Lucy hesitated. She didn't want to put up the blackout, it seemed so unwelcoming, but she couldn't see any more to knit and she couldn't make the children sit in the dark. Besides, even the firelight would send out a glow that would bring the warden knocking on the door. She sighed and let the curtain drop. Wilmot would have to come home in the dark after all.

A movement on the corner of the street caught her eye and she lifted the curtain again, her heart suddenly in her throat. Yes. There was someone there. Someone coming this way. Someone who strode with a free, slightly rolling gait; someone who carried a kitbag; someone who—

'*Wilmot!*'

Not caring that the light from the fire would spill into the street, Lucy flung open the front door and rushed outside. He caught her in his arms just as she tripped on a loose paving-stone, and held her there, hard against him.

Laughing and crying all at once, she clung to his blue-clad arms and burrowed her face against his rough serge chest.

'Oh, Wilmot – Wilmot . . . I thought you'd never come home again . . . I thought you were *dead*.'

'Dead?' he said, and the sound of his voice brought a fresh flood of tears. 'Dead? It'll take more than a few Germans to kill me, Lucy. Now, let's get inside out of the cold and I'll tell you about the penguins.'

They were the only ones who wore evening dress, he said. He sat beside the fire, built halfway up the chimney to welcome him home, and demolished half a dozen of Lucy's cutrounds, spread lavishly with blackcurrant jam and topped with cream. They were the funniest birds you ever saw, waddling along on their hind legs – well, he knew they were the only legs penguins had, but it *looked* as if they were up on hind legs, like a performing dog – and coming up to you so trusting. And the way they stood about in groups, like little old men having a natter, it was a proper comical sight.

'We had to stop down there in the Falklands quite a while to get all the repairs done. Good job they're British, those islands. Mind you, the South Americans are mostly neutral, they'd have taken on any job, but it would've been a queer thing to have been in one of their harbours alongside a German ship. But the islands being ours, they looked after us like heroes.'

'And so you were,' Lucy said. The family was clustered about him, as tightly as they could get, everyone wanting to be close. Geoff and Patsy were on the floor, each with an arm wound around their father's legs, and he had Zannah on his lap. Lucy sat opposite in her own armchair, but she'd pulled it closer so that she could touch him still, and she knew she'd get her chance to be closer later on. 'The papers have all been full of you, and you've been on the wireless and everything.'

'There's talk of us going to London,' Wilmot said, half shyly. 'Going to see the Lord Mayor. And there'll be a reception here in Plymouth too, with Lord and Lady Astor.'

Lucy's eyes sparkled. The Astors almost ran Plymouth between them. Lord Astor was Lord Mayor, and his wife – even though she was born an American – had become the first woman Member of Parliament. Seeing them both at once was as good as seeing the Lord Mayor of London any day.

'Well, you deserve it,' she said. 'You deserve medals, all of you.' Her face grew sad. 'But what about all those men who were killed, Wilmot, and their poor families? They can't be feeling very happy now, with the ship back and their men never coming home again. I feel ever so sorry for them.'

'I know.' Wilmot's face twisted then hardened. 'And I've promised to go and see one or two of the wives, Luce. Tell 'em a bit about it – not much.' His eyes seemed to see something she would never see, never even know about. 'Couple of my oppos copped it – we always said we'd look out for each other, do anything we could. Well, there's nothing left to do now, and I don't suppose they really want to know what happened. I don't want to go into it all anyway, but it don't seem right to just not bother. I mean, I've got to go and pay my respects.'

'Yes, of course. I'm sure it's the right thing to do.' Lucy thought back to those moments when she had thought herself a widow. 'I'd have wanted someone to come and see me.' She remembered the names of men Wilmot had said were his best mates. 'Teddy Endacombe, or Knocker White. I'd have liked it if they'd come.'

'Well, they won't be coming anyway,' he said quietly. 'It's Teddy Endacombe and Knocker White's missuses I've got to go and see.'

The leave passed all too quickly. Most of the time they spent at home or going round to see Maud and Arthur.

Once or twice they left the children at the guest house and spent an afternoon at the pictures. They saw Laurence Olivier and Vivien Leigh in *Wuthering Heights* and took Geoff and Patsy to see Judy Garland in *The Wizard of Oz*. Generally in the evenings they put up the blackout curtains to shut out the weather and played cards or listened to programmes like *ITMA* or *Band Waggon* on the wireless. After the nine o'clock news they would listen to Lord Haw-Haw and jeer at his sneering, plummy voice and futile efforts to scare them.

As Wilmot had said, there were receptions held for the crews of the ships both in Plymouth and in London. He came home bemused. 'We marched all through London with a band in front of us, and people waved flags and cheered like we were royalty. And then we had our dinner – lunch, they called it, but it was a proper dinner really – at the Guildhall. You've never seen anything like it, Luce. It's like a huge church. And there was all long tables and china plates that I swear had gold on them, and cut glasses to drink out of. I tell you what, the ratings' Mess is going to seem a bit of a comedown after that.'

'You wouldn't like to live like it all the time, though,' Lucy said, half afraid that their small terraced house and few bits of china would also seem a comedown. 'I mean, it's not like real life, is it?'

Wilmot grinned and pulled her close. 'Don't worry, maid. I wouldn't swop our home for all the Lord Mayors' palaces and parlours in the country. I reckon I've got all I want here, with you and our little tackers. And once this war's over I'll be content to stop here.'

'You mean you really will come out of the Navy? As soon as you can?'

'As soon as I can,' Wilmot promised her. 'And it can't be too soon for me.'

It didn't look as if the war would soon be over after all.

Christmas had come and gone, and the Battle of the River Plate brought it home to everyone that a war really was being waged. The merchant ships that had been so much at the mercy of the enemy were now protected by convoys of naval ships, but that didn't stop the battles. It seemed as if the Navy was going to be at the forefront of this war, rather than the Army or the Air Force.

'Mind you, the weather's got a lot to do with it,' Arthur said. 'Look at it this way: it's been a rough old winter and the Germans aren't any keener to fly their planes than we are. That'll change, come the better weather, you see if it don't. I reckon things'll start happening come spring.'

He was right. The war seemed to be happening everywhere but in Britain. It seemed, during those cold months when rationing had bitten deeper and all kinds of rules and regulations been imposed, that Hitler had forgotten his threats to invade. Instead, he was concentrating on Scandinavia and troops were being sent there. Denmark had already fallen and the situation in Norway didn't look much better.

And so far there hadn't been a single bomb dropped.

'Not that we want them,' Emily said when Lucy went to spend Easter in Portsmouth. 'And there's more people than ever come back from the evacuation. Your dad reckons it's just a lull. They're getting themselves ready, that's what he says.'

'That's what Wilmot's dad says too,' Lucy said. She looked up at the sky, glittering with barrage balloons. 'D'you think those'll really keep the planes away?'

'Well, they're not going to want to fly into them, are they? And if they come in below them our lads'll shoot them down straight away.'

Vic and Kenny had both been called up. Vic, who had got married a month before war was declared, had gone into the Army, into the local regiment, and had already done his training – six weeks' square bashing and peeling potatoes, he said when he came home for his first leave. It had changed him, Eileen said. He ironed his own trousers and he'd learnt to be tidy. 'If being tidy's going to win the war, he'll do it all on his own. We can't leave anything lying about but what he picks it up and polishes it.'

Kenny was in the RAF. They didn't seem to be so bothered about tidiness. He wore a white scarf carelessly round his neck and talked about training as a mechanic, maybe even a pilot. He took Geoff up to Hilsea and they watched planes coming in to the small airport at Airspeed.

'Uncle Kenny's going to fly a Spitfire,' Geoff said, and spread his arms wide, making zooming noises as he ran round the room. 'I hope there's still a war when I'm old enough to fly Spitfires.'

'Geoff!' The edge in Lucy's voice betrayed the fear she still felt for Wilmot, now back at sea again. 'Don't you dare say such wicked things!' But it was all a game to nine-year-old boys, and she didn't even want him to understand the reality of it all.

Even her sisters were preparing to do their bit. Alice was married too, and her husband Ted was in the same regiment that Vic had joined. They were expecting to go to France soon. They had no children and Alice had decided to go back to her job as a nurse. There would be plenty needed soon enough, she said grimly.

Kitty, who was only just twenty, was talking about going into one of the Women's Services. They'd started the WRNS up again after disbanding them after the Great War. Emily was horrified at the idea and Joe inclined to put his foot down, but what could you say? The girl would be twenty-one in less than a year and the Government was talking about conscripting women anyway.

'I don't know what the world's coming to,' Emily said, as she did a hundred times a week now. 'To think of women fighting!'

'I keep telling you, Mum, we won't be fighting.' Nobody

looked less like fighting than Kitty, standing on tiptoe to look in the mirror and curl her glossy dark red hair. She wrapped a scrap of fur round her neck like a scarf and looked like a tiny, bright-eyed fox. 'We just do the shore jobs and that means more men can go to sea.'

'I'd rather you didn't bother,' Lucy said. 'I wouldn't mind a scrap if my Wilmot didn't have to go to sea.' But she knew that nobody was going to get release in this war. It was going to be all hands to the pumps and get it over with.

The Allied Forces withdrew from Norway after only a couple of weeks' fighting. Mr Chamberlain resigned as Prime Minister and Winston Churchill took his place. A week later, the Germans started their air attack on the Low Countries, and the word *blitzkrieg* entered the language.

'I told you, my pretty,' Arthur Pengelly said when Lucy was back in Plymouth. 'I told you what it'd be like. They'm softening 'em up with dive-bombers and then sending in the tanks. And nobody seems able to stop 'em.'

'They can't do that here,' Maud said. 'They can't get tanks across the Channel.' But she spoke without conviction and nobody argued with her. They all knew, in their sinking hearts, that the Germans could.

'Our boys will stop them,' she said. 'There's plenty of troops over in France now, and we've got the finest Navy in the world. And the RAF . . .'

'The RAF haven't been proved,' Arthur told her. 'They only just got going in the last war. Nobody knows how they'd manage, not really.'

They were soon to find out. In less than a month, British troops came back from Dunkirk, white faced, bandaged, exhausted – and those were the lucky ones. There were many others left dead on the beaches and in the fields of Normandy. Amongst them was Lucy's brother Vic.

There was no doubt now that the war was real.

The summer brought the Battle of Britain, and now nobody could say the RAF was untried. Another flock of young men was killed, like doves in the air, and the family had a new worry. Kenny had achieved his ambition to be a pilot and was based near Chichester. He flew Spitfires, just as he had promised Geoff he would, and when he came home his talk was peppered with 'flaps' and 'prangs' and 'ditches'. He seemed to lead a charmed life, always returning from operations, always with a grin on his face, though to Lucy, when she saw him, the grin seemed fixed, and behind the merry eyes lurked a soul that was filled with dread.

So far, the Germans had aimed all their attacks at the British airfields, determined to kill the only power that could really prevent their invasion, but as the Battle of Britain drew to a triumphant close and the people began to draw breath, they changed their tactics. And in September 1940, the bombing began in earnest.

Many of those who had returned from evacuation during the 'phony' war now hurried back again to new billets. The authorities still considered Plymouth to be safe, and at first it seemed that they were right. The first raids were over London: as night fell on 7 September the docklands were already ablaze, the fires caused by hundreds of tons of bombs falling like rain throughout the day. This time, the RAF seemed powerless to stop them. Even the Thames was set on fire as blazing stocks of rum, sugar and paint were scattered from the ruined warehouses to float on the water. And when a river was on fire, one fireman remarked grimly, you really knew you were in trouble.

All through September it continued. In October, Londoners began to forsake the street shelters for the safety of the deep Tube stations. Photographs appeared in the newspapers and film on Pathé Pictorial, of shattered streets, destroyed buildings. And it wasn't just London. Other cities were getting their share too: Liverpool, Bristol, Southampton, Coventry . . .

Before the bombing started, Lucy had been thinking of going back to Portsmouth for Christmas. Vic's widow Eileen had had his baby now, a little girl with really red hair, she wrote to Lucy, and she was going to call her Victoria after the daddy she'd never know. Lucy badly wanted to see the new baby, but now she hesitated and decided against it.

When she heard about the huge bomb that had been dropped on Portsmouth on Christmas Eve, demolishing an entire street, she was glad she'd stayed in Plymouth, and when the blitz hit Pompey on 10 January she was frantic.

'How do we find out what's been happening? How can they let us know?' The guest house was on the phone, but the Travers' little terraced house in Portsmouth wasn't, and phone lines were down anyway. Emily couldn't even have got through from a phone box. 'They could all be dead.'

'No news is good news.' Maud was staunch as usual, but they both knew that these days no news could just as well be bad news. They both waited anxiously, listening for the phone to ring, looking out of the windows for the telegraph boy on his red bike.

It came at last, a buff envelope that Lucy opened with shaking fingers. 'They're all right,' she said, her face twisting in a grimace of a smile that turned quickly to a sob. Her legs trembled suddenly and she sat down. 'Oh Mum, they're all right.'

After the first of Portsmouth's blitzes there was a mass burial in Kingston Cemetery. Everyone hoped this would be all they were to suffer, but there was another blistering attack on 10 March. Once again, Lucy was beside herself with fear until the telegram came to tell her the family had survived.

And still there had been no major raids on Plymouth. True, there had been a few bombs dropped, apparently by planes that had passed over on their way to Bristol and flown off-course, but the danger still didn't seem especially great, and there was no mention of evacuation.

'They'm right after all,' Maud said. 'Plymouth's not going to get it. They can't get right down here, see, they'm just concentrating on the places that are easy to get to.'

Coventry? Lucy thought. Liverpool? Surely Plymouth wasn't any harder to reach than these cities, and look what had happened to them. And why should Bristol be bombed and not Plymouth? She was conscious of dread every night when she went to bed, dread every morning when she woke.

Only ten days later, on the very day when King George VI and Queen Elizabeth came to visit Plymouth and take tea on the Hoe with Lady Astor just as if it were peacetime, her dread was fulfilled. The Germans came at last, that night and the next, and began systematically to flatten Plymouth. Lucy had never missed Wilmot so much. She could only be thankful that she had by her side another man who had come to be, not only her friend, but a friend to the whole family, David. David Tremaine, who had suffered his own terrible loss and knew all too well what a German bombing raid could do.

Chapter Four

David Tremaine was born in Cornwall in the summer of 1903, seven years before Lucy. His father, Pascoe Tremaine, editor of a local newspaper had gone to war in 1914 and was killed at Passchendaele. His mother, Kathleen, a London girl, had stayed long enough to bring David up in the village where he was born, and then gone back to look after her ageing parents.

David took after his father. As a boy, he had spent many hours in the newspaper office, helping to produce the paper. He had even been entrusted with one or two small reporting jobs – going to the local flower show and listing the winners, writing a story about a ship that was wrecked in a nearby cove. It wasn't a big ship and nobody was killed, or he wouldn't have been given the story, but it was a thrill for him to see his words in print all the same.

When he was old enough, he got a job on the same newspaper, under the editor who had taken over when David's father joined the Army, and after he had served his apprenticeship and achieved some independence he began to work his way up, first joining the staff of the *Western Morning News* and then going to London, where he lived for a time with his mother and grandmother, his grandfather having by then died. By the time the Second World War started, he was married with a twelve-month-old baby son.

For some time during the late 'thirties, David had been working for a specialist Government publication and had become an expert on naval matters. Not much of his work appeared in newspapers these days: he spent his time gathering information to be published in Government reports, or in advising those civil servants who would in turn advise their ministers. His work involved travelling between the main naval ports of Portsmouth, Plymouth and Chatham, and for some time he had been in the habit of staying at Pengelly's. He found it homely and comfortable, he said, nicer than the big, impersonal hotels, and after a while he was as much a friend as a paying guest.

'He's a nice sort of a man, that David Tremaine,' Maud remarked. He had been on his way out just as Lucy came in with Geoff after school, and immediately offered to take the two older children up on the Hoe. It was long before talk of war had seriously begun, and the newspapers were full of talk of Edward VIII and Wallis Simpson. Zannah was still a baby, still called Susannah, and she was red faced and crying that afternoon with teething problems. Lucy thanked him gratefully and watched him walk away up Lockyer Street, tall and loose limbed between the two children, Patsy holding his hand and skipping, and Geoff talking away nineteen to the dozen about what he had done at school that day.

'He's bringing his fiancée down to stay soon,' Lucy said, soothing Zannah with a bottle of cool water. 'There, there, lovey, that's better, isn't it? You've got yourself all hot and bothered . . . They're getting married at Christmas. Heather, she's called. He showed me her photograph.'

'I hope they'm wanting separate rooms,' Maud said a little sharply. 'I'll have no goings-on in my house. Mind, he doesn't seem that sort of a chap, I'll say that for him. Decent, like.'

David brought Heather down a few weeks later. Maud gave them not only separate rooms, but she put them on different floors, too: David on the top floor, where the rooms were really attics, and Heather on the first floor in one of the best rooms.

'Tell us all the best places to go,' David said to Lucy. 'I want to take Heather down to Cornwall to meet my auntie there and see where I grew up, but she wants to see Devon as well. We're going to hire a car for a day or two and then go on by train.'

'You need to ask Wilmot really. He's the one who was born here.'

'You've lived here for quite a while though, haven't you?' Heather asked. She was a pretty girl, with soft brown, naturally curly hair and wide hazel eyes. She obviously adored David and it was clear he thought the world of her. They held hands all the time and Lucy had inadvertently caught them kissing on the landing, just outside Heather's room.

Wilmot was in port just then, and at David's suggestion the four of them spent Saturday afternoon and evening together. While Maud looked after the children, they all squeezed into the Baby Austin David had hired and set off for Dartmoor. They roamed about the wide, empty spaces and picnicked beside the bubbling East Dart before returning to spend the evening in Tavistock, calling in at the Royal Oak in Meavy for a last drink on the way back.

'That was lovely,' Lucy sighed, leaning her head on Wilmot's shoulder as they sped back across Roborough Down. 'We hardly ever get out like that, all on our own. It was as good as being on holiday.'

David and Heather left next day, taking the train down into Cornwall over the Brunel Bridge that spanned the broad reaches of the Tamar.

When they got married, Lucy sent them a telegram (rejecting Wilmot's suggestion of a rude one and settling for 'Best wishes for your new life together'), and the next time David came to stay at Pengelly's he was a happily married man with a baby on the way.

David never talked about his work. He came to Plymouth

about once in eight weeks, and she knew that he went to Portsmouth and Chatham with about the same frequency. Wherever else he went and what he did in between, he never said and she never asked. You didn't ask anyone anything these days; there were too many posters up exhorting you to 'be like Dad, keep Mum', or telling you that walls had ears. She knew, however, that an attack of TB had left him unable to join the services.

In that first winter of the war, when he came to Plymouth he walked down Lockyer Street of an evening and sat with Lucy in the small back room. He played with Geoff and Patsy and sat Zannah on his lap and told them about his own baby son, little Stevie. Lucy was busy knitting balaclava helmets and socks, but with a few scraps of wool she made little pom-pom balls for him to take back to Stevie. She asked if Heather and the baby were going to go into the country, but David shook his head.

'I want her to come to Cornwall and stay with Auntie Meg, but she won't hear of it. Says she wants to keep our home going. And then there are the mums, of course.' His own mother was getting on and still living with the ancient grandmother, and Heather's mother was also still alive and in poor health. 'She doesn't feel she can leave them.'

'It's not easy,' Lucy said, and told him how her mother had thought she ought to get out of Plymouth. 'She can't believe it's any safer than Portsmouth.'

'She may be right,' he said soberly. 'Isn't there anywhere you could go?'

'Not really. We don't know anyone outside Plymouth, and if they're not evacuating it means you have to pay.'

'Mm.' He thought for a minute or two, then fished a piece of paper out of his pocket. 'Look, I'll give you my aunt's address down in Cornwall. I'm sure she'd know somewhere you could go, if you do want to leave the city. I'm still trying to persuade Heather to go down there – she might agree if she thought you were going to be there too.'

Lucy thanked him, but she knew she wouldn't use the address. Her home was here in Plymouth now, and she couldn't leave Maud and Arthur. Arthur hadn't been at all well lately, he always suffered with his chest in winter and just lately he'd been getting pains when he climbed the stairs or walked up to the Hoe.

Lucy thought of the three children as David gave her the address of his aunt in Cornwall. She still shared her mother's anxieties about the safety of Plymouth. It would be better for them out in the country, and there couldn't be anywhere much safer than Cornwall, but just at present she couldn't see any justification for leaving.

'I'll remember it, if they do look like bombing us,' she said, and smiled at him. 'Now, before you go I'll make us a cup of cocoa.'

They sat together before the fire, companionably drinking cocoa. The children were all in bed now, and it was nearly time for the nine o'clock news. David didn't seem inclined to move, and Lucy didn't feel like reminding him. It was nice, the two of them sitting here together, nice company, and she got little enough of that, when all was said and done.

'What d'you think's going to happen?' she asked after a few moments' silence. 'It wasn't over by Christmas, was it? Will it be over by next Christmas? They say the fighting's awful in Denmark and Norway now. It's as if he wants to take over everything.'

'I think he does. And he's got a lot of power. We can't just sit by and let him walk all over the world. If he was a good man it would be different – except that a truly good man wouldn't even want that sort of power. But he's not good. He's not even bad. He's evil, Lucy, and we've got to fight evil.'

Lucy looked at him. She had never heard David speak in such a serious tone before, and he knew what he was talking about. 'David, that sounds awful.'

45

'It is awful,' he said soberly. 'It's a bad business altogether, Lucy, and I'm very much afraid it's going to get a lot worse before it gets better.'

They sat silent for a few minutes, looking into the fire. Lucy tried to fight down the dread that was rising in her. She had already been through it once, when Wilmot was involved in the Battle of the River Plate, and after that triumphant return she'd thought her own battle over. Now she knew that as long as the war lasted, it would never be over.

'I don't know how I'll manage if anything happens to Wilmot,' she said in a trembling voice. 'I try not to think about it. I try not to think about the danger and the fighting and people getting killed. But we can't push it away and pretend it's not happening, can we? Some people *are* going to get killed – men and women and children. Some people are going to feel like I feel now, trying not to think about it, and they're going to have to face it. So we've all got to. We've all got to face it together.'

'I'm afraid we have.' He turned his head and looked at her. 'And that's what will help us win, Lucy. The feeling that we're all in it together – that if we pull together and help each other, we'll get through it. It isn't just what happens in the fighting, you see – it's what happens behind all that.'

'At home,' she said. 'All the way down from the Government to little back rooms like this. D'you really believe that, David? D'you really believe that people like me, just staying behind with the kids and keeping a home together, can have a real effect on the war? It sounds daft, put like that.'

'Not daft at all,' he said, and there was a new, strange note of tenderness in his voice. 'No, Lucy, it doesn't sound daft at all . . .'

They stared at each other. Lucy noticed for the first time how very dark his eyes were, almost black with a narrow rim of deep blue. She saw the tiny movement of a muscle in his jaw, and felt a tremor deep inside.

'David –'

'Lucy,' he said, and moved slowly closer. 'Lucy –'

The kiss was brief, a quick, hard touching of lips before they both drew back, startled and confused. Lucy turned away, her hands over her face.

David muttered something she couldn't hear and then said swiftly, 'Lucy, I'm sorry. That shouldn't have happened. Look, I'd better go.'

'No.' She turned back. 'It's all right, David. It doesn't matter. It – it was just one of those things.' She lifted her hands away from her face. 'It was talking about Wilmot and the war and everything. I was upset and you wanted to comfort me – that's all it was.'

'Yes,' he said slowly, 'that's all it was.'

'Let's listen to the news,' she said, and switched on the wireless. 'And I reckon you could do with another cup of cocoa before you go back. It's bitter out there. You'd never think we were nearly halfway through April.'

David hesitated, then sat back. The usual burbles and whistles filled the room as the wireless warmed up, then they heard the measured tones of the BBC announcer start to read the news, and they looked at each other in dismay.

Denmark had surrendered. Hitler had won another country.

David continued to stay at Pengelly's during the summer and autumn of 1940. The kiss was never repeated, nor even referred to, but he and Lucy drew closer as friends. Sometimes, guiltily, she thought of that moment by the fireside and knew that if circumstances had been different, there could have been a different relationship between herself and David. If there had been no Wilmot, no Heather . . . But she turned such thoughts away as soon as they arose. Entertaining even for a second the idea of never having known Wilmot – of there never *being* a Wilmot – was wicked. And if there had been no Wilmot, there would never have been a Geoff, or a Patsy. Or Zannah.

No. David was not, nor ever could be, more than a friend. Nor did either of them want to be more than friends to each other.

He was in Plymouth when battle-scarred ships returned from Dunkirk, bringing the shattered remnants of the BEF. He was there again when the Battle of Britain was at its height. Walking on the Hoe together, with Geoff and Patsy running ahead and Zannah stumping between her mother and David, a chunky fist clasped by each, he and Lucy looked up at the hot blue sky and imagined the fighting going on over other parts of the country. Lucy thought of her brother Kenny, up there in his Spitfire, and she wept again for her other brother Vic, who was lying dead somewhere in France and would never see his baby.

David disengaged his hand from Zannah's and reached across to her. 'I know,' he said quietly, and she thought that he did know, that he needed no explanation.

The bombing raids had begun now. The first had been on 6 July, only a month after Dunkirk; Plymouth had heard its first air-raid siren a week before but there had been no bombs then. Now, a lone aircraft flying high came in almost unnoticed and from a clear blue sky brought sudden destruction to a row of houses in Devonport and killed three people, one of them just a boy.

'So they can get this far after all,' Maud said to her husband, but the words were scarcely out of her mouth when the second raid came, less than twenty-four hours later, and this time five people were killed, and Home Sweet Home Terrace, which bore the brunt of the attack, became suddenly a place of horror and fear. After the worst of the daylight attacks towards the end of September, when more than a dozen people were killed at Stonehouse, Lucy made up her mind and moved the family into Lockyer Street.

David's baby son Stevie was a two-year-old now, and Heather had given David a snap of his birthday party to show Lucy the next time he came to Plymouth. He looked fat and jolly, a big grin on his face and chocolate smeared round his mouth. Heather had made a cake and there were two candles on it – ordinary white household candles, but Stevie didn't seem to care. David was in the picture too, looking proud and happy.

'I wish he could bring her and the baby down some time,' Maud said when Lucy showed her the picture. 'I liked her, she's a real nice young woman.'

'I like her too.' Lucy and Heather had started writing to each other, mostly talking about the children, but Heather had said how difficult it was for her to get out at all now, what with the baby and three old ladies to look after. David helped as much as he could, but you couldn't put too much on to a man in wartime, and he was often away anyway. She wrote cheerfully, without grumbling about this – indeed, she often said how lucky she was to have her mother still alive, and for Stevie to have two grannies and a great-grandma – but Lucy could tell she was tired sometimes, and David confirmed this.

'She looks worn out. I do all I can to help when I'm there, but the lion's share falls on her shoulders. It might be a bit easier if they were all under one roof, but my mother refuses to budge out of her own home, so Heather's backwards and forwards all the time.'

'Won't your mum go down to Cornwall? She used to live there, after all.'

'I've suggested it, but she wants to be near Stevie. He's her only grandchild – so far.' He gave Lucy a funny, rather shy little smile and she looked at him with sudden excitement.

'What do you mean – so far? Is Heather expecting again?'

'Well – yes, we think so.' He couldn't stop his smile from spreading now. 'Only it's early days – not even two months – so don't say anything yet. Just in case it's a false alarm.'

'No, of course not. But you don't really think it is, do you?'

'No,' he said, looking inordinately pleased. 'We're pretty sure.'

'Oh, that's lovely. Well, you haven't hung about, have you? What will Stevie be when it's born?' She began to count on her fingers. 'Let's see, it's September now – another seven months you think, so it'll be born some time in April – and he'll be just two and a half. Goodness, Heather's hands are going to be fuller than ever.'

'I know. I'm a bit worried about that myself, but she hasn't turned a hair. Says the mums can help out, it'll keep them occupied.' He grinned again. 'They'll probably be fighting over the pair of them.'

'Well, I think it's lovely.' Lucy looked a little wistfully at Zannah, who was on the floor playing with a set of coloured wooden bricks that Geoffrey had had when he was two years old. 'I'd like to have had another one. Just one more, a year or two younger than her. But what with the war and Wilmot being away all the time . . .'

'He's bound to come home soon,' David said, but she shook her head.

'It doesn't seem the right time now. It doesn't seem right to bring children into the world when things are so awful. It's different for you, you've only got the one kiddie and you've got to get your family together, but we've got three and I think we'll have to be satisfied with that.' She leant forward and gathered Zannah into her arms. 'And this one's such a little pet – I can't believe God would give us another treasure like her.'

David went back to London on the night train. When Lucy woke next morning, it was to the news that London had been bombed yet again.

'Why doesn't he *make* her go down to Cornwall?' Lucy fretted. 'He's got an auntie there with a big house and nice garden, he's told me all about it, he ought to tell Heather she's *got* to go.'

'You ought to know why,' her mother-in-law said. 'You wouldn't go if it was you, and you had Wilmot coming home.'

Lucy had to admit she was right, and it seemed almost as if people were, in a strange way, getting used to the bombing. In her letters, Heather described how young girls were shrugging off the danger and going out with their boyfriends just the same, to the pictures or dancing. They'd got fed up with letting Hitler rule their lives, she wrote.

By Christmas, there was no more doubt that the whole of Europe and beyond were gripped in the fiercest war the world had ever known, surpassing even the horrors of the Great War of 1914-18. The cities which had not yet been hit waited, and in January Lucy began to suffer the nightly torments of not knowing what was happening to her family in Portsmouth. On the same day that she received her first telegram, telling her that they had survived the worst night of bombing yet, she also received a letter from David.

'I'm so thankful to be able to tell you that Heather's agreed at last to go down to Cornwall,' he wrote. 'All the mums are going with her, so the whole family will be safe. I'll be bringing them down next week, after I've been to Portsmouth, and we want to break our journey in Plymouth for a night on the way. Book us three rooms at Pengelly's for next Wednesday!'

'Oh, I'm so glad,' Lucy exclaimed, and wrote back immediately, telling David that the best rooms in the house would be ready for them, and enclosing a note for Heather, to say how much they were all looking forward to seeing her, and that Zannah was already getting excited at the thought of seeing Stevie.

However, Zannah was to be disappointed. While David

was in Portsmouth, while he was actually visiting Lucy's family and sitting in Emily and Joe's back room, eating cottage pie and going with them down to the shelter as the siren sounded yet again, there was another raid on London. The house he and Heather were buying, where Heather and her mother and baby son were living, received a direct hit, and all three were killed outright.

Chapter Five

It was on 20 March that David came back to Plymouth for the first time since the death of Heather and his baby son.

As usual he said nothing about his reason for being there but Lucy knew that it was something to do with the visit of the King and Queen. They had come, as they were doing to so many other cities, to see the destruction, and they didn't just go to the smartest parts of Plymouth, they went to shabby backstreets that had been made more squalid still by the bombs that had torn the mean little houses apart. They looked about them, their faces sad and stricken, and talked to the people who were struggling to repair damaged homes or rescue their few possessions; they talked to them just as if they were personal friends.

'They've been bombed themselves,' Maud said. 'Buckingham Palace itself has been hit. They know what it's like.' But Lucy didn't think they did. They hadn't seen their entire home smashed to pieces, and had to go to some refuge post and queue up for hours and ask for ten shillings to buy clothes for the family. They hadn't had to wonder where they would lay their heads that night, or the next, and know that they'd never see their possessions again, that all they'd worked and striven and scraped for had gone for ever, or, worse still, that they'd never see loved members of their family again.

But that wasn't really their fault, and Lucy supposed they were doing their best, so with Maud and Arthur and the two girls she went up to the Hoe and cheered the King and Queen as they walked about with Lord and Lady Astor.

Geoff was there with the school, all looking very smart with their hair brushed until it shone and their socks held up smooth and unwrinkled by new garters. They had each been given a small paper Union Jack to wave, and the bright flags fluttered bravely in the March breeze, the red stripes echoed by the broad red bands on the Smeaton Tower.

David was there too, mixing unobtrusively with the press reporters and photographers. A visit by the King and Queen would be reported in all the local newspapers, to boost morale. They had already toured the city, through streets lined with cheering people. Lucy managed to get quite close, gazing with admiration at the shy, pleasant face of the King and the bright cornflower-blue eyes of the Queen.

David came to the guest house later that evening. He dropped his suitcase in the hall and came straight into the kitchen, looking tired. Lucy, who was slicing onions for supper, turned and went over to him, holding out her arms.

'David. Oh, David –'

He looked at her and his face was full of anguish. It was only a few weeks, she thought, and the shock probably hadn't even started to hit him until then. But somehow, seeing her, with onion tears on her cheeks and real sorrow in her eyes, broke down all the defences he had built up in those few weeks. He stumbled towards her and as she folded her arms about him he laid his head on her shoulder and began to weep.

His tears weren't the sort she would have expected. Not quiet, not restrained, but loud and noisy, with gulps and snorts, the sort of tears a child sheds, and his body shook and shuddered in her arms. He put his own arms around her and clung to her, and amidst his sobs there were words, words she could only just make out; pleas for his wife and baby to be returned to him, a tormented outpouring of sorrow.

Lucy stood quite still, only her hands moving as she

patted his shoulders and stroked his heaving back. She murmured to him as she would to a child, but her voice was thick and shaking with her own grief. She was aware of someone coming into the kitchen but only knew who it was when she felt her mother-in-law's arms around them both and heard Maud's voice in her ear.

'There, there. The poor lamb. The poor, poor lamb.' Nobody knew, perhaps not even Maud herself, whether the 'lamb' were David himself, the baby Stevie or Heather. Or even the old woman who had died. 'Let it out, then. Let it all out. You'll feel better when you've let it out.'

'All at once,' he said in a choked voice when at last he could speak. 'All at once. I saw the house when I went back . . . There was nothing left, nothing.' He lifted his head and looked into Lucy's eyes. 'Nothing.'

'Oh, David. It's terrible. It's awful.' At no other moment, even when she had thought herself a widow, even when she had waited in terror to hear if her own family had been killed, had the reality of the war been brought home to her quite so savagely as at this. Heather, the laughing bride; Stevie, the fat, jolly two-year-old – and the new baby, the unborn child growing in Heather's womb. All gone. Nothing left. The tears that ran down her face now had nothing to do with onions.

'I wanted to go in,' he said. 'They wouldn't let me. They said it was too dangerous. I could see there was nothing left – it caught fire, you see, it was burnt out, there were only a few roof-timbers all blackened and scorched, and great slabs of crumbling plaster hanging off the walls. It stank of burning . . . I knew there couldn't be anything to find, but I wanted to go in just the same. I wanted to be there – just to be *there*.'

'Of course you did. Of course.'

He looked at her. 'You understand that? They all thought I was crazy. Perhaps I was, for a while. I fought with them . . . I was a bit of a nuisance, I'm afraid.'

'It was your home,' Lucy said. 'Of course you wanted to go in. You wanted to be there with them.' You wanted to say goodbye, she thought, but didn't say it. Of course David hadn't actually wanted to say goodbye – he hadn't wanted to lose his family at all, he'd wanted it not to have happened – but he'd wanted, for just a while, to stand where they had died, to try to share it with them.

Maud had been busy with the kettle. Now she laid her hands on David's shoulders and pressed him gently into a chair at the kitchen table. 'Here's a cup of tea,' she said. 'I've put in a drop of Arthur's whisky. He doesn't drink it really, we just keep it for medicinal purposes, but he likes a drop in his cup of tea at bedtime sometimes.'

David's tormented face twitched with a faint smile. He rubbed one hand over his face and looked with surprise at his wet palm. Maud handed him one of Arthur's handkerchieves which had been airing on the rack that hung above them.

'Mop yourself up. And don't bother to say you're sorry. It does us all good to shed tears at times like this, and goodness knows you've got more cause than plenty of others.'

'And no more than many,' he said, his voice still shaking. 'You don't know what it's like up there.'

'We've heard,' Lucy said. 'We've seen pictures. And in Portsmouth.'

'I know. I'm sorry. I've seen it there too. The Guildhall gutted, shops destroyed, whole streets flattened. Liverpool as well. And Coventry – Coventry's a nightmare.' He shook his head. 'The worst of it was she'd just agreed to go down to Cornwall. I was going to bring them all, just a few days later. They'd have been safe . . .' His voice shook and thickened again and he bowed his head, covering his face with the big khaki handkerchief.

'Oh, David.' Lucy could think of nothing to say. There were no words for this kind of occasion. She put out her hand and laid it on his head, feeling the crispness of the thick, curling hair beneath her fingers. I'm so glad we never let that kiss go any further, she thought. I'm so glad he doesn't have anything to feel guilty about.

Clearly, though, he did feel guilty, horribly guilty that he hadn't argued more, insisted that Heather leave London. It didn't have to be Cornwall, it didn't have to be so far away, she could have gone to Hampshire or Berkshire or into the Cotswolds, anywhere she wanted to go. She didn't have to be evacuated, to go to whatever billet was chosen for her, he would have paid, paid willingly, for a cottage they could rent, a house big enough for them all. He should have kept on at her, worn her down as in the end he had done, but he should have done it sooner.

It all poured out as he drank Maud's tea without noticing it. All his guilt and grief and anger, flooding out in the kitchen of the guest house as he hadn't been able to let it loose anywhere else. 'She would have been all right,' he said hopelessly, over and over again. 'They would all have been all right.'

It was useless for Lucy to say that Heather had made her own choice, that she was a strong-minded woman, that it wasn't just her, the old ladies had refused to leave as well and that she'd felt obliged to stay to look after them. David listened politely but it was obvious that he either didn't hear her or just didn't believe it. He should have insisted, and he hadn't.

'But you did. You told me you did.'

'Not enough,' he said with a curious obstinacy. 'I didn't do it enough.'

By the time she took the children up to bed, Lucy was exhausted. Her own sorrow had come to the surface again and, with it, all her old anxieties about Wilmot and the family in Portsmouth. But there was no comfort for her while David was in such distress and she felt a desperate sadness that she could not be more comfort to him.

David went out, saying he wanted to walk up to the Hoe again now that it was quiet after the royal visit, and she felt a guilty relief as he closed the door. The children were fractious after the excitement of the day and she washed them quickly and bundled them into their pyjamas.

'Now, say your prayers.' She knelt beside them and added a special prayer for Uncle David. 'And for Auntie Heather and baby Stevie up in heaven.'

'Why do we need to say prayers for them?' Zannah enquired. 'Doesn't God know they're in heaven?'

'Don't be a twerp,' Geoff said scornfully. 'There's millions of people in heaven. He can't know them all.'

'He can,' Patsy argued. 'It says in the Bible, he knows even the sparrows, they told us that at Sunday School. If he knows sparrows, he's bound to know all the people.'

'I bet he doesn't. I bet he doesn't know all the people who've gone up in the past year,' Geoffrey said, making it sound as if going to heaven was like moving up a class in school. 'There's millions of people getting killed in the war. He can't know them all at once.'

'Yes, but they're not all going to heaven. The Germans won't be going to heaven. They'll be going to—'

'That's enough!' Lucy interrupted sharply. 'You don't have to talk like that, either of you. Just say "God bless Auntie Heather and Stevie, and their grannies," and then get into bed and let's hear no more chatter till tomorrow.'

'Can I say God bless the Queen as well?' Patsy asked. 'I thought she was ever so pretty.'

'Yes, you can say God bless the Queen.'

'And the King,' Geoffrey said.

'*And* the King.'

'And Princess Elizabeth and Princess Margaret Rose.'

'Yes, and that's all. Just say "and everyone else I know".' Lucy was desperate to see them asleep in bed. It seemed dreadful to feel cross with them over prayers, dreadful to want their chatter to stop when little Stevie and others like him would never chatter again, but her nerves felt stretched almost to breaking-point. David's anguished tears had upset her more than she'd realised at the time, when she was trying to give him comfort. Now, all she wanted to do was sit down by herself and pour out all her own feelings, first on paper to Wilmot and then, at last, to herself in her own tears.

'And everyone else I know,' the children said obediently into their steepled hands, and then scrambled into bed. Lucy bent and kissed them tenderly and they wound their arms around her neck.

'I'm sorry baby Stevie's dead,' Zannah whispered.

'Yes. So am I.'

'I don't see why babies have to get dead. It's not their fault there's a war.'

'I know.'

'Stevie wouldn't have wanted to be a soldier even when he was grown up, so why should he get dead?'

'I don't know, Zannah. I just don't know.' She looked down at the little girl. 'How do you know he wouldn't have wanted to be a soldier?'

'His face isn't like a soldier's face,' Zannah said, already half asleep. 'He's too kind. He wouldn't ever have wanted to hurt people.' She rolled her head away and her eyes closed. Lucy saw their movement under the thin skin of her eyelids and pulled the bedclothes up around the small, still-chubby body. What a little oddity Zannah was. She often came out with these remarks about people – and so often, Lucy reflected, she was right. Would she have been right about Stevie?

No one would ever know now.

Lucy kissed the older children goodnight and went downstairs. Maud and Arthur had left the kitchen to sit in the living-room. She could hear the *Band Waggon* tune being played on the wireless and the sounds of the comedians' voices. Richard Murdoch and Arthur Askey – normally she enjoyed their jokes as much as anyone else but tonight she just didn't feel like laughing.

Now, at last, she had time to herself, time to release her own suppressed feelings, yet now that she was alone, she did not know quite what to do after all.

When the first drone of enemy aircraft came, she was still sitting idle in her chair, her letter to Wilmot unwritten, her tears unshed. By the time the planes departed she had news of a different sort to impart. And her tears were the most bitter yet.

The wail of the siren wasn't any different that night from all the other times it had sounded. Many times already it had brought death and destruction to some part of the city, but never on the scale of that night of 20 March 1941. There was nothing to tell the people who ran to their shelters, or those who shrugged and didn't bother, that tonight was going to be so different.

'Quick. Down to the cellar.' Arthur was halfway downstairs, dragging his trousers on over his pyjamas, his braces dangling. 'Get the little 'uns up.'

'Oh, I'm so *sick* of this.'

Lucy brushed past him on her way up. They had evolved a routine. Maud made for the kitchen where she put on kettles and made flasks of cocoa and tea. Arthur gathered together a bundle of blankets and pillows which were kept ready on the landing. Lucy got the children up and dressed and, together with any guests who were staying, they all made their way down the steps to the dank, cavernous cellar which had only ever been used for storing things that nobody really knew what to do with.

The children had been deeply asleep after their exciting day and were hard to rouse. Patsy, at six, was of an age to be afraid of the snarling drone of the bombers as they approached, and the harsh rattle of the ack-ack gunfire.

She trembled as Lucy pulled her, still barely awake, from the bed, and whimpered.

Geoff was awake in an instant, making ack-ack noises back. He made for the window to look out and Lucy dragged him back sharply. 'Don't be so stupid! You know we mustn't show a light. Do you want them to see us and drop bombs right on top of the house?'

'I was only going to look for a second,' he grumbled. 'It's not fair, you never let me see. I shan't have anything to tell my grandchildren.'

'You won't have any grandchildren to tell if we don't get down to the cellar quickly. Now get dressed and go downstairs to Grampy.' She turned her attention to Zannah, who was snuggling back under the bedclothes. 'Wake up, sweetheart, we've got to go downstairs. Come on, lovey.' She drew the warm body into her arms, feeling a moment of hatred for the enemy who were threatening her children's lives. 'Let's just wrap this blanket round you.'

Zannah yawned and stretched, her heavy eyelids quivering with sleep. Lucy lifted her into her arms and Zannah let her head droop on her mother's shoulder. Pausing now only to snatch up the blanket, Lucy scurried out of the bedroom and down the stairs.

The drone had increased to a roar, drowning out all other sound. As the family and guests crowded down the cellar steps, it throbbed about them, reverberating in the stone walls, shaking the earthen floor, vibrating in the lath and plaster ceilings, in the floorboards, in the joists and in the deepest, most fundamental framework of the whole house. It wouldn't stand it, Lucy thought, the noise itself will shake it to bits, shake us all to bits. And she clamped her hands to her ears and then thought how much worse it must be for the children. She looked at Geoffrey's face, alive with excitement and fear; at Patsy's, white and quivering; and at Zannah's, the colour of ashes, her mouth wide and stretched in a scream of terror that nobody could hear.

'Zannah! Oh, Zannah, my baby, my poor, poor baby.' She clasped the little girl against her and reached out for Patsy and Geoffrey, pulling them close. The roar was all about them and even though it seemed to fill the air so that no more sound could possibly find room to be heard, even though it was so loud that you felt you could reach out and touch it, the thuds and crashes of exploding bombs made it seem no more than a whisper, and the family cringed and cowered together beneath the black and heavy weight of it.

It went on for hours. It had been just half past eight in the evening when it had started, and by the time the all-clear sounded and they raised their heads and stared shakily into the gloom of the cellar, it was almost dawn.

'Whatever's happened out there?' Lucy whispered. 'What are we going to find?'

Nobody answered. Maud was huddled on a blanket with Arthur, their hands so tightly clasped that the skin was white and stretched. The two or three guests – a sailor whose ship had put into Devonport for repairs and whose wife had come down from Scotland to spend a few days with him, and an old man who had been bombed out of his home in London – were also crouching on the cold, damp floor against the wall. David was close to Lucy. His arms had been around her and the children all night, but now he moved away slightly and she saw that his face was taut and streaked with tears and dust.

'At least they're out of it now,' she said quietly, touching the arm that had held her so strongly throughout the tumult. 'At least you know they don't have to suffer any more.'

He turned and looked at her as if she were a stranger. Then his face cleared a little, and he nodded. 'Yes. I know they're not afraid and suffering. But – oh, Lucy –'

'I know.' Painfully, she disengaged cramped arms from around the children and stretched stiffened legs. The others were moving too, slowly as if they had forgotten how. One by one, they stood up, moving uncertainly, looking at each other, nobody wanting to be first to go up the cellar steps and see what lay above.

'Come on,' David said, taking hold of himself. 'We can't stay here for ever. I'll go first. We'll need to be careful . . .'

Nobody asked why care was needed. Even little Zannah knew that there might be no house above them now, that nothing but wreckage might await them, that they might not even be able to open the cellar door. We might be buried alive here, Lucy thought with a sudden sick fear.

David and the sailor went up the cellar steps together and when they pushed gently on the door it swung open, and they saw to their relief that everything seemed just as usual above.

'Oh, thank God,' Maud kept saying as they moved through the rooms. 'Oh, thank God, thank God . . .'

The rooms were heavily curtained. No light filtered through, yet they seemed faintly lit by a dim redness, a glow that was perhaps a particularly fiery sunrise. And in the silence, that had seemed so absolute after the planes had gone at last and the explosions ceased and the rattle of ack-ack stopped, could be heard a growing hum, a more subdued kind of roar, like the voice of a giant beast woken from slumber and still half-snoring.

'I think it's light enough to open the blackouts,' David said quietly, and Lucy turned out the lights while he pulled back the curtains and then lifted the wooden frame away from the living-room window.

There was a moment of silence. The red, flickering glow flooded into the room. There was daylight in it, though not much yet, but the daylight was lost in the ferocity of the crimson and orange and black of the flames that burned over Plymouth after the destruction of that night.

'Spooners has gone,' Arthur said later. He and David had gone out, picking their way through the debris, trying to make sense of this new, flattened Plymouth. 'Spooner's, and the Royal Hotel, and God knows what else. Derry's Clock's still there, but you can't make out where you are, half the time. There's bits of buildings – you can recognise some, but then there's others that don't look like anything at all. And some have just gone, nothing but rubble left. You couldn't even say there was *streets*, let alone buildings. And there's still fires burning and firemen trying to put 'em out, and miles and miles of hosepipes. We gave up and come home, there wasn't no use trying to get through it all.'

'We were just in the way,' David said. He looked exhausted, Lucy thought, and she knew that his own grief was very close to the surface. He had seen what London had been like, what his own home had suffered, and the pictures of Heather and Stevie, and Heather's mother and grand-mother, were still vivid in his mind. She laid her hand over his and wondered if he had noticed. 'I should have helped . . . I ought to have been able to do something.'

He had come back because he was worried about Arthur. The older man had looked ill and grey, the skin around his mouth a bluish white. He looked better now he was back, with a cup of tea in front of him, but his breathing was still ragged. He ought to see the doctor, Lucy thought, but what doctor would be holding surgeries this morning?

David got up suddenly. 'I'll go and see if there's anything I can do. I can't sit here.'

'But what can you do? What can anyone do?' Maud was in tears again. She had started crying when David had first opened the curtains to reveal the glow of flames as the city burned. 'It's all up – they've beaten us. We can't –' She sat upright in her chair, her body quivering, tears running down her face.

Lucy spoke sharply. 'Don't talk like that, Mum. We're not beaten. London, Pompey, Coventry, Liverpool – they've all been through this, and so've a lot more places, and *they're* not whining about being beaten. So don't let's

64

hear any more talk like that, if you don't mind.' She looked at David, knowing he had to go. 'You'll be careful, won't you?'

He nodded wearily and she felt a sharp stab of pity for him. He had lost so much. 'We're still here for you,' she said quietly. 'You matter a lot to us, David.'

He looked at her, and still she wasn't sure that he really saw her. 'There may be people,' he said. 'People buried . . . I must go and help.'

They heard him stumble along the passage and out of the front door. It closed behind him, leaving only the sounds of Arthur's ragged breathing, and Maud's quiet sobs.

Chapter Six

David spent the day in the devastated streets, scrabbling under piles of rubble for the bodies of survivors. In many places, the fires were still burning, defeating the firefighters' efforts to put them out, and no one could get near. Too often, the bodies he did find were of those who had not survived, and he came home that evening white and shaking from what he had seen.

They spent the second night, as they had spent the first, crouching in the cellar beneath the house, listening to the holocaust as it burst above them.

'How long can we go on like this?' Lucy whispered. 'All our cities destroyed – they're tearing the heart out of Britain. We'll never be able to get back to normal.'

'Don't let's say "never",' he murmured, and she knew what it must cost him to say that, when he had lost so much already. 'We've got to get through it somehow. Nothing will ever be the same again – but we've got to survive, or there's no point in any of it.'

They came out next morning, fear gripping their hearts as they took down the blackout. There was hardly a window left with glass in it. The splinters were buried in the fabric of the curtains, shards that were too grimed with smoke and dust even to glitter. Amidst the flames that still burned were billowing clouds of black, oily smoke that blotted out the orange glow. And as the daylight grew stronger and the sun's rays managed to penetrate the gloom, they could see that a thick pall of dust hung over the entire city.

Lucy left the children with Maud and Arthur and went

with David to see the damage. Little as she desired to look at the destruction, something in her wanted desperately to understand it, to share the horror of the experience with those who had lost everything they possessed. It was the same desire that she had felt after the blitz on Portsmouth, a need to share it with her family. But she hadn't been able to go then, and she'd had to rely on her mother's letters, the newspapers and the BBC news for information. Now, she could see it for herself, and knew that all the terrible stories she had heard were merely the tip of an horrific iceberg.

Together, with others who had come out to stare in stupefaction, they wandered aimlessly through streets that had once been familiar and were now the stuff of nightmare.

Many of the buildings had simply been blown apart by the bombs and great craters pocked the ground while bricks and blocks of concrete and girders of wood and steel lay strewn around them. In some places, it was impossible to see where the road had been and where the buildings had stood. Of the walls that remained standing, most were crumbling and broken, their roofs smashed and caving in. A few bits of furniture hung at crazy angles and possessions lay mixed together, some broken beyond any hope of repair, others inexplicably untouched.

Other buildings had been set on fire, and in many of them the flames still raged. As before, the streets were a tangle of hosepipes and the firemen, white with exhaustion beneath the grime, were battling grimly to contain flames that had been out of control for hours and would never be contained but must, in the end, be left to burn themselves out.

'Plymouth's gone,' Lucy said, staring at the inferno. 'Plymouth has gone for ever.'

But Plymouth had not gone.

Much of it had been destroyed. The centre, the tangle of streets, the great shops – Spooner's, Dingle's, Jay's the furniture store, and many others – were smashed to pieces. Drake's Circus had been completely burned out. Old Town Street, Cornwall Street, George Street, Union Street and the Octagon – all had been devastated. Charles Church and St Andrew's Church – the cathedral of the city – were gutted shells.

It was said that the fire had been so intense that gold in a jeweller's shop window had melted and run away down the gutters.

But some buildings still stood, inexplicably untouched amongst the ruins. Derry's Clock still ticked defiantly on its tower, a landmark for those bewildered by the desecration of the city. Leicester Harmsworth House, where the newspapers were produced, still stood in Frankfort Street, surrounded by wreckage. And in those shops and offices which remained, people still went to work, picking their way through rubble to get there.

For a fortnight they were left in peace to collect themselves. Help came from all over the country: firemen already worn out with the bitter experiences of fighting the raids in their own cities, arrived to help Plymouth in her hour of need. Bulldozers came to help clear the streets, and builders and roadworkers to make the damaged buildings safe. Burst water pipes and gas mains were repaired, electricity restored. It all took time and people were forced to struggle on without for days that looked like stretching into weeks or even longer. Nevertheless once their initial shock was over, the Plymouthians bounced back, refusing to be beaten. Like those others in similarly hit cities in other parts of the country, they thumbed their noses at Hitler.

David went back to London. Before he left he hugged everyone in the family, promising to come back soon, making them promise to take care of themselves. 'Go down to the cellar every night,' he said. 'Never mind whether there's a warning or not. Just go.'

They did, for the first few nights, but the cellar was cold

and damp, and as the warning siren remained silent night after night, they began to hope that the enemy had abandoned Plymouth. There wasn't much left to bomb, after all.

'If we could only leave a few mattresses down there it wouldn't be so bad,' Maud complained, 'but they'd be covered in mould in a week. And it isn't doing Arthur's chest no good, having to spend all night in that damp atmosphere.'

'I still think David's right,' Lucy said. 'We just don't know when they'll come back.'

Inevitably there came a night when Arthur refused to go. He had a bad cold, and he blamed the nights in the cellar for it. 'It'll be pneumonia if I goes down there tonight, and it'll be the death of me. I'd rather die in me own bed.'

Maud wouldn't leave him, so Lucy took the children down by herself. There were no guests in the hotel now. They dragged a mattress down the stairs and lay there alone in a corner of the dank little dungeon, watching the flickering light of the hurricane lamp on the green-patched walls.

'I don't like it,' Patsy whimpered. 'I don't like it down here by ourselves.'

'I don't see why we have to come,' Geoff said grumpily. 'Grampy and Grammy have stayed in bed. Why can't we?'

'You know what Uncle David said.' Lucy would rather have been upstairs in bed herself. 'There might be another raid, and you know how bad they've been.'

'There hasn't been for ages. Not for *weeks*.' He poked with his finger at the skin forming on his cup of cocoa. 'Why can't we go out to Dartmoor, then, if it's so dangerous here? Lots of people do. Billy Madge's mum and dad do, they go out every night and take their tent. Billy says it's smashing, just like real camping. There's lots of people go.'

'We haven't got a tent.' Lucy knew about the thousands of people who trekked out of the city each night. They slept where they could, with or without tents. She'd thought about it, thought about going out to Yelverton or Tavistock, or perhaps to Ivybridge. Or just getting on a train and getting off at some tiny station – Clearbrook or Whitchurch, perhaps – and finding shelter where she could. But it wasn't as easy as that. You had to get everything together, you had to make your way back next morning – it took half the day, just going and coming back. And she didn't like the idea of sheltering in some barn or under a hedge in all the cold of night and the bad weather, with all sorts of people about.

'This cellar's safe enough. As long as we're down here we're all—'

The wail of the siren interrupted her and she gasped and grabbed for the children's hands. They clutched each other, even Geoff's bravado gone as they listened to the familiar snarl of the approaching planes.

'Oh no,' Lucy whispered, and gathered Zannah close against her heart. 'Oh, not again. Not again, not again . . .'

It was several minutes before she thought of Arthur and Maud.

'Grammy and Grampy,' she gasped. 'They're still upstairs. Why haven't they come down?'

'Perhaps the house has been bombed,' Geoff suggested, and she was so terrified that he might be right that she cuffed him sharply.

'Don't say such things!' Gently, she shifted Zannah from her lap on to the mattress. 'I'll go and fetch them. They mustn't stay up there.'

'Don't go and leave us alone!' Patsy was obviously terrified. 'Mummy, please –'

'I've got to fetch them. I can't leave them.'

'*Mummy* –'

'I'll only be a minute.' She tried to unpick Patsy's fingers. Zannah was clinging too. 'Let go – let *go* –'

'I'm coming too –'

'*I'm* coming –'

'*No!* Stay here – I'll be back before you know I'm gone. Geoff, look after them. Patsy, do as Geoff tells you – look after your sister.'

'*Mummy!*'

The crash of a bomb almost immediately overhead obliterated Lucy's voice and the voices of the three children. Almost without knowing it, she was up the cellar steps, only half aware that the children were close behind her. The bomb did not seem to have fallen on the house, but the walls were crumbling, sheets of plaster dropping away as she ran panic-stricken up the main stairs towards the bedrooms, and she could hear the roar of fire from somewhere outside, and the crash of breaking glass.

'Mum, Dad – where are you? Why haven't you come down?' She was aware suddenly of someone behind her, of the light from a torch throwing her shadow on the walls, and she jerked round. 'Whatever are you—*David!*'

He stood a step or two below her, lowering the torch so that the beam did not shine in her face. 'I came in on the last train. The raid hadn't started – Lucy, why aren't you in the cellar? What are you all doing up here?'

She looked past him at the children, crowding past to clutch at her skirt. 'I told you to stay downstairs. I *told* you.' She looked helplessly at David. 'I came to fetch Mum and Dad. They wouldn't come down. I don't know why they haven't come out of their room.' Half fearfully, she looked back up towards the bedroom door. 'I can't leave them there.'

'Go down. Take the children down.' He pushed past them. 'I'll bring them. They're probably still asleep.'

'In *this*?' But Lucy knew that the two older people had managed to sleep through a number of the raids, and that Arthur had started to use earplugs. It was quite possible that both were lying there, their ears stuffed with cottonwool, oblivious of the uproar in the skies.

'Go on. Go downstairs. Get the children out of this.' He gave her a push. There was another explosion, closer than before, and the house shook. Lucy heard a crash from one of the rooms, as if something heavy – a wardrobe or a dresser – had toppled over. She felt a scream rise in her throat and stumbled down the stairs, dragging the children with her.

'Quick. Back in the cellar.' They were at the foot of the stairs now, only yards from the cellar door. It stood open, the darkness of the steps yawning below. And as Lucy blundered towards it, it seemed to lift away from its hinges and hang trembling in air that had become suddenly visible, a shimmering curtain of darkness shot with blinding white light. The stairs themselves lifted away and hovered for a moment before falling slowly back into place. The walls became fluid, billowing outwards with the flimsiness of net curtains blowing in a fierce wind, and the wallpaper fluttered and was shredded to a million tiny flakes. The house was filled with a sharp, hot wind that brought with it a flash of light, like a bright, gleaming sword, and screamed a banshee scream before it fled away into the night. In an instant of clarity Lucy felt she understood everything: the secret of the world, of the universe, of life itself, and she knew that she had seen what men since time began had seen, and what they had described as the Angel of Death.

The explosion came last of all. But Lucy did not hear its sound.

The house was not completely gutted. Enough rooms were left habitable for the family to live in, and the experts said that rebuilding would be possible. Nobody knew when it would be possible – there was already far too much rebuilding needed in the city for anyone to give a date or make any promises – but the walls could be shored up and the torn roof patched, and the doors and windows replaced so that what was left could be made secure.

Arthur and Maud had both been saved. They had woken shortly before the bomb had fallen and had been struggling into their clothes even as David and Lucy met on the stairs. Arthur's hand had been on the doorknob when the explosion had shaken the house and the blast flung him across the room, landing mercifully on the bed. Maud, sitting down to put on her shoes, had been narrowly missed by a shard of glass as big as a spear, which had impaled the pillow where, only ten minutes earlier, her head had been resting.

David had saved Geoffrey's life, and Patsy's too. Seeing that Arthur and Maud were all right, he had turned his attention to the children. The blast had scattered their bodies over the passageway but Geoff was already staggering to his feet, blinking and holding his head. He looked up at David and his eyes filled with tears.

'I didn't mean it to happen. I didn't mean it.'

'Of course you didn't, old chap. It's not your fault.'

'I should have done what Mum said. I should have stayed in the cellar.'

'It doesn't matter.' David's eyes were on the ceiling above Geoffrey's head. He spoke quietly. 'Just go over by the front door, old son, will you? Just go and wait for me there.'

'I want Mum.'

'By the door, Geoff.' David's voice was tight. He came slowly down the stairs and moved towards the two girls, lying huddled by their mother's body. 'Go on now, there's a good chap.' The ceiling above the stairwell was shaking, the walls buckling slowly outwards. Off the stairs now, he quickened his steps, moving swiftly down the hall to the three huddled bodies. *'Geoffrey!'*

The boy was beside him, catching his sleeve. David felt his panic and bit back the anger that was born of his own fear. The boy was only eight or nine years old . . . He bent and touched the three faces, feeling their warmth. Please God they were still alive. He could hear the creaking, tearing sounds of wood being pulled apart. The stairs. The walls. The ceiling. He flung a glance of dread and apprehension upwards, caught a glimpse of Arthur and Maud stumbling down, yelled at them to get out, away from the stairs that were about to give way, away from the walls and the ceiling that were about to come crashing down. He grasped Lucy's shoulder and dragged her along the floor, brought her to the front door just as Arthur wrenched it open, ran back for the girls. Geoff was in his way and he thrust him out, then bent towards the two crumpled bodies, lifting both in his arms, turning to stagger back along the passage, towards the open door, towards the red and flickering heat that was pouring in from the street.

The walls buckled and the ceiling drooped, slowly, like a bellying hammock slung between the rafters. The stairs folded inwards and crashed. A beam dropped from some-where high in the roof. It fell across David's path and caught him a stunning blow across the shoulders. It knocked the two girls from his arms and he fell across their bodies, pinned to them by the long and heavy slab of wood.

When Lucy was well enough to hear what had happened, they told her that David had a broken shoulder and had lost his left arm. Her daughter Patsy was in another part of the hospital. Her back had been injured and it was unlikely that she would ever be able to walk again.

Zannah – her baby Zannah – had been killed outright.

Chapter Seven

When Lucy looked back at that time, after the war had ended and before Wilmot returned, she thought of it as the lowest point of her entire life. Nothing, she thought, could be any worse than that moment when they told her that Patsy was crippled and Zannah, her lovely Zannah, killed.

It was as if darkness had descended on the world, a great engulfing blanket of solid blackness that swallowed everything it touched. She moved in an enshrouding fog which barely parted to let her through, and there was no light, not even the tiniest flickering pinpoint of light, to show her the way. The fog dulled sound as well, so that she couldn't properly hear what was said to her, couldn't make sense of the noises she heard, and her ears were offended by laughter and music so that she shut them out and ignored them. Her only interest, as she slowly and reluctantly awoke to life around her, was in the war news, and she listened avidly to reports of air-raids and battles at sea, and followed on a map the advances of the German forces in Europe, stabbing little black-headed pins in to show where the Front was at its most active.

'I don't like it,' Maud said to Arthur. 'It's not healthy. It's morbid.'

'I don't know what we can do about it,' he said. 'I've tried. I told her, it's the living you ought to be bothering yourself about now, maid, not the dead. They're safe enough. It's that little Patsy who needs her mum, and young Geoff. But she just looked at me as if she didn't know what I was talking about.'

Maud shook her head. 'It's the worst thing that can happen to a woman, losing a child. And Zannah was like a little princess. We all miss her.'

''Course we do. 'Course we miss her. But Patsy and Geoff are the ones that need their mum now – specially Patsy, poor little toad.'

Patsy had been brought home from hospital. There was nothing more that could be done for her, the doctors said, and she lay propped in a bed brought down into the living-room, staring out of the window during the day and reading or listening to the wireless in the evenings. Geoff played games with her when he was home from school, but Patsy tired quickly. She suffered from headaches and asked for the curtains to be drawn because the light hurt her eyes. At eight o'clock she was carried into the small room next door that had been used as a store-room and was now converted to a bedroom for her to use, and when there was an air-raid warning she was carried down the cellar steps.

The main stairs had been replaced. The blast had done no more than rip them from their roots and bring down a ceiling with them, leaving most of the rooms intact. By the time Lucy came home from hospital, the house had been patched up a bit, and when Patsy returned it was taking guests again. There were still people coming to Plymouth, needing accommodation, and the few rooms that Maud and Arthur kept open were nearly always full. But the work of just these few rooms kept them as busy as if the whole building were packed night after night, and they looked to Lucy to help.

'It's not the bed-making and washing, that's the same as ever it was,' Maud said. 'It's the shopping. Getting their ration books and standing in queues hour after hour and trying to get stuff to make a decent dinner of an evening and a breakfast to send them out with. And we couldn't even do that at first, what with all the gas being cut off all over the city.' She sighed and rubbed her face wearily. 'And you can't get a girl to come in and work now, they're all off doing war work, joining the Forces or going into munitions or driving buses – there's no end to it all. They're even talking of putting them in the dockyard.'

'I can't help it, Mum. I'm just so tired all the time. And Patsy takes up a lot of my time, you know that.'

Maud did know. Patsy wanted a lot of attention these days, and you couldn't blame her. It was terrible for a kiddy to have to spend her days in a bed, looking out of the window at the others, or in what was no better than a pram. And knowing she'd never be any different, that was the worst of it. Nothing but a lifetime of just sitting and being wheeled about.

'All the same, there's a war on,' she said. 'I know it seems awful, Lucy, but we've all got to pick ourselves up somehow and carry on.'

David said the same when he came to see them. He spent less time in hospital than they'd expected, considering he'd lost an arm, but it was a while before he came back to Plymouth. He'd gone down to Cornwall to stay with his auntie, taking his mother with him, and he came up in the train one day. It was in the middle of May, not long after Mr Churchill had come to Plymouth. Churchill had driven through the streets in an open car, perched up on the back of it so that everyone would get a good view, and he'd waved his cigar and made the V–sign. Arthur was still talking about it.

'Didn't know he was coming till half an hour before,' he told David. 'The police went round in a van, telling folk. Well, a lot of 'em were on their way out for the night – getting on for four o'clock, it was – so there weren't that many crowds, but those of us that did stop got a proper sight of him. And he got a proper sight of us too, and of Plymouth. You could see he was upset. Tears in his eyes, they said he had. "God bless you all," he said. I heard him with my own ears. "God bless you all."'

'His wife looked proper smart,' Maud said. 'I was surprised – I mean, he's no oil-painting, is he? You can see why they call him the British bulldog. But she's lovely, and she was dressed lovely too, a spotted fur coat – snow leopard, it said in the paper – and a scarf over her head with bits of his speeches printed on it. I thought that was handsome.'

'Mind you, not everyone was pleased – got a bit superstitious about it, some did. Thought there'd be a raid that night, like when the King and Queen came. But there wasn't. I don't reckon Hitler's got the nerve to bomb old Winnie!'

'And how's Lucy?' David asked when their reminiscences had run dry. There'd been no sign of her since he had arrived, and he was afraid that she didn't want to see him. He hadn't heard from her since the raid, and had been torturing himself by thinking that perhaps she blamed him for Patsy's injury and, worse still, for Zannah's death.

Maud and Arthur exchanged glances.

'Well, she's well enough in herself,' Maud said. 'I mean, she had a bit of a knock on the head and a few bruises here and there, nothing much to make a song and dance about, and they're all healed up. But she's taken it bad, there's no saying otherwise, and she don't seem able to pull herself out of it somehow. I've told her, there's many have had to suffer as bad and worse, and we can't all sit about crying all the time – not that she does, it might be better if she did have a good cry and let it all out, but she—' Maud stopped abruptly and flushed scarlet. 'Oh, I'm *sorry*. I forgot you'd lost your little one just the same. And Heather too. Oh, what must you be thinking of me!'

David shrugged and made a wry grimace. 'Don't worry, Maud. You're right. There are a lot of us going through the same thing. That's why I wanted to see Lucy. It sometimes helps to be with someone who – well, who's been through it too.'

Maud nodded. She rested her eyes on his empty sleeve, pinned up on his shoulder. 'And how are you keeping yourself? It's a bad job, that.'

'Bad enough,' he agreed, 'But at least it's not my right arm. I've still got the useful one! Mind, you don't realise just how much you use an arm till it's not there any more – not to mention the fingers and thumb. I've had to learn a lot of new tricks.'

The door opened and Lucy came in. She stopped when she saw David and hesitated for a moment. Her face whitened and then the colour came flooding back and tears sprang to her eyes. She ran the last few steps and flung herself into his one-armed embrace, weeping against his chest.

'David! Oh, *David*.'

'It's all right,' he said softly, holding her firmly against him. 'It's all right, Lucy. I'm here. I'm here. Just cry it out, now, just cry it out. It'll make you feel better. You will feel better.'

'I'll never feel better,' she sobbed. 'David, didn't they tell you? Zannah—'

'I know. I know about Zannah.'

'And Patsy – she'll never be able to walk again. Oh, David, it's not fair, it's not fair.'

'I know. War isn't fair to anyone. *Life* isn't fair. But we all expect it to be. That's why it comes as such a shock when we find out the truth.'

'Why Zannah?' Lucy whispered. 'Why did it have to be her? She was such a lovely little girl, David.'

He said nothing, just kept stroking her shoulders with his one hand. Maud and Arthur got up and quietly left the room. David drew Lucy down into a chair and pulled another close. He placed his arm around her shoulders again and she leant her head on his shoulder.

'I don't think I can bear it, David, I don't think I can go on living.'

'Of course you can,' he said firmly. 'Of course you'll go on living. You've got Patsy and Geoff depending on you. And Wilmot. What do you think he's going to say if he comes home and you're not here? If you haven't waited for him.'

'I want to. I want to be here, but – it's so hard. It hurts so much. I don't think –'

'Listen,' he said, and cupped his hand under her chin, making her look into his face. 'Listen to me, Lucy. I *know* how much it hurts. I *know*. And I've gone on living. Don't you think there have been times when I've felt like this too? When I've felt the pain was just too much to bear? And do you know what I tell myself when it gets too bad?' She shook her head. 'Shall I tell you?' He waited for her answer.

'Yes, please, David,' she whispered at last.

'I think of the people who will be even more hurt if I stop living. My mother. My aunt. *You.* Your children, Arthur, Maud, even Wilmot who's away fighting, risking his life for us. And others, people you don't know, friends and family who are less important to me, but who would all be affected in some way, however small. And who am I to say how small the effect would be?' He looked at her for a moment and then said quietly, 'My pain would be ended, but theirs – well, whatever pain they already have, I would just be adding to it. Spreading mine around all of them, all of *you.* I don't think I have any right to do that, Lucy. I think it's my job to keep that particular pain to myself.'

Lucy was silent. Then she said, 'And it's my job to keep mine.'

'Do you think so?' David asked. 'I'm not saying I'm right, Lucy. It's just what I believe.'

'I know. But Zannah – I'm not the only one, David. There's Wilmot, and all the rest of the family. And Patsy, she's like a ghost. And even Geoff – he's not the same. It's hurting them too.'

'And will it hurt them any the less if they lose you as well?' he asked, and she bowed her head.

They sat quietly for a while, then Lucy said, 'I'm a selfish pig, David. You went through all this and you lost your wife as well as your baby. And I haven't even asked about your arm.'

'My arm?' he said lightly, shrugging so that the stump, reaching halfway to where the elbow ought to have been, moved. 'Oh, I haven't seen it for a few weeks now. Ask about the rest of my body.'

Lucy laughed, and the unexpected sound seemed to warm the air. She lifted her head and looked at him, then gave him a crumpled grin and rubbed the back of her hand across her nose. 'I really have been a selfish pig, haven't I?'

'No,' he said. 'No, you haven't. Not at all. You've been an ordinary young woman who's gone through a terrible time.'

'But there are so many people going through just the same. Worse.'

'And they all hurt just as much as you. We all suffer the same, Lucy. We just have to get through it as best we can, and nobody has any right to tell us how we should do it.'

'All the same,' she said, 'this is war. We can't give way. We've got to carry on, like you said. We can't let Hitler beat us.'

David smiled and took her hand. 'That's the stuff.'

'I shan't let him beat me,' she said seriously. 'For a while, I thought he had. But I'm not going to let him do it. None of us is going to let him do it. We won't give in to him, David. We won't.' For a few minutes, she was silent again, as if summoning all her strength to fight this new and so much harder battle. And then she looked at him again and smiled. 'Well, come on, then, David. Tell me about the rest of your body . . .'

Slowly, Lucy dragged herself out of the despondent slough into which she had fallen immediately after

Zannah's death. There really was too much to do, she told herself, to give in. And it was up to everyone to make it clear, in whatever way they could, that they were *not* giving in. That was the answer, she thought. Show people. Show Hitler. Show them all.

That was why someone had gone down to St Andrew's church the day after it had been bombed. The roof had been blasted away, although the walls still stood, and the bells hung undamaged in the tower. And over the main door someone had hung a plank of wood with the single word '*Resurgam*' carved roughly on it.

Rise again, Lucy thought. That's what that person had been saying. We'll rise again, all of us. We won't give in.

'Come on,' she said, going into Patsy's bedroom on 1 June. 'We're going out. We're going up on the Hoe, dressed up in all our best clothes, and we're going to show everyone that we're not beaten.'

Patsy turned from the window and stared at her. 'On the Hoe? In our best clothes? But why?'

'I told you. We're going to show Hitler we won't be beaten.'

'But he won't see us. It's only people round here who'll see us.'

'I know. And they're the ones who matter.' Lucy knelt beside her daughter's bed. 'You see, if we look miserable we make other people miserable. But if we smile and look bright and cheerful – why, that helps them to feel better. And it spreads, like ripples when you throw a stone into a pool of water. And if we start it off this morning – and other people do it as well – well, it could spread as far as Hitler himself in the end. And that's how we can show him we won't be beaten. Just think, if everyone did it—'

'The war would stop,' Patsy said. 'It would just stop.'

She held up her arms for Lucy to remove her nightie and wash her. Lucy dressed her in a summer frock she hadn't worn since last year, a favourite that had been just a little bit too big and now fitted perfectly. For a moment, she felt a lump in her throat, thinking of Patsy as she had been when she last wore that frock, running along the grassy Hoe, laughing and playing tag with Geoff and Zannah. The tears stung her eyes and she brushed them away impatiently.

She didn't think the war would come to an end just because she and Patsy went walking on the Hoe, but who knew what great effects stemmed from small beginnings? And it had to be better than looking miserable.

It was all she could do, after all. All she could do, and the least she could do.

Chapter Eight

The worst of the blitz was over. As May passed into June, and June into July, and the blazing days of summer softened to the mellowness of autumn and then the first sharp frosts of winter, the raids grew more sporadic and less intense. There was still damage done, still people injured and killed, but there were no more nights of terror spent listening to the incessant, unbearable barrage of explosions, and no more dawns of fire.

'Us mustn't sit back and think it's all over, all the same,' Arthur said. 'There's still a war going on, and the Germans won't leave us in peace till it's finished with.'

Peace! It was a word from an age gone by, a word from fairytale. Lucy could scarcely believe that there had once been a time when she and Wilmot had strolled arm in arm on the Hoe and gone swimming in the little rockpools. She looked down at the big semicircular pool that had been opened soon after she'd first come to Plymouth, and thought of how she'd taught Wilmot to swim, how he'd raced her and won. How they'd taken Geoff and Patsy across the Cremyll ferry to Cawsand and played with them on the beach. How they'd caught the train out to Yelverton, even as far as Princetown once, and walked on the moor and picnicked in the heather.

She hadn't liked Princetown much. It was a gloomy place, its houses all grey and uniform – prison officers' houses, Wilmot said – and she hated the huge stone prison itself, a great barracks of a place with hundreds of windows. There must be prisoners behind each of those windows, thieves and murderers, and she loathed the idea that they were there, looking out at her and the children.

She wondered now what it was like to be in prison during a war.

She wrote to Wilmot every day, even if it was no more than a line or two before she said goodnight. Letters came sporadically from him. He couldn't say much but she guessed he was in the Mediterranean, and then, after Pearl Harbor, in the Far East.

By the middle of April 1942, a year after the bombing that had killed Zannah and left Patsy in her wheelchair, the news was all of a new battle – the Battle of the Java Sea. The *Exeter*, it seemed, was fated to be involved in these great sea encounters. This time, however it seemed the *Exeter* was fated altogether.

Lucy was in Portsmouth when the news came through. She sat white faced in her mother's back room and listened to the wireless. Patsy was lying in her grandfather's big armchair, her legs propped on a little wooden stool he had made for her. Geoff, now ten years old, was playing with some old Meccano that had once belonged to Vic.

'*Exeter*'s gone down,' she whispered through lips that suddenly refused to move properly. 'Mum, did you hear that? They've sunk the *Exeter*.'

'It could be just a rumour,' Emily said. There had been rumours like that before. But they both knew it wasn't. The BBC was very careful about the news it broadcast and never told you anything that wasn't true. 'And the men could have been saved. There were other ships about as well.'

Despite her words, Emily was as frightened as Lucy. They sat close together, their arms about each other, listening. Geoff, sensing something wrong, looked up and opened his mouth to speak, but Lucy shushed him with a quick flap of her hand.

There had been three ships lost, they heard then and later, as more news filtered through. HMS *Encounter* had gone, and an American ship, the USS *Pope*. It had been a tremendous battle, and *Exeter* had already been hit and damaged when she was caught between four enemy cruisers. She had no power left, and no chance against such force.

'But what about the men?' Lucy asked desperately. She asked the question again the next day, and the next, but there was no answer. Nobody knew what had become of the sailors aboard her.

'They think a lot survived,' Joc said, reading the *Daily Express*. 'They think they managed to get ashore. They were probably taken prisoner. We'll hear soon.' But no word came, and Lucy went back to Plymouth not knowing, once again, whether she were widow or wife.

'I can't bear to think about it,' she said to David. 'And I can't *stop* thinking about it. I think of him going down on the ship, swallowed up in the water.' She shuddered. 'There'd be sharks, wouldn't there? And then I think about him trying to swim about, trying to stay afloat . . .' She remembered his words to her before the war, when she'd discovered he couldn't swim. *If the ship went down, I'd probably be a thousand miles from land anyway* . . . 'And even if he did get ashore – what happened then? Did they just wander about in the jungle?' She had only a vague idea of what the jungle might be like, and pictured tigers stalking through dense, tropical undergrowth, and snakes rearing broad, vicious heads and spitting venom from hissing mouths. 'Or did they get caught? And if they were caught, why hasn't anyone let us know? They're supposed to let people know, isn't that one of the rules?'

'The Japanese don't follow the rules,' David said grimly. Nobody had wanted to believe this to start with, but it had been growing increasingly clear. Some of their prisoners had been allowed to write home, more as a sop to international demands than anything else, but the cards and letters had been little more than brief scrawls, all saying much the same thing – that the prisoners were being treated well. And this was something that fewer and fewer people now believed.

'You hear such awful stories,' Lucy said. 'We don't know what they might be doing to them, David. I can't bear to think of Wilmot being – being *tortured*.'

It was a year before they heard from Wilmot, a year during which Lucy lived with a gnawing anxiety that couldn't be ignored or forgotten. Outwardly, she continued as normal, hiding her fear with a ready smile and keeping a joke always on her lips. She had never forgotten David's remarks about pain; that if you didn't keep it to yourself, it would be passed on to everyone else, and would multiply as they in turn passed it to others. She came to see her own anguish as something to be kept imprisoned in her own heart. Like the men in Princetown, it must be incarcerated where it could do least harm.

When the telegram finally arrived, she could not believe it. She stood with the buff envelope in her hand, staring at the scrappy piece of paper with its uneven lettering, shaking her head, the tears running down her face. After a moment, she felt the weakness in her legs and sat down on a kitchen chair.

'He's safe. He's alive. He's a prisoner. He's *alive*.'

Arthur had yelled up the stairs for Maud as soon as he saw the telegraph boy's red bike propped against the kerb. She came running down and they both stared at Lucy, who was still clutching the sheet of paper. Arthur reached over and took it out of her fingers.

'She's right. He's alive. Our Wilmot – he's a prisoner. He'll be coming home. Once this lot's over, *he'll be coming home*.'

'I knew it,' Maud breathed. 'I knew my boy couldn't be dead.'

They hugged each other, she and Arthur who scarcely ever touched each other in public, then Arthur went over to the cupboard where they kept the medicines, and the half bottle of whisky.

'I reckon this calls for a bit of a celebration.'

None of them particularly liked whisky, unless it was in one of Maud's hot toddies, made for colds and coughs, but they sipped at the thimblefuls he poured into sherry glasses, and choked a bit and wiped their eyes and laughed. It relieved the tension. Lucy even held out her glass for more, and Arthur gave her a reproving look.

'Now then, maid. No need to turn to the bottle now.' But he poured a drop more, just enough to wet the bottom of the glass, and she tipped it into her mouth. 'Where are the children? We ought to tell them their dad's safe.'

There was no need to ask where Patsy was. She was in her room, reading one of Lucy's old storybooks, *The Phoenix and the Carpet*. Patsy had taken to reading a lot, and her appetite for books was voracious. Her present book was about a family of children who had found a magical creature and a magic carpet to go with it. It was as if she had discovered the joys of travelling by imagination, now that she could no longer do so physically.

Geoffrey was a different matter. Now eleven years old, he was seldom indoors. With other boys, he roamed the ruined streets, clambering on heaps of rubble, making dens in bombed-out houses. It was useless to warn him of the dangers, useless to forbid or punish. He was a growing boy, hungry for adventure, and the streets of Plymouth, ripped apart by war, were an adventure playground.

The only person who had any influence with him was David. David had saved his life that night when the house had been bombed and Zannah killed. He had dragged him clear just as the heavy beam came crashing down, had taken the blow himself and lost his own arm. David was a hero, with the hero's badge of an empty sleeve, and Geoff worshipped him.

David's visits were infrequent, however. He was kept

busy in London mostly and came to Plymouth about once a month, usually staying no more than a night or two, taking the opportunity whenever he could to go on down to Cornwall to see his mother and aunt.

'Where is that boy?' Arthur demanded impatiently now. He was still holding the telegram in his hand. 'He ought to be here. Here's his dad in a prison camp and *he's* out running the streets. You ought to keep a firmer hand on him, Lucy.'

'He's a boy. He's got to have his freedom.' But neither of them had the heart for this well-chewed bone of contention. The whisky was warming them, along with the knowledge that Wilmot had survived the sinking of the *Exeter*.

Next day, it was all over the papers. Pictures of the ship, sailing from Plymouth, the story of the hunting of the *Graf Spee* all over the South Atlantic until she was trapped in Montevideo harbour and scuttled by her captain. The story of the *Exeter* sinking a year ago in the fearsome battle of the Java Sea, and the long silence before news came of the miraculous survival of her crew.

There was plenty of cause for celebration. The men hadn't, after all, been eaten alive by sharks. They hadn't been machine-gunned in the water, nor run down by Japanese ships. They hadn't struggled desperately until the waves closed over their heads and they were drowned.

'It's a miracle,' Lucy said, the relief flooding through her in great sweeping waves. 'Oh Dad, it's a real miracle.'

'You're right, maid.' He lifted his glass. 'You're right.'

They smiled at each other and touched their glasses together, and Maud began to sing 'Pack up your troubles in your old kit bag – and smile, smile, smile.'

None of them, just at that moment, gave much thought to the reports of what was happening to the men in those Japanese prisoner-of-war camps.

Chapter Nine

By the time the news about the *Exeter* survivors had been received, the war had progressed on several different fronts.

Japan had rolled over the Far East like a mighty tank. Singapore had already fallen. Now Hong Kong had been taken, and in Parliament members listened appalled to the stories told them by Anthony Eden of the terrible atrocities the Japanese had committed there. Soldiers bound hand and foot before being bayoneted to death, nurses raped and tortured, civilians butchered . . . The stories went on, each one more sickening than the last. It was almost impossible to believe the evil that had been unleashed upon the world, and impossible to believe that it would ever end.

'Once this sort of thing's started, how is it ever going to be stopped?' Lucy asked in despair. 'It's everywhere. It's like a horrible plague, all over the world, and every country's being infected. I don't see how it can ever be stopped.'

David was with her. They had taken the children up to the Hoe, and stood there on the broad, grassy expanse, staring at the grey waters of the Sound. Somewhere out there, thousands of miles beyond the horizon, was Wilmot. What was he suffering under the rule of these barbaric people?

Geoffrey had other problems. Sweets had been put on ration last summer and they hadn't been allowed to have any icing on the Christmas cake. He was fed up with having only one pot of jam with his name on, to last a whole month. He'd almost forgotten what bananas looked like, and the only time oranges had been in the shops was just before Christmas; even then, there had only been one each. He kicked his feet moodily on the grass and looked up at the sky.

'We used to be able to fly kites. We're not even allowed to do that now.'

'You know why,' Lucy said.

'Doesn't stop them flying huge great barrage balloons, does it? I don't see what harm a tiny little kite would do amongst all that lot.' He glared at the huge grey balloons, floating like a herd of elephants above them. 'I'd fed up with the war. It's just spoiling everything.'

Lucy sighed. She couldn't argue with that. It had spoilt years of her marriage, years of the family life she and Wilmot ought to have been sharing. It had spoilt years of Wilmot's life, and God knew what he was enduring now.

'Mum, I can see Janet and Betty over there,' Patsy said. 'Can I go over and talk to them?'

'Take her over there, Geoff, there's a good boy,' Lucy said, and Geoff pushed the wheelchair away. He wouldn't have done that if David hadn't been here, she thought, he would have argued and sulked at having to go and talk to a crowd of girls. He was being specially difficult about Patsy just at present. It was natural for a boy of his age, of course, not to want to play with girls, but surely he could show her a bit of kindness. He could run off at any time, after all, and climb and jump just as he'd always been able to do. Sometimes, she thought that was why he stayed out so much, so that he wouldn't have to help with Patsy.

'We've got to keep believing we'll win,' David said. 'I know it's hard, but it's the only way.'

They leant on the railing and looked down at the little rockpools. The sea washed in and out of them, the water clear and silky. Nobody was swimming there. Even though it was still only early spring, a day like this would have had some of the bigger boys out with their trunks and ragged towels, leaping off the rocks into the waves, yelling with the excitement of it. But now a lot of those youths were already training for the Armed Forces, and many of those who had been here when she and Wilmot came to swim a few years ago were dead.

She wondered if an afternoon diving off rocks would ever seem exciting again to those who survived, who had seen action at sea, in the air or on land in all those many countries now fighting out the biggest and worst war the world had ever known. Perhaps by then even boys would have had enough excitement.

'It's been going on for nearly four years,' she said. 'Four *years*! I'd never have believed it.' She paused. 'Zannah would have been six now.'

'I know. And Stevie would have been five.'

'Oh, David. Will we ever get over it?' She looked at him, standing beside her. He was looking out to sea, his profile sharp against the sweep of the waterway, his fair hair beginning to shade to grey. He looked tired and worn. Whatever work he did, it was exacting, and although he'd adjusted to having only one arm, she knew that it couldn't be easy. There were all the things you did that really needed two: carrying things, getting dressed of a morning, buttering a slice of bread (when you could get the butter). All the little things that people did all the time without even thinking of them, but which must add to the burden of his days. 'You must miss Heather terribly,' she said, thinking of how much Heather would have helped him.

'I do. I miss her all the time.' He turned his head and looked down into her eyes. 'But it helps a lot, having you.'

Lucy felt a small shock and remembered, without warning, that kiss they'd once shared, the kiss that had told her that there could be so much more between her and David, so much that was forbidden. She stared back at him speechlessly.

'I can't tell you how much it means to me, coming to Plymouth,' he went on. 'There's nowhere else that means home to me now, only Pengelly's. And you and Maud and

Arthur and the children – you're my family to me now.' He glanced away to where Geoff and Patsy were the centre of a group of children, boys and girls. They were all laughing, and one of the girls broke away to do a series of cartwheels across the grass. 'Geoff especially. I feel sometimes as if I was given the chance to save him to make up – a bit – for not being there for Stevie.'

Lucy stared at him. She felt enormously touched. She put out her hand and laid it on his empty sleeve. 'But you lost your arm –'

'I'd rather lose both my arms than have lost Geoff, or you or Patsy that night,' he said, almost savagely. 'I wish I *had* lost them both, if it could have kept Zannah alive. Listen,' he went on his voice low. 'Listen, Lucy. I know I shouldn't be saying this. Wilmot's alive and in prison and God knows what conditions he's living under. And I'd never do a thing to hurt either of you, you know that. But while this war's on – well, I want you to know that you are the most important person in the world to me. I love you, Lucy. I love you as deeply as a man can love a woman. And I don't think that's ever going to change.' He stared at her and she saw the truth deep in his eyes, and beside it the misery of its hopelessness. 'I know it can never go anywhere. I know you'll never be able to love me, but – I want you to know. And to know that if you ever need me – *ever* – I'll be there.'

Lucy tried to speak but her throat had closed up and her lips were like stiff bands across her frozen face. She shook her head a little and felt the hard ache of tears in her throat find release in her eyes. The salty water scalded her cheeks. She reached out a hand that shook and laid it again on his sleeve, but there was an arm in this sleeve, a warm, living arm in which tiny muscles jumped at her touch.

'Don't say anything,' he begged. 'I shouldn't have. I never meant to tell you. Don't let it make any difference.'

'But of course it makes a difference.'

He looked away, his mouth tightened. 'You won't want me to come again. I've spoilt everything.'

'No. *No*. It – just takes me a little while to get used to, that's all.' She laughed a little, breathlessly. 'David, I thought we were just friends.'

'We are. We *should* be. We will be. That's if – if you don't tell me to go away.'

'I'm not going to tell you to go away,' she said quietly. 'I'll never tell you to go away. I couldn't bear it if you weren't coming to see us whenever you can.' She lifted her eyes and looked him full in the face. 'I want you to go on thinking of us as your family, David. We *are* your family. Geoff – wouldn't be here if it weren't for you. And besides that – I love you too.'

The silence seemed to encompass the entire Hoe. It was as if everyone walking there, all the children playing, had stopped and turned to stare. Lucy gave a quick look round, unnerved, but it was her imagination, nobody had stopped, they were all continuing as before, the children were screaming and laughing, the adults strolling, just as if nothing had happened. She looked back at David.

'It won't come between me and Wilmot,' she said. 'It's a different sort of love. I won't ever be unfaithful to him, or anything like that. But after him and the children, you're the one who means most to me, David. And I don't think *that's* ever going to change.'

'I don't want us not to be friends,' he said a little unsteadily. 'I don't want it to spoil that.'

'Neither do I. And it won't.'

He put out his hand and she took it in both of hers. They smiled at each other and, as they stood there, Geoff came running up and tugged at their linked arms to gain attention.

'Mum! *Mum!* Terry Leeming's got a football. A real one. He got it from his uncle in Birmingham. He says I can be in his team if I go for practice now. I said I would, I can, can't

94

I? Can't I, Uncle David? You'll tell her I can, won't you, she'll let me if you say so, you will say so, won't you, *won't* you?' He was hopping from foot to foot with excitement and David and Lucy both laughed.

'All right, I'll say so,' David said, and Lucy nodded, her face suddenly alight as it had not been alight since Wilmot had last been at home. 'But what about Patsy? Bring her back over here first.'

'I can't. I haven't got time. I've got to go now, or I can't be in the team –' Geoff was already racing away across the grass. 'Janet's bringing her back, she'll be all right. See you at teatime, Mum.' He was gone, disappearing into a motley gang of twelve-year-old boys yelling football slogans as they disappeared across the Hoe.

'Boys!' Lucy exclaimed, and remembered her wonderings of a few moments earlier. 'Well, it's good to know that they're still boys after all. I was beginning to wonder.'

'Boys,' David said as if uttering a great truth that no one had ever perceived before, 'will *always* be boys.' And he set off across the grass to retrieve Patsy in her wheelchair.

There were raids throughout 1943, less frequent but always destructive. However, the defences were better now and enemy aircraft were met by a determined barrage of anti-aircraft fire and rockets. The searchlights lanced the night sky with a vivid web of long white spears and sometimes you could actually see the plane caught in the beam before it was shot down. One crashed at Stoke and its crew died in the flames. During the same raid, a huge bomb landed on the police headquarters, bringing down half the roof and coming to rest, unexploded and menacing, on the landing just outside the courtroom.

There were now thousands of houses in Plymouth waiting to be repaired. Some could still be lived in, their roofs patched up with tarpaulin and their windows boarded over. Others were smashed beyond repair and stood with gaunt jagged walls over craters that had once been cellars or foundations. Gardens that had once been lovingly tended were now tangled jungles of weeds. It never seemed to be the useful or pretty plants that ran riot, Lucy observed. You never saw cabbages or roses taking over and flourishing like dandelions and thistles did.

'They say the Germans are making coffee from dandelions,' Maud said. 'Or is it acorns? I don't fancy it anyway. Mind, I don't say no to a nice drink of dandelion and burdock, but I don't know how you make it.'

'People ate rats in the siege of Paris,' Patsy said. She couldn't go to school; most of those that hadn't been bombed had by now evacuated their children to the countryside, and the one or two still functioning were too far away, and in any case they couldn't take a child in a wheelchair. But Lucy was doing her best to see that Patsy's education didn't slip. Every week she walked through the ruined streets to the temporary library and got out as many books as she could, using the whole family's library tickets. She brought home books about history and geography, and read them herself so that she could talk about them with Patsy. Geoff brought home his own homework and Patsy did it too, and Arthur suggested she could help with the accounts for the hotel.

'It's only adding up. She could manage that. And look at it this way: it'd be a sight more useful than working out how long it takes to fill a bath when some daft fool's left the plug out, like that homework young Geoff had last week.'

Plymouth was full of Americans now. They came on ships that were larger and somehow more warlike than British ships, but when they came ashore they were ready for a drink just like the British tars. They filled the pubs in Union Street and washed like a tide through the city, scattering chewing-gum, chocolate and dollars amongst the children who soon learnt to follow them, chanting 'Got any gum, chum?' When Geoff came home the first time, displaying his prizes, Lucy was furious.

'It's no better than begging. You're not to do it.'

'But they chuck it at us anyway.' He spoke in an injured tone. 'And I brought the chocolate home for you and Patsy and Grammy. I thought you'd *like* it.'

Lucy sighed. What could she say, when he was giving his sister a bar of chocolate such as never came her way these days? She knew that a lot of people welcomed the Americans, and why not? They were like a breath of fresh air, bringing with them an air of freedom from the constant sense of dread that had become part of the British way of life. The Americans hadn't been bombed, they hadn't suffered from food shortages or rationing, they knew their folks at home were safe, they were young and energetic, well fed, strong and healthy. It was like a glimpse of another life to see them swinging through the streets and hear their talk. Nearly as good as being at the pictures.

All the same, it worried her a bit to see them flashing their money about and throwing sweets and things at the children. And it wasn't just the children. They were interested in the girls – it was only to be expected, they were young men with lots of energy – and they'd brought things to entice them as well. More chocolate, and things like scent and pretty underwear and stockings made of nylon, that were as sheer as silk and had real seams down the back.

Lucy began to hear the phrase that was to become so commonly used amongst young British men, bitterly jealous of their American rivals: 'Overpaid, oversexed and over here.' You couldn't blame them, she thought, but you couldn't blame the Americans either. They were all human beings.

The last raid came at the end of April 1944. Nobody knew then that it was the last, as the cloud of aircraft came snarling in over the Sound to drop its bombs over Oreston and the waterfront, burning out the Western National bus depot. Nobody even dreamed that it could be the last, for immediately afterwards the coasts and rivers of Devon and Cornwall became a hive of naval and military activity, with ships massing in the Channel and tanks and lorries filling the roads and lanes.

'We'll be a bigger target than ever,' Arthur said. 'It's handing it to them on a plate. The Jerries'll be over and bomb the lot.'

But they didn't come. The tanks went on arriving, the ships gathered, and suddenly, one morning in June, vanished as if they had never been. And on the wireless came the news of the invasion of Normandy. D-Day.

'Let's hope it won't be like Dieppe,' Maud said, listening anxiously, but it wasn't like Dieppe. This time, the Germans had been caught unaware and the Army forged into France. At last, the tide seemed to be on the turn.

'I can really dare to start thinking we might win after all,' Lucy said to David. 'It really does seem as if it might all be over.'

'It does,' he said. 'Not by Christmas, perhaps, but – maybe not too long after.'

Geoff was disappointed by D-Day. It was exciting that the Army had invaded Normandy, he conceded that, and he took a lot of interest in keeping track of their movements, sticking pins in the big map Arthur had put on the wall to show where the different forces had got to. But the streets that had been so full of vitality as the Americans roved about, scattering largesse, were now empty again. The colour had gone, leaving them no more than the grey ruins they had been before. And the chocolate and chewing-gum had gone with them.

He wasn't the only one disappointed. There were a lot of young girls in Plymouth, Lucy thought, who were also going to miss the fun and excitement, although in their case, a good many of them had something else to remember their new, big-talking boyfriends by.

'He said we'd get married,' was the cry now. 'He said he'd take me to *Hollywood*.'

Well, Lucy thought again, they were all human beings. And war was a lonely time for the girls they left behind.

Nineteen-forty-five. The sixth winter of the war. Lucy could barely remember what peace had been like. The carefree, youthful days at home in Portsmouth, when she had spent her days working at the naval outfitters, and her life with her friends, her family and Wilmot, seemed like a distant dream. Had they ever really happened?

The fighting continued, and now it was the Allies who were pushing home their offensive. The Russians were marching into Europe; they drove a spearhead through Poland, the country that had been at the heart of the war, and took Warsaw, the city which had suffered more than any other under the Germans. By the end of January they were just a hundred miles from Berlin and it really began to look as if the war might be coming to an end.

'But not in Japan,' Lucy said. 'And that's where Wilmot is.'

Her own family were caught up in it all. Alice had lost her husband Ted at Tripoli. She had stayed in her nursing job at the Royal Hospital in Portsmouth, and she'd been on duty the night it was bombed. All through the barrage she'd rescued patients from the damaged wards and afterwards she'd been awarded a medal. Once the worst of the blitz seemed to be over she'd volunteered as a nurse in the WAAFs, and when D-Day came she flew to France in Dakotas, bringing home the wounded.

Kitty was doing well in the Wrens. She went across the Gosport ferry every day to work at HMS *Dolphin*, the submarine base. Later on, she was posted to Portland and she managed to 'wangle' a few trips down to Plymouth to see Lucy. She was as pretty as ever, like a bright-eyed little furry animal with her curly red hair, and she seemed to be thoroughly enjoying the war.

'The main thing is to have as much fun as you can,' she said. 'Life's too short to be miserable. Keep smiling through, that's what they say, and that's what I do. Anyway, it's our patriotic duty to keep the boys happy when they're at home.'

Lucy wondered how many boys she'd kept happy, and what her mother and father thought about it, but Kitty laughed at her fears.

'I shan't get caught. You don't have to, these days. And I don't go with them for money or anything. I mean, some girls will do anything for a pair of nylons or a bottle of scent. I'm not like that.'

'I bet you don't say no, all the same,' Lucy said, unable to keep a tinge of disapproval from her voice.

Kitty gave her a sharp look. 'Listen to me, our Lucy. I don't go with just any bloke that comes along. I've been with a few, yes, because I like them and they're lonely and might go off and be killed next day – but I don't do it for what they can give me. I enjoy it too, you know. And it isn't serious. It's just fun.'

Lucy couldn't look at it like that. To her, making love with a man was a very serious thing indeed. Something she'd only ever done – only ever would do – with her husband.

'Don't tell me you've never fancied anyone else,' Kitty said, watching her and seeming to read her mind. 'Not all this long time, with Wilmot away for years.'

'Well, I haven't, then,' Lucy said indignantly, and then stopped and bit her lip. There wasn't much point in looking down on Kitty if she couldn't tell the truth herself. And there had been someone else. She had never made love with him, never done more than kiss – just once – but she'd told him she loved him, and meant it.

David.

'Well? You see?' Kitty's voice was triumphant. 'Who was he, then? One of the Yanks?'

'No! It wasn't like that at all.' Lucy was scarlet, and as angry with herself as with her sister. 'It – it's completely different.'

'Oh yeah?' This was an expression Kitty, with many others, had picked up from the Americans. 'How different?'

'It's not the same as what you're doing, not the same at all. We – we love each other.'

'Lucy!' This time, to Lucy's surprise, the disapproval was in Kitty's voice. 'Oh, Lucy, how can you? With Wilmot in a Japanese POW camp. Oh, I think that's dreadful. At least I make sure my boys aren't married.'

'*No!*' There was nothing for it, Lucy saw, but to tell her the truth. 'I told you, it isn't like that. We've never – we've never done anything about it. We never will. And I haven't stopped loving Wilmot, it doesn't make any difference to Wilmot and me. It's just happened, that's all. We love each other, but we'll never do anything about it, never.' She paused, unable to take the final step of speaking David's name. 'He's Wilmot's friend as well,' she said at last in a low tone. 'He'd never do anything to hurt him.'

Kitty stared at her, and Lucy saw the light dawn on her face.

'It's David, isn't it?' she said slowly. She knew David well; he always came to visit the family when he was in Portsmouth. 'It's David. David and you.'

'Not David and me. I told you, we've never—'

'It's all right. I believe you.' She added, almost from habit, 'Thousands wouldn't.' Her eyes softened and she reached out her small, strong hand and covered Lucy's. 'Oh, Luce. You poor thing.'

The tears sprang to Lucy's eyes. She felt their heat with some astonishment. She had never wept for herself and David, never seen their story as a sad one. There had been too many other things to weep for, and the affection between

101

them had been a source of strength to them both. But now she saw it with Kitty's eyes – a loss, a deprivation, a bud that could never flower, a flower that could never fruit.

'It's all right,' she said a little harshly. 'There's plenty of worse things happen at sea.' And the truth of that phrase, so commonly used, hit her afresh; and she thought of Wilmot, struggling in a sea of flames, and the suffering he might be enduring even now.

Beside that, an unfulfilled love seemed little to weep about.

Lucy's brother, Kenny, piloted a Lancaster. He flew on sorties over Germany, and one night he went to Dresden and came back with death in his eyes. He had looked down, he said, and seen a firestorm below him; a holocaust of flame which surely nobody could have survived. The bombing had been so intense that their blast and the fires they had started had created their own wind, fanning the flames into an inferno. It was like looking into the jaws of hell.

'Well, they done it to us,' people said. 'Serve 'em right, don't it?'

But Kenny shook his head. For the first time, he had realised that there were people down there, not just 'Germans', the mythical storybook trolls of imagination, black and evil hobgoblins, but children still at school, babies in prams, girls and boys just growing up, pregnant women and elderly people. People who hadn't asked for war, who had thought themselves safe in a city that was known only for its beauty and had nothing to do with the conflict.

'It's supposed to bring the end of war closer,' he said, 'but that's not much comfort to them, is it?'

After a while, he was taken off bombers and given a desk job. They said it was for health reasons, and indeed Kenny was never quite the same again. The ready smile had vanished, the jokes disappeared, and when he went for a walk he walked alone.

Lucy felt as if she had lost both her brothers.

All the talk now was of the end of the war. The blackout was taken down, some of the streetlamps lit. Church bells rang out wherever there were bells to ring and ringers to ring them. The Allies crossed the Rhine and the Russians marched steadily nearer to Berlin. Hitler was said to be in hiding, and his mistress, Eva Braun, with him. And then, at the beginning of May, came the news of his suicide.

'It's all over. It must be all over now.'

David found Lucy up on the Hoe where they had walked so many times during the past six years. They stood silently together, looking out over the waters, looking towards Drake's Island and the breakwater and the tiny pencil shape of the Eddystone Lighthouse far beyond.

'I know what you must be feeling,' he said after a while. 'It may be over in Europe, but it's not ended in Japan. The war still goes on there.'

'I sometimes wonder,' she said, 'if I'll ever see Wilmot again.'

The desolation in her voice struck him to the heart. He put his arm round her shoulders and held her firmly against him. 'You will. You must. He's survived all this time.'

Lucy had received infrequent and scrappy letters from Wilmot. The Japanese allowed their prisoners only the minimum of communication, and nobody believed those who said they were well treated. Lucy could barely guess at what was happening to Wilmot.

'We can't be sure of anything,' she said to David. 'You know that. We may think terrible things can't happen, but they do. They've happened to us already. Why should they stop?'

'Well,' he said, 'at least if the war's over in Europe we'll be able to concentrate on the Far East. It won't go on much longer, Lucy. The end really is coming.'

It came – for Europe – only a few days later.

*

VE Day.

The streets of Plymouth rejoiced. A grand parade of all the Services, the Home Guard, ARP wardens, nurses and everyone else who had a uniform to wear, marched through the city from St Jude's to Stonehouse, with a Royal Marine band at its head. People strung bunting from their houses, pianos were dragged out into the streets and dancing went on into the early hours. They looked up at the skies which for six long years had brought death and destruction, and they cheered to see the stars above. Those same stars had looked down impassively, uncaring, when the bombs had fallen, blotted out by the searing flames. Now, however, the skies were clear and brought no threat, and once again they could be loved.

Lucy joined in the celebrations. You couldn't not join in – you had to be glad. There were many others like her, she knew, who smiled through stiffened lips, who felt the hollow ache for loved ones who were still away, still imprisoned or fighting. How did they feel, knowing that it was over for so many while they still toiled on in peril of their lives? But you had to be glad. You had to join in.

And then it was all talk of rebuilding. Plans for the new Plymouth city centre. Plans for houses – the new prefabricated houses, more like shoeboxes than something you'd want to live in, but welcomed with enthusiasm by their new occupants. Lucy went to see one and couldn't help being impressed. It all looked so new, so clean, and they even had bathrooms. Bathrooms, for people who had always been accustomed to a tin bath hanging on a nail outside and brought indoors on Saturday nights! And refrigerators, too. Those who hadn't been bombed out were quite jealous: there was little chance of bathrooms and fridges for them.

So many buildings were still in ruins. The shells of St Andrew's church and the stately Guildhall, both gutted, towered over the still-flattened streets. They had gone on holding services in the church ever since the bombing, and the word *Resurgam* was still in place over the church door. Inside the roofless building they had planted flowerbeds which glowed with the colour missing now from the smashed windows, so that despite the damage it was an inspiration to go inside and hear the familiar prayers and the voices of the choir lifted in the well-known hymns.

But life still wasn't easy. Big stores like Spooner's and Dingle's had had to move their premises, just as the smaller shops had done. You couldn't shop easily any more, going from one to the other; they were all miles apart. With the incessant queueing, which hadn't improved even though the war was over, it made every shopping trip a major expedition.

After the first euphoria had died down, the realisation slowly dawned that things weren't going to improve overnight. There would still be rationing – in fact, even more foods were going to be rationed now, including bread, which had never been short before. There would still be power cuts and shortages of coal. You still wouldn't be able to get decent furniture, or pretty crockery, only 'utility'; nor lace tablecloths, nor nice paint and wallpaper to do up rooms that hadn't been touched for six long years.

Still, at least you could go to bed knowing that you weren't going to be woken by the wail of the air-raid warning, though. At least you knew your men were safe and would be coming home for good.

Except, of course, for those still in the Far East.

In the end, it was only eight weeks that the world had to wait. A long, slow eight weeks, and a terrible end, when all was known. But at last, when Lucy had almost given up, came the August morning when her son Geoff came racing in from the streets, his hair standing on end, shrieking the news.

'It's over! It's finished! The war's *over*!'

Chapter Ten

It was January 1946 before Wilmot finally came home.

First of all, the prisoner-of-war camps throughout the Far East had to be located and the prisoners freed. There was some urgency in this, for there were fears that the Japanese would execute their captives. However the terrible wrath of the Western world, evinced in the atom bombs dropped on Hiroshima and Nagasaki, had had its effect and the occupying troops were in the main able to march in and take over without resistance. Emperor Hirohito had declared surrender, and that was enough for his defeated people.

Wilmot's first letter didn't seem so very different from those he had sent from the camp. It was scribbled and uninformative, but Lucy knew that he was going to hospital and would stay there until they were sure he was fit to travel home.

'What does that mean? What have they been doing to him?'

Other prisoners began to return. The stories of what had gone on in the camps began to circulate, horrifying accounts of brutality. If you didn't bow your head as the camp commander passed by, it was likely to be chopped off. If you were lucky enough not to be killed, you risked a punishment so cruel that you might well wish you had been. The food was very nearly at starvation level, and the diseases of malnourishment were rife. Boils, sores, digestive disturbance became commonplace, and this led to other diseases. Everyone suffered from dysentery, and every day someone died.

Lucy wrote long letters to Wilmot, telling him how much she was looking forward to seeing him again, telling him about the family and the hotel, but even that wasn't easy. She couldn't tell him about the children without referring to Patsy's wheelchair, and she was acutely conscious of the fact that she wasn't mentioning Zannah. It didn't seem right to be talking about two of their children when they'd had three – but what could she say about Zannah? When Wilmot had gone away, she'd been a chubby toddler, all smiles and cuddles. Now – she just wasn't there any more. He knew this, of course, had known it for years, but somehow now it seemed to be happening all over again, and the pain was just as sharp as ever.

As Wilmot's return grew nearer, Lucy found her initial excitement gradually replaced by apprehension. He had been gone for five years. It was longer than they'd enjoyed married life, when you counted all the times he'd been away before the war. They'd both been through so much in that time; they must have changed, both of them. She went to the mirror and looked at her reflection. Six years of war had tired and aged her; she was no longer the bright-faced bride or the happy young mother he would remember. She was thirty-five years old and there were lines at the corners of her eyes. The deep violet was still there, and the burnished red-gold of her hair, but there were a few white hairs amongst it now, and she dared not pull them out for fear that seven more would appear in place of each one.

Suppose he was disappointed with her. Suppose he didn't love her any more.

Suppose she didn't love him.

Lucy pushed the thought away, angry with herself for even letting it touch her mind. Of course she still loved him. And of course he wouldn't have changed. Nothing could change the Wilmot she remembered, the fresh-faced sailor full of jokes and cheeky remarks. There might be a few adjustments to make, but there would be too much to do to let silly fears spoil things. A home to find, for a start. And a job for Wilmot, for surely he'd be coming out of the Navy now. If it hadn't been for the war, he'd have come out years ago.

'I'm sorry now I let the house go,' she said to her mother-in-law. 'It's been good of you to let me and the kids stop here all this time, but we ought to have our own place. And you'll want the rooms now, to get the guest house on its feet again.'

'Don't talk so daft. This is your home for as long as you want it. And I don't think you'll find it so easy to get a place of your own anyway. There's more people looking for homes than there are places for them to live, you know that. And you'd never get a prefab, not while you can go on living here.'

Lucy knew this was true. She sighed. It would have been so much better to start off with Wilmot on their own together. Good as Maud and Arthur had been, a couple needed to be private, especially when they'd been separated as long as she and Wilmot had been.

'Besides,' Maud went on, 'I'm a bit worried about Arthur. He's not looking right to me. I don't like the idea of him trying to do all the work here on his own when you've gone.'

'Oh, I wouldn't let him do that,' Lucy said at once. 'I'd still call in every day and lend a hand with things, same as always. After all, when Wilmot's at work—'

'And what work,' Maud asked, 'do you think a man who's spent the past four years in a prisoner-of-war camp is going to get?'

Lucy stared at her.

'You know what they say about those places,' Maud went on. 'Torture camps, that's what they call them. Wilmot's not going to be the man he was, don't you expect it. And he'll be thankful to have some work to do here, without going out tramping the streets to look for it.'

108

'But he's got a trade.'

'Which he's not touched for four years.'

'Mum, how can you talk like that?'

'Because we've got to face it.' Maud folded her lips tightly together. 'Don't think I *like* it, Lucy. It's my own son we're talking about, I haven't forgotten that. But you've seen what's happening already. Men coming home in their demob suits, all full of what they're going to do to get the country on its feet again – and then, a few weeks later, what are they doing? Knocking on the door asking you to buy brushes, that's what. And they're the lucky ones! Look, I've seen it before, after the first war – men coming home to jobs that weren't there any more, men who'd been good enough to fight for their country and now weren't wanted any more. Chucked on the rubbish heap.'

Lucy was silent. She felt a sick horror descend on her like a grey, slimy sponge, wrapping itself about her face and head. Putting up her hands as if to brush it away, she cried, 'But Wilmot won't be like that! He's clever, he'll get something—'

'My friend Mrs Endacott's George is clever,' Maud said. 'He couldn't even get a job selling brushes.'

Lucy's apprehension grew. Wilmot was supposed to be coming out of the Navy. Suppose he decided to stay in. They would never have a proper life together. Suppose the Navy didn't want him anyway – how would he feel? Suppose Maud was right and he couldn't get a job. It would be so cruel, after all he had suffered, to find that his country didn't want him.

Perhaps the hotel was the answer after all.

Lucy thought about it. Pengelly's had never been more than a guest house, taking in a few visitors at a time. It had brought in enough income to keep Maud and Arthur, and Wilmot when he was a boy. There had been just enough guests through the war to keep it going, and Lucy's naval allowance had helped, but there wasn't enough to keep two families if Wilmot left the Navy, especially with some of the rooms needed for her and Wilmot and the children. And the whole house needed refurbishing. It hadn't been redecorated in over six years. The outside looked shabby, the once white walls grubby and peeling, and blackened by smoke from the fires of the blitz. The window-frames were in poor condition and some of the sashes were broken. And inside, when you came to look at it properly – for you got used to it when you lived there all the time – was downright scruffy. Skirting-boards knocked and chipped by Geoff's bike and Patsy's wheelchair; wallpaper discoloured and starting to come away; ceilings yellowed by tobacco smoke; paintwork scraped and carpets threadbare. The whole place needed gutting and then starting again, she thought.

It would have been too, if it had been bombed properly. And she almost laughed at herself for wishing that the Germans had made what Arthur would have called 'a proper job' of it.

Well, there'd be plenty to keep Wilmot occupied, getting the place up to scratch. And plenty for her to do as well. New curtains to make, bedlinen to sort out – all it needed was the money. Just a minor problem, really.

They had hoped that Wilmot would be home for Christmas, but as the winter drew on and November came, they knew that there would be no chance of this. Ships from the Far East took a good eight weeks to get home, and Wilmot hadn't even been given a date for leaving. And then, suddenly, came the news that he was on board an aircraft-carrier, together with a crowd of other ex-POWs, and leaving Singapore next day. He would be home some time in January.

'January!' Lucy gasped.

'We'll have our proper Christmas then,' Maud said. Tears were running down her cheeks and Lucy had to remind herself that Wilmot was as precious to her as he was to Lucy herself. Her only son, her only child . . . She thought of Zannah and the grief that was always in the back of her mind, and thought of how it would have been if she hadn't had Geoff and Patsy as well. The whole world gone at once. She hugged Maud with sudden understanding and made up her mind that she wouldn't be possessive, she'd let Wilmot's mother have her share of him. And at the same time, she wished again that they had their own home. It wasn't going to be easy.

Upstairs in her bedroom, she looked again in the mirror. Her eyes went past her own reflection to the bed. She'd slept on her own now for over four years, and pretty well most of the time before that. It was going to seem queer having someone else in bed with her. *Someone else?* she thought with a tiny flicker of hysteria. It was Wilmot she was going to share with, for heaven's sake! Wilmot, her husband. And they wouldn't just be sleeping, either . . .

They'd be making love. That was something else neither of them had done in all those years. She looked back at her reflection, seeing the doubt in the wide violet eyes, wondering if she would be able to remember what to do, how to do it. She'd thought of it often enough at first, and then tried not to think about it, pushing it away, successfully for the most part, except when she lay bitterly lonely in the middle of the night, and when she dreamed about it. She'd remembered how it felt then, all right.

Suppose it didn't work. There had been the odd occasion even quite early in their marriage when Wilmot just hadn't been able to do it and no amount of cuddling or stroking had made any difference. Usually it was because he was tired or had a cold or perhaps had drunk a beer too many in the Mess, and they'd just laughed it off. It didn't matter because they could cuddle and kiss anyway, and there was always the next night. But what would four years such as he had just endured have done to him?

I'll just have to play it all by ear, she decided. I'll have to let him set the pace. Work his way back into life the best way he knows, and I'll help him all I can. There's going to be so much for him to learn again, and he's the one who's been through the worst time. It's my job to help him and make him strong again.

The thought seemed to bring her the comfort she needed. The thought of drawing on her own reserves, her own strengths, to help the husband she loved so much and had missed so badly. And I *am* strong, she thought with sudden surprise. I've grown strong during all these years – I've had to. Bringing up the children on my own, helping Wilmot's mum and dad, practically running the guest house at times . . . even losing Zannah and having Patsy crippled, and learning to get on with things just the same. It's all made me strong.

She looked with some wonder at the reflection in the mirror. Her eyes had darkened to the deep purple of pansies, and the white hairs amongst the burnished gold didn't seem to matter quite so much after all. It was her strength that mattered, her strength and her love, and that was what Wilmot was coming home to and what she would offer him.

They had Christmas, of course, the first post-war Christmas, with a thin layer of icing on the cake, roughed up with a fork to look like snow, and a Father Christmas made by Patsy out of brown paper with a scrap of red paint to stand on top of it. There was a Rupert book for Patsy, who had followed the little bear's adventures in the *Daily Express* right through the war, and a *Hotspur* annual for Geoff. There were sweets and chocolates from the whole family's ration, saved up for weeks, and there was a bowl of oranges on the sideboard, a chicken and a proper pudding for dinner, and a tin of peaches and clotted cream for Christmas Day tea.

'It's almost as good as pre-war,' Maud said, looking at the laden table. What with sandwiches and a dish of tinned pilchards and some salad, the feast looked good enough to compete with any pre-war memories. David, who had come to spend Christmas with them, raised his eyebrows and laughed.

'It looks as if you're expecting an army!'

'It's a practice run,' Lucy said with a smile. 'We're going to do it all again when Wilmot comes home.'

'Of course. And when d'you think that'll be?' He slid Patsy's chair up to the table and made sure she could reach her knife and fork. 'Some time in January, isn't it?'

'About the middle, we think.' Lucy felt her heart skip. It did that a lot these days. 'You'll come, won't you, David? For the party?'

'Oh.' He looked a little nonplussed. 'I don't know – do you think Wilmot will want me here? I mean, he'll just want his family.'

'You *are* family. You know that. You've been here all through.' She glanced at Geoff. She didn't need to add, *You saved his life*.

David was less certain. He didn't think Wilmot would necessarily see him as part of the family. He would want Lucy to himself, without another man hovering in the background. They'd been friends four or five years ago, and before the war, but that didn't mean he had a place here now. Wilmot was hardly likely to have spent the last four years aching to see another man.

'I think it'd probably be best if I don't come down to see you all until after Wilmot's had a chance to settle in,' he said, passing Geoff the sardine and tomato sandwiches.

Lucy stared at him, surprised by her own dismay. Somehow, without really thinking about it, she had assumed that David would be here. He'd been here through all the most important parts of the war, good and bad, and although they'd agreed that they could never let their friendship deepen, he was special to her. More special than she'd realised; more necessary.

'But –' she said, and then caught his eye and stopped. There was a tiny warning in it, and a flicker towards Maud and Arthur. Lucy bit her lip and glanced at her mother-in-law. To her relief, Maud wasn't even looking at her but was concentrating on cutting into the Victoria sponge, but she knew what David's look had meant.

'Things will be different from now on,' he said to her later as they said goodnight outside her room. 'They have to be. We can't be the same sort of friends as we have been. It wouldn't be right.'

'But there was nothing wrong. We never—'

'That's not the point. I'm glad, very glad, that we never let anything happen.' He sighed a little. 'It could have done, so easily . . . but things have been very different during the war, Lucy, and now they've got to change again. You do see that, don't you.'

Reluctantly, she nodded. She did see it, really, she had just never thought of it until now. There had been too much else on her mind and somehow she'd just taken it for granted that David would always be there, just as he always had been.

'We'll all have to go back to where we were before,' she said and heard him sigh again.

'Do you think that's possible? I think we're going to have to find new ways. It isn't going to be easy, Lucy, for any of us.' He paused for a moment. He was very close and she could feel his breath on her cheek, could even, she thought, feel the beating of his heart. For one moment she wanted to forget everything, to throw all this caution and sensibleness to the winds and take him into her bedroom and make love together, just this once, just this last chance . . . but it wasn't possible. It wasn't possible for either of them.

She reached up and touched his cheek, feeling a deep sadness that something was slipping away from her, something she needed and would now never have.

'Goodnight, David.'

His eyes turned upon her in the dim light. He bent his head and brushed her lips with his, very gently, very tenderly, and she gasped with the shock of it and knew that he felt it too. The moment came again, more powerfully than ever; and once again, they let it pass.

'Goodnight, Lucy. Goodnight.'

January came. Lucy was restless, unable to settle. She roamed about the house with a sheet of paper in her hand and a pencil, trying to make notes about what needed doing. The amount of wallpaper would run into acres, she thought, and what wallpaper was there to be had anyway? None of that sort of thing had come into the shops yet. It took time, she supposed, to get organised again. Factories had been taken over for other things, for munitions and uniforms and utility furniture. Army blankets had been made on looms previously used for carpets. It would take time to get them into production again. And paint, they'd need gallons and gallons of it. Nothing wrong with a nice drop of distemper, Arthur said when she mentioned her worries, do a nice pale green or blue everywhere, that was all that was needed to freshen things up.

'I'd just like a bit of real colour,' Lucy said wistfully. 'And some nice patterns. It's years since we've had that sort of thing. It would make us all feel so much better.'

'Why do you want to feel better?' Arthur asked. 'Isn't winning the war enough for you, my beauty?'

It ought to be. It ought to be enough for anyone. And to begin with, of course it had been. But once the singing and dancing in the streets had stopped, once the bunting had come down and the Union Jacks been put away again, once winter had come with its rain and its greyness, it didn't seem to be quite enough any more. There were no more raids, no more fighting, no more killing and being killed, it was true. There were no barrage balloons like herds of elephants in the sky, no searchlights at night, no banshee siren, no rattle of ack–ack. You could see your way at night in lit streets, you could use a torch, you didn't have to worry about the blackout. It ought to have been enough. And yet . . .

If it had been summer, it might have been better, Lucy thought, picking her way through streets that were still heaped at the sides with rubble, still pocked by craters. A bit of sunshine would have helped, but the greyness seeped into everything, into the jagged ruins of once fine buildings, into the mud of tangled gardens, into the weary grind of having to put it all right again. A scruffy guest house, a ruined street, a wrecked church, a gutted Guildhall. Everywhere you looked, there was damage to be repaired, and the task seemed too enormous even to contemplate.

And in the midst of it all, she had this terrible, gnawing feeling of excitement mixed with dread. I ought to be happy, she thought. I ought to be over the moon. Wilmot's coming home. He's coming home. And sometimes I feel so scared I almost wish he'd stay away . . .

No. That was an *evil* thought. She hated herself for letting it into her mind. She wanted him home, she was looking forward to it, it was all she'd dreamed of all these years, and to prove it she tossed aside her plans for the guest house and threw herself into a frenzy of preparation.

'I don't see why *I* have to help scrub the stairs,' Geoffrey objected. 'Patsy doesn't have to do anything.'

'Daddy's coming home, Geoff. Don't you want him to see our home looking as nice as possible? Don't you want him to feel happy to be here?'

'I bet he'd be happy even if we didn't do all this washing and stuff. Men don't bother about all that.'

'Sailors do,' Lucy retorted. 'They keep their ships spick and span all the time. Now stop arguing, Geoff, and when you've done that you can clean the front windows.'

She knew she was overdoing it. She knew that Geoff resented the extra work, and she knew that he was right, that Wilmot probably wouldn't even notice, but she was driven by something deep inside, a sense of something that wasn't just excitement, something she was afraid to examine. And it made something to do while she waited.

The middle of January. The ship was thought to be coming into Southampton, but nobody really knew. It could be Portsmouth or Portland or even Plymouth itself. Nothing seemed certain, these days. All you could do was wait. Every morning, Lucy woke with a fluttering heart, wondering if this would be the day. Every ring on the doorbell brought her to her feet. Every time she went out, she returned with her heart in her mouth, wondering if he'd arrived in her absence and was even now sitting in the kitchen, his hands wrapped around a mug of tea, talking and laughing with his mum and dad, the old Wilmot, fresh faced and cheeky, with a joke always on his lips.

When she'd hurried along the pavement and up the steps to the front door, down the narrow hallway and into the kitchen, to find that he wasn't there at all, she never quite knew whether she was disappointed or relieved.

'He'll let us know when he's coming,' Maud said. 'Soon as the ship docks, he'll send a telegram. We'll get warning.'

Other men were coming home too. There was hardly a day went by without some street being decked with bunting and Union Jacks, and houses with 'Welcome Home' banners strung from their windows. You couldn't go down the street without passing some chap in a greatcoat, carrying a kitbag and looking tired and excited all at once. The street parties were over, but there was always the sound of singing and piano-playing coming from some-where, and children going to school boasting of 'my dad' who had come back from the war with medals all over his chest and a coconut in his kitbag.

And there were the men who had come back earlier, the ones Maud had talked about, who trudged the streets with a different sort of bag: a cardboard suitcase filled with brushes or books to sell, men whose faces were weary and disillusioned, who wondered what it had all been for and why they had ended up like this.

The front door opened and closed. Lucy, alone in the kitchen, didn't even bother to lift her head. It would be Maud back from her friend Mrs Endacott, or Arthur home from the pub where he sometimes called in for a pint. Or Geoff, back from the game of football he'd at last been released to play.

The kitchen door opened before she had time to register that the footsteps in the passage were none of these. The figure in the doorway cast an unfamiliar shadow. There was a bulky look about it that she didn't, at first, recognise. It was only when she saw the two kitbags and the dark blue greatcoat that she began to understand.

'Aren't you going to say hallo to me, Lucy?' the man in the doorway asked. 'Aren't you going to give your husband a kiss after all these years?'

Chapter Eleven

'*Wilmot!*'

He stood there in the doorway. Wilmot. In that first, dazed and blinding moment, she caught a glimpse of the changes – the weathered, yellowish skin, the folds around the eyes, the narrow lines running from his nose to the corners of his mouth – but she wasn't looking for changes: she was looking for things she had known before, remembered, dreamed about.

It was all that she had ever dared hope for.

She was on her feet, her chair thrust back so sharply that it toppled, and he moved towards her at the same moment. They met in a hug so fierce she thought she wouldn't survive it, a clasping of arms about bodies that strove to forget, to obliterate the years that had stood between them; and a kiss that almost drowned and swallowed them both.

'You didn't let me know –'

'I couldn't. I wanted to surprise you –'

'Wilmot, I've missed you so much – it's been so awful.'

'Lucy. Lucy. *Lucy.*'

They kissed again and again. Their tears mingled, salty on lips and tongue. She felt his warmth, his solidness, and marvelled. It was really Wilmot, Wilmot himself here in her arms, no longer a dream, no longer a fantasy. She touched his hair and felt almost sick with the enormity of it all. He was here. After so much had happened, he was here at last.

'Wilmot, your hair –'

'What? What about it?' He was kissing her face, burying his nose in her neck.

'It's grey. Some of it's quite grey.'

He stood back abruptly and she looked up into his face, catching her breath. She had never seen that look before, that sudden withdrawal, that stoniness.

'Well? It's hair, isn't it?'

'Wilmot, don't look like that. It doesn't matter – of course it doesn't matter. We're older, we're both older.' She was panic-stricken, thinking she had spoilt it already. 'I've got grey hairs myself, look, lots of them.' She would not have believed, a few days ago as she stared into the mirror and wondered whether to pull them out and risk the seven more, that she would have actually pointed them out to him. 'Just think, I'm thirty-five, that's middle-aged!' She laughed, trying to make him laugh too.

'And I'm thirty-eight.' There was a twist to his mouth and she wished she hadn't mentioned ages. Thirty-eight was only two years off forty, and didn't they say something about being too old at forty? But he doesn't deserve it, she thought, he was only thirty-two when all this started, he doesn't deserve to have the best years of his life taken away from him like that.

'Oh, Wilmot,' she said, reaching up to kiss him again, 'it's *so* lovely to have you back.'

He caught her against him and covered her mouth once more with his. To her relief, the moment seemed to have passed and once more they were caught up in their joy at being together again. And all too soon, their privacy was invaded. The front door opened again and they heard the tramp of feet as they were wiped on the doormat, the sound of voices. The usual murmuring as Patsy's wheelchair was manoeuvred into the passage, the sound of Geoff's voice as he recounted the highlights of the afternoon's football game. And then they were in the kitchen, all of them, filling it with noise and movement which stopped abruptly as they saw who was there. And Wilmot was buried beneath a rush of bodies as everyone – everyone except Patsy – rushed to embrace him.

'Wilmot! Oh, my boy, my boy.'

'Wilmot –'

'Dad! *Dad!*'

And from the wheelchair, left pathetically out of it all, 'Daddy, Daddy.'

They broke away at last. Lucy touched her husband's arm – it took her a second to overcome the immensity of being able actually to touch his arm – and glanced towards Patsy. Wilmot, still in the midst of hearing Geoff's excited and largely incoherent account of the football game, looked across the kitchen table towards his daughter.

There was a tiny silence.

Patsy was now nearly twelve. Sitting there with her legs covered by a blanket, it was difficult to believe that there was anything wrong with her. She looked like a normal little girl, with hair tied back in pigtails, her slim figure just beginning to develop. She looked as if she was just sitting there, could jump up and walk and run at any moment like any other twelve-year-old girl, but they'd been told this would never happen. She would never do any of these things again. The family were used to it now, but how would Wilmot feel?

'Patsy?' he said quietly, almost wonderingly, and he went across to her and knelt beside her chair, putting his arms around her. She wound her own arms around his neck and he laid his face against hers, and Lucy saw that he was crying. 'Oh, my little Patsy.'

Geoff, cut off abruptly in his chatter, looked downcast. Lucy flicked her fingers towards him.

'Now, you don't need to look like that, our Geoff. There'll be plenty of time for us all to talk to Daddy and tell him all we've been doing. But what he wants now is a cup of tea, so put the kettle on for me, there's a good boy, and then

take those kitbags up to my – *our* – bedroom. Show Daddy
how strong you are. He's a real man now,' she said to
Wilmot, conscious that she was talking too quickly, her
voice running on with aimless chatter. 'He looks after us
all.' There wasn't a scrap of truth in it. Geoff was an
ordinary thirteen–year–old, more interested in football and
getting out with his mates than in being the 'man of the
house'. And in any case, Arthur was that.

Wilmot turned. 'No, don't take them both. Leave that
one down here.' He grinned. 'It's got some presents in.'

'Presents!'

Geoffrey was alight again at once. He dragged the kitbag
into the kitchen, forgetting his mother's instructions, and
began to unpick the cords around its neck.

Wilmot laughed. 'Don't get too excited, old son. There's
no toys, I'm afraid. Just a few tins of fruit I managed to get
hold of in Singapore. They told us you didn't get much of it
at home so we all brought as much as we could carry.'

'Tins of fruit!' Lucy stared as the cans of peaches and
apricots came out of the bag, and then began to laugh. Her
laughter was high pitched and uncontrollable, and after a
few minutes Maud pushed her into a chair where she leant
her head on her hand and laughed herself into a weak
silence.

Wilmot stared. 'What's so funny?'

'It's the tins of fruit,' his mother told him. 'We didn't
think you'd have had much of that kind of food all these
years, either. So when they were in the shops just before
Christmas, Lucy got some specially. Queued up for hours,
she did. We had one at Christmas and then we saved the
other two for when you came home. They're in the
cupboard now.' She nodded her head and Geoffrey
opened the cupboard door and took the two cans out, one
in each hand. 'You see? Peaches and apricots . . .'

The first few weeks were a mixture of joy and dismay.

They would have been better in their own place. A married couple needed time and space and privacy to feel their way back after years of separation. Years in which each had suffered misery unknown to the other, misery they would never be able to convey because there was just too much of it and anyway the memories were too sharp, too painful to recount. And yet they needed to know. How else, Lucy thought, could they ever understand?

'We heard such awful stories,' she said to Wilmot. 'Men being beaten and tortured. I worried about you all the time.'

'And don't you think I worried about you?' he demanded, as if she had criticised him. 'You're not the only one who worries about other people. You don't know what it was like out there.'

'I know. I know. Don't take it like that,' she begged. 'I didn't mean it that way. I just wanted you to know – I love you so much, Wilmot, I was frantic.'

He stared at her, then he reached out and pulled her towards him. 'I love you too, Lucy. I'm an ungrateful sod. It's just that – well, you don't know, you'll never be able to picture it. I can't tell you –'

'Try. Try. I'll never be able to understand if you don't try. I'll never be able to share it with you.'

'*Share* it!' He gave a harsh bark of laughter. 'Lucy, you don't know what you're saying. You can't *share* it. How can you? It's over – thank God – and I don't want to have to go through it all again. It was bad enough the first time. I just want to forget it now, that's all, forget all about it, forget it ever happened, *forget* it, can't you understand that?'

'Yes, yes, of course I understand. I'm sorry, Wilmot. We won't talk about it again.'

But he couldn't leave it alone. Nothing that had been suffered in Plymouth, nor anywhere else, was as bad as being in a Japanese POW camp. As he walked the ruined streets and stared at the shattered buildings, his lips curled a little. Why hadn't anything been done? Why was it still in such a state? Bombing? He and his mates had been bombed at sea, bombed by aircraft and fired on by other ships. 'And *we* didn't have shelters to go to. We just had to take it.' The big shops smashed, the churches left as gutted shells? 'Yes, but you still *had* shops, didn't you? Spooner's and Dingle's and all those, they just moved somewhere else, didn't they? They still kept going, you could still buy things. And they kept on having services at St Andrew's just the same, never mind that the roof was gone.' Rationing? 'Look, don't talk to me about rationing, everything's rationed on a ship at sea, everything, all the time. Didn't you ever realise that?'

And he was right, Lucy thought sadly. Everything they had suffered, Wilmot had suffered too. And more, so much more. More than she would ever know.

She had clues to it, though. They came without Wilmot knowing it, in his behaviour during the day and even more so at night, when she lay awake, listening to his fevered mutterings, or woke to his screams.

'No! *No!* You can't do that – oh my God . . . Let me out of here, let me out, *let me out* – oh, *Christ* . . .'

She woke him as soon as she could, only seconds after he had woken her with his cries, and he would stare at her with wild unrecognising eyes, eyes that had fear in them, and pain, and murder. There were moments when she almost feared that he would turn on her, as if she were one of his tormentors, as if he truly believed himself back in that nightmare world.

'Wilmot. Wilmot, it's me, Lucy, your wife. Oh Wilmot, my poor darling, my sweetheart.'

And suddenly he was awake, trembling and soaked with sweat, quivering in her arms, sobbing like a baby, muttering incoherent words that might perhaps have told her every-thing, had she only been able to understand.

He might indeed have told her at those times, deep in the night, but she soothed and shushed him, unable to bear his pain, wanting only to smooth away the terrors and give him the comfort he so desperately needed.

'It's all right, darling. You're here with me. You're home again. It's all right. They've gone now. Nobody's going to hurt you. Nobody's ever going to hurt you again.'

It was as if she had another child, she thought when his sobs had quietened at last and he had drifted back to sleep, still cradled in her arms. Another child to tend and care for, to give her strength to and to shield from the world.

But what of her own need for comfort and strength?

Wilmot had been home for three weeks when David came again. He was sitting in the kitchen reading the paper, a mug of tea at his side, and he turned his head slightly sideways and frowned as the other man walked in.

David stopped in the doorway, then moved quickly forwards, holding out his hand. 'Wilmot. It's good to see you again. How are you?'

Wilmot rose slowly. He didn't take the hand David was offering. His eyes went to the empty sleeve but he made no comment. Instead, he said rather coldly, 'I didn't know the guests were allowed in the kitchen.'

David let his hand fall. 'I'm sorry. I don't suppose you remember me. David. Tremaine. I used to come here before – before the war. We spent quite a bit of time together.'

'Oh, I remember you,' Wilmot said, but not as if he had only just recognised David. Clearly, he had known him the moment he opened the door. 'I remember you all right. Even if I didn't, they all talk about you all the time.'

David flushed a little. 'Oh, I'm sure they don't,' he said uncomfortably. 'Not all the time! They must be much too pleased to have you back to bother with me.'

'Yes, you'd reckon so, wouldn't you?' Wilmot agreed without pleasantness. 'You'd think they'd be glad to have me back. The returning hero. The long-lost son and husband and father. You'd *think* they'd be pleased.'

David looked at him. 'Look, perhaps it would be better if I went . . .'

'Do what you like,' Wilmot said indifferently. 'Mind you, you'll have to pay for your room even if you don't stay here. That's only fair, isn't it? 'Tisn't easy running a hotel, can't have guests ratting on their bookings, we'd be bankrupt in no time if everyone did that.'

'Wilmot. What's the matter? We used to be friends.'

'Yes, that's what I thought.' Wilmot's voice was cold, and bitter. 'And you've been friends with Lucy too, haven't you? All through the war, all the time I've been away.'

'For God's sake, Wilmot. You're not suggesting there's been anything wrong between me and Lucy? There never has been. There never would be. You can't believe we'd—'

'Listen,' Wilmot said. 'I can believe anything of anyone. I've *seen* what people can do to each other. I've seen worse things than you can imagine. Anything's easy for me to believe.'

David sighed. 'But that's different.'

'Is it? How is it different?'

'Lucy's your wife. And she's – well, she's Lucy. She would never betray you. She's absolutely loyal.'

'Be your age,' Wilmot said. 'I've only been home three weeks but I can see it. Blokes who've come home and found their wives living with other men. Found they've got more kids than they thought. Found their homes empty and the missus disappeared to God knows where. And how about the ones who've buggered off to America, eh? Couldn't even stay in the same country. That's how loyal women are.'

'But that's not Lucy. She hasn't done any of those things. She's still here. She loves you.'

'So she says,' Wilmot said gloomily. 'So she says.'

He sat down again and leant both elbows on the table,

burying his face in his hands. 'Oh my God. I'm sorry, David, I don't know what I'm saying. I don't know what gets into me. When something unexpected happens, someone walks in and takes me back to those days, it seems like something happens in my mind. It's like a click. I can't explain it. I'm *sorry*.'

David moved swiftly round the table and laid his hand on Wilmot's shoulder. 'It's all right. It's all right.' He felt the bones beneath his fingers. Wilmot didn't look as thin as he'd feared. They'd built him up in hospital, nursed him back to health. He'd been down to six stone when he came out of the camp, Lucy had told David when she wrote, though it was difficult to believe. He must have looked like a skeleton. Now he was up to ten stone, and although that was still light for his build, it wasn't more than just ordinarily thin. David reminded himself that Wilmot had suffered more than anyone could dream, and that his real recovery would need more than just feeding up.

'You don't have to worry,' he said, pulling out a chair and sitting down. 'It'll get better in time. It will.'

Wilmot lifted his face and David saw with pity that it was wet with tears. 'Will it? And how would you know?'

His truculence was returning. Lucy had hinted at something like this. It's been so bad for Wilmot, he can't take in the fact that anyone else has had a bad time, she'd said. It isn't his fault.

David disliked referring to his own suffering, but now he shrugged his shoulder, lifting his empty sleeve. 'I've had my ups and downs.'

Wilmot stared for a minute, then nodded. 'Oh, yeah. You lost that in the blitz, didn't you? And what did they do? Take you to hospital, did they? Made it all neat and tidy, sprinkled you with Dettol, bandaged you up, sent you home to Mum. Made sure no nasty germs got into it . . . Shall I tell you what happened to a bloke in our camp who lost his arm? Shall I? It just got left, that's what. I don't know why he didn't bleed to death. We bandaged it with what we could, we gave bits of our own shirts and wrapped them round his stump, and there was no anaesthetic for him, nothing to put him off to sleep, not even a drink. It didn't stop him bleeding, either. The blood kept on coming through the rags. You could always tell where he was after that from the flies.' He paused and lifted his mug, took a long draught of tea. 'It went bad, of course. Bound to, wasn't it? Stank to high heaven – God, I never smelt such a pong.'

'What happened to him?' David asked after a pause, and Wilmot threw him a contemptuous glance.

'Well, what d'you think happened? Went mad, of course, and died. It didn't take all that long, but I reckon it was too long for him.'

There was a silence. David felt sickened by the story and all that it implied. He felt a deep pity for Wilmot and all the men who were tortured by such memories.

'You lost that the night Patsy copped her lot, didn't you?' Wilmot said suddenly. 'And Zannah. You lost your arm. Patsy lost both her legs, and Zannah – we lost Zannah.'

David wished he had not referred, even obliquely, to his own losses. He knew that if he tried to identify with Wilmot, if he mentioned Stevie and Heather, it would only add to the other man's bitterness. And Wilmot was right, after all. In the context of Patsy and Zannah, his arm was little enough to lose. He thought suddenly of the saying one quoted at times. *I'd give my right arm* . . . He hadn't even done that. He'd only given his left arm.

'I'd have given both my arms to have saved them,' he said quietly. 'I'd have given my life.'

'Yeah,' Wilmot said, too wearily even to mock, 'yeah.'

It was with deep relief that David heard the front door open and Lucy's footsteps coming along the passage. She opened the door and came in, already chattering about the shops, the queues, what she had managed to buy at the butcher's. She stopped abruptly just inside the kitchen.

'David! You're early – I didn't expect you till this afternoon.'

He smiled and stood up. Normally he would have gone to her, given her a light kiss. This time, he didn't move, simply held out his hand and, with a flicker of a glance towards Wilmot, she shook it gravely.

'How are you, David?'

'I'm well. And you?' Their eyes met and their feelings communicated with the ease they had grown used to: half sadness at having to suppress their normal easy, friendly delight in each other's company, half amusement. It seemed so farcical, Lucy thought, and wondered what had happened between David and Wilmot.

'Your room's ready for you,' she said, and then decided that this was ridiculous, they couldn't go on like this, 'but you'll have a cup of tea first. I'll put the kettle on. And you'll have your supper with us as usual. I know Wilmot will want to talk to you.'

The faces of both men told her, in different ways, that she knew no such thing, but she ignored them and went to the sink to fill the kettle. She lit the gas, keeping her back to them, and heard with relief the sound of David moving his chair slightly to sit down again. When she turned back, Wilmot was finishing his tea.

'So how's it going, then?' he asked David in perfectly normal tones. 'Still in the same job, are you?'

Patsy had been out with her grandparents. They didn't often take her out these days because the wheelchair was too heavy for them to push up hills, but it was a bright afternoon and Maud said it seemed a shame for the child to sit indoors all day. They could get her up the slope of Lockyer Street and on to the Hoe if they both gave a hand to it, and Geoff could walk that far with them and help too, even if he did want to go off with his friends straight after. So that was what they'd done, and they came back full of news.

'The Promenade Pier's being all cleaned up and the rubble taken away. I wonder if they're going to rebuild it.'

'No, they'll do the houses first. They're just making it safe.'

'I reckon they'll get the big swimming-pool going, though. Look at it this way, people will want it, in the summer.'

'David!' Maud was first into the kitchen, pulling off her woolly gloves and unwinding her scarf. 'Oh, you're early.'

'Is Uncle David here?' Patsy manoeuvred her chair through the doorway. 'You haven't been to see us for ages,' she accused him. 'There's all sorts of things I want to tell you. And I've read that book you lent me, have you brought the next one?' Patsy was working her way steadily through the stories of Arthur Ransome. 'I've read *The Wouldbegoods* as well, Mum got it from the library. Have you read that? I like Oswald Bastable best, he's so clever. It isn't magic though, like *Five Children and It* and *The Phoenix and the Carpet*, it's just about an ordinary family.'

David laughed and pulled her wheelchair towards him. 'And what's wrong with ordinary families?'

'Well, they're just ordinary, aren't they? I wish I had a magic carpet and could go anywhere I wanted.'

'You wouldn't like it when you got there,' Wilmot said. He had been watching his daughter, his eyes veiled behind half-closed eyelids. 'And what about your dad, don't I get a kiss?'

'Oh yes.' But there was a tinge of doubt in Patsy's voice. Wilmot didn't normally ask for a kiss every time she came in. 'But you're here all the time now, aren't you, and we only see Uncle David now and then.'

There was nothing anyone could say in response to this. David's 'now and then' was seldom more than six weeks between visits, whereas Wilmot had been away for years, but nobody missed the innocent implication of Patsy's words.

'Well, is there any tea in that pot?' Maud asked, a shade loudly. 'Or have you drunk it all?'

'It's not long made.' Lucy refilled the kettle and got out more cups. Suddenly, everyone moved and became busy, Arthur pulling off his cap and unwrapping his muffler, Maud helping Patsy out of her coat and Lucy putting away the shopping she had queued for. The kettle whistled and she dropped another spoonful of tea into the pot and poured boiling water on top. Maud filled a jug with milk and set the little bottle of saccharin tablets on the table.

'I'll just get the sugar out for David.'

'Oh, David has sugar, does he?' Wilmot's voice, like Maud's, was a trifle over-loud. 'Why's that, then, David? Saccharin not good enough for you, is that it? Rather use our sugar, would you?'

'David doesn't use our sugar,' Lucy said quietly. 'He brings his own.'

'You're giving him our bowl.'

'Which was filled with David's sugar the last time he came.' Lucy set the bowl down and put a spoonful of sugar into David's cup. She gave her husband a look as she did so, a look that dared him to question her further. Wilmot's eyes narrowed and the skin around his mouth whitened and looked taut.

David said quickly, 'It doesn't matter, Lucy. I'd just as soon have saccharin.'

'Why? You don't like it. It's your sugar and you can choose how you have it. You leave more here than you use, anyway.'

'It doesn't matter,' he said again, and Lucy sat down, biting her lip. Maud gave her a quick glance and poured tea for everyone. The rest of them passed the saccharin bottle around in silence.

'They say there's been snow up north,' Arthur remarked,

apparently oblivious of the atmosphere. 'Had any up London way, David?'

Lucy laughed a rather brittle laugh. 'London's not exactly "up north", Dad.'

'Well, it's more north than Plymouth is,' Arthur said with irrefutable logic. 'They could have had snow. Mind you, we don't want it, do we, not now the football's getting going again. I've been telling our Wilmot, he ought to come and see Argyle play, but he don't seem interested.'

'I've been up to the ground,' Wilmot said. 'It's a shambles.'

'Well, it was bombed, wasn't it? Same as everything else round here. It don't mean the team doesn't play, it don't mean we can't go and support them.' Arthur sucked at his tea. 'We've all been through it. We've all got to carry on.'

Lucy looked at him. Arthur was sixty-seven years old and showing it. He ought to have retired years ago, ought to be able to take life a bit easier, but instead he'd been forced to carry on, struggling to run a small hotel all through the war, seeing the houses all around him bombed and blazing, seeing his own house damaged. He probably wanted nothing more than just to sit in his armchair and smoke his pipe and listen to the football and the boxing on the wireless, and stroll down to the pub and have a yarn with his mates. But instead, he had to carry on.

And Maud too, although she'd always been a big woman, she looked worn and tired, as if she'd had enough. They've both had enough, Lucy thought, and it's up to me and Wilmot to take it off their shoulders.

She talked to Wilmot about it later that evening, as they got ready for bed. It was the only time they could be private together, in this half-hour before sleeping, but that didn't mean Wilmot was always ready to take advantage of it. Already, Lucy had learned that she was wise to choose her moment for raising a difficult subject.

'Your dad looks a bit run down,' she remarked, pulling off her jumper. 'I think it's getting a bit too much for him, running this place.'

'Well, he doesn't do all that much, does he?' Wilmot was already in his pyjamas. He took off his clothes in two movements – vest, shirt and jumper in one go, trousers, pants and socks in the second – and left them heaped on the floor. He used to be so tidy, she thought. All sailors were – you had to be, on a ship. Now, he didn't seem to care any more. 'You do the books and all the paperwork.'

'I know, but he still does quite a bit around the place. And your mum, she's run off her feet with the beds and cooking. I do as much shopping as I can to take it off her, but it's still a lot of work. And there ought to be more, now that we'll be getting more guests.'

'God knows why.' He was in bed now, dragging out the sheets and blankets that Lucy had tucked in that morning, punching his pillows into a crumpled ball. 'I can't see why anyone would want to come to this godforsaken hole.'

'Wilmot! It's your *home*.'

'It's a godforsaken hole,' he repeated. 'Plymouth *and* this so-called hotel. I mean, look at it, Lucy. Think what it used to be like – a place you could ask people to. It's a dump now.'

She wasn't clear whether he meant the city or the house now, but his words could be fairly applied to either. 'Well, it's up to us to get it back again, isn't it?'

'How d'you mean?'

He didn't really want an answer to that, she thought. His tone was truculent again, daring criticism or even the mildest suggestions which could be construed as criticism, but she went doggedly on.

'Well, we could start by keeping it clean and tidy.' She couldn't help the acidness in her voice as she glanced at his heap of clothes. 'We could do a bit of decorating. Freshen up the guest rooms. There's some new curtain material at the Co-op, I thought I might get some. It'd be so nice to have pretty curtains after all that blackout.' She bit her lip. Blackout was something that was likely to start Wilmot off again. *You were lucky to have lights to hide.* 'And we ought to get some new crockery. I know it's only utility, but at least we could have cups and saucers and plates that matched. It would look much nicer in the dining-room.'

Wilmot whistled. 'You've got big ideas, haven't you? New curtains, tea sets – you'll be wanting to carpet the place from top to bottom next.'

'Well, it wouldn't hurt to do that either. Carpet makes a lot of difference to a place. And we've never replaced the carpet that was ruined when we had the bomb.'

'And where's all the money coming from?'

'We'll have to earn it,' Lucy said quietly.

Wilmot's demob papers had come through. He was no longer in the Navy. Lucy had wondered how he would take this, but he just looked them over and then pushed them aside as if they were of no interest and went back to reading the strip cartoons in the *Daily Mirror*. *Jane* was his favourite, of course, but he liked the lantern-jawed *Ruggles* as well. He seemed far more interested in their careers than in his own.

'What do you mean, earn it?' he demanded now, firing up at once. 'Are you telling me I'm lazy? Workshy, is that it?'

'No, of course not.'

'I'd have thought I'd done my bit for a while,' Wilmot said, as if addressing a third party, a whole crowd of third parties massed somehow in a corner of the bedroom. 'I'd have thought four years in a Jap prisoner-of-war camp – not to mention two years at sea before that, fighting enemy ships, living in fear of bombs and torpedoes – I'd have thought that was enough for a while. I'd have thought I was entitled to a bit of time off. Not a holiday, I wouldn't ask for anything as much as that, but just a bit of peace and quiet to get over it all. I'd have thought that was the least I could ask.'

'Wilmot, don't,' Lucy begged. 'I didn't mean that, you know I didn't. Of course you're entitled to some time to yourself. I just meant – well, someone's got to do the work, and your mum and dad are getting on, it's not fair to expect them to . . . I'm not saying *you're* not being fair,' she added hastily, seeing his face, 'just that we've got to sort things out. *Think* about it. That's all.'

'Well, that's not what it sounded like to me,' he muttered, watching her pull her nightdress over her head. 'It sounded to me as if you expected me to come up with something. All this talk about carpets and curtains and so on. *You've* had the use of the money all this time, Lucy. I didn't spend it, stuck there in POW camp.'

'I know.' She slipped into bed and put her arms around him. 'I didn't mean anything like that, Wilmot. I shouldn't have brought the subject up. I'm sorry.' She tried to draw him close but she could feel the resistance in him and her despair grew. 'Cuddle me close, love, like you used to do,' she whispered. 'Cuddle me close and forget all that. Let's just be us for a little while, shall we?'

Slowly, the resistance melted and he became soft in her arms. And then his body hardened in a different way and she gave a small sigh of relief and uttered a soundless prayer of thanks as she welcomed him and surrounded him with her own softness and her strength. And afterwards, as he fell asleep still wrapped in her arms, she prayed again that this night, at least, he would sleep without dreams.

For herself, however, the nightmare seemed scarcely begun, and as she lay awake, staring into the darkness, she felt more lonely than ever she had felt during those years of separation and fear. During that time, she had always been able to believe that the Wilmot she had known and loved still existed, and now she knew that he did not. Somewhere out in the Far East, at some time during those terrible years, the Wilmot she had known and loved so much had died and gone for ever.

Chapter Twelve

There were other times when Lucy was almost able to believe that Wilmot was recovering from his experiences. Times when he seemed no different after all from the Wilmot she had known, the cheeky sailor she had fallen in love with and married. He would wake from a good night's sleep, clear eyed and refreshed, reaching for her in the big bed. Their loving then was good, leaving her warmed and comforted. It was just a matter of time, she told herself. You couldn't expect him to get back to normal overnight. Look how long it had taken her to get over losing Zannah. Well, she still hadn't got over it, she never would, you couldn't ever really get over losing a child. And it was the same for Wilmot. He had to learn to live with his memories, just as everyone else did, and he *was* learning. He just had to take his own time.

'Let's take the kids over to Cawsand,' he said one morning just after Easter. 'It's time young Geoff learnt to swim.'

'Geoff can swim,' Lucy said, surprised that Wilmot didn't know this, then bit her lip. Of course he didn't know. There were a thousand things he still didn't know. 'David taught him.'

'Oh? That can't have been easy, with only one arm.' She wondered whether he was jealous, but there didn't seem to be any hidden meaning in Wilmot's tone. 'Well, I daresay he won't mind too much swimming with his dad, will he?'

'Of course he won't. He'll love it. They'll both like a day

out. So will I.' She snuggled up to him. 'It's nice of you to think of it.'

'Why shouldn't I think of it? I can still remember what it's like to be a father, you know.' He took in a breath and then said, 'I'm sorry, Lucy. I shouldn't have said that. I just get riled at times.'

'It was my fault.'

'No, it was mine. Let's forget it and start again. How about taking the kids to Cawsand today? We could go swimming.'

'They'd like that,' she said, smiling at him in relief. 'You can give Geoff a race. He's quite a good swimmer already.'

They got up and told the family their plans over breakfast. Patsy's face lit up, but Geoff scowled.

'I said I'd go up Central Park and play football.'

'You can do that any time,' Lucy said, 'but it's a lovely day and Daddy and I want to have a day out together.'

'We could do *that* any time.'

'But I want to do it today,' Wilmot said. 'You can run round and tell your mates you won't be coming. Tell 'em you'll play football tomorrow.'

'They might not play tomorrow. They might want to go fishing.'

'Then you can go fishing with them.'

'But I wanted to play football—'

'For heaven's sake,' Lucy said in exasperation, 'stop arguing, Geoff. You spent the whole war wishing Daddy was home, and now he is, you can't be bothered to spend a day out with him. Now, go and tell them you won't be playing football today and then come back here as fast as you can. It's much too nice a day to spend hanging about waiting for you.'

Geoff pushed out his bottom lip but said no more, and when he came back he looked more cheerful. Some of the other boys were spending the day with their families as well, and the idea of a day on the beach was evidently more appealing.

'Don't make things difficult, Geoff,' Lucy said to the children in a low voice, as they waited in the passageway for Wilmot to come downstairs. 'We have to be very careful with Daddy. He's had a terrible time and it's affected him. It's almost like an illness.'

'You mean he's gone barmy,' Geoff said bluntly. 'That's what happened to everyone who was out there.'

'Geoff!' Lucy stared at him, shocked. 'That's a terrible thing to say.'

'Well, it's what everyone else says. The men who've come back from Japan just aren't the same any more. They've all come back funny in the head.'

'I don't care what people say. *You're* not to say such things. Daddy's not – not *any* of those things. He's just had a horrible time, worse than anything you can even think of, and he's got to have time to get over it all. And we've got to help him.'

The bedroom door opened and closed above them. Wilmot came down the stairs. He had found a pair of grey flannel trousers and a sports jacket that Lucy remembered from before the war. He had no tie on and his shirt was unbuttoned at the neck. He looked an ordinary father, ready to take his family out for the day, and when he gave them all his old cheerful grin Lucy's heart contracted with love.

'Right, then. Let's go, shall we?' He picked up the basket Lucy had packed with sandwiches, a Thermos flask and a bottle of water. Arthur appeared with an old deflated car inner-tube and dumped it in Geoff's arms. Lucy piled the towels and swimming costumes on to Patsy's lap.

'Aren't you useful,' she said, smiling at her daughter.

'Just a pack-mule, that's me,' Patsy said. 'A trolley. I sometimes wonder if there's any room for me in this wheelchair, when you've finished piling stuff into it.'

'Oh, we always put you in first, just to make sure,' Lucy

assured her. 'What I'm saving up for now is a chair with an engine and a trailer, so that we can all get in as well and save on bus fares.'

They manoeuvred the chair out of the front door and down the steps to the pavement. They were to take the ferry to Cawsand, and getting Patsy's wheelchair on to the boat was something of a problem. But the ferryman was helpful and soon she was installed between the seats, waiting eagerly for the short voyage across the Hamoaze.

Lucy sat with Wilmot, her hand on his arm. The sun was warm on her face and there was just the lightest of breezes. Gulls swooped around the boat and filled the air with mewing cries. The Hamoaze was busy with craft, much of it taking holidaymakers on trips up the river or across to Cornwall. Men and boys were fishing from Devil's Point, and the beaches at Bovisand and along Tinside were already thronged with people.

'They *are* starting to come back,' she said. 'Visitors. I know the centre's still in ruins, but the beaches are here still, and all the pools, and the lovely scenery. People need holidays, Wilmot, and they're starting to take them. It'll be even busier in the summer.'

'I suppose it will,' he said, and she tugged a little on his sleeve.

'Don't you see what it means? The hotel business will get better. It'll be worth making those improvements, Wilmot. It's worth thinking about expanding.'

He turned his head and stared at her. '*Expanding?*'

'Yes.' She hesitated. This was meant to be a holiday, but Wilmot seemed to have recovered his good mood and she had to take her chances when they arose. 'I was thinking – next door was much more badly damaged than our house was. I don't think the people are ever going to live there again. We could buy it – extend the hotel. It would be one way of making it pay while we all lived there. There just aren't enough rooms otherwise. It makes sense, Wilmot,' she went on eagerly. 'I've been thinking about it a lot and—'

'You've been *thinking* about it?' he interrupted. 'Without mentioning it to me? Shouldn't we be talking it over together? Just remember, *I'm* home now. I know you've done all the work for the past few years but I can take over from now on. You just concentrate on your own job – running the house and looking after us all.'

He turned away again and Lucy sat silent, watching the green heights of Mount Edgcombe come closer. She felt confused and uncertain.

Wilmot was right, she told herself. He was the man of the house and it was for him to decide what course their future took. She ought to be pleased that he was taking an interest, that he wanted to take on the responsibility. And yet, she was the one who had been at home, who had helped run the hotel, who knew its problems. Surely her voice counted for something.

And she wasn't at all sure that Wilmot was yet ready to take over the reins of the household, let alone a business. He was still suffering, she knew that. She hardly dared to guess at what was going on in his mind sometimes, when he sat staring into space, his face white under the yellowish tinge he still bore, his eyes cloudy with pain. What visions did he see then, she wondered, what agony did he relive?

He needed her help desperately. But sometimes she felt that she was losing her way and did not know how to give it.

Going to Cawsand was like going abroad, to some foreign fishing village on a Greek island, perhaps, or a tiny Italian harbour. The village was like a haven after the turmoil of Plymouth, untouched by bombing, the little stone cottages all set higgledy-piggledy in the twisting streets. The beach was a perfect horseshoe, with bright, clear water shimmering over the golden stones, bordered by low cliffs and thick, green woods.

Wilmot carried the basket with their lunch in while Lucy pushed the wheelchair and Geoff raced ahead with his towel still tightly rolled under his arm. A few other people were making their way to the cove, but there was plenty of room for everyone to find a space and soon Geoff had stripped off his clothes and was running into the sea.

Lucy spread a towel over Patsy's lap and started to get her clothes off. Wilmot stared in surprise.

'You're not putting her in the water?'

'Yes, why not? She loves it, don't you, Patsy?'

'But will she be all right? I mean, she can't walk . . .'

'That doesn't matter. We can carry her down the beach. Once she's in the water, she can float on the tyre. Blow it up now.'

'But people might stare at her.' He sounded really upset.

Patsy looked up at him. 'It's all right, Dad. I don't mind. I'm not ashamed of my legs – why should I be? Anyway, who cares if they want to spend their day looking at me instead of having fun?' He still looked doubtful and she added, 'I've been in the water before, Dad. I like it. My legs feel all right then – they feel like they used to. I can float and I can even swim a bit, using my arms.'

'Well, so long as you're sure,' Wilmot said. 'I don't want people staring at you, that's all.'

Lucy went on getting Patsy ready. When she was decent in the costume Lucy had made for her, she lifted her out and took her down to the edge of the water. She sat her down with her legs in the shallow, softly bubbling foam, and then came back to Wilmot. He had started to blow up the big inner-tube with a bicycle pump.

'You're not ashamed of her, are you, Wilmot?'

'Of course I'm not! She's no different from any other kiddie, she's just been hurt, that's all. Just like a soldier or a sailor who got wounded in the service of his country. I just don't like the idea of people looking at her.'

'Look,' Lucy said. 'Patsy's going to be like this for the

rest of her life. Another sixty or seventy years, probably. She's going to want to do things just the same as any other person, and she's going to have to get used to people staring. It's only the rude, ignorant ones who'll stare anyway.'

'That's all very well, but—'

'But what?' Lucy asked when he fell silent, glowering down the beach at Patsy, who was taking her weight on her hands, letting the waves lift her body as they came in. 'But what, Wilmot?'

'I just don't like to see it,' he burst out. 'My daughter, with her legs like that. I don't like people looking at her and knowing—' He stared at her, and to her dismay she saw tears in his eyes. 'I'm not ashamed of her. I'm *proud* of her. Maybe it's myself I'm ashamed of – that I wasn't here to look after her, to look after Zannah, *all* of you . . . Look –' he began to fumble with his clothes, his fingers shaking – 'I'll go in the water with her now. I'll do anything. Anything you want – for all of you.' His voice was trembling as if he were on the brink of weeping. He pulled off his shirt and dragged his trousers down. Like the rest of them, he had come out already attired in his swimming costume, navy woollen trunks. He stood up and picked his way down the beach.

'Oh, Wilmot—' Lucy felt a great pity well up in her and her own tears rise. She mustn't give way to them, mustn't let Wilmot's changes of mood upset her. Only a few months ago he'd still been in a Japanese POW camp, watching his friends suffer and die, not knowing when it would be his turn. It wasn't surprising he was having problems settling down.

She slipped out of her sundress (cut down from an old frock) and went down to join her family. Wilmot had lifted Patsy in his arms and was taking her out into deeper water. He let her float on her back and when Lucy joined them Patsy was laughing, relaxed, her useless legs drifting like a mermaid's tail. She was suddenly struck by a resemblance between Patsy and her father. All the children had inherited Lucy's red hair although none had quite the depth of violet-mauve of her eyes – except Zannah, she thought with a pang – but there was something in the shape of Patsy's face, in the curve of her lips, that was taken directly from Wilmot. The same cheeky smile . . .

It struck Lucy then how seldom Wilmot smiled like that now. The cheekiness had gone. Even when he tried, there was a difference, a touch of bitterness, a hardness that hadn't been there before. It was only in Patsy's laughing face that she could discover the Wilmot she had known and loved.

'Come on,' Wilmot said. 'Show me how you can swim.' He turned her over gently in the water, keeping one hand beneath her chin, the other under her stomach. Patsy moved her arms in the breast stroke. Wilmot moved along with her and they progressed through the water together with Lucy watching. A small wave broke over Patsy's face and she spluttered, then turned her head to laugh at them. Lucy and Wilmot caught each other's eye and smiled, and Lucy felt the warmth of her love once again in her heart.

Geoffrey had been swimming with some other boys, their bodies plunging and splashing in the water like porpoises. He came dashing up to his father.

'Race me, Dad! Race me to that rock.'

He was off before Wilmot had a chance to respond, his wiry body flashing through the waves. Wilmot, startled, took his eyes off Patsy and hesitated, then swam more slowly after his son. He didn't look at home in the water, Lucy thought. He probably hadn't been swimming since the beginning of the war – except when the *Exeter* had been sunk and he'd been left floundering in the Java Sea.

If the ship ever does sink I'll probably be a thousand miles from land anyway.

143

Geoff had reached the rock and was hanging on to it, watching his father's approach. Even at this distance Lucy could see the surprise in his eyes. Clearly, he'd expected to be overtaken and beaten in the race. He'd *wanted* to be beaten. He'd probably told the other boys all about his father, boasted to them.

Suddenly, Lucy knew she couldn't bear to see the contempt in his eyes. She steadied Patsy and called out.

'Time for lunch! Come on, Geoff, you've been in the water long enough now. I'm taking Patsy in and we'll have our sandwiches.'

Geoff stared at her. 'But we've only just got here –'

'I know, but we're all hungry. We'll have our picnic now.' She was walking into the shallows, Patsy drifting lightly beside her. 'Don't argue, Geoff. You'll be able to go in again later.'

'Not for an hour,' he grumbled. 'You never let me go in for an hour after I've eaten anything. Can't I stop in a bit longer, Mum? I'm not that hungry, honest.'

'I said, don't argue.' They were on the beach now, and she had to carry Patsy up to her wheelchair. The stones hurt her feet and she half staggered, then felt Wilmot beside her.

'I'll take her. Don't want you falling down, the pair of you.'

'Thanks.' She smiled at him and he took Patsy from her arms, as gently as if she were a baby.

Geoff came grumbling up the beach but cheered up when given a marmite sandwich and a whole boiled egg to himself. This was one of the great treats of the day, boiled eggs all round, and later came the second when Lucy gave Geoff a sixpence and told him to go and buy ice-creams for himself and Patsy. Ice-cream was one of those things you just hadn't been able to get during the war, and it was still a novelty. Even now, you couldn't get cornets, only thin slices off a block, sandwiched between two wafers, but it was ice-cream and already dripping as Geoff came back along the beach.

They waited for an hour and then Wilmot took Patsy into the water again and let her 'swim' for as long as she liked, while Lucy and Geoff raced to the rock several times, reaching it neck and neck. Lucy touched it first twice and Geoff twice. The fifth time, she said, would be the decider, and she slowed up just enough to let him get there first, knowing that although he'd wanted his father to beat him he wouldn't want to come second to his mum.

They came up the beach together, laughing. The tide had come right in since they'd arrived and was now half out again. Wilmot and Patsy were back on the beach, surrounded by the debris of the picnic, but there were a few biscuits left and Lucy nibbled one, suddenly hungry. She sat on the blanket and leaned against Wilmot.

'It's been a lovely day. I hope you've enjoyed it, Wilmot.' She looked anxiously up into his face.

He grinned down at her. 'It's been a smashing day. You know, I've never been all that much of a one for beaches – not till I knew you, anyway. Couldn't ever see the pleasure in it, somehow.'

She wondered at that, knowing that he had grown up in Plymouth, within a few hundred yards of the Hoe and all those bathing pools, within easy reach of such beaches as this. But in Portsmouth, even in Southsea, she'd known people who weren't fond of the water and never went swimming. You didn't have to be a fish just because you lived beside the sea.

'Well, now you know what fun it can be we'll have to come again. And the children have enjoyed it. It's so nice to be all together again and to come out like this for picnics.' She began to pack up the bags and roll up the damp towels and bathing costumes. 'Let's have another day out before Geoff goes back to school. We could get the train and go out on the moor.' She paused suddenly, folding the blanket.

Geoff had already started to push Patsy's wheelchair up to the road. 'Wilmot – let's have another baby.' The words were out before she could stop them and she heard them with astonishment. She hadn't even known she was going to say them, hadn't known she was thinking about it.

He turned and stared at her. '*What?*'

Lucy flushed a little. 'I was thinking – when I said we were all together again – we're not, are we? We haven't got Zannah. And we never will have, and I know another baby would never take her place, nobody could . . . But I would like another one, Wilmot, I really would. Perhaps even two. We always said we'd have three or four, didn't we? You always wanted a big family. And now the war's over –'

To her dismay, Wilmot's face clouded over. More than clouded – it was like thunder. She gazed at him, feeling suddenly frightened. What had she done?

'My God!' he burst out. 'Don't you think I've got enough on my plate? No job – no proper home of my own – a family to support already – and you want *more*? You want us to start all over again, with a bawling kid keeping us awake at night, needing new clothes and nappies and all the gubbins . . .? Lucy, there's been times since I came home when I've thought I was going mad, but now I wonder if it was me at all. It's you. You're off your rocker.'

'Wilmot—'

He had turned away, was already taking his first stride up the beach. Lucy started after him and the blanket unfolded in her arms, came loose all around her like a flopping skirt and almost tripped her up. 'Wilmot – don't, please. I'm sorry. I shouldn't have said it. It was just – I don't know, I just suddenly felt . . . oh, *Wilmot.*'

At the pleading note in her voice, he turned. He was standing slightly above her on the beach and looked taller and somehow, she thought in her distress, stronger. He looked down at her and she reached out her hand, trying to sort out the blanket with the other.

'I'm sorry,' she said again, helplessly.

He grunted again. The anger had faded from his face. 'Well, all right.' He watched her struggle with the blanket. 'But don't let's hear any more about it, all right? It's not the right time, Lucy. Okay?'

She blinked rapidly, hoping he would not see her tears. The blanket was tightly folded again and she came level with him and took his arm. 'I do love you, Wilmot.'

He nodded. 'Come on. We'll have to hurry if we want to catch the next ferry.'

Lucy didn't think there was any need to hurry. If they didn't catch the ferry, there would be another one, and there weren't many nicer places than Cawsand to while away the time in the sunshine. But she said nothing and they walked up the beach together to where Geoff and Patsy were waiting, and then they walked back through the narrow streets like any other happy family after a day at the seaside.

Chapter Thirteen

Gradually Plymouth, like the rest of the country, dragged itself up out of the slough and began to construct a new life. For Plymouth, perhaps more than for any other city save Coventry, this meant an entirely new centre.

'We have an opportunity now to make a new Plymouth,' the City Council said. 'The old Plymouth which we loved has gone for ever. Now we must make the most of our opportunity to build a modern city, a city that will go forward proudly into the second half of the twentieth century.'

The local papers were full of the plan for the rebuilding of the great shops, the theatres and hotels which had been destroyed. Paton Watson, the city engineer, and Sir Patrick Abercrombie had designed it back in 1943 after the blitz had reduced so much of the city to rubble, but the work did not begin until March 1947, almost two years after the war had ended.

The winter of 1947 was the most bitter of a series of cold winters. The snow started in January and kept on falling. Lucy's mother wrote from Portsmouth to say that the King and Queen and the two Princesses had come to Portsmouth at the end of the month to set sail on HMS *Vanguard* for their visit to South Africa. The platform at the Harbour Railway Station had had to be swept clear of snow so that the red carpet could be laid. They were coming back in May and it would be nice if Lucy and Wilmot and the children could come for a visit then and see the Royal Family.

'They're saying that Princess Elizabeth might get

148

engaged then,' Lucy said, reading the letter at breakfast time. 'She's fond of that young Prince Philip of Greece. The King's said that if they still feel the same about each other when she comes back from this trip he'll let them get married.'

'I don't know how "they" know so much about it,' Arthur grunted. 'I wouldn't be telling the world and his wife if it was my girl getting sweet on a sailor. Mind, he's wise to take her out of the way for a bit, stands to reason a young girl like that isn't going to know her own mind.'

'Arthur!' Maud protested. 'What a way to talk, when your own son went into the Navy and brought home a nice young wife.'

Lucy smiled, pleased with the compliment. She and Maud hadn't always seen eye to eye, you couldn't expect it with two women sharing a house, especially a kitchen, but they'd got on well enough. 'I'd like to go to Pompey in May,' she said. 'It would be nice to see the King and Queen and the Princesses. Geoff won't be able to, of course.' Geoffrey had left school now and started work in the dockyard as an apprentice. 'But you and me could go, Wilmot, and take Patsy.'

'Well, we'll have to see about that, won't we?' Wilmot said. 'Depends how busy we are.'

Wilmot had more or less settled down, though he still suffered from the terrible nightmares which made him cry out at night and tore his temper to shreds for days afterwards, but Lucy had learnt to cope with his moods. She tried never to reproach him, knowing that he suffered deep remorse whenever he had been unfair to her or one of the children, telling herself that it wasn't really the true Wilmot who shouted and swore and stamped about the house, or who sat sullen and silent for hours on end. It was the man the Japanese had made of him. Somewhere deep inside, the real Wilmot still lived and, if she were only patient enough, one day he would come back to her.

Wilmot's main comfort at this time was Patsy. From the moment he had first seen her in her wheelchair, unable to jump up to greet him, he had shown her a tenderness that not even Lucy received from him. Irritable, even surly, for so much of the time, he rarely failed to find a smile for his daughter, and he would take her up on the Hoe and for long walks through the ruined Plymouth streets, pushing her wheelchair tirelessly, the two of them chatting endlessly, or sometimes companionably silent.

Lucy was thankful that he could find such comfort, and glad to see it strengthened after the day on the beach. If she could not reach him herself these days, at least their child could touch his heart, and anything that could save him from the torment of his memories was to be welcomed. It was a shame he couldn't find a similar bond with his son, she thought sadly, but Wilmot and Geoff seemed to be drifting further and further apart and it was as much Geoffrey's fault as his father's. Or perhaps it was nobody's fault, but just another sad result of the war and the separations it had forced upon families. And perhaps Wilmot's return had been just at the wrong time for Geoff, who had been for so many years without his father and had perhaps built him into a hero in his boyish mind.

Nobody could describe Wilmot now as a hero. When he wasn't with Patsy, he resorted to his only other comfort – the rum bottle.

He had grown used to his daily 'tot' when in the Navy: from the age of eighteen onwards all sailors were given the traditional issue of strong, dark rum. They were supposed to drink it at once but some of them saved it so that they could have a 'bender' at the end of the week. Nobody had been given rum in the POW camps, of course, but it had been one of the things they all longed for and Wilmot seemed intent on making up for lost time.

'Just because Lord Nelson was pickled, it doesn't mean you've got to be too,' Lucy said once, acidly, referring to the story that Nelson's body had been brought back from war preserved in strong brandy, but she didn't have the heart to nag him. He'd had little enough pleasure from life in the past few years.

She had said no more about another child, and put the longing away from her. She knew that Wilmot would not be able to cope with the added responsibility, nor to the division of her own attention. How could she give a baby the devotion it needed, when Wilmot was as likely to wake crying in the night, and demand more? It wouldn't be fair to any of them, least of all the baby. But despite all her resolve, there were times when she could hardly bear to look into a pram or to see the joy on a young mother's face.

After a few desultory attempts to find a job Wilmot had agreed that it was best to take over the running of the hotel, and Arthur and Maud were now officially retired, although they still helped out here and there. It was the only way a living could be made: wages to staff of any kind would have eaten up any profit. Once again, Lucy had suggested expanding.

'I've told you before, you're talking daft,' Wilmot said. 'We can't afford to buy property. Especially ruins that have got to be rebuilt. We've always managed to make a living out of this place before.'

'That was before the war,' Lucy said, 'and you had more rooms to let then. Wilmot, it just isn't feasible to run this place as it is at present. Look at the figures.'

Wilmot shrugged the figures away and grew annoyed when Lucy persisted. He was in charge now, he told her, and she'd be better off looking after her own side of things than interfering with his. And couldn't he smell burning coming from the kitchen?

Lucy went back and took the potatoes off the heat. They'd boiled dry while she was talking to Wilmot in the little office, but they'd only just caught. He must have a nose like a bloodhound's. She poured some more water into the pan and it hissed fiercely, in much the same way as Lucy would have liked to do at her husband. There were times, she thought, when it was hard to keep a still tongue.

For most of the war, Lucy had helped both Maud and Arthur with the running of the hotel. She had done every job there was to do, from making the beds and cleaning the lavatories to cooking breakfasts. In the last few years, she'd more or less taken over the accounts and done all the ordering, the paying and the tax returns. She knew those accounts as well as she knew her own purse.

At the same time, she had encouraged Wilmot to take over. She'd wanted him to feel he was worth something, to know that he could do a proper job. He'd been lucky to have a business to walk into, but he'd needed all the encouragement and support Lucy could give him, and she'd given it willingly. She'd shown him how to work out all the figures, how to order food and the various materials needed for cleaning and maintenance, how to cope with all the official forms which seemed to multiply daily. He listened and looked and nodded, and said he understood, but it was probably better for Lucy to go on doing the work as a sort of secretary. She continued, maintaining the fiction that he was now in charge, but it came as a shock now to realise that he actually believed it, and that her work was virtually discounted.

It was the same for many women, she knew. Women who had taken on men's work during the war and now found themselves pushed aside. Naturally, the men wanted their jobs back. They'd been torn away from them and made to go and fight when they didn't want to, gone through all sorts of hell, and now they wanted to come back and resume their lives. However, that didn't make it easy for the women who had driven buses and worked in offices or on farms, and even done dangerous war work, like driving ambulances or joining the Services. They'd tasted freedom and independence. They'd lived their own lives, made their own decisions, not had to answer to anyone. And now, suddenly, they were back in the kitchen, treated like skivvies. Like some sort of lower order.

'We've got brains and we've learnt to use them,' Kitty said to Lucy when she came down to Plymouth for a few days' holiday. 'We aren't going to say yes sir, no sir, three bags full sir any more.'

That was all very well when you weren't married, Lucy thought, but a husband needed to be looked up to. He needed to feel he was master in his own house.

And yet she knew that she was right over the hotel. Unless they let more rooms, they wouldn't be able to make a living, and the only other road led to bankruptcy.

The winter brought a halt to most of the plans to rebuild Britain. For months, snow lay like a frozen blanket over the country. The frost went down to twenty degrees, the coldest since records had begun in 1890. Power cuts were imposed to save fuel, and police patrolled the streets warning shopkeepers against using lights or any other electrical appliances during the prohibited hours. From nine in the morning until four in the afternoon, except for the dinner-hour, the power was cut to every home. Street-lights went out again and it was as bad as it had been during the blackout itself. What traffic dared to take to the streets, creeping slowly along the icy roads, was brought to a halt more than once, unable to negotiate the hills, and people who were on their way home from a long, cold day at work, had to get off the buses and walk for miles. And at home, as often as not, they found only a meagre fire, for coal was rationed and hardly ever available.

People died of cold.

The city transport department did its best. Men came out with water tenders and sprayed the roads with saltwater, which was supposed to melt the thick icy covering. Instead, it too froze, adding a new layer to the solid crust. Along the edge of the beaches the sea itself froze, forming a foamy ridge of crystalline billows. Out on Dartmoor, ponies and sheep perished in their hundreds.

'We'll have a hot summer after this,' one man said to Lucy as he shovelled away the latest fall of snow from the pavement in front of his house. 'You see if we don't.'

So we might, she thought, but it wasn't much comfort just now, with the country as cold as Siberia.

The thaw came in March, though they said that on Dartmoor it would be June before all the snow, frozen in hollows, would melt. It came only slowly, though, and was followed by more bad weather. In April, a gale swept the city and left a trail of destruction, sweeping away newly built walls and hoardings. The task of rebuilding, which had barely begun, had to be started all over again.

In May, Lucy took Patsy to Portsmouth. Geoff wasn't interested in seeing the King and Queen anyway, and Wilmot grumbled that there was too much work to do in the hotel for him to be able to leave. Lucy, knowing that he wanted her to feel guilty about going away, took no notice. It was time she went to see her own mum and dad, she said; they were getting on the same as Arthur and Maud were, and didn't see much of her and the children.

Wilmot came to the station with her and they got Patsy's wheelchair into the guard's van and lifted Patsy into a seat in the nearest carriage. Kenny was coming to meet her at the other end, Lucy said, and she put her arms round Wilmot's neck and kissed him.

'I'll miss you.'

Guiltily, she realised that she always felt fondest of Wilmot when they were about to be parted. She could see him then as he had been, not as he had become, knowing that tonight she would not be disturbed by his nightmares nor saddened by his lovemaking. It didn't happen so often now – he found failure in that area even harder to bear than his other failures – but he still turned to her from time to time, at first loving and gentle, and then gradually despairing, berating her for not exciting him, complaining that it was her fault, she wasn't ready quickly enough, he'd been all right a few minutes ago and now it was too late . . . He beat at the pillows with his fists in frustration and Lucy lay beneath him, helpless. If she moved it was wrong, if she didn't move it was wrong, she must caress him, yet she must not touch him *there*, or in *that* way, or at all. It was her fault, her fault, her fault . . .

There was only one way out of the awful state he was in. Lucy tried everything she could think of, loathing herself all the while, and eventually she would succeed. By then, she was usually in tears, and perhaps it was her tears that helped him, for he smiled then as he raised himself above her, smiled as he looked down into her sobbing face. And afterwards he collapsed on her body, almost unconscious with exhaustion and she wrapped her arms around him, sobbing still, but whether for herself or for him she scarcely knew any longer.

For a few nights now, away in Portsmouth, she would at least be able to sleep undisturbed.

The train steamed along the coast, up the estuary towards Exeter, along the cliff at Dawlish, through the tunnels in the red rock at the edge of the shore. Patsy sat with her face pressed to the window. She was thirteen now. Her face had lost its childishness and acquired an attractive thoughtfulness. Her vivid eyes sparkled with life. If she weren't in a wheelchair, Lucy thought sadly, she'd have the boys after her any time now.

But what boy would want a girl who couldn't even walk?

It was several hours before the train finally pulled in at Portsmouth Town station. Patsy had wanted to go on to the harbour, only another five minutes; she enjoyed the sensation of being almost at sea, with the water visible below the boards of the steps and platforms and the big Isle of Wight paddle steamers waiting at the end. But the town station was nearer for Kenny to come, and Lucy was at the window waiting as the carriage came to a halt on the bridge overlooking the Guildhall Square.

'We'll have to be quick. We've only got a few minutes to get the wheelchair off and you into it.'

'Well, if you get left on the platform you'll have to come and meet me at the harbour anyway,' Patsy said with a grin. 'At least it can't go any further than that without dropping into the sea.'

It might have been a good idea to have done that after all, Lucy thought. She was always anxious about getting Patsy, the chair and all their luggage off in time, before the guard blew his whistle. People were usually helpful and there was generally a porter to help, but you never knew . . . And suppose Kenny wasn't there, suppose for some reason he hadn't made it? She leant out of the window, ignoring the warnings not to do so, and stared down the platform, looking for her brother's red head.

There was no sign of him.

Oh, Kenny, she thought in exasperation, where are you? It was almost impossible for her to manage everything by herself. If he didn't come, she'd have to get a porter to help her out of the station and find a taxi, if there were such a thing to find, and goodness knows what that would cost. She turned her head as the train came to a halt, looking for red hair. He might have a hat on of course, but Kenny seldom wore anything on his head. And then she heard her name being called.

'Lucy. *Lucy*.'

It wasn't Kenny's voice. Unbelievingly, she turned her head again, and watched as a tall figure came down the platform towards her. She stared into his eyes and then, as he lifted his hand and opened the door, she stepped down and found herself held against his chest.

'Lucy,' he said, folding his one arm about her and burying his face in her hair. 'Lucy. It's so good to see you.'

'David,' she said, and felt the tears sting her eyes.

David had withdrawn from their lives during the last few months. His work in Plymouth had ended with the war and although he still came down to Cornwall to see his mother, he seldom broke his journey to visit the Pengellys. His presence in Portsmouth came as a complete surprise to Lucy.

'David! I never thought you'd be here.'

'I'm writing a piece on their trip to South Africa.' David had returned to ordinary journalism after the end of the war. 'I couldn't come to Pompey without seeing your parents and when they told me you were coming – well, I'm afraid I couldn't resist the temptation to come and meet you.'

'I'm glad. I've missed you.'

They looked at each other, standing on the station platform surrounded by Patsy's wheelchair and their luggage, the feeling between them acknowledged without words – the feeling that had grown early in the war, perhaps even before that, perhaps had been there since their very first meeting. The feeling that had grown and deepened to love, and would never alter.

David wasn't staying with the Travers: he had a room in a small seafront hotel at Southsea, about fifteen minutes' walk away. The next morning he came down after breakfast and spent the day with Lucy and Patsy, and at Emily's insistence stayed for supper.

'I can't eat your rations,' he objected. 'I had to give my book to Mrs Watson at the Seahorse, I ought to eat there.'

'Go on, we can squeeze in an extra one,' Emily said, giving him a push. 'Anyway, didn't you bring us that lovely tin of ham and those eggs? I reckon we can spare you a few veg out of the garden to go with them.'

The *Vanguard*, carrying the King and Queen and the young Princesses, steamed back into Portsmouth Harbour on Sunday evening. Lucy and David pushed Patsy's wheelchair to the Sallyport and carried her up to the top of the walkway. From here, they could see straight across the narrow entrance to the harbour and across to Gosport on the other side. The tall tower of Holy Trinity church stood out behind the buildings of HMS *Dolphin*, the submarine base, and all along the seawall at Haslar as well as on Gosport Hard itself, people could be seen waiting to see the ship bringing Their Majesties home.

'You'd never think this little entrance was big enough to let big ships through,' Lucy said, looking at the neck of the harbour. 'And there's all that huge space hidden away behind.'

'That's what's made Portsmouth so important.' David gazed out towards the Isle of Wight. 'It's sheltered, too. Look, Patsy, there she comes.'

The smooth grey ship slid through the water towards them, surrounded by the tugs and yachts which had gone out to meet her. *Vanguard* was a warship, but she was used by the King whenever he needed to go to sea. He was a sailor himself and had served in the Royal Navy in the days when he'd never dreamed he would one day be King. Now *Vanguard* was dressed overall, flags of all colours flying from her masts to her bow and stern, and her decks were lined with sailors, their white cap-covers gleaming in the evening sunshine.

'It's lucky they've come back after May the first,' Patsy observed. 'It wouldn't have looked nearly so nice with the sailors still in black caps.'

The ship passed so close that they could clearly see the King and Queen, with the two Princesses, standing on the bridge. Patsy waved and cheered with the rest of the crowd

158

and Lucy felt a lump come into her throat. The King and Queen had stayed with their country all through the war, refusing to leave for the safety of Canada, refusing even to leave London. It was said that the Queen had even said she was glad when Buckingham Palace had been bombed because now she could 'look the East End in the face'. Only now, when their country was safe at last, had they left to visit another part of their empire.

'I wonder if they'll let Princess Elizabeth get engaged to Prince Philip now,' she said as the ship proceeded up the harbour. Faintly, on the still air, they could hear the thin, high whistle of the bosun's pipes as *Vanguard* passed the Semaphore Tower and the masts of HMS *Victory*, lying in dry dock in the dockyard. All ships entering Portsmouth Harbour made this mark of respect to *Victory* and her admiral, Lord Nelson. 'It would be nice to have a royal wedding.'

'I bet they will,' Patsy said as they made their way back down the steps and began to walk through the streets of Old Portsmouth. 'I bet she'll have twelve bridesmaids, too. Can we go and see them again tomorrow, Mum? They're going to drive all along the road from the dockyard to the Guildhall Square and the Lord Mayor's going to have a big reception for them there, and then they're going to catch the train to London. We can go, can't we? Grandma was showing me the route in the *Evening News*.'

Lucy laughed. 'Of course we can. So long as you don't mind the crowds. You might not be able to see much, you know.'

'Well, it's worth a try,' Patsy declared. 'And I certainly won't see anything if I stop at home. You don't mind helping to push me, do you, Uncle David?'

He smiled at her. 'I don't mind at all.'

They walked on through the streets, so many of them still showing the damage of war. There had been very little rebuilding here yet, and the craters and ruined houses had become overgrown with dandelions, thistles, grasses and the arching bushes of buddleia. For a few moments nobody spoke, and Lucy glanced sideways at David.

She was still rather shaken by the surge of joy she had felt upon seeing him again. It was several months since they had met, and she had received only two letters from him, both addressed to Wilmot as well as herself. She had tried to hide from herself just how much she had missed him during that time, knowing that he was right to distance himself. Wilmot had made it more and more clear that he did not welcome David's position in his family. 'Getting his feet under the table' had been one of his kinder references. It was in vain that Lucy tried to convince him that there was nothing more than friendship between them, and even though she did not think that Wilmot genuinely believed she had been unfaithful to him, there was a tiny core of honesty in her that would not let her forget the kiss they had shared, nor the longings that had torn at her heart. Perhaps Wilmot sensed it; perhaps although he wanted to believe in her, some subconscious knowledge fed his jealousy.

The crowds who had come to see *Vanguard* return to Portsmouth were dispersing, many of them wandering along the seafront past Clarence Pier towards Southsea. Lucy pushed Patsy's wheelchair, feeling more content than she remembered feeling for a long time. It's as if we were a family, she thought. And yet she had walked like this with Wilmot and Patsy and Geoffrey often enough, along the Hoe, the four of them a real family, and not felt so content.

She glanced again at the man walking by her side. He was tall and rather thin, his empty sleeve pinned tidily against his jacket as always. He was forty-four years old now and his hair was beginning to grey at the temples. He looked faintly tired, his eyes shadowed, but she knew the shadow was not of weariness but of grief. He still mourned the family he had lost in the blitz; he would mourn them always.

Sadly, Lucy wished that she could give him comfort, but that was forbidden them.

The next morning dawned rather dull, with a light drizzle damping the air. It seemed that everyone in Portsmouth was intent on seeing the King and Queen and their daughters drive through the city. The streets were decked with flags, and every schoolchild was lined up along the route, each clutching a Union Jack. David came early to collect the family, and he, Emily and Lucy made their way to the Hard, taking turns to push Patsy's chair.

'It's a shame your father didn't feel up to coming,' Emily said. 'He thinks a lot of the King and Queen.'

'Wilmot's dad was always one for the Duke of Windsor,' Lucy remarked. 'While he was Prince of Wales, anyway. He doesn't think so much of him now.'

'Well, nobody does. Spent the war nicely out of the way, didn't he? And they say he was a Hitler sympathiser anyway. Still, we don't want to talk about that today. Here's a good spot.'

They settled themselves at the edge of the pavement to wait. It seemed as if the whole of Portsmouth and Gosport was there that morning, waiting to see their King and Queen. Lucy remembered the day they had come to Plymouth and walked on the Hoe, six years ago. She had gone up to see them, with Maud and Arthur and her two daughters. Patsy had run in front of her, she remembered, her pigtails flapping. Zannah had been so excited at the thought of seeing the King and Queen, and so comically disappointed that they hadn't worn their crowns.

The crowd began suddenly to cheer and the sound swelled about her like the roar of waves on a stormy shore. The car containing the King and Queen and the two

Princesses was coming out of the dockyard gates and along the thronged road. Lucy turned her head again and watched, and saw their smiling faces and their gently waving hands.

They're just people, she thought in some surprise, and then laughed at herself. What had she thought they were? Creatures from a fairytale? She remembered Zannah's disappointment that they were not wearing crowns, but she was glad of it. They were people, like herself and David.

Almost too late, she began to join in the waving and cheering, and to her great delight, the Queen's head turned at that moment and the china-blue eyes met hers. Just for a moment, Lucy felt that the Queen – the Queen of England herself – knew of the existence of Lucy Pengelly.

Chapter Fourteen

As had been expected, Princess Elizabeth became engaged to Prince Philip of Greece soon after her return from South Africa, and the wedding was announced for November. It was the lift the country had been waiting for. Suddenly, everyone was in a turmoil of excitement.

'They say she's getting presents from all over the world.'

'I wonder how many toast-racks they'll have!'

'They'll probably have to be gold-plated or they won't let them on the table.'

'Never mind nattering on about toast-racks, I just want to see her wedding dress.'

Predictably, most of the men professed boredom with the whole affair, but it was men who were doing most of the organising, Lucy pointed out, and men who wrote the newspaper reports and read out the news on the wireless. And it was a man's wedding too, as well as a woman's!

'You'd never think it was,' Wilmot grunted. 'I haven't seen any of the papers wondering what *he's* going to wear to get married in.'

'He'll wear his naval uniform, of course, same as you did.' Not that Prince Philip's uniform would be anything like Wilmot's – he was an officer, with lots of scrambled egg on his cap and gold rings on his sleeves, whereas Wilmot had been in the matelot's square rig. Still, it was the uniform of His Majesty's Royal Navy, and something to be proud of.

Prince Philip would look really handsome in his uniform, she thought. Half the women in the country were in love with him now, and envied the pretty young Princess her luck.

Wilmot was doing his best to forget the years he had spent in the 'Andrew'. He still called Plymouth 'Guz' and talked about his friends as 'oppos' and rum as 'grog' but the time at sea and in the POW camp were something he preferred to push out of his mind. Mostly, with the help of his daily 'tot', he managed it, but he couldn't control the dreams he still had at night.

Lucy didn't know what to do. When he'd had too much to drink, Wilmot was surly and unapproachable, and when he was sober it seemed a shame to upset him by bringing the subject up. Anyway, she would rather use those times to talk to him about the business.

'The place next door is up for sale,' she told him, coming back after another interminable morning spent queueing for this and that. 'The people are never coming back. They've moved out to Tavistock to be near their daughter. It's our chance, Wilmot.'

'Our chance? Our chance to do what – chuck our money down the drain?'

'Our chance to expand. Wilmot, we'd be daft not to. That place is going to go for a song. And next-door-but-one could go the same way. We could stretch right along three buildings. These houses would knock into one easily. Pengelly's could be a real hotel.'

'I thought it already was a real hotel. Why do we keep making all those beds if it's not a hotel? Why do all those people keep coming to stay?'

'Not enough beds,' Lucy said, refusing to rise to his sarcasm. 'Not enough guests. We've been into all this before.'

'And I said no before.' He was beginning to get angry, as he always did when he felt himself to be losing an argument. 'You say we'd be daft not to do it – I say we'd be daft even to think about it. Do you have any idea what it would cost?

We haven't got money like that. Where's it going to come from? Tell me that.'

'The bank,' Lucy said calmly, although her heart was thumping. 'The bank will lend it to us.'

'In a pig's ear!' Wilmot said scornfully.

'They will,' she said quietly. 'I've asked them.'

Wilmot stared at her. 'You've *asked* them? You mean you've been to the bank, without even discussing it with me, and you've *asked for money*?'

Lucy nodded. She kept her eyes fixed on his, as if this would help her keep control. She saw the dawning of real anger.

Wilmot came slowly to his feet. His face was suffused with a dark, angry red, his eyes were bloodshot and small between narrowed lids.

'You went to the bank without me? You didn't even mention it?'

'I've mentioned it often enough. I went to see if there was a chance, that's all. I haven't *done* anything, Wilmot.'

'Haven't *done* anything?' he repeated on an angry laugh. 'I should say you've done quite a lot. Taken matters into your own hands, made me look a fool – I should say you've done a bloody sight too much.'

'I haven't made you look a fool. I just went to ask, that's all. I haven't made any arrangements or signed anything.'

'I should hope not! I should hope they'd have more sense than to let you.'

Lucy controlled her anger. 'I managed to look after things pretty well while you were away, Wilmot.'

'That's right,' he said, 'chuck that at me. It always comes back to that, doesn't it? The brave little woman at home, keeping the world turning while her good-for-nothing husband goes off to play soldiers. Or sailors. It doesn't matter which, we're all tarred with the same brush, aren't we? It's all our fault there are wars in the first place, so why shouldn't we—'

'Wilmot, stop it! I've never said any of those things. Of course I don't think that.'

'Oh, pull the other one, it's got bells on,' he said wearily. 'Look, Lucy, I'm not a fool. I know what you think of me. I can see it in your face. A drunk and a fool who'll never be good for anything. Run a hotel? Provide for a family? Don't make me laugh!'

'Wilmot, that's *enough*.' Lucy realised that she'd been clutching her bag of shopping all this time. She put it on the table. Why had she started this now, of all times? She'd meant to wait until this evening, get them both settled down with a good supper inside them and get round to the subject gradually. Blurting it all out the minute she came in was bound to be a disaster.

However, it was done now. She unbuttoned her coat and went to put the kettle on. A cup of tea would do them both good and perhaps bring the temperature down a bit. And the matter had to be discussed some time. The talk she'd had with the bank manager had brought that home to her.

'Life isn't going to be easy for any of us,' he'd told her, 'but for some, there are opportunities and it's just a matter of recognising and taking them. I think you may be right – this is just such an opportunity for you.'

Lucy had felt a quiver of excitement. 'You mean you think we'd be right to expand the hotel?'

'It's certainly worth thinking about,' he said. 'We'd have to go into all the figures, of course, but you're in a very good position where you are, and if there are adjacent buildings becoming available . . .'

Lucy had come out almost dizzy with excitement. The bank manager had spoken cautiously, but she knew that even the slightest encouragement would not have been given if he hadn't felt there was a worthwhile chance. She would talk to Wilmot about it first, she'd thought, and then they could put their plans to Maud and Arthur . . .

And now it was all in ruins, before she'd even got her coat off.

She made the tea. Wilmot was sitting at the table, watching her. She could feel his eyes on her as she moved around the room, getting a bottle of milk out of the safe outside the back door, taking cups off their hooks, warming the teapot just before the kettle came to the boil, then dropping in a spoonful of tea and pouring the water on. She put the knitted teacosy over the pot and put sugar in Wilmot's cup before pouring out.

'Well, you might give it time to draw,' Wilmot said sullenly.

'It had three minutes.' She put the cup in front of him and then sat down opposite. 'Look, I'm sorry I let it out like that, I didn't mean to.'

'No, you meant to keep it a secret till you'd got it all worked out, I suppose.'

Lucy sighed. 'I didn't mean that either. I meant to wait till later so that we could talk about it properly. I've done some sums. I can show you the figures.'

Wilmot said something very rude about the figures, and Lucy felt her temper rise again. 'It's our living I'm talking about, Wilmot. Or maybe you're not interested? Perhaps I should have just handed you the bottle of rum instead of making tea?'

'And what's that supposed to mean? You're saying I'm a drunk now, is that it?' His eyes glared at her. They looked smaller than ever, like a pig's. She felt a wave of revulsion.

'Well,' she said, 'aren't you?'

The silence dropped between them like a stone into water. Lucy heard her words echo in the room. Appalled, she jumped up and ran round the table, putting her arms around his neck and cradling his head against her breast.

'I'm sorry! I'm sorry, Wilmot. I didn't mean to say that, I didn't mean it. I don't think that about you. I love you. I want us to work together. Wilmot . . .'

He drew away from her. She could feel the stiffness in his shoulders and neck. Desperately, she caressed his face, his hair, she bent over him and kissed him, pleading as she did so.

'Don't look like that, Wilmot. Don't hold yourself away from me. Please. *Please*. I love you, I didn't mean any of it, you know I'd never do anything without talking to you first.'

'But you did,' he said, 'didn't you?'

'*No!* I just went and asked, that's all.'

'Without talking to me first. Without even *mentioning* it to me. How can I believe you, Lucy? How can I trust you? When you go behind my back like that? You talk about us working together, but you don't do it, do you? How do you think that makes me feel? It makes me feel that *you* don't trust *me*. You don't think I'm enough of a man to work for my own family.' His voice had changed as he spoke, from sullen indignation to reproachful sadness. He tilted his head to one side and looked at her, and she saw a shadow of the old Wilmot and felt her tears begin.

'Of course I trust you. I'm sorry, Wilmot. I'm sorry.'

'There's no point in any of it, is there, if we can't trust each other? If we can't talk things over together, we can't work together. I suppose it never occurred to you that *I* might be making plans as well? Plans for our future.'

'Plans?' she said. 'You've been making plans?'

'Well, why not?' He stared at her. 'You're not the only one round here with a brain, Lucy.'

Lucy flushed. 'I didn't mean –'

'That's just it, isn't it?' he said. 'You say a lot of things you don't mean.'

Lucy was silent. She stood with her hands still on his shoulders, aware that if she moved away he would take that as a sign of offence, and be offended in his turn. She closed her eyes, feeling slightly sick.

Wilmot put up his hands and removed hers from his

shoulders. He stood up and turned to face her, then laid his hands on her shoulders. He looked down into her eyes and she knew exactly what he was going to suggest. It was what he always suggested, whenever they had had a disagreement, whenever she had begun to appease him; whenever he sensed that the balance of power between them had shifted his way. It was as if he knew that only then could he successfully make love to her.

'Let's go upstairs,' he murmured. 'Everyone's out. Never mind the shopping – or the tea. Let's go upstairs, and then we can talk about these plans we've both been making.'

There was nothing Lucy wanted to do less, but she knew that if she refused, Wilmot would revert immediately to his surly bad temper, and there would be no chance of further discussion for days, if not weeks. And there was always the chance – she told herself this every time – that this time he would be happy again, become the old Wilmot, the one she had fallen in love with.

She followed him up the stairs.

Wilmot's plans, it turned out, were not so very different from Lucy's. A cynic might have suggested that he had had none of his own at all, but Lucy was determined not to be cynical. She was simply thankful that he was prepared to discuss them.

'Of course, I thought of buying next door myself, ages ago,' he said as Lucy brought him a cup of tea in bed half an hour later. 'I suppose you didn't think to lace this tea a bit? It makes it taste much better . . . never mind. Yes, I remember mentioning it at the time. I suppose that's why you thought of it now, you remembered what I said.'

Lucy looked at her cup. She knew he was watching her, waiting for a reaction, but she was determined not to make one.

'It's getting the money that's the problem, but since

you've been into the bank and enquired it looks a bit more hopeful.'

'They'd want to talk it over with you, of course,' she said quickly. 'With both of us.'

'Oh, you won't need to be there,' he said off-handedly. 'I'll take over now.'

Lucy didn't speak for a moment, then, very carefully, she said, 'I think I ought to come too. I can explain the figures.'

'I think,' Wilmot said dangerously, 'that I can understand your little sums, Lucy.'

Lucy took in a breath. She got out of bed and pulled her dressing-gown around her. It was the one she'd made for her trousseau, a warm camel-coloured wool, and it had seen her through sleepless nights with the children, through the even more sleepless nights of the blitz. Without either speaking to or looking at Wilmot, she went out of the room and along the landing to the lavatory. She shut herself in and then stood there, leaning her head against the wall.

It doesn't matter, she told herself. As long as we just *do* it. As long as he's happy and feels he's in charge. As long as we can make a living, none of it matters.

She looked at the chain hanging from the cistern. Wilmot had told her very little about the camp, but he'd said once that men were whipped with chains like that. She reached out and drew it towards her, looking at the links, feeling them against her palm, imagining the pain. I mustn't get angry with him, she thought. I don't know what he suffered out there.

She went back to the bedroom and started to get dressed. Wilmot was still in bed, cradling his cup in his hands. Lucy smiled at him, but she knew that the smile was stiff and unreal.

'All right,' he said, in one of those tones most calculated to annoy women, 'what have I done this time?'

'Did I say you'd done something?'

'You don't have to say. It's written all over you. The way you stormed out –'

'I didn't storm out. I walked out quietly.' It would be better not to answer him at all, yet if she kept silent he would go on needling until she did. Lucy felt the frustration rise in her again, the helplessness.

'You were muttering to yourself!'

'I was not.'

'Well, anyway, I can see you're working yourself up to something,' Wilmot said. 'Another quarrel, I suppose. My God, why is it women can't talk about anything without turning it into a quarrel? Doesn't matter what it is, it's always got to be an argument. The next thing is, you'll start crying, and then I'll be supposed to feel guilty and tell you it's all right, don't upset yourself, we'll do whatever it is you want. Oh, I know the whole thing word for word, we've been through it all before, times without number, we—'

'*Shut up!*'

Lucy's voice cut across Wilmot's like a chopper cutting into a tree. He stopped abruptly, his mouth still half open, staring at her.

'Lucy –'

'I said, shut up.' She stood in her blouse and petticoat, her skirt in her hands, glowering at him, all her resolve gone. 'I've heard enough. You do this every time, Wilmot. You do your level best to make me feel in the wrong, to make me feel guilty – and it doesn't matter what we've been talking about, we always end up like this. We never ever talk properly because *you* turn it into an argument. Not me – you. And we don't even argue about whatever it is we're talking about. It's always a list of your complaints, all the things I do wrong, until I'd do anything to stop it, just to keep the peace. And I've had just about enough of it.'

Wilmot raised his eyebrows. 'Now who's complaining? Now who's making a list?'

'Oh no,' Lucy said. 'You don't get round it that way. You

171

don't make me feel guilty this time, Wilmot. I told you, I've had enough.'

'So what are you going to do about it? Put a gag on me?' He giggled suddenly. 'Or wear one yourself. That'd be a better idea.'

Lucy gave him a withering look. 'I'm not doing either. I'm going to go downstairs and unpack the shopping. Then I'll get dinner ready. Then I'm going to go into the office and spend the afternoon working on the figures I talked about with the bank manager, and when I've done that—'

'Yes? When you've done that?' He was sneering, but in his eyes was a gleam of something that looked like fear.

'I'll talk them over with your father,' Lucy said deliberately. 'The hotel does belong to him still, unless I'm very much mistaken. And neither of us can do anything without his agreement, in case you've forgotten.'

She pulled her skirt over her head and fastened it about her waist. Then, without another glance at her husband, she went out of the room and down the stairs.

Wilmot lay back on the pillows. His heart was beating jaggedly and he could feel the heat on his skin. He reached under the bed and dragged out a bottle, half full of strong brown rum, and he poured a generous measure into his teacup and drank it down.

'Women!' he said on a swaggering note, and then, bitterly, 'Bitch! *Bitch!*'

It was Patsy who brought him round in the end. She listened as her parents and grandparents discussed the plans at mealtimes, and watched her father's face, sulky and glowering. Later, she asked him to take her out for a walk and he pushed her chair up to the Hoe where he could sit on a bench and they could gaze at their favourite view.

'I don't think I'll ever get tired of coming up here,' Patsy said. 'It's always different – all blue and shining on fine days and then grey and stormy like this afternoon. I never know which I like best.'

Wilmot glanced at her in surprise. He hadn't really wanted to come out this afternoon, he'd wanted to stay at home and pick another argument with Lucy, but he found it difficult to refuse Patsy. She was so dependent. She couldn't just walk out and bang the door behind her when she wanted a bit of fresh air, she had to ask someone to take her. And she was the only one who seemed able to soothe these moods of terrible frustration that gripped him, when he felt almost as powerless as he had in the Japanese camp. That's what it is, he thought, staring out at the grey, choppy waters of the Sound. I feel just like I did back then, trapped in a world I can't control, and it scares me. It's daft. I know I'm not going to be hurt or tortured like we were there, yet I feel just as scared. No wonder I want to hit out and scream and bash the nearest person. I just wish it wasn't Lucy I wanted to bash. It's not fair on her. It's not fair on anyone.

'I'd have thought you'd like the fine days best,' he said to Patsy, but she shook her head.

'I like it whatever it's like. The fine days are lovely, but the stormy days are exciting. Look at it now. Look at the way the wind's blowing the tops off the waves and making them break. You can see why they're called white horses, they look just like horses' manes, galloping across the water. And look at the sky. The clouds are really racing each other – and that one's crying, see? You can see the rain, like a black curtain. It'll blot out all Rame Head and Mount Edgcombe in a minute, just as if they weren't there at all. It's gorgeous.'

Wilmot looked. He had seen storms at sea, the waves forty feet high and the bow of the ship ploughing through them, rearing until the vessel stood almost on its stern before dropping into the trough beyond, and then lifting again, up and up, endlessly through the roaring ocean.

Sometimes it seemed like fun. More often, it was something to be endured, something that could be dangerous and frightening and, at best, deeply uncomfortable. He supposed there had been a wild sort of beauty in it too, but he hadn't appreciated it at the time and didn't think he would now, if he were out there.

'You're a funny kid,' he said to Patsy, seeing for the first time the light in her eyes, eyes as changeable as the sea itself, sometimes a soft blue, sometimes – as today – a strange, greenish grey. Her red-gold curls were whipping round her face, stinging it with colour, and she turned to him and laughed.

'I'm not. I'm ordinary – I just can't walk.' A restlessness flickered across her face. 'Maybe that's why I love the sea so much, and the stormy weather. I feel sometimes as if the wind could blow me away, as if I could just fly with the clouds, up there in the wild sky.' She stared upwards for a moment or two, then added, 'It's why I love swimming, because in the water I'm not trapped any more.'

Trapped. That word again. And she feels it too, Wilmot thought, watching the exhilaration in his daughter's face. That's what we've got in common, why we understand each other. We're both trapped, she in her wheelchair, me in my memories.

Patsy turned to him suddenly, fixing her eyes on his. 'You will agree to what Mum wants to do with the hotel, won't you?' she said, and the unexpectedness of her question took him by surprise, so that he answered without thinking, and heard his words with astonishment.

'Yes. Yes, I suppose I will. It makes sense really, I know that. It's just that –' He shrugged helplessly. 'I don't know what it is, I just want to argue with whatever she suggests. It's daft, I know.'

'It's not,' Patsy said quietly. 'It's because for years you weren't allowed to argue at all.'

And maybe she was right, he thought, wheeling her back

174

down Lockyer Street. Maybe that's all it was. But Lucy wasn't a Japanese guard. She was his wife, who loved him, who'd worked hard and endured her own suffering all these years, and didn't deserve to be treated so badly.

I'll do better from now on, he resolved. I'll change. I'll beat these trapped feelings and sulks and tempers. I'll forget about the camp and all the things that went on there.

I'll be the man I used to be, and I'll start to pull my weight.

Changes, however, weren't so easy to bring about, and it was not long before Wilmot was floundering again. The trouble was, he thought, he didn't even know it was happening, and how could you change what you didn't even know you were doing? And the feelings of frustration, of fear, of being trapped, were too powerful for Wilmot to fight. They swept over him and overwhelmed him, like those forty-foot waves he had known at sea, and his only defences were to swagger, to boast and, in the end, to drink.

Lucy was cautiously pleased when he told her that he was willing to look into the idea of expanding the hotel. She made an appointment with the bank manager, who looked at the figures again and talked them over with Arthur and Wilmot. Lucy stayed at home, thinking that three would be a crowd in the manager's office, and when the men returned she looked at them anxiously.

'What did he say?'

Wilmot gave her a cocky look. 'Ate out of our hands, just like I said he would. Didn't he, Dad? He says my idea of buying up next door and the place next door to that when it comes up is a good one, but he says we ought to make an offer now for next-door-but-one — make sure we get it before anyone else steps in. Then we can do the whole conversion at once.'

Lucy stared at him. She let pass the implication that the plans had been all Wilmot's — she had already resigned herself to the fact that she would never be given credit for all her hard work. But she hadn't dared believe that the bank manager would be prepared to loan them enough for the whole job at once.

'You mean he'll let us have all the money? Straight away?'

'Well, not straight away,' Arthur said. 'We've got to get the work done, see, and then the bank'll pick up the bills as they come in. Then we don't take out a big loan. I wouldn't have thought of that myself, but he had it all worked out.'

'Well, you're not a businessman, you see, Dad,' Wilmot said. 'I mean, you've never had to worry yourself about that sort of thing. But me and Mr Dyson, we get along just like that.' He made a circle with his thumb and forefinger. 'Pengelly's will be all right now, you wait and see. We'll be as big as the Duke of Cornwall before we've finished!'

Lucy sighed. The Duke of Cornwall was the biggest and best hotel in Plymouth. It had been specially built as a grand hotel and took up a whole corner all to itself. Three houses knocked together in Lockyer Street were never going to be able to compare with that.

'Don't let's get carried away,' she said. 'There's a long way to go before we can even begin to compete with the Duke. There's getting the money organised, getting plans drawn up, working it all out . . .'

'Yes, well, I might have expected you'd throw cold water on it,' Wilmot said. 'It's always the same with women. Got to stick their five eggs into any discussion, and when you let them it's all cold water and wet blankets.' He glared at Geoff who had begun to giggle. 'And you can keep your nose out too. I don't know what you find so funny about the idea of trying to build up a business.'

'It's not that, Dad,' Geoff said. 'It's cold water and wet blankets.' He snorted with laughter again.

Wilmot glowered at him. 'You've had too much of your

own way. Not enough discipline. You'll get a shock when you're called up for National Service, Geoff.'

'I'm looking forward to it,' Geoff said. 'It'll be a chance to get away from this place.'

'Geoff!' Lucy exclaimed and he shrugged and gave her a half-shamefaced, half-sullen look.

'Well, wouldn't you? I mean, I've never been anywhere but Plymouth, and half my life I've spent hiding from bombs. And look what a dump it all is. It's going to be years and years before it's all rebuilt. I'm fed up with it. I want to see a bit of life.'

'And just where do you think you'll see that?' Wilmot asked scornfully. 'Every town and city in the country's been bombed, and most of the rest of the world as well. It's the same everywhere. You won't see any different sort of life anywhere else.'

Geoff shrugged. 'I reckon it was better in the war. There was a bit of excitement then. It's just dull now, dull and dreary.'

Lucy looked at him. He was fifteen years old now, growing fast and filling out. She had wanted him to stay at school and do School Certificate, but he'd refused and got his apprenticeship instead, abetted by Arthur, who said there was nothing like an apprenticeship to set a young chap up in a trade. Now he went off to Devonport dockyard early every morning in working clothes, with his lunchbox under his arm, and didn't come back till nearly six.

'You don't know when you're well off,' Wilmot said to him. 'You don't know you're born.'

'Oh, you can't say that,' Lucy said. 'He works hard, and he only gets Saturday afternoons and Sundays off. It doesn't give him much time to have any pleasure. He's still a boy, Wilmot.'

'When I was that age, I was already in the Andrew. I was away at HMS *Ganges* and they didn't give us much rest there, I can tell you. There was no one to make my bed for me either, and we only got a bit of pocket money.'

Lucy said nothing. Geoff made his own bed, but he didn't do much else to help around the hotel. Why should he, when he worked long hours and handed over his pay packet unopened of a Friday night, regular as clockwork? Lucy took what she wanted for his keep and gave him the rest back to spend as he liked, hoping he would save some.

'Leave him alone, Wilmot,' she said. 'It was different when you were a boy. And you had some good times in the Navy before the war, you can't deny that.'

'That's not the point. The point is that the boy's always moaning. He ought to be thankful for what he's got.'

'Like you are, I suppose,' Geoff said.

Wilmot started to rise from his chair and Lucy reached out swiftly and grabbed his arm. '*No*, Wilmot! Geoff, apologise at once for being cheeky.'

'Why should I? It's true. He's always griping on about something. I get fed up listening to it.'

'You don't have to sit in the same room as me if you don't want to,' Wilmot began, and then, as Geoff started to get up, '*Sit down!* I'm talking to you.'

'Well, make up your mind,' Geoff said, and Wilmot's face flushed a dark red.

Lucy recognised the signs and groaned inwardly. There had been more and more of these quarrels between father and son lately and Geoff was growing less willing to accept Wilmot's authority. It was understandable in a way: he had hardly seen his father until he was thirteen years old, and the Wilmot who had returned after the war was a stranger to him. Whatever Geoff had expected of his father, Wilmot had been a disappointment to him, and whatever Wilmot had expected of his son, he hadn't found it in Geoffrey.

David and Geoff were more like father and son than Wilmot and Geoff were, she thought sadly. Wilmot had evidently thought so too, and had made no bones about his resentment: 'It's easy enough to be a hero when you've got a comfortable bed to lie in at night.'

'David's had a hard war too,' she had pointed out. 'He lost his wife and his baby in the blitz. And he lost his arm saving Geoff's life. It's no wonder he takes a lot of interest in him.'

'Well, it's time he stopped taking an interest,' Wilmot said. 'There's nothing to stop him getting married again and having a son of his own.'

David hardly ever came to Plymouth to see them now, but it hadn't made any difference to Geoff. He wrote regularly and talked about going to London during his holidays. Or down to Cornwall, where David's aunt still lived.

Lucy sometimes felt as if she spent her days trying to keep the peace between Wilmot and his son. Patsy was all right, she was the apple of her father's eye and could do no wrong. And at least there was no problem with her staying out late at night or having unsuitable boyfriends. But Geoff just seemed to set out to aggravate – deliberately making remarks that would inflame Wilmot's temper, and then being cheeky and making it all worse.

'Stop it, the pair of you,' she said sharply. 'I'm fed up with all this squabbling. We used to be such a happy family.'

'When I wasn't here, you mean,' Wilmot said.

Before Lucy could deny it, Geoff muttered, 'You said it.'

There was a dead silence. Lucy closed both eyes. If he doesn't hit him now, she thought, he never will, and there isn't a thing I can do about it.

Nothing happened. She opened her eyes again. It was as if the whole world had come to a standstill. Nothing had happened, nobody had moved. Geoff and his father faced each other across the kitchen table. Wilmot's eyes were bulging and Geoff looked half challenging, half scared.

179

Patsy, in her wheelchair at the other end of the table, was gazing from one to the other, terrified.

Slowly, Wilmot began to rise to his feet. Both fists were clenched. He leant across towards Geoff.

Geoff scraped his chair back. Big though he might be for his age, he didn't have Wilmot's bulk. He glanced sideways at his mother and she recognised the panic in his eyes, the realisation that he had gone too far, and jumped up.

'All right,' she said, raising her voice to just below a shout. 'All *right*. That's enough. Stop it now, both of you. *Stop* it, Wilmot. Sit down and listen to me.'

For a moment, she thought it wasn't going to work. She didn't have the authority after all. But then, perhaps because they both wanted to stop but wanted to be told to do it, the two relaxed. Wilmot unclenched his fists and laid his hands flat instead on the table. Geoff sat back in his chair. And then, slowly, Wilmot sat down too.

'That's better,' Lucy said. She stayed on her feet, looking from one to the other. 'Now listen to me, both of you. I told you, I've had enough of all this bickering. This used to be a happy home, and I mean when we were all here together. Now, we've all had a hard time, but so has everyone else. There's nothing different about the Pengelly family. And some people have had a lot worse. There's always someone worse off than yourself, remember that. What we've got to do now is pull together and make things better again. They're better already. Two years ago, we were looking forward to being like we are now. We were still at war. You were still in camp, Wilmot. We were looking forward to what we've got now, thinking it would be paradise.'

'Some paradise,' Geoff muttered.

'I said *stop* it!' She had rarely spoken to him so sharply, and she saw the hurt on his face. 'Now look. Your father's trying to look to the future. He wants to build up Pengelly's to a really good, big hotel – not as big as the Duke of Cornwall, perhaps, but one of the best in Plymouth. And I want to help him. And that means a lot of hard work for us, and a lot of help from you. *And no more arguing*. Do you understand? We'll never get anywhere at all if we're always arguing and squabbling.'

She paused. Wilmot was looking pleased, Geoff sullen. She felt a pang of remorse, as if she had let him down. It wasn't his fault, after all, if he'd found it difficult to accept his father after so long. And Wilmot had never really been fair or understanding of Geoff's problems. He'd expected to be hero-worshipped, and indeed Geoff had been quite ready to do that at first, but he'd been rejected and criticised from the very first. You couldn't expect a boy to put up with that.

I'm sorry, Geoff, she said silently to his bent head, I'm sorry, but I've got to keep your father happy. It's the only way.

She could only take one step at a time, and at least Wilmot was now willing to work at building up their future. That was the biggest step they had taken yet.

Chapter Fifteen

By the time Princess Elizabeth and Prince Philip were married, in November, the plans for the conversion of the hotel were well under way. The house next door had been bought, and although the owners of the next one hadn't yet decided whether or not to sell, Lucy was hopeful and had got the architect to draw up plans that could include the extra building if and when it became available. She stopped outside whenever she came back from the shops, gazing along the façade, hardly able to believe that they had already achieved so much.

Maud and Arthur were leaving most of the work to her and Wilmot now. In their late sixties, and having lived through two world wars, they were both tired out and wanted nothing more than a few years' peaceful retirement, but they still owned the hotel and nothing could be done without their approval. And that was just as well, Lucy thought, for if Wilmot had had the freedom to do as he pleased, there was no knowing what would have happened. During the past few months, he had veered wildly from proposing extravagant schemes they would never be able to carry out, to moods of deep gloom in which he prophesied ruin for them all.

'Look at all this money we're borrowing. We'll be paying it back for the rest of our lives. We'll *never* be able to pay it back. I don't know why I let you talk me into this.'

'I thought it was your idea, Wilmot.'

'That's right, blame me! It's always *my* fault, isn't it? *My* fault we're on the verge of going bankrupt, *my* fault we'll all end up in the gutter.'

'We won't. Look, it's all right, everything's going to plan.'

'*Your* plan. I should never have listened to you.' And he disappeared upstairs where, as Lucy knew very well, he would pour himself a glass of rum and sit gazing sullenly out of the window as he drank.

She had grown used to his moods. The best course, she had discovered, was to carry on as if nothing had happened. Eventually, he would come downstairs, stumbling and slurring his words, either truculent or restored to a good humour which brought him to her side, pinching her bottom and kissing her neck with slack lips. Either way, the rest of the day would be a tightrope for the whole family to walk, and the end of it would come in bed that night, with Wilmot's increasingly desperate efforts to make love to her and Lucy's equally desperate efforts to help him.

'It's your fault. You're frigid. How can a man make love to a woman who's frigid?'

Perhaps I am, Lucy thought miserably, but I never used to be. And she would hug and caress him, striving to bring him the release he longed for. Just let him do it and get it over with, she prayed.

Even when he was successful, she sometimes wondered if he actually enjoyed it. She could feel no passion in him, no tenderness. I could be a doll lying here, she thought, and when it was finished at last she would turn over and lie staring into the darkness, conscious of a sensation of having been dirtied all through her body, and her tears would creep silently down on to the pillow.

The Royal Wedding occupied the newspapers for weeks and everyone brought out their bunting and celebrated just as they had at the end of the war. Lucy, Maud and Patsy listened to it on the wireless. The commentator talked about the people who were gathered in Westminster Abbey, mentioning them by name – foreign kings and queens, dukes, duchesses, prime ministers, lords and ladies – and describing the women's clothes. He seemed to know them all. When the Princess herself came into the Abbey on the arm of her father, the three women leant forward, eager to picture the wedding dress as he described it.

'Oh, I *wish* we could see it all,' Patsy lamented.

'You will tomorrow. There'll be photos in all the papers. And we'll go to the pictures next week and see it on the newsreel.'

'It won't be in colour, though. I'd like to see it in colour.'

Lucy made up her mind to get Patsy a book of the Royal Wedding, just as soon as one was published. She had books of the Coronation of George VI in 1937, with beautiful colour pictures of the King and Queen in their robes, and of their crowns and the orb and sceptre. A book of the wedding would be a lovely present for Christmas, if it came out in time.

Lucy had done a good job with Patsy's schooling, even Wilmot had to admit that. Nobody else had bothered much, and even after the war was over the schools didn't want wheelchairs – even if you could have got one up the steps and through the narrow corridors that they all seemed to have. However, Lucy's own education had stopped at fourteen and there didn't seem to be much more she could teach Patsy now. She still brought home books from the library, but the girl was bored and restless, wanting something more to do.

'I reckon that girl could help with the accounts,' Wilmot said one day soon after the Royal wedding. 'She's as bright as a button with figures.'

'She's just a child still,' Lucy said, but he shook his head.

'There's plenty her age out at work. She's coming up to fourteen. And she's always got her head in a book, she could add up our sums standing on her head, couldn't you, my pretty?' he added as Patsy herself wheeled her chair through the door.

'It's about the only thing I can stand on, then,' she said with a grin. 'What sums d'you want added up?'

'The hotel sums,' Lucy said. 'Your dad thinks you could do the accounts.'

Patsy's face brightened. 'What, me? Do the books and the ledgers? Oh yes! And I could be a receptionist as well. Sit in the front hall behind a desk and give the guests their keys and answer the phone, and all that. I don't need to be able to walk to do those things. Oh, Mum, please say yes! I'd be doing a proper job, just like our Geoff. Say yes, *please*.'

Lucy looked at her. Patsy's eyes were sparkling, her face shining with eagerness. Wilmot too looked pleased and excited, and it was that more than anything that made up her mind.

'All right. You can try it, anyway. We'll give you a month, just like any other girl. But you'll have to treat it as a proper job, mind, you'll have to work the right hours and everything.'

'I will! Oh, I *will*.' Patsy hugged her father's arm. 'I'll be the best receptionist you've ever had.'

'That won't be hard,' Wilmot said with a flash of his old humour. 'You'll be the *only* receptionist we've ever had.'

There was a lot of accounting to do, and a lot of costing. The new parts of the hotel would need complete rebuilding and refurbishing. As well as new carpets, curtains and furniture throughout – none of them easy to come by in these days of austerity – that meant washbasins in every room and a bathroom and lavatory on every floor. All the floorspace had to be calculated, and materials chosen. Every smallest item had to be costed before the bank would give them the money.

The work of rebuilding made life harder than ever. It seemed that everywhere you went, there were builders, creating rubble and dust wherever they moved. Windows were taken out and either boarded up or covered with tarpaulin, which flapped in the wind and kept everyone awake at night. Lucy had hoped that next door could be rebuilt first, leaving the original Pengelly's to be run as normal until the last minute. For a while, this seemed to work well enough, but there came a day when the builder in charge told them they'd have to break through.

'That means we won't be able to take guests,' Wilmot said. He stared accusingly at Lucy. 'We won't be able to make any money at all.'

'I know. We knew that would happen.'

'But what are we going to live on? The bank's not going to pay our grocery bill.'

'It's all been costed in,' she explained. 'It's all right, Wilmot. It's all been taken into account.'

He stared at her and she could see his mind working. He'd known it was all taken into account, of course, but he'd forgotten it. Then he'd panicked and now he was feeling a fool. She felt sorry for him.

'I'd forgotten it myself,' she said, telling a white lie. 'It was only when I looked at the figures . . . There's so much going on, nobody can keep it all in their head.'

'No,' Wilmot said, relaxing a little, 'they can't. Of course, I remembered as soon as I started to think about it properly. It just took me by surprise, that's all.'

'Me too,' she agreed, and gave a small sigh of relief that the moment had passed safely.

The few guests who had booked in were passed on to another guest house in the next road. Lucy promised to send them details of the new Pengelly's when it was open again and hoped they'd all come back, if only out of curiosity. Once they'd got through the doors, she was sure they would stay.

'We've got to make the foyer really attractive. Nice and bright, with carpets and chandeliers.'

186

'*Chandeliers?*' Wilmot gasped. 'Blimey, what's this going to be, Buckingham Palace?'

'Well, just one, hanging from the middle. Not a real chandelier – more a sort of cluster of separate lamps.' The narrow passageway was being done away with and the two front rooms turned into a wide hallway. Lucy had spent hours ensconced with the architect, discussing plans and ideas, keeping some, discarding others. Wilmot had been there too, at first, but he'd found the whole process irritating and eventually declared that it was 'women's work'. Now, she thought resignedly, he seemed to have taken on the task of vetoing all that had been decided.

He'd stopped coming to the bank too, leaving everything in Lucy's hands. She spent hours in the manager's office, going through the figures and making sure that nothing had been forgotten, as well as keeping a strict eye on the spending. She had no intention of putting them into any more debt than was absolutely necessary. She knew Mr Dyson well now and trusted him, and she thought he trusted her too.

'I'll leave it to you to explain that to your husband, Mrs Pengelly. You've got a very good understanding of it all.'

'We're not doing anything we can't afford,' she said to Wilmot now, 'but we're never going to get a chance like this again. We've got to make the best use of every penny.'

'And chandeliers are the best use, are they?'

Lucy wished she hadn't used that word. 'I told you, it's not really a chandelier, just a hanging lamp. It's not really expensive, Wilmot.'

'It's the only thing that's not, then. What with enough carpet to cover Argyle football ground, curtain material to stretch from here to Tavistock and enough light bulbs to keep St Andrew's church going for a twelvemonth, I'm beginning to wonder if we're not paying for the whole of Plymouth to be rebuilt. I tell you, Lucy, it frightens me, it really does. How long is it going to take to get ourselves out of this debt? I wish we'd never gone in for it, I do really. We should have been content with running a decent little guest house, like I wanted to in the first place.'

So now it's my fault again, Lucy thought. She said, 'We went through all that, Wilmot. We couldn't make enough to keep us all.'

'Well, I could have got a job.' He stared at her, daring her to tell him he couldn't or hadn't wanted to. 'That would have been better than shackling ourselves to a millstone like this.'

'*Do* you shackle yourself to a millstone, Dad?' Geoff inquired, coming through the door in time to hear the last words. 'I thought you tied it round your neck.'

'And you needn't be so cheeky, clever-clogs!'

'Sorry. I was only joking—'

Wilmot swung round furiously. 'Joking!' he exclaimed. '*Joking!* Yes, that's what's wrong with this house. There's too much joking going on. Too much bloody silly *joking*.'

'Oh, for Christ's sake,' Geoff said disgustedly, 'a bloke can't say a word in this house these days without getting his head bitten off—'

'And you can stop that swearing. You know your mother doesn't like it.'

'She has to put up with it from you, though, doesn't she,' Geoff said rudely. 'But then, you're the boss around here, aren't you. Head of the household, the brains of the business and all that. I *don't* think!'

Wilmot stood quite still, glaring at him. Lucy saw his fists clench at his sides, saw the ugly colour flood his skin. She stepped forward, holding out one hand, knowing that if he lost control of himself there would be nothing she could do about it.

'Wilmot –'

He flung her a glance of furious exasperation and turned angrily away. 'Oh, don't worry, Lucy. I'm not going to touch your precious boy. I wouldn't soil my hands. But you'd better do something about that tongue of his, or I warn you, I'll hurt him one of these days, hurt him badly. I won't be able to help myself.'

He pushed past the wheelchair and Lucy heard his feet stamping up the stairs. She looked at Geoff and her eyes filled with tears.

'Oh, Geoff. If only you'd stop goading him so much. To hear him say a thing like that . . .' She shook her head in a wave of sadness. 'There used to be nobody who liked a joke better than your father. Nobody I ever knew . . .'

The rebuilding of the hotel took up most of Lucy's attention. The worst part was over and their living accommodation was more or less back to normal. Instead of the old family kitchen there was a new, bigger kitchen with proper big cookers and two sinks. It wasn't homely, but Lucy didn't intend that the family should use it; they were to have their own place, where they could make tea or their own meals if they wanted, but mostly, she thought, they'd eat what was being cooked in the main kitchen.

'I can just as easily make the family's dinner while I'm cooking for the guests. Your mum will help too, and the girl, of course.'

'Girl? What girl? It's the first I've heard about a girl.'

Lucy sighed. They had been through it all before, but Wilmot greeted each stage of the development as if it had been sprung on him entirely unawares.

'We'll need a bit of help around the place. Your mum and I can't do it all. You know that, Wilmot. We discussed it. We thought we'd advertise a bit nearer the time. There must be plenty of young girls around here who'll be pleased to have a job.'

Wilmot grunted. Apart from intermittent bursts of enthusiasm, he now took little interest in the new plans. He spent the mornings getting in the builders' way and then went out, saying he had appointments, but really,

Lucy knew, to go to the pub. She let him go without comment. He was better out of the way. In fact, she dreaded his occasional interference, which invariably led to problems and had twice brought the builders to the point of walking out.

Wilmot was drinking continuously now. In a way, he seemed better for it. He was seldom drunk, at least not noisily or belligerently. In the mornings, he was slow and grumpy, and usually had a headache which he attributed to 'nerves', and liable to be quarrelsome, but once dinner time was approaching and he could go out for his 'appointments' he became more cheerful. He returned at one o'clock, then spent the afternoon either snoring in a chair or up on the Hoe, where he sat for hours staring out at the ships in the Sound. By teatime he had already started on his bottle of rum – his 'daily issue', he called it – and this kept him placid during the evening.

Lucy tried to make sure he had no more than two glasses each evening. If he just stuck to that amount and it kept him happy, she thought, there couldn't be much harm in it, but sometimes she thought the bottle was going down quicker than that.

The decorators had arrived now and all the walls were being painted. Lucy had suggested that Wilmot should help with this, but after seeing his first attempts she steered him towards the family rooms. Geoff helped too, at the weekends, and even Patsy could paint the dados from her wheelchair.

'I'm not a bad hand with a brush meself,' Arthur said, and took on the decorating of his and Maud's room.

'I don't think much of the colours,' Wilmot said, finding fault as usual. 'Couldn't you get something a bit brighter?'

'We're lucky to be able to get the paint at all,' Lucy told him. 'You'd think it was against the law. Well, so it was for quite a long time. Remember that, Dad, when all we could get was brown? I quite like this nice green and cream myself, it looks fresh.'

When the painting and decorating had been done, the linoleum arrived, and the carpet squares Lucy had bought to go over it. She walked from room to room and along the new corridors, marvelling. You wouldn't think it had been two houses once. Wilmot was right – it really was almost as good as the Duke of Cornwall!

She had leaflets printed and sent them out to all their old guests. When she came to David's name she hesitated, then made up her mind and wrote a letter to go with it.

'Why not be our first guest?' she suggested. 'It's such a long time since we saw you, and Geoff and Patsy would love it if you came. You ought to be here, if anyone should.'

Wilmot might not like it, she thought, sealing the envelope and sticking a penny stamp on it, but just this once she wasn't going to worry about what Wilmot thought. She didn't know what they would have done without David all through the war, and it wouldn't be right to leave him out now. And she wanted to see him herself.

For the first time for months, Lucy admitted to herself just how much she wanted to see him.

Pengelly's Hotel reopened for business on 2 May 1949, a Monday. As usual, in all naval ports – everywhere there was a sailor, in fact – the first had been marked by the sudden blossoming of white cap-covers. The world seemed suddenly a brighter, sunnier place.

'It's going to be all right now,' Lucy said, hugging Wilmot's arm as they stood in the new 'foyer' – a grand name for what had once been two rooms and a passage. 'We'll make it work, you'll see.' She was feeling extra excited because David was coming today. Wilmot hadn't seemed to mind after all, perhaps because they'd also invited the bank manager, Mr Dyson, to lunch in the new dining-room, with the architect and the lawyer who had guided them all through the intricacies of planning. Wilmot was dressed in a new suit for the occasion and looked proud and, she thought, rather distinguished. She touched the greying hair at his temples with her fingertips. 'Pengelly's is going to do very well for itself.'

'Well, so it ought to,' he said. 'We've worked hard enough on it.'

Lucy bit her lips together and tightened her forehead to keep her eyebrows from shooting up into her hairline.

'And you've done your share,' he conceded generously. 'You've turned your hand to a lot of things you've never thought you'd have to do. I appreciate that, Lucy. You've been a good wife to me.'

She smiled at him. Perhaps from now on things would be better after all. Perhaps he'd get his confidence back, start at last to forget those dreadful things that had happened to him in Japan, perhaps he'd stop having nightmares and stop drinking quite so much and be able to make love again properly. Perhaps the old Wilmot would come back at last.

'I love you, Wilmot,' she said, hugging his arm close against her. 'I really do, you know. I love you.'

The new front door swung open. They both looked towards it. And Lucy gasped and felt her knees begin to tremble as David Tremaine walked towards her.

'You've done a marvellous job, Lucy.'

The day was almost over and she and David had walked up to the Hoe to watch the sun set. Wilmot had disappeared, probably to the pub, and Patsy, tired out by all the excitement, stayed at home reading and listening to the wireless. Geoff, who had come home from the dockyard only when it was all over, was still eating his own supper and said he might walk up to meet them later on.

'It's been hard work,' she admitted, 'but I've enjoyed it – most of it.' She gave him a wry grin, thinking of all the frustrations they had suffered, when materials didn't arrive or the wrong carpet was delivered or the builders had complained about Wilmot. 'It's wonderful to see it all finished. I just hope we can make a success of it now.'

'You will. You must be the first hotel in Plymouth to have really pulled things together and started fresh. The first small one, anyway. Most of the others still seem to be struggling along just as they were.'

'It seemed to be an opportunity. We were able to get help from the city planners as well as the bank. That's not likely to happen again. And being able to buy next door so cheaply . . .'

'It took courage, all the same. And that's why I know you'll make a success of it now. Someone like you is bound to be successful, Lucy. You're strong.'

'Am I?' She turned and looked up into his face. 'I don't always feel strong, David.'

'I doubt if anyone does. It's keeping going through those times that shows who's strong and who isn't. Hanging on when you feel most like giving up. There must have been times like that.'

Lucy leant on the railing and looked down at the rockpools and the big semicircular bathing-pool where she had taught Wilmot to swim.

'Yes, there were. I wondered if we were doing the right thing. Maud and Arthur never said anything, but they must have wondered too. And Wilmot –'

'Wilmot did say so.'

'Yes. Over and over again.' She gave him a rueful smile. 'Everything that went wrong was my fault, my idea. And quite honestly, most of it was, so I couldn't argue with him. I used to pray that it would all turn out right in the end so that I wouldn't have let them all down.'

'It's not what he's saying now,' David observed, looking out across the Sound at the golden pathway made on the sea by the setting sun. 'He's like a dog with two tails, and taking all the credit.'

'It's nice to see him so happy. He's been through a terrible time, David.'

'And does that give him the right to make you miserable as well? He *has* made you miserable, hasn't he?'

Lucy said nothing for a few moments, then she said slowly, 'It's not about rights. Life isn't like that. We can't talk about *rights*, as if we were born with a contract made with the rest of the world. We don't have any rights over the way other people behave or treat us.'

'Don't you think so? Don't we have a right not to be hit over the head as we walk down the street, or robbed, or our houses set on fire? Don't we have a right to live in peace?'

'We haven't for the past ten years,' Lucy said. 'Those sorts of rights are made by law, and when the law wants to take them away it just does. We didn't have those sorts of rights in the blitz, did we?'

'Things are different in wartime.'

'Things are different whenever the big high-ups want them to be,' Lucy said with a touch of bitterness. 'But that's not the sort of rights we were talking about, David. We were talking about ordinary people living together. I don't have any right to expect Wilmot to be different from what he is. Especially after all he's been through. He didn't ask to be sunk at sea or spend years in a POW camp being tortured and beaten and seeing his friends die. What happened to his rights then, David? And doesn't he have a right to expect me to understand and help him? I'm his wife. It's what I promised to do.'

'So Wilmot has rights, even though you don't,' he said after a moment.

'He has the rights I give him,' she said. 'Those are the only rights we have, the ones other people give us freely and willingly. There aren't any others, and expecting them only brings trouble.'

A small silence fell. They stood close together, leaning on the rail, their fingertips almost touching. At last David said quietly, 'It's a harsh philosophy, Lucy. Hard on yourself.'

'I can't help that,' she said. 'It's the way I feel. Maybe if we were all harder on ourselves it would turn out to be quite easy after all.'

He pursed his lips slightly and tilted his head, as if half acknowledging the truth of such a paradox. 'And where does it leave us?'

'Us?' Lucy said.

'You know how things are with us,' David said softly. 'We both know. It hasn't changed, has it – the feeling we have for each other?'

Lucy shifted her glance away from the golden pathway. She turned her head and met his gaze. The violet in her eyes had deepened to the purple of the encroaching dusk. Her face was pale.

'No. Nothing's changed.'

'And nothing is going to, is it?'

'How can it?' she asked with sudden passion. 'You can see how my life is. How can I walk away from all that? How can I walk away from *them*? It isn't just Wilmot.'

'I know.'

'They have the *right*,' she said, using the word deliberately, 'they have the right to expect me to be there. To keep faith. I have to keep faith, David.'

'Because of them?' he asked. 'Because of their needs?'

Lucy looked away. He saw the torment in her face, the struggle to face her own truth.

'No,' she said at last, 'because of mine.'

David stayed for a week. He was writing a book about the rebuilding of the three major naval ports, Plymouth, Portsmouth and Chatham. As he had always done, he ate his meals with the family, talking easily with Maud and Arthur, having long conversations with Patsy and setting off in the evenings for walks with Geoff. They took the ferry to Torpoint or to Saltash and strolled along the foreshore of the rivers that fed into the Hamoaze, and one evening they took the train to Yelverton and walked back across the moor, coming home by moonlight.

What they talked about on these jaunts, Lucy never knew, but she could see the contentment in Geoff's face when they returned, the pleasure he had felt in the company of the man who had been like a father to him.

Wilmot said nothing. He behaved as if David were not there. Now that the hotel was open he had undertaken certain duties – mostly those of welcoming new guests, supervising in the dining-room, keeping an eye on Patsy as she did the daily accounts. He dressed smartly every morning and stood at the new front door, proud to be seen as the proprietor of Pengelly's. But by eleven o'clock he had begun to look at his watch, and at twelve he disappeared, returning at one for his dinner – the family still ate their main meal of the day then, leaving Lucy free to cook for the guests in the evening – and spending the afternoon either on the Hoe or dozing in an armchair.

Lucy never said that she thought the hotel would run just as well if Wilmot were not there. She didn't even allow herself to think it. She told herself that he would find his own level, that he was a support to her and the rest of the family just by being there, that the place would fall apart without his presence in the background.

There were times, quite long periods in fact, when she almost believed it.

She said goodbye to David at the end of the week, knowing that he would leave an emptiness behind him. They said goodbye in the foyer, with other guests leaving at the same time, and no chance for a private moment.

'It's been so lovely to see you again,' Lucy said, giving him her hand. 'Don't leave it so long next time. Come and see us again.'

'I will.' His eyes looked into hers. 'Lucy –'

'We'll always be friends,' she said quickly. 'Nothing is ever going to change that.'

'I know.' He hesitated, then smiled at her. 'It's all right. I won't say anything to embarrass you. I just want you to know – you have a *right* to my friendship, Lucy. A lifelong right.'

She smiled, remembering their conversation on the Hoe. Rights could only be given, not claimed. 'And you have a right to mine.'

A final look, a final moment of silence and a brief, firm handclasp, and then he was turning away, was gone through the new front door. And Lucy stood there, feeling bereft, unable for a moment or two to move. The hotel seemed suddenly empty.

Chapter Sixteen

Now that the hard work of getting the hotel refurbished was over and guests had begun to arrive, Wilmot began to try to mend his relationship with Geoffrey. He had been very hurt by Geoff's sarcastic remarks, and ashamed of his own behaviour. It's time we both grew up, he thought. Geoff's not a nipper any more and maybe it would be better if I treated him like a man.

As always, he went to the other extreme and when Geoffrey's eighteenth birthday came around he took him off shopping and, without a word to Lucy, bought him a motorcycle. When they brought it home, Wilmot driving it rather uncertainly with Geoffrey wobbling on the pillion, Lucy was horrified.

'Oh, Wilmot. I don't like motorbikes. They're dangerous. What did you want to give him that for?'

Wilmot shrugged. 'He's a man now. Eighteen years old. I was serving on ships at that age. Anyway, you can see how pleased he is with it.'

Lucy could. For once, Wilmot had done the right thing as far as Geoff was concerned. He was like a dog with two tails, propping his new toy up on its stand outside the hotel and polishing it almost every time he came back from a ride.

'You've got to admit, Mum, it's a real smasher. It's a single carburettor Triumph TR5 Trophy. It's a competition bike – been made for scrambling or trials – but it's just as good on the road. I'm thinking of joining a club.'

'What do you mean, competitions? What are scrambles and trials? You're not going racing on it!'

'Well, scrambles are sort of races. Only on rough ground, not on race-tracks. It's fun, Mum. And trials are where you do sections like hills or streams and bits of rocky track, anything rough where you can get a bike through. You've got to be able to ride really well. You can come and watch, you'll enjoy it.'

Lucy didn't think she would enjoy it at all. She looked at her son, standing tall and broad, his red hair glinting in the sun, and realised suddenly that Wilmot was right. He was a young man now, no longer a boy. He was growing up, away from her, and the motorbike would take him away even faster.

Geoff took out his handkerchief and polished away a minute speck of dust. He had other ideas about the bike, ideas he wasn't going to tell his mother. Girls liked a chap who could take them about without having to use buses, and a motorbike was glamorous and exciting.

He couldn't do anything about that, however, until he had passed his test. As a learner driver, he could only ride alone or with a qualified rider on the pillion. Wilmot had got his licence years ago, so the two of them went off together several times a week, heading out towards Dartmoor or along the coast into Cornwall or eastwards to the South Hams. They went to Newton Ferrers and Noss Mayo, where Maud and Arthur had spent their honeymoon, and parked the bike on the cliffs, looking down at the blue lake of the estuary.

'It's smashing being able to get out of Plymouth,' Geoff said as they unpacked the sandwiches Lucy had given them. 'That bike's the best present I ever had.'

Wilmot felt a glow of pleasure. For once, he'd done the right thing. He saw himself and Geoff going off on long jaunts together, maybe taking a tent and staying away for several days. It would be like being young again. It would be his second chance to be a proper father, teaching his boy about camping and lighting fires and cooking in the outdoors. Perhaps they could even run to a small boat later on and go sailing or fishing.

'I can't wait to go to scrambles with it,' Geoff went on dreamily. 'I reckon it'll go really well. I might even be a racer, like Geoff Duke. He won the Manx Grand Prix, only of course he was riding a Norton. Did you know, Dad, Nortons made bikes for the Army during the war . . .'

His voice chattered on and Wilmot adjusted his dreams. Well, he supposed they could go to scrambles together, and even to races, though he didn't think Lucy was going to approve of Geoff's ambition to take part in either of them. Trials weren't so bad, they were all about skill and there wasn't much danger involved, but maybe that wouldn't suit Geoff. Boys liked the spice of danger, he thought ruefully, as long as they didn't know what it really meant.

It didn't matter anyway. It didn't matter what he and Geoff did, so long as they did something together, so long as they could be a proper father and son, and it looked as if the bike had succeeded where all the other things he had tried had failed.

Geoff put in for his test at once, and passed straight away. Wilmot banged him on the back and took him down to the pub for a drink. To his dismay, however, Geoff went off on his own next day, without inviting his father to come with him.

'What did you expect?' Lucy asked. She still didn't like Geoff having a motorbike, and now he'd passed his test it stood to reason he was going to be off on his own. 'Next time we see him, he'll have a girl on the pillion.'

'I thought we'd go on having rides out together,' Wilmot said aggrievedly. 'I thought he'd been enjoying it.'

'I daresay he did.' Lucy felt sorry for him. He'd tried so hard, and now he looked like a woebegone little boy, deserted by his friends. 'But he's eighteen years old, Wilmot. He's not going to want his dad along with him. Did you want Arthur with you when you were that age?'

'I was in the Navy when I was that age,' Wilmot said, but he had to admit she was right. He'd been after the girls, like his mates, flaunting their sailors' uniforms and snogging in the back row of the pictures, wondering how far they could go. And some of those girls had been ready to go quite a way, too, the trollops.

He thought of Geoff, picking up some flighty piece of goods and taking her out on the back of his bike. Down to Newton Ferrers, or out on Dartmoor. I ought to have given him some advice, he thought, I ought to have told him what's what. Now, it seemed suddenly too late and he found a new anxiety to add to his disappointment at being left behind.

'I thought the bike'd bring us together a bit,' he said. 'You said we ought to find something, and I reckoned that was it.'

'Well, so it was. But he's growing up. You can't expect much different.' Lucy laid her hand on his arm, feeling a glow of affection. He really had tried, and it was a shame he was disappointed. 'But he won't forget it was you who gave him the bike, Wilmot. He'll always remember that.'

Geoff quickly acquired a string of girlfriends who were eager to ride pillion. Jilly became one of them very soon after arriving at the hotel.

Jilly was the maid at Pengelly's. She had been there for two years now, mostly helping Lucy with the cooking. Soon, she would take full charge, leaving Lucy free to concentrate on the management, and there would be another maid, perhaps two, as well as the daily cleaning woman who had been coming in for the past year, for Pengelly's was expanding again. The third house in the row had been bought at last and the conversion to turn it into part of the hotel was almost complete. Even Wilmot had not been able to complain that the venture had been anything but a success.

Jilly had come to Pengelly's from Cornwall, where her

mother had been looking after David's aunt ever since she first began to be ill. Her illness was one of those creeping diseases of old age, creeping slowly in the case of David's aunt, but everyone knew that she would gradually become more and more helpless. Mrs Penfold had done housework for her ever since she first moved to Cornwall, and they had become friends. Now Mrs Penfold had let her own small cottage and moved in, so that she could be a permanent nurse and companion, and David had suggested that Jilly might be just the sort of girl Lucy wanted for the hotel.

'She needs a live-in job and she wants to come to Plymouth – see a bit of life, she says.' He grinned. 'But she's a nice, decent sort of girl – you won't have any trouble with her.'

'Send her to see me,' Lucy had said, and Jilly had arrived with one small suitcase and an old carpet-bag given her by David's aunt. She was small and dark, with sooty-lashed blue eyes and a soft, burring voice, and she seemed willing enough to turn her hand to anything she might be asked to do.

'She'd make a good waitress,' Lucy said. 'Or a receptionist. She's bright enough, and she's very pretty.' But Patsy was receptionist. They had made her a little office behind a tiny counter in the entrance hall, and she sat there all day, her wheelchair barely visible, welcoming new guests, giving them their bills as they left, and doing the accounts. It was a cook that they really needed, and Jilly loved cooking.

By now, Lucy had got used to the bike and the girlfriends and she didn't take much notice. Geoff was young and enjoying life, and she was too busy to wonder what her maid was doing during her time off. She didn't realise that as soon as the evening meal had been served and as soon as Geoff had come in from work and finished his own supper, Jilly's apron was hung on the hook behind the door and the two of them were off on the motorbike. By then Lucy was in the family living-room, thankful for the chance to put her feet up after a long day's work.

Running a proper hotel was very different from looking after the simple guest house Pengelly's had been before the war, she reflected. The country was at last getting back on its feet. Most of the rationing was coming to an end, and things were coming into the shops – new things, well made, not utility any more. People were earning better money and starting to go on holidays again, and Devon was, as always, a favourite destination. A lot of people came to Plymouth, even though there was still so much rebuilding still to be done. The new Royal Parade had been opened by the King in 1947 and shops were being built all along one side. There were going to be a new Dingle's, a big Spooner's and John Yeo's, and a new Co-op. A lot of the shops were still trading from the row of Nissen huts that had been put up all along George Street, and when they were gone at last the new Civic Centre would be built in their place, and there was even talk of a new Theatre Royal. Plymouth was going to rise again, like a phoenix, from the ashes.

All this work brought people to Plymouth – people from other cities, wanting to see what was being done, men from the ministries in London, architects and businessmen who were all interested in the new Britain. And they all wanted good accommodation.

'It's solid value for money we've got to give,' Lucy said. 'Comfortable rooms with good beds, and decent food for their bellies. None of your fancy French cooking – what men want is a proper meal. Roast beef and Yorkshire, and good bread-and-butter pudding or a nice apple pie with clotted cream. The sort of food they've longed for all through the war.'

Clotted cream was the most popular item on the menu. They had it on scones, on toast and jam, and on breakfast cornflakes, as well as on their apple pies. They had to be shown how to eat it, on top of the jam rather than underneath it, and without butter, but to a man they loved it and asked for it again and again. Lucy started to serve afternoon teas as well as lunch and dinner, and non-residents came in especially for her Devonshire scones.

'We'll be able to fill the new rooms three times over,' she said, doing the accounts with Patsy. 'It's just a pity we can't buy up any more of the houses in the row!'

'For God's sake,' Wilmot said, coming into the office, 'give it a rest. Champagne tastes on lemonade money, that's your trouble, Lucy. Let's be satisfied with what we've got.'

'Being satisfied with what we'd got didn't get us where we are today,' Lucy said tartly. 'The old guest house wouldn't have been able to survive as it was. If you'd had your way, we'd be out on the streets now, and how satisfied would you have been with that?'

'If I'd had my way?' Wilmot glanced around him at the newly painted walls, the real chandelier that had replaced Lucy's 'cluster', the dark red patterned carpet that covered the floor where they had put linoleum a few years before. 'I thought I *had* had my way. Wasn't it all supposed to have been my idea in the first place?'

Lucy gave him a withering look and turned back to the accounts. She had little patience with Wilmot these days. At some point since the evening when the new hotel had first opened and she had stood on the Hoe with David and talked about rights, she had hardened towards her husband. She knew he was drinking more than was good for him, but all her efforts to help him stop had been in vain and she had finally shrugged her shoulders and left him to it. Sometimes, she was aware that she had shrugged her shoulders of him altogether.

However, there was never time to think about that now. Always, there were other things to claim her attention. New furnishings for the hotel, as more and better products came back on the market. New menus, as more ingredients became available, and new suppliers as local businesses got back on their feet.

'I want to support local farmers as much as possible,' she said. 'It's good for them as well as for our guests. Strawberries from Bere Alston, that sort of thing. The produce is good and it's fresher than buying from London, but it's got to be the right price.' She drove a hard bargain, but she generally got what she wanted.

Arthur and Maud had never bought from London, never even thought of it. They had bought locally all their lives. Lucy seemed to be moving in different circles these days, and they couldn't keep up with her.

'Best if you retire properly,' she said to them. 'You've worked hard all your lives, you deserve a rest. Put your feet up, go to the pictures of an afternoon or up on the Hoe and sit in the sun. Leave it all to me now. You don't have to worry any more.'

Arthur was glad of a rest, but he found it hard to give up entirely. After breakfast he went out into the front hall – he'd never got his tongue around the word 'foyer' – and sat on the little green chaise-longue, keeping Patsy company and having a chat with the guests as they paid their bills or went out for the day. But once the early morning bustle was over and the hotel quiet, he drifted into the back room with Maud. On fine days, he went out and sat up on the Hoe as Lucy had suggested, hobnobbing with his cronies there, or he walked round the new streets, watching the rebuilding. To her relief, he found this a fascinating new hobby and came back every day with something to grumble about.

'I told you, it's just like a kid's building blocks. All square. No character to it.'

'It'll be convenient, though.' They went through all the old arguments about wet feet and roofing over the lot, with Arthur and Wilmot like a Greek chorus, chiming in with each other as if they'd rehearsed for hours. Sometimes,

Lucy wanted to scream at them, but she held her tongue. So long as it kept them happy . . .

Happy? When she had a rare moment away from thoughts of the hotel, she caught up the word and wondered about it. What was 'happy'? She'd thought she knew, back in the early days when she had first known Wilmot. Happiness then had been the excitement of waiting for him to arrive on the doorstep, grinning that cheeky grin, his kitbag dumped beside him. Happiness had been strolling along the front at Southsea, her arm in his. Happiness had been getting married, those first nights of loving, the days of sunshine when she'd taught him to swim in the big new swimming-pool. Happiness had been when he'd come home when Geoff was a year old, and when Patsy had been born, and Zannah . . .

Had there ever been any happiness since then?

It was useless to think about it. Since then, there had been fear and dread and terror, and a constant, gnawing anxiety. During those dark days, what she had now would have seemed like paradise. It *was* paradise, in comparison. You had to admit that. You had to be satisfied with what you'd got.

This is where I came in, she thought, as she remembered her own reply when Wilmot himself had told her that. Being satisfied with what you'd got didn't get you anywhere else.

I don't know where we would all be if I'd been satisfied, if I'd just sat back and waited for other people to get on with life. Mum and Dad both getting older, and tired after all they'd been through, Wilmot a bag of nerves after all *he'd* been through, Patsy in her wheelchair . . . Only Geoff could have been any help at all, and he'd been no more than a boy when the war ended, with a boy's interests, and when he'd got old enough to leave school he'd wanted his own life, and it wasn't in the hotel. And why should it be?

The responsibility had rested squarely on Lucy's

shoulders. For all she'd pretended to defer to Wilmot, for all she'd let him take credit, the responsibility had been hers. The bank manager had known that, and if he hadn't believed she could do it – she, not Wilmot – they would never have got that loan.

She went to the bathroom and looked in the mirror. She'd hardly had time lately to examine her own face, but she did so now. There were lines appearing round her eyes and the crease of a frown in her forehead. But her skin was still pale and fine, and her eyes as deep a violet as ever. And although there were a few white hairs appearing on her head, they were sparse amongst the thick, springing waves of auburn, only slightly faded from when she was a girl.

Happiness was whatever you chose to make it, she thought. Twenty-five years ago, it would have been a kiss from a good-looking young sailor. Twenty years ago, the birth of her first baby. Ten years, just to have her family safe around her.

And today? In ten years' time, would she look back and see that happiness had been hers now all the time?

Perhaps happiness was, after all, just being satisfied with what you'd got.

The first time Geoff took Jilly out on his motorbike was in the spring of 1951. He took her for a ride on the moor and when they came to the town of Tavistock he parked the motorbike in the square and they walked down the road to the bridge. They leant over the parapet and looked down into the river.

'You can see quite big fish here sometimes. Salmon. They jump up over the weir. Those steps at the side were made for them to jump up when the water's too low for the weir.'

'It's pretty.' People were walking along the broad stone pathway beside the river. 'Where does that go?'

'To the Meadows. It's the local park. It's nice.' They left

207

the bridge and walked down the steps to the pathway. It ran high above the tumbling, rock-strewn river. The old walls of the Abbey ran alongside, and there was an arch to go through before they reached the Meadows. The opposite bank was thick with trees and bushes, and ducks swam in the rushing water or preened their feathers on the rocks.

The Meadows was a broad open stretch of grassland, with large oak and beech trees shading its walks. It reached right down to Drake's statue, at the corner of Plymouth Road, and across to the narrow canal which ran the four miles from Tavistock to the mining village of Morwellham, on the banks of the Tamar. There was a children's paddling pool and a sandpit, and in another part there were a few swings and an old steamroller that someone had left there for them to clamber over. Between the canal and the road there were rose gardens, tennis courts and a bowling green.

'It's lovely,' Jilly said as they wandered hand in hand along the canal banks. 'It's my favourite place in the whole world.'

Geoff grinned. 'And how much of the whole world have you seen? You've never even been as far as Exeter.'

She turned wide blue eyes on him. Her hair gleamed in the sun with the iridescence of a starling's wing. 'I've seen pictures.'

'It's not the same as going there.' Geoff swished the water with a stick he'd picked up. 'I want to go all over the world. I want to see everything.'

'You ought to join the Navy then, like your dad.' But she spoke wistfully, hoping that he'd say he didn't want to do that.

To her surprise, he did. 'I'm not joining the Navy! All they ever do is go to sea. I don't want to spend months just staring at the water. No, when I get my call-up I'll go in the Army. They get sent all over the world.'

'I thought most of them went to Germany.'

'Well, that'd be a start. And some go to Cyprus or Israel
– there's plenty of other places. Anyway, I don't care where
it is, so long as it's somewhere. I'm fed up with Plymouth,
Jilly. I've never been anywhere else either. Well, I've been
further than you.' He grinned. 'I've been to London.'

'Have you? Have you really? What's it like?'

'Well, it's still a bit of a mess, but they're getting a lot of
it rebuilt. Of course, they're getting the Festival of Britain
all ready now. That's going to be worth seeing. I'm going in
the summer, when I get my holiday. Here –' he looked at
her, his eyes bright – 'why don't you come with me?'

'Me? Come to London with you?' She stared at him.
'How could I do that?'

'Easy. We'd just get on a train and go.' He laughed at her.
'You just buy a ticket at the station.'

'Oh, you – I don't mean that. I mean – well – you and
me, going to London together. What would people say?'

'They'd wish they were coming too. You ought to come,
Jilly. You ought to see London. And this Festival, it's going
to be smashing. Everyone will want to go.'

'I know, but . . . It would take more than a day, wouldn't
it? I mean, we couldn't go and come back on the same day.'

'Good Lord, no. We'd need nearly a week. There's going
to be all sorts there – the Dome of Discovery, the Skylon,
the fair at Battersea Gardens. And I could show you all
the other things too. The Tower, and St Paul's, and
Westminster, where Princess Elizabeth got married, and
Madame Tussaud's – oh, everywhere.' He looked at her.
'We could stay with Uncle David.'

'Uncle David? You mean Mr Tremaine?'

'Yes. Your mum lives with his auntie, doesn't she? He's
got a house in London, he could put us up. I stayed with
him last time. He's got plenty of room.'

'I don't know – I mean, my mum just did cleaning and
that sort of thing.'

'So what? She looks after his auntie now, she's a sort of

companion. Anyway, what difference does that make? It's you I'm asking, not your mum.'

'Yes, but I'm just a hotel assistant.'

'And I'm just a dockyard apprentice.' Geoff shook his head. 'I don't know what you're worrying about. Uncle David will be pleased to see us.'

'Well, he's always been very nice to me,' Jilly admitted. 'But going to stay with him – I'm not sure.'

'Well, *I'm* sure. I'm sure I want you to come and I'm sure he won't mind a bit. He won't even make you share a room with me.' He grinned at her blush. 'It'll be much better fun than going about on my own.'

'Go on, you'll find another girl to go with you. You've got loads of girls wanting to go out with you.'

'Maybe I have,' he said, suddenly serious, 'but I'm not sure I want anyone else. I think I just want you.'

They walked on, suddenly silent. They had walked the length of the Meadows beside the river and then back along the canal. They went out into Plymouth Road and met the children coming out of the primary school on the opposite side. The bus station was crowded with green double-decker Western National buses, coming from and going back to Plymouth, Okehampton, even Exeter and Bude.

Tavistock was like the hub of a wheel. As well as the bus station there were two railway lines, one the main line between Plymouth and Exeter and the other the branch line between Plymouth and Launceston. It must always have been busy, Geoff said. It was one of the stannary towns, where metals had been brought for weighing in the mining days. He took her back to the big square, surrounded by the handsome buildings of the Town Hall, the big church and the old Abbey gateway, and showed her the plaque that told you all about it.

They went into the pannier market behind the Town Hall where people were selling produce – crusty, yellow cream in big bowls, mounds of vegetables and fruit, cheeses and bacon. Someone had a stall where they were selling garments they'd knitted or sewn, someone else had things made of wood. It was like an Aladdin's cave where you could buy anything you wanted.

'I'd like to live here,' Jilly said, fingering a handknitted cardigan. 'I'd like to do all my shopping here.'

'Well, maybe you will one day.' Geoff took her out again, and through an archway into the main street. 'I'll tell you where you can get the best doughnuts in Devon, shall I?'

They walked up the hill and almost at the top found a small bakery. It smelt richly of new-baked bread and cakes, and there was a queue right out on to the pavement. They joined the queue and bought hot pasties and a bag of doughnuts, rosy with jam squeezing out through their sides, then carried them down a steep flight of steps and went back through the Meadows to sit beneath the big oak and beech trees by the river, eating their lunch.

'You will come to London with me, won't you?' Geoff said presently.

Jilly sat quiet for a while, looking at the river. She knew quite well that she was in love with Geoff, and she was pretty sure she wasn't the only one. She'd seen those other girls on the back of his motorbike before he'd asked her out. What she didn't know was whether he was in love with her. It didn't seem likely, with all those other girls hanging about. How many of them had he already asked?

'I don't know,' she said. 'I don't want to decide straight away.' She turned her head and looked at him with her sooty-lashed eyes. 'Let's wait a while, shall we?'

Geoff looked as if he was about to argue, then thought better of it. He laid his hand on hers. 'I'd really like you to come.'

I'd really like to go too, she thought. And he did look as if he meant it. His face was open and his eyes looked straight at hers, darker than usual with just a blue rim round the wide black pupil. And he hadn't made any passes at her, not like some of the boys she'd been out with at home.

'I'll think about it,' she said a little breathlessly. 'I'd like to – but I'll have to think about it.'

'Think yes,' he said, and his eyes were intent. 'Think yes – yes – *yes*.'

They went in August. By then, Lucy had got used to their friendship and as long as they stayed with David she knew they wouldn't come to any harm. She didn't think there was anything serious in it – Geoff was much too young for that, and Jilly was even younger, only seventeen – and she'd rather he was in London with a girl than wandering about on his own. You never knew what might happen to a young lad in the big city.

'Mum thinks I'll get snatched away and sold as a white slave,' Geoffrey said with a grin as they settled into their seats on the train. 'Good thing I've got you to look after me.'

'What's a white slave?' Jilly asked. 'I didn't think there were any slaves now, anyway.'

'Well, they're –' He glanced at her and decided not to go into it. 'I don't know, really. It's just a sort of saying. I like going on this line, don't you? All along the beach, in and out of the cliffs – it's like something out of an Enid Blyton story. I used to read her books when I was a tacker.'

'I bet she'd been down to Devon and Cornwall,' Jilly said. 'A lot of the places she wrote about are just like the little coves and villages round here.'

They spent the journey gazing out of the window, giving themselves marks for spotting church towers or spires (one for a tower, two for a spire) and doing the crossword puzzle in the paper Geoff had bought at the station. Jilly had made some sandwiches and brought a bottle of lemonade, and they had these at about twelve o'clock, and soon after that the train pulled into Paddington station.

'It's enormous,' Jilly said in an awed whisper. 'Look at the roof, Geoff, it's like those pictures of the Crystal Palace. You'd never think it had been built just for railway trains.'

'Wait till you see the Underground.' Geoff was already striding away towards the exit, a suitcase in each hand. Jilly hurried after him with her old carpet-bag and followed him down the steps. She wrinkled up her nose.

'It's a bit smelly. D'you really mean to say people came down to places like this to shelter during the air-raids? It must have been horrible.' She waited while Geoff bought tickets, and then followed him to the top of the escalator. 'Oh, we haven't really got to go on that, have we?'

'It's all right. It's just a moving staircase.' He hefted one suitcase under his arm and took her hand. 'Just step on and stand still. You don't have to walk down if you don't want to.'

Jilly stood rigid, her hand resting tentatively on the moving banister. As they approached the bottom she gave him a nervous look, and he grinned and held her hand tightly.

'Now just step off. That's right. It's a good job you've got me to look after you. Now we have to look on that map and see how to get to Chalk Farm station.'

They emerged at last on the corner of a busy road. Jilly took a deep breath.

'Well, it's not what you'd call good fresh air, but at least it's air. I don't know what that stuff down there's called.' She looked at the shops and the traffic and giggled. 'Not much like a farm, is it?'

David lived in a side street a few hundred yards up the hill from the station. The street was quite different from the main road, which was lined with small shops and, like most streets in London, still pocked with occasional bomb sites. David's street was built of tall houses with steps going up to their front doors and more steps going down to basements. There were tall poplar trees shading the hot pavements, and

213

in some of the small front yards there were babies in prams or plants growing in pots.

'It looks ever so posh,' Jilly said.

Geoff led the way up a flight of steps and rang a bell. There were several bells, Jilly noticed, each with a different name on. She remembered that Mr Tremaine had told her mother that he had divided his house into flats. He had just kept the ground floor and the basement for himself, and there were two floors above that. It sounded sensible, though she wondered why he hadn't just sold the house if it was too big and moved somewhere smaller.

She glanced up and down the road, feeling nervous again. It was all so different from the village in Cornwall, even from Plymouth. She had never realised how big London was, so big that you could get on a train and travel for half an hour or more and still be in the city, with not so much as a bit of lawn to remind you of the country. She wondered what Mr Tremaine was going to be like. She knew him of course, she'd known him for quite a long time, but that was down in Cornwall where people were different – slower, more relaxed. Here, they all seemed to be anxious and in a hurry, pushing past you in the Underground, frowning, grey faced. Would Mr Tremaine be different too?

Then the door opened and he was there, dressed a little differently in rather smart trousers and a white shirt rather than the grey flannel bags and old Fair Isle jumper he wore in Cornwall, but otherwise looking just the same with his friendly smile and crinkly grey hair. He held out his hand in welcome and as Jilly rather shyly gave him hers, he pulled her gently towards him and kissed her cheek.

'Welcome to London, my dear. Welcome.'

The Festival was all Geoff had promised it would be. They went twice to the main Exhibition, wandering for hours amongst the stands and demonstrations. It was to be a celebration of Britain's recovery from the war, the King had said when he first suggested the idea, a resurgence of the Great Exhibition of 1851 when the Crystal Palace had been built and all the world had come to show its wares. It was like that now, a gathering of countries that less than ten years ago had been at war, a symbol of peace.

Geoff's favourite was the Dome of Discovery, a huge, steely saucer-like structure that looked as if it came straight from a science-fiction film and had displays of what the future would be like that left them gasping and incredulous. Just outside this was the tall, slender Skylon, a graceful ellipse that pointed skywards like a sign of hope.

But best of all were the evenings, when they went to Battersea Park. The fair was the biggest and the best ever seen in England, and Geoff and Jilly became children again, riding on the scenic train, tiptoeing along the swaying bridges of the Treetops Walk to look down through the fairy-lights at the heads of people beneath; laughing themselves helpless in the hall of mirrors or on the cakewalk. They went on switchback rides, roundabouts and ghost trains, and it was late at night when they finally made their way back to Chalk Farm on the last bus, sitting in the front seat at the top and holding hands as they gazed dreamily at the lights of London swaying past.

'It's been a gorgeous holiday,' Jilly said on the last evening. 'I've never had such a lovely time in my whole life.'

'Nor have I.' Geoff took her hand in his and stroked the fingers gently. 'I didn't know it was possible to be so happy. I don't really want to go back, do you?'

'I don't know. I wouldn't want to live in London, not all the time.'

'Nor would I, but – going back seems so ordinary. Going back to the dockyard, the same as usual, only seeing you in the evenings.' He hesitated and she glanced at him and saw the colour came into his face. Suddenly, her heart began to beat a little faster. 'Jilly,' he said, speaking quickly now so that his words almost tumbled over themselves. 'Jilly, I love you. I want us to get engaged. Will you? Will you marry me, when we've got enough money? Please, Jilly – say you will. Say yes.'

'Geoff –'

'I know we can't get married for ages,' he went on desperately, 'but if we could just be engaged – you see, I'll have to go away before long, I'm bound to be called up and I might have to go anywhere.' The idea of seeing the world seemed suddenly to lose its appeal. 'If we were engaged before I went – well, I'd feel better. I'd know you were waiting for me. Oh Jilly, I do love you. Say you love me. Say you will.'

'Oh, Geoff,' she said tremulously, 'of course I love you. Of *course* I'll marry you.'

Chapter Seventeen

Geoff's call-up papers came just before Christmas. To everyone's surprise, he had chosen to go into the Army rather than the Navy or the Air Force. Lucy, recalling his early ambitions to fly a Spitfire, was relieved by this – a motorbike was bad enough. Wilmot was slightly put out that his son didn't want to follow him into the Navy, but he didn't argue. It seemed that he was learning at last that Geoff was a man now and would make his own decisions.

By the middle of January, he would be gone. Geoff and Jilly decided that they could not wait another two years or more to be together. They wanted to be married now.

'Now?' Lucy said blankly when they told her. 'Get married? But you're not even engaged.'

Jilly blushed. 'We were thinking of getting engaged at Christmas. I've been looking at rings.'

'Have you asked Mrs Penfold?' Lucy asked her son, ignoring the idea of rings. 'Have you asked her if Jilly can get engaged? She's not even eighteen. I don't know how you can be thinking of such a thing.'

'I knew it was daft, letting them go jaunting off to London together,' Wilmot said. 'Bound to lead to trouble. Here –' his brows came together in a frown – 'you're not in trouble, are you? Geoff?'

'No. *No*. Of course not.' Geoff's face was scarlet, Jilly's a bright pink. 'I've never – we've never –'

'All right, all right,' Lucy said hastily. 'So long as that's all right. Now look, you must see you can't get married. You're both much too young. And with Geoff going away straight after, what sort of a marriage would it be?' She was painfully conscious that her own marriage had begun in a very similar way. 'You both need to grow up a bit more,' she went on quickly. 'You'll be separated a long time – suppose you meet someone else? It can happen, you know. I know you don't think so now, but it's true. It won't hurt you to wait a couple of years till Geoff's out of the Army, and then if you're in the same mind—'

'We will be. We know we will be.'

'You *think* you will be,' she said, but she remembered the certainty of youth, the knowledge that nobody else, *nobody* – with the exception perhaps of Romeo and Juliet – had ever felt like this, had ever loved so intensely. She looked at them helplessly, and silently thanked God for a law which prevented youngsters like this from making dreadful mistakes, at least until they were twenty-one.

'Just get engaged at Christmas,' she said. 'Geoff's not going off to war. You'll have plenty of chances to see each other. By the time he comes out again you'll be that much older and more sure. It's the best way.'

'Two years!' Geoff said when they were alone again. '*Two years!* It's a lifetime. I can't wait that long, Jilly.'

'I don't know what else we can do,' she said miserably. 'If they won't give you permission . . . And even if they did, I don't think my mum would. She doesn't approve of young marriages either.'

It was David who came in for the most censure. They had stayed with him in London, and for some reason everyone had got the impression that if it hadn't been for that holiday Geoff and Jilly would never have fallen in love. There were plenty of girls in Plymouth just as pretty and just as keen on Geoff, Lucy said, and plenty of boys who would be pleased to take Jilly out. It was bound to lead to trouble, letting them go off for a whole week on their own. What had David been thinking of? Hadn't he kept an eye on them?

'I didn't do anything,' he protested when Lucy rang him up to tell him what had happened. 'They went off on their own every day to the Festival, or to see the sights. They slept in separate rooms—'

'I'm not saying they didn't. I hope I can trust my own son.'

'Well, what are you complaining about?' he asked reasonably. 'If they'd stayed in Plymouth instead of coming to London, they could have gone off all day just the same, out to Dartmoor or down to Cornwall. They would still have felt the same about each other. What's the difference?'

There was a difference, but Lucy couldn't explain it. She put down the telephone receiver feeling dissatisfied and unhappy. It was the nearest she and David had ever come to a quarrel and she lay awake that night, tears she couldn't explain drifting softly on to her pillow. I wish I hadn't gone on at him, she thought sadly. I never see him these days, and I have to ring him up and grumble at him, and he's right, it's not his fault.

She wasn't the only one. David's aunt complained to him as well. Mrs Penfold was very upset, she said, and half inclined to tell her daughter to come home straight away. No doubt Geoff was a nice enough boy, but she didn't want Jilly tied down so soon. Twenty-one was quite early enough. She didn't even approve of their getting engaged.

'I suppose I can't stop that though,' she said to Lucy when she came to Plymouth to talk over the situation. 'I can't stop her wearing a ring or saying they're getting married one day. I just wish they'd not got serious so quickly.'

'So do I,' Lucy said. 'Mind, I've nothing against your Jilly, she's a nice girl and a lovely little cook, and I daresay she'll make a good wife some day. Same as my Geoff will make a good husband. It's just too soon.'

The two women nodded at each other. They got on well

and Mrs Penfold stayed a day or two longer, seeing the sights of Plymouth and admiring the new shops before she returned to Cornwall.

Geoff and Jilly went shopping for an engagement ring and on Christmas morning Geoff put it on Jilly's finger. She gazed at it, turning her finger so that the light flashed on the three tiny diamonds, and her eyes sparkled as brightly with tears as she looked up at him.

'It's lovely, Geoff. It makes it seem so real.'

'I wish it was a plain gold one, without any stones,' he said, and she nodded.

'So do I. But it'll come. Now we're engaged – they won't really make us wait all that time, Geoff.'

'It's having to go away makes it so much worse,' he said. 'They're sending chaps out to Korea now. They only get a few weeks' basic training and then they're gone. I might be away the whole two years.'

'You'd think your mum and dad would understand,' Jilly said. 'Them having been separated all that time.'

However, that was just why Lucy understood, just why she didn't want them tied to each other too soon. Wilmot had been a fresh-faced, laughing young husband when he'd gone to war – and he'd come back a changed, bitter man. She couldn't believe such a thing would happen to Geoff, but suppose it did? And even if that didn't happen, there was the chance that Jilly might not stay faithful. It was all too easy for a young, attractive girl to fall in love with someone else.

Just as she had fallen in love with David.

For a long time now, Lucy had suppressed her feelings for David and her deep sadness that they could never be together. She had used the hotel as a means of escape from them, immersing herself in the work of the conversion, of the development of the hotel, building up the business to the success it now was. All the time she had told herself and Wilmot that it was essential as a means of making a living for the family, she had known that there was more to it than that. It was a means of survival without the man she loved.

Now, with Geoff and Jilly's story unfolding before her, she could not blind herself any longer to the deep love and the deep wretchedness that still smouldered inside her body, her mind, her heart.

During the day, by keeping busy, she could keep the thoughts at bay; but at night, exhausted though she might be in body and mind, she could not hide any longer from her heart. Her feelings flooded in and she would lie beside Wilmot for hour upon hour, torn by the misery, the loneliness, the thought of the wasted years.

I can't let it happen to those two children, she thought. If they're meant to be together, if they really love each other, two years will not be too long to wait. And if they can't wait – well, I may have saved them both from this.

But it was not something she could tell them. There was nobody she could talk to, except for David. And for the first time in her life, and over this very matter, she had quarrelled with him.

Geoff went for his basic training in January. He was away six weeks and then came home for a brief leave. It was only a month since the King had died, and the whole country was saddened, but in Geoffrey's face Jilly saw more than that. She touched his cheek and felt the ache already in her heart.

'You're going away.'

He nodded. 'Korea.'

Jilly sat down on the settee and he sat beside her, holding both her hands. She turned her face against his shoulder and he put both arms round her and held her tightly, feeling the dampness of her tears on his shirt.

'It's not fair. It's not *fair*.'

'I know.'

'If only we'd been able to get married. We could have

221

been married at Christmas. What difference would it have made to anyone else? I'd be your *wife*.'

'Oh, Jilly.'

'It's all I want,' she said passionately. 'Just to be your wife. It's going to be so horrible, knowing you're all that way away, on the other side of the world, and us not married. Why couldn't they let us, Geoff, why?'

'I suppose they meant it for the best—' he said helplessly, but she broke in angrily.

'The best? How could it be for the best? It's just old people being mean to young ones, that's all. Just because they've got the power to stop us! It's not right, Geoff. We're not children, we're adults, we're grown up, we work for our living. Why shouldn't we be able to decide for ourselves?' She stared at him, her face white. 'Look at you. You're a soldier, you can go off and fight for your country, even for someone else's country, but you can't get married. It's stupid. It's *cruel*.'

'Oh, Jilly – Jilly, don't upset yourself. There's nothing we can do about it. Don't let's spoil the last few days we've got together.' He held her against him again and for a few minutes she submitted, weeping against his shoulder. Eventually she gave a long shudder and pulled away. Her wet face was set, her eyes narrowed with determination.

'I tell you what, Geoff. They're not going to stop us being married. Oh, maybe not in a church, we can't do that – but we can be married as far as *we're* concerned. I feel as though we are already anyway. I'm your wife, Geoff, even if some bloke in a frock hasn't said a lot of words over our heads. And this weekend is going to be our honeymoon.'

He stared at her. 'Jilly, what are you saying?'

'I'm saying we're going to go away together.' She lifted her chin. 'We'll tell your mum we're going down to Cornwall to stay with my mum for a couple of days. We'll find ourselves some nice little place to stay – a bed and breakfast or something, in Torquay – and we'll be married, just for a few days.' She looked at him and grasped his hands. 'It's all we've got, Geoff,' she said urgently. 'It's all we're going to have for maybe two years. But at least we'll have that, and they won't be able to take it away from us.'

Lucy wasn't best pleased to hear that Geoff and Jilly were going down to Cornwall for most of his leave. She didn't mind giving the girl her time off, she said to Wilmot, but she didn't see why they couldn't spend it in Plymouth. Didn't they realise Lucy was the boy's mother and would want to see as much of him as possible before he went away?

'They're being selfish,' Wilmot agreed. 'All youngsters are selfish. But there's nothing you can do about it. You can't lock Geoff in his room.'

They went on the motorbike. It wasn't particularly good weather for motorcycling, but they couldn't afford the train, they needed all their money for their accommodation, and besides, Lucy might have wanted to come and see them off and she would have known they weren't getting on the train for Penzance. Going on the motorbike, nobody knew which way they were heading.

The motorbike puttered through Plympton and along the road to Ivybridge and through Buckfast, past the big abbey that the monks were building. The road twisted between high banks, not much more than a country lane in places. They came to Newton Abbot and then Totnes. The earth was very red around here, and the banks were starred with huge yellow primroses, their faces as big as half-crowns. The hills rolled gently on either side, the grass already lush. When they came within sight of Torbay, Geoff stopped the bike and they sat and gazed for a few minutes.

'It's lovely,' Jilly said softly. The bay curved in a great horseshoe, bounded by the long, high cliffs of Berry Head on one side and the arm of Babbacombe on the other. Torquay lay at the heart of the bay, with the town of Paignton close beside it, like a sister. The sun was out and the whole scene was bright with the green of fields and woods, the glowing auburn of the earth and the stretching, glittering blue of sea and sky.

'We'll come here for our proper honeymoon,' Geoff said, and she squeezed his arm.

'This is our proper honeymoon. Only, nobody will ever know it but us. It'll be our secret all our lives.'

'If it's our honeymoon,' Geoff said, 'we ought to be married, and you ought to be wearing a ring.' He felt in his pocket and brought out a small box. Inside was a plain golden ring. Jilly took it out and held it reverently, her eyes sparkling with tears.

'It's a proper wedding ring. Oh, *Geoff*.'

'Well, what did you expect?' he asked. 'A curtain ring from Woolworth's? This is our proper wedding, Jilly.' He took the ring back and held her hand in his. Then, looking into her eyes, he said, 'I, Geoff, take thee, Jilly, to be my wedded wife. To have and to hold, from this day forward, in sickness and in health, for richer for poorer, for better for worse, so long as we both shall live.' He grinned a little and said, 'I hope I got it in the right order, but it doesn't matter, so long as it's all there. I love you, Jilly.'

'I love you too,' she whispered, and in a husky voice she repeated the vows. The tears were pouring down her cheeks as he slipped the ring on her finger. 'No, let me take the engagement one off first, or they'll be the wrong way round. There.'

They stared at the gold band on her finger. Jilly's heart was beating fast. She looked at Geoff and saw in his face the same awe that trembled through her body. The wind in the trees was like a choir, and when she heard a blackbird call it was like a peal of bells.

'We're married now,' she whispered. 'We're married.' And then, with a flash of mischief, 'You may kiss the bride!'

They went on into Torquay. The road ran right along the seafront, where palm trees grew along the pavement, just as if they were abroad. The pier jutted out into the sea and there were two harbours, an outer harbour and a small inner one, filled with little boats that were all heeled over on the mud because it was low tide. The shops were clustered around the harbour and the main road ran up the hill.

Geoff drove on to Babbacombe and they stopped on the cliff road and looked again at the broad sweep of the bay and the red escarpment of Berry Head on the far side. The sea met the sky with only a thin, dark rim of horizon to separate them, and sailing boats danced with white horses on the glittering blue.

'Let's find somewhere to stay here,' Jilly said.

It was still only the beginning of March and the holiday season hadn't begun yet, but there were a few small guest houses and some private houses advertising bed and breakfast. They looked at them and finally chose a small guest house with green window-frames and daffodils growing in the garden. It stood high up on the cliff, with the same view out right across the bay to Berry Head. The woman who answered the door looked at them a little doubtfully.

'I don't know. I've only got one room vacant.' She glanced at Jilly's left hand and Jilly lifted it proudly.

'We are married. This is our honeymoon. My – my husband's a soldier, he's going away next week. We don't have much time.'

The woman's face softened. She looked about sixty, small and plump, motherly looking. 'You poor things. It was like that for me and my first hubby. Married just after the war started and then he went away. We had two days together, and that was all.'

'Was he away a long time?' Jilly asked as they followed her into the house and up the stairs.

'Oh, he never came back, maid. Killed at sea, he was. No, that two days was all I had of married life. Then I met my

Harold and we've been married thirty-five years come next August, but I still think of my poor Bill, you know.'

Thirty-five years! It was the first war she was talking about, the 1914–18 war. The little chill that had touched Jilly's heart faded. It was all so long ago, it was like history.

'This is the room.' The woman stood back to let them see. It was small, almost filled by the double bed, and there was a narrow utility wardrobe in one corner and a dressing-table in front of the window. The bed was covered by a brown satin bedspread and looked fat and bulky, as if there were a thick eiderdown underneath.

'It's lovely,' Jilly said. 'Isn't it, Geoff?'

'And that's the bathroom door, opposite. I usually charge a shilling for a bath, but you can have one for nothing.' She had obviously taken a fancy to them, or perhaps she had some fellow-feeling even though her own short-lived marriage had been so long ago. 'If you want to bring your things in and get settled, I'll have a cup of tea ready for you in the lounge.'

Mrs Turner, her name was, and she was kindness itself. The only trouble was that she had taken such a fancy to Geoff and Jilly that she didn't want to let them go. She kept them talking in her overstuffed front room with its fat, billowing sofa and armchairs smothered with satin cushions and lace antimacassars and plied them with tea and bisuits until they began to despair of ever being alone. Then, quite suddenly, she got up and said briskly, 'You'll be wanting to go out for a walk now. Get some of our good fresh sea air into your lungs. I do high tea at six, so you've got an hour. My Harold will be home then, he'll be pleased to meet you.'

They found themselves out on the pavement. Geoff had brought the motorbike into the little front garden and they left it there, not daring to take it out. They'd been told to go for a walk, so go for a walk they would have to. Side by side, they set off on the route Mrs Turner had pointed out, which took them towards the cliffs.

'I thought we'd never get away,' Jilly said, giggling. 'She's ever so nice, but she can't half talk!'

'I wonder what time she'll let us go to bed,' Geoff said. They were on a cliff path now, high above the sea. 'I know she means to be kind but we've only got these two days. I don't want to spend them listening to her, I want to be with you.'

'You will be with me. We've got all night and all tomorrow night.' She blushed a little and held his hand tightly. 'And we can be out all day tomorrow. We're going to have a lovely time.'

To their relief, Mrs Turner seemed to have exhausted her fund of chatter. She welcomed them back an hour later and served them a high tea of steamed plaice with tinned peas and new potatoes and bread and butter, and sponge cake. Then she told them they could sit in the lounge until ten o'clock if they wanted to, and retreated to the back room where they could hear her talking to her husband. They sat on the sofa for a while, wishing they dared to go upstairs, and then went out for another walk. It was dark now, though, and a chilly wind had sprung up, so they went back. They hesitated in the hallway, and then Mrs Turner popped her head out.

'I'm just making a cup of tea. I'll get Mr Turner to bring it in to you.'

'He wants to have a look at us too,' Geoff whispered to Jilly, and she giggled. 'After this I reckon we can go upstairs.' They sat down again on the sofa. The cushions were glossy and elaborately stitched, not the sort of cushions you could ever really lean against. Over the mantelpiece there was a mirror cut out in a fancy design, and the light was shaded by a lampshade made of shapes of glass. On one wall there were three plaster ducks in flight.

At last they were able to go upstairs. They took turns in the bathroom, washing and cleaning their teeth. Neither wanted a bath now. The day seemed to have dragged interminably towards this moment and they didn't want to put it off any longer. All the same, while Geoff was in the bathroom and Jilly took the opportunity to scramble hastily into her nightdress, she wished suddenly that she could prolong it after all. Her heart was skipping unevenly in her breast and she felt shaky and almost sick. She got into bed and sat up, her arms round her knees, listening anxiously to the sound of Geoff letting water out of the washbasin.

He came in wearing his pyjamas. They looked at each other and smiled nervously.

'I feel a bit scared,' she said with a little laugh. 'It's silly – I feel as if we hardly know each other.'

'I know. I feel like that too. But it's just us. We're just the same people really.' He came closer and sat on the bed. 'It seems so funny, doesn't it? Getting into bed together. I mean, it isn't really anything to do with loving each other. It's just a bed. We could love each other anywhere. In a field. Behind a haystack.'

She giggled. 'Not so comfortable, though.'

'No.' He put his arms round her and she leant against him. 'I really do love you, Jilly. I love you all the time. I always will. If – if you don't want to do this – well, you don't have to. I don't want to do anything you don't want.'

'I know. I love you too, Geoff.' She took in a deep breath. 'And I want us to love each other properly. We – we're married, remember?' She freed her left hand and lifted it so that he could see. 'Proof!'

They laughed, and suddenly it was all right and they held each other close and began to kiss. Geoff's arms tightened, like iron bands around her trembling body, and he kissed her lips and then her cheeks and eyes and ears. He buried his face in her neck and his hands moved over her body, stroking her back and shoulders and then her waist and breasts. Jilly caught her breath. His fingers splayed out across her breasts, his palms cupping their fullness. He pushed aside the open neck of her nightdress and touched

228

the skin, and he pushed her gently back on the pillows and laid his body alongside hers.

'Jilly. *Jilly*.'

'Take off your jacket,' she whispered. 'I want to feel your skin.' With shaking fingers, she unbuttoned his pyjamas and pushed the cotton back, spreading her hands over his chest. He had no hair on his chest, it was smooth and lean and young, but there was muscle there, shifting beneath the skin, and there were muscles in his arms too, quivering with power. She felt weak.

Geoff undid the rest of the buttons on her nightdress and she moved so that she could pull it up over her body. He had never seen her in anything less than a bathing suit. She sat up and pulled the nightdress over her head lifting her arms in a motion that was unconsciously graceful, like a statue he had seen once in a museum, or like an old painting. Her breasts were smooth, lifting with the movement of her arms, and he put out his hand and touched one of them, as tenderly as if he were touching a baby's cheek. She laid the garment aside and looked at him, shy and proud.

Geoff stroked her body, very gently. He was aware that there would never be another time like this, never another first time. He wanted to savour it, to make it last. He trailed his fingertips tenderly over her shoulders, down the valley between her breasts, circling in the crease underneath, outlining their curves. He lifted one slightly towards him and bent to lay his lips upon the swelling flesh, folding them about the stiff, hard nipple. He slipped his other arm around her shoulders and held her firmly, letting his hand slide down her body, exploring the slight curve of her belly, the indentation of her waist, the swell of her hips.

Jilly put her arms around him and lay back, her body arched towards him. He could feel the rapid beating of her heart, like a bird in his hand. He slid his hand down again, touching her thigh, marvelling at its silkiness, and very gently, with the tips of his fingers, touched between her thighs.

Jilly gave a shuddering sigh and he felt his heart leap. His fingers were moist. He stroked more firmly and felt her move beneath him. Suddenly, his pyjama trousers were an encumbrance and he dragged them off. A powerful urgency invaded him and he forgot about making it last. He forgot about everything except the desperate rapture of the moment. He flung himself down against her, on top of her, and thrust himself hard against her.

Jilly cried out and tried to move him. 'No. Not there.' She wriggled beneath him and the movement inflamed him further. He thrust again. 'Geoff. *Wait.*'

'I can't –'

'Yes, you can.' Her voice was soothing, though it still trembled. She put her hands under his hips and lifted him slightly, shifting her body beneath him, and then she took him in her hand, the touch of her fingertips an almost exquisite torture, and gently guided him. 'There.'

It didn't feel any different to Geoff. There was still a resistance. He pushed cautiously, aware now that he might be hurting her, and he heard her gasp a little. A wave of despair broke over him. He wasn't doing it right, it wasn't going to work . . . And then, quite suddenly, the resistance gave way as if something tore, something thin and fibrous like a piece of silky fabric, and although Jilly cried out again she also gripped him firmly with her arms and pulled him tighter against her. And he was conscious of being in a different place, as if he had slipped with his whole body into a warmth, a comfort, that he had never imagined existed, and he gave a shudder of his own, a long rippling quiver of delight.

'*Jilly.*'

'Geoff, I love you.'

'I love you.'

Their bodies moved together, gently and slowly, skin

sliding on skin like silk on silk, the warmth and excitement flowing between them as if they were truly one person, one body. Jilly put her hands on his head, one each side, and brought it down to hers and they kissed, a long, slow kiss that seemed to complete the union of their bodies. But it was more than bodies. It was as if their souls too had met and flowed each into the other.

It could not last long, that first time, however much they wanted it to. The excitement was too much for them. All too soon, they were lost again in the swoop of passion, drawing them up and on, all else forgotten. It was like climbing a mountain, a shimmering glass and crystal mountain. And then they were at the peak, poised briefly before that final lift into space, into a place where none could follow and they clung to each other, shaken and dizzy, and then fell slowly, slowly, back to earth and awareness.

'I never thought,' Geoff whispered in her ear when they could speak again at last, 'I never *dreamt* it would be like that.'

'We're truly married now,' she murmured back. 'We're truly, truly married . . .'

Chapter Eighteen

The Korean war was at its bloodiest that winter. To those at home, it was difficult to comprehend. The unfamiliar names – Osan, Kumyangjang, Suwon and Seoul – came uneasily to British tongues. The concept of the battle against Chinese Communism, coming so soon after the six-year war against Hitler's Nazism was almost too much to grapple with. And as those at home always did, Lucy and her family focused their attention on the one thought that meant the most to them: the thought that Geoff was out there, that he might at any moment be fighting, wounded, killed.

'It's just too much,' Lucy said to Wilmot. 'We've been through it all before. Why does he have to be taken away from us, just when we were getting ourselves together again?'

Wilmot grunted and she gave him a despairing look. Since Geoff had gone he had become more uncommunicative than ever, and she was sure he was drinking more. The bottle of rum he kept openly on the shelf and opened immediately after their evening meal wasn't going down so fast, but she had discovered another one, half full, under the bed and a third hidden in the coal-bunker. How many more bottles were secreted about the house, and how often did he drink from them?

'Is it like Japan?' she asked, her voice trembling a little. 'I mean, if he's taken prisoner, will they –'

'How the *hell* do I know?' Wilmot came to his feet and swept his hand across the kitchen table, sending a bottle of sauce flying. His face, always unhealthily sallow these days, was flooded with dark colour, so that he looked bruised all over. 'How the hell do I know what those little yellow bastards will do? I've been trying to forget it all these years – d'you think I want it all brought back to me? D'you think I want to think of my own son, caught in the same bloody trap I was in? I tell you, Lucy, if you had my memories –' He closed his bloodshot eyes, squeezing them tightly as if to shut out the unbearable pictures.

Lucy sometimes thought she had. She had lived through so many of his nightmares that it was almost as if she had shared the experiences themselves. Normally she would not have dreamed of bringing them back to him, but now Geoff was out there, and she tortured herself with her imaginings.

'Anyway, he's not been taken prisoner and probably won't be,' Wilmot growled, sitting down again. He was looking really ill, she thought, blotchy faced and red eyed. She had thought several times lately of asking him to see a doctor. Yet what would a doctor do but tell him to stop drinking? 'He's just a National Service squaddy, he won't get sent into battle.'

Lucy didn't know whether to believe that or not. If the National Servicemen weren't going into battle, why had they been sent there? She listened to the news and read the papers, and if she went to the cinema she watched the scenes shown on Pathé Pictorial and her fears returned. Geoff, she thought, Geoff. He's just a baby still.

She thought again of the last few days before Geoff had departed. He'd spent all the time he could with Jilly and, seeing them together, Lucy had wondered if she'd been right to forbid their marriage. They were so obviously in love, and they seemed well suited. If only they'd been a few years older, she would have been happy to give them her blessing – but she could not believe that two youngsters not yet out of their teens were ready to pledge their whole lives.

They needed the protection that she and Mrs Penfold, aided by the law, could give them.

'I know it hurts,' she had said to Jilly, coming on her crying in the kitchen. 'I know you feel the world's come to an end, but it hasn't, you know. Geoff will be back almost before you know it, and if you're of the same mind then—'

To her astonishment, Jilly whirled on her. 'You *know*? How can you possibly know? You've never been in my position! You don't know anything about it at all.'

Lucy shook her head. 'I may not have been in exactly the same position, but I do know what it's like to see my man go off to war.'

'But he was your husband, wasn't he?' Jilly said. 'You'd been married for years. You had children. At least if he didn't come back, you would have had all that just the same.'

'It still hurt just as much to see him go. More, probably. And then we had all those years of waiting. I want to save you from that, Jilly.'

'Save me?' the girl said bitterly. 'How can you save me from that? I'm having to wait just the same. And just how is stopping us getting married going to save me from a broken heart? Do you realise, if anything happens to Geoff they won't even let me know? It'll be you they tell – not me.'

'But I'm his mother—'

'And *I* ought to be his wife. That's what he wanted me to be.' Jilly stared at her and Lucy was shocked by the expression in the girl's eyes. 'And you stopped us from getting married. *You*.'

'It wasn't just me,' Lucy protested weakly. 'Geoff's father didn't want it either – nor did your own mother. We all—'

'They'd have agreed if you had. You could have persuaded them. They'd have listened to you.'

Lucy tried to deny this, but she knew in her heart it was true. She could have persuaded Mrs Penfold, overridden

Wilmot. She gazed helplessly at Jilly, seeing how thin and pale the girl looked, her cheeks pinched, her vivacity dimmed. But I *was* right, she thought, I *was*. This will pass. Everything passes.

'Please believe me, Jilly,' she said gently. 'The time will go and I'm sure Geoff will be all right. And if you both still love each other when he comes back, then we'll arrange the biggest wedding you want, with the most beautiful dress in Plymouth and a reception here in the hotel, everything you could ask for.'

Jilly looked at her, then she reached behind her back and untied the strings of her white apron. She took it off and laid it on the kitchen table.

'I don't want a big wedding, or a white dress,' she said coldly. 'I don't want a reception in the hotel. Don't you understand? I just want to be married to Geoff and I want to be married to him *now*.'

She turned and walked out of the kitchen, leaving Lucy staring after her, feeling at a loss, and as if she were the young girl and Jilly the woman, with a woman's wisdom.

That was ridiculous. What Jilly was feeling now was nothing more than calf-love, the first stirrings of desire as felt by any young girl. Intense enough, to be sure, and easy for such a young girl to mistake for the real thing. And it might well turn out, as time went on, to be the real thing. Young love had developed into maturity before now. But more often, it didn't, and that was why there was a law to protect such young lovers, to protect them from themselves.

I *was* right, she told herself. I *was*.

Whether she had been right or not, there was nothing to be done about it now, and Lucy's attention was soon distracted by a telephone call from her sister Alice, in Portsmouth. Her father had had a heart attack and was in hospital. Could she come at once and see him?

'Oh dear. Oh, how awful. Poor Mum.' Lucy's brain raced, trying to think of ways and means to leave the hotel. It wasn't a busy time for guests, but they had decorators in, and refurbishments going on, work being done on the new part . . .

'Of course you've got to go,' Patsy said, seeing her mother's indecision. 'I can look after everything, and Jilly will help me. Pompey Gran and Grandad need you now.'

Lucy set off next day from Plymouth North Road station, still with misgivings in her heart. Since her confrontation with Jilly, there had been an atmosphere of strain in the hotel and she felt as if a grey shadow hung over her life. It was almost like a premonition, she thought, staring out at the sea lapping the red cliffs as the train ran along the shore. As if something awful is going to happen, changing all our lives.

Well, so there probably was. Her father was ill, wasn't he, and perhaps going to die. Wasn't that enough to have premonitions about? Wasn't that enough to cast a shadow over her spirit?

And yet . . . Somehow, Lucy felt that there was something more than that, and her thoughts turned, inevitably, to her son.

Geoff had written that he was going on a few days' leave soon. The news had given her hope. Things couldn't be too serious, if they were being sent on leave, although the news hadn't cheered either Jilly or Wilmot.

'Have you seen where they're sending him?' Wilmot demanded, as if it were a personal insult. 'Japan! *Japan!* He'll be spending his leave with a lot of little yellow buggers who don't know the meaning of humanity, and what sort of a leave is that going to be, eh? You tell me that. Why, he'll be afraid to go to bed at night for fear one of 'em'll creep in and murder him while he sleeps.'

'Wilmot, don't talk like that. We're at peace now.'

'Peace!' Wilmot echoed. '*Peace!* Those swine will never be at peace.'

Lucy hoped he was wrong. Surely the H-Bomb had cowed the Japanese for ever; they would never rise above the threat of such damage again. The papers still talked about it from time to time – the aftermath of the huge bomb, the radiation sickness, the cancers . . . It was a terrible thing that had been done, more terrible than anyone could have imagined, but it would surely prevent anything worse.

'It hasn't stopped wars though, has it?' Wilmot had said. 'It hasn't stopped boys like our Geoff from being sent out there to fight all over again.'

Lucy bit her lip and stared out of the train window. She'd thought that once the war was over and Wilmot home again for good, all their troubles would be over, but that wasn't what life was like, was it? Somehow, as soon as one trouble was over a new one came to take its place.

While Lucy was away in Portsmouth, Jilly did her best to help about the hotel. She had taken over all the cooking and now oversaw the work of the two girls who came in each day to make beds and clean rooms – not that there was much to do at present, with the hotel taking so few guests. She helped Patsy too, for independent as Patsy had become in her wheelchair there were still a few things she could not manage.

'You're as good as a sister to me,' Patsy remarked as Jilly helped her to take her bath. 'There's not many people I'd let help me like this. I'd sooner go dirty than let some near me!'

'Well, if Geoff and me had had our way, that's what I'd be.' Jilly hung up the towel. 'And you'd be—' She stopped suddenly and Patsy looked at her curiously.

'I'd be what? Here, was that a letter you had from our Geoff this morning? I thought you looked a bit upset afterwards.'

'Yes.' Jilly glanced away and when she looked back Patsy was dismayed to see her eyes full of tears. 'Oh, Patsy, it all seems so awful – you just can't imagine. Here–' she fished it out of her apron pocket – 'I'll tell you some of what he says. I just don't know how he can bear it.'

'Bear what? I thought he was on leave.'

'Yes, in Japan, and he doesn't like it much, I can tell you. He says it reminds him too much of what his dad went through out there. He doesn't like the people at all, although I suppose you can't blame him for that. But that's not the worst of it.' She glanced at the letter.

'So what is? What's the matter with him?'

'It's what they've been doing in Korea. Listen, Patsy.

I would never have thought I could do things like we're expected to do out here, Jilly love. Killing people. Not just soldiers, that would be fair fighting – but ordinary people, people who've done nothing to hurt me nor ever would. Last week my mate Billy Watkins shot two old people who were just working in their paddy-fields, for nothing. All they did was come out of their house to work – an old man and an old woman, like Grammy and Grampy. And he shot them dead. And I tell you what, Jilly, if he hadn't done it I would probably have done it myself. That's what they've done to us, you see. That's what they've turned us into out here – brutes. Savages. And cowards too, because we know that if we didn't do it the sergeant would shoot us.

I don't know what's going to happen when our leave ends. A lot of the blokes are saying they won't go back. Billy Watkins is almost going mad with thinking about it all. And some of the others – Jilly, I've seen things I don't want to tell anybody about ever, people torn to bits, bits of people that were still alive, begging to be killed and put out of their misery like you'd put an

238

animal out of its misery, men screaming and crying and asking for their mothers . . . Sometimes I think I've died and gone to hell, and I know that hell can't be any worse than this. And you're all I've got to hold on to, you and the memory of our—'

Jilly stopped abruptly and folded the letter up as if Patsy's eyes could read through the paper to the words he had written.

'I thought we'd finished with all that,' Patsy said, her voice shaken. 'I thought the war was over and this was supposed to be peacetime. People like Geoff and you – you were supposed to be able to look forward to living a normal life.'

'Normal!' Jilly said bitterly. 'Does anybody know what normal is any more? Maybe we've all got so used to war that we think *that's* normal.'

'But it was supposed to be so good. Love and laughter –'

'And peace ever after,' Jilly finished. 'Well, we can stop thinking that, I reckon. There's boys like Geoff getting killed out there, and even if they do come back, what are they going to be like? Look at your dad. He was supposed to have been like Geoff once, all full of jokes, and look what happened to him.'

Nobody looked less full of jokes than Wilmot these days. He had given up all pretence that he wasn't drinking heavily, and took his first drink of rum when other people were having morning coffee. The strange thing was that he didn't really seem drunk a lot of the time. Or perhaps it was so long since anyone had seen him truly sober that his slightly slurred speech and unsteady gait had just become a part of his everyday being and simply went unnoticed. And if he was depressed and surly most of the time, that was how he'd been ever since he came back from Japan, and it was excusable in view of what was happening to Geoff. He knew what it was like out there, he told anyone who would listen, he knew what those boys were going through.

'I blame myself,' he said, sitting at the kitchen table with his head supported in shaking hands. 'I should have stopped him. I should have made him go into the Navy. I put him off that. It's all my fault.'

'Don't talk daft,' his mother said sharply. 'Geoff made up his own mind, it was nothing to do with you.'

'Nothing to do with me? I'm the boy's father, aren't I? How can it be nothing to do with me? A boy looks up to his dad, takes notice of him. I shot my mouth off too much about what it was like below decks and that's what turned him off the Navy. But for me he'd have been sitting pretty on a messdeck now, seeing a bit of the world. Instead of that he's going through bloody hell out in Korea and chances are we'll never see him again.'

'Wilmot!' Maud glanced at Jilly, sitting white faced at the end of the table. 'Watch your words, for goodness' sake.'

'Why? She knows. He's written enough to her, for God's sake. Told her more than he's told the rest of us, I'll be bound. Well, hasn't he?' he demanded belligerently, looking at Jilly.

Jilly bit her lips. 'What Wilmot writes to me is private between us, Mr Pengelly.'

'Oh, I'm sure it is. All that lovey-dovey stuff. I know, I used to do a bit of that meself. And much good it did me, too.' He glowered around the table, as if daring anyone to challenge him.

Nobody did. Maud got up and started to clear the table and Jilly helped her. She wondered whether she should tell them the truth about herself and Geoff, but she could not bear the look on Wilmot's face if she did. She carried dishes to the sink, feeling his eyes on her. Since Geoff had gone, she had felt this more and more – Wilmot's stare, cold and inimical. As if really, deep down, he blamed her for Geoff's departure, however much he might claim to blame himself.

'I suppose you blame me too,' he said suddenly. 'You think it's all my fault he's gone, and my fault you didn't get married before he went.'

Jilly glanced at Maud. The older woman sighed and frowned slightly, shaking her head.

Wilmot sneered. 'All right, I know what you're thinking. Don't rise to the bait. That's it, isn't it? You think if you don't say anything I'll shut up, and it won't matter what I say or what I think. Nothing matters so long as it isn't said, that's the way of it, isn't it? Keep it all bottled up inside, keep it to yourself, don't bother other people . . .' There was an edge of raw pain in his voice and Jilly turned quickly, responding to the pain, wanting to soothe and comfort it, but he sensed her reaction and warded her off with an upraised hand. 'Well, and maybe that's right after all. Because you can't do anything about it, nobody can, it's there inside me for ever and nothing can help, *nothing*. D'you hear me? I've got to live with it burning me inside, eating me away, and there's *nothing anyone can do about it, ever.*'

'Wilmot —'

'Mr Pengelly —'

Maud and Jilly spoke together, both moving towards him, but Wilmot was on his feet, his hands held out before him, shaking his head from side to side.

'Don't come near me. I don't want you near me. I don't want anyone.' His pain was almost too much to bear. 'I told you, it's all my fault Geoff's gone, my fault, and if anything happens to him it'll do for me too. And maybe that'd be the best thing all round, for I'm no use to man nor beast here, I know that.'

'Wilmot, don't talk so stupid.'

'Stupid? Stupid? And what's so stupid about facing up to the truth, eh? Tell me it's not true, tell me what good I've been these last four years or so, and then tell me who's talking stupid.'

241

'Wilmot, you're not well.'

'I haven't been well,' he said, 'since a little yellow bastard with slit eyes took a bayonet to my backside and chucked me into a chicken-coop for a fortnight.'

'Oh, Mr Pengelly,' Jilly said, her eyes filled with tears, 'you had a terrible time. We all know that.'

'And I'm still having it,' he said. 'I go through it all over again, night after night, just as if it was happening to me same as before. And during the day I think about it.' He picked up the half-empty bottle of rum which had been standing on the table. 'And you wonder why I drink. This is the only friend I've got.'

'If only we could help –'

'You,' he said to Jilly, 'you could help. And shall I tell you how? By getting out. By going away from here and never coming back. Every time I look at you, I think of my boy, out there where I've been, living in hell. Every time I look at you I think of him, taken prisoner, killed, tortured like I was, like I've seen other blokes tortured. Every time I look at you, you make it all worse.'

'Wilmot! You can't talk to poor Jilly like that!'

'I can. I have. And if she really wanted to help me, she'd go.'

Maud turned to Jilly. 'Take no notice of him. He's not responsible for what he says.'

'But it's what he feels,' Jilly said quietly, her face ashen. 'He can't help what he feels.' She looked at Maud. 'I can't stay here if I make it so much worse for him. I can't do it.'

Maud stared at her. 'You're not seriously thinking of going?'

'I don't see what else I can do.' Jilly turned her eyes on Wilmot. He had sunk back into his chair and lain his head on his arms and now he was sobbing, his shoulders heaving. 'Look at him. He's suffering such a lot. Perhaps I'd better go, just until Mrs Pengelly gets back – but maybe she won't want me either. Not if it hurts him so much.'

242

She walked quietly out of the kitchen.

Maud stared after her, one hand lifted as if to prevent her going, then she let her hand drop to her side and moved instead to give what comfort she could to her son. Like Lucy, sitting now by her father's bed as she watched his life ebb away, she was beginning to wonder what it was all about, and why life seemed to be crumbling just when they had all thought it would be so good.

Chapter Nineteen

Joe died a week later. He regained only a confused consciousness, occasionally aware of where he was, opening his eyes to stare around him with a kind of bemused dismay, clutching at the hand of whoever sat beside him. His legs had swollen with dropsy and the nurses said he shouldn't be given too much fluid, but his mouth was dry and he begged constantly for water, for a drink. Lucy dipped her finger in the glass and wet his lips, but he shook his head painfully. 'A *drink*. A proper drink.'

'It's cruel,' Kitty said. She had got special leave and spent as much time as she was allowed beside his bed, sitting there as smart in her Wrens uniform as if she was going on parade. She was an officer now and full of cool authority, but even she was daunted by the nurses. Lucy could see that she longed to pick up the glass and hold it to her father's mouth, let him drink his fill, but she didn't quite dare.

'What would it matter? He's dying anyway. Why shouldn't he have a drink to make him feel better?'

'Kitty! Don't talk like that.'

'Why not? You know it's true. So do they. They told us. It's terrible to refuse him a drink. He's *thirsty*.'

They had moved away from the bed while the nurses sponged Joe's flaccid body, and were talking in whispers, but Lucy glanced anxiously towards the bed. 'He might hear you.'

'He can't hear anything. Lucy, you know he's only got a few days. Perhaps no more than hours. We're going to have to face it.'

'Yes. I do know.' The nurses had finished and the two women moved back beside the bed. Lucy reached out and touched her father's cheek with one hand, smoothing the skin gently. He was sleeping now, relieved for a while of his misery. She wished he would just slip away like that, without knowing any more.

Lucy started to speak, but the words would not come, Instead, she began to cry, silently, her head bowed, the tears dripping on to her laced fingers. One of the nurses, tending a patient on the other side of the ward, noticed and hurried over, looking with professional anxiety at Joe, but Kitty waved her away.

'It's all right. It's not Dad. My sister's rather upset.'

The nurse nodded and went back to her other patient. Kitty slipped her arm around Lucy's shoulders and held her close. 'What is it, Lucy? Is it Wilmot? Or Geoff?'

Lucy started to speak again and lifted both hands instead, holding them up for a moment or two before letting them drop in a gesture of despair that told Kitty more clearly than any words. It was both. It was everything.

'You're tired out,' Kitty said quietly. 'You're just tired out. And you need David.'

Lucy lifted her head and stared at her. 'How do you –?'

'I'm not blind,' Kitty said. 'I know how you feel about him, and how he feels about you. Oh, it's all right – nobody else knows, or if they do they're keeping quiet about it. And nobody would blame you, anyway. Not with Wilmot the way he is.'

'We've never –'

'I don't suppose you have,' Kitty said with the ghost of a smile. 'Not that I'd blame you if you did. Quite honestly, I think you're mad not to. I would, like a shot, but then I'm not married, and never likely to be.'

'We don't even see each other.'

'I know. It's all right, Lucy. You don't have to explain to me. I know you'd never do anything wrong – not like me.'

245

Kitty grinned cheerfully. 'I'm the black sheep in this family! All the same, it's David you need, isn't it? That's why you're so unhappy – because the one man you really want, the man who could take all those burdens off your shoulders and make life worth living, is the man you can't have.' She shook her head compassionately. 'No wonder you say life isn't fair.'

'It's not just that. It's all the other things. Much worse things. It's much worse for other people.'

'So it may be. But that doesn't make our own pain any the less,' Kitty said. 'And it doesn't mean we have to be ashamed of feeling it.'

They sat quietly for a few minutes. Joe was still asleep, his breathing quieter than it had been for some hours. Kitty reached out and smoothed back his thin grey hair.

Lucy opened her mouth to speak, but before she could utter a sound there was a strange rattling from their father's throat. They both turned swiftly, reaching out to help him, but Joe was beyond their help. He lay rigid, his eyes suddenly wide open, hands reaching up like stretching claws.

'Dad –'

'Nurse! Nurse! Come quickly –'

The nurse was at the bedside, leaning over him. She took him by the shoulders, raised his body from the pillows, held him for a moment. And then Lucy and Kitty, watching in frozen dismay, saw the final shudder convulse his body, heard the last breath sough from his body.

There was a moment of silence. The nurse laid him back gently on his pillows and closed the staring eyes. She looked at the two sisters. 'He's gone. I'm sorry.'

They nodded, unable to speak, then Lucy leant over and kissed her father's still-warm cheek. Kitty pressed the heels of her hands against her eyes for a minute or two and then did the same.

'We'll have to go and tell Mum.' She looked at the nurse.

'Can he stay here for a while? So that she can come in and see him?'

They left the ward slowly, their arms around each other's waists.

The family gathered for the funeral a week later. Vic's widow Eileen, who had married again, came with her new husband, Bob, and twelve-year-old Vicky. Alice, who was living at Cosham, came with her husband John and son Michael. Kenny, who hadn't married and still lived at home but had a string of girlfriends, brought none of them. He was beginning to look older, Lucy thought, seeing the lines of tiredness on his face and wishing he would settle down. Other, more distant, relatives came as well; aunts and uncles and cousins from Portsmouth and Gosport and further afield than that.

Neighbours and friends came. People who lived in the streets where Joe and Emily had spent their marriage, mates who had known Joe at work in the dockyard, men who said they had been at school with him years ago. The throng grew and grew as they poured into St Mary's church, and Lucy felt a lump in her throat as she gazed around her. She would never have believed that her father had known so many people, made so many friends.

Wilmot had travelled alone on the train from Plymouth. Lucy had gone to the town station to meet him, watching anxiously as he descended a trifle unsteadily from the carriage. Don't get drunk, she prayed, don't make a show of us. Not now . . . She went forward to greet him and smelt the rum on his breath. If you let me down now, she told him with her eyes, it'll be all over between us. I warn you.

Wilmot saw and understood the warning. He glowered and said, 'You needn't look like that. Stroll on, a bloke's got to have a drop to sustain him on these godawful trains. Even your dad wouldn't have begrudged me that.'

Lucy ignored the 'even'. She wondered if she had been

wise to ask him to come, whether she shouldn't have told him to stay at home, but people would have wondered. 'Just keep off it now you're here,' she said, and reached up to kiss him. 'It's good to see you, Wilmot.' And just for a moment, it was. She had been lonely here by herself, she realised, with no one to turn to for her own comfort. She rested her head against his shoulder.

Wilmot grunted and put his arm round her shoulders, but the moment passed quickly. He turned to get his luggage from the train and, stumbling, dropped a shopping bag on the platform. Lucy heard the clink of bottles and then the sound of breaking glass. Her husband swore.

'Bloody hell. We'll have to go to an off-licence on the way to your mum's.'

'I said, keep *off* it,' Lucy snapped. 'It's my dad's funeral tomorrow. Do you want to turn up drunk?'

'Do you want me to turn up at all?' he demanded, and the brief rapport was gone. He threw the broken bottle into a litter-bin and marched ahead of her, indignation keeping his gait steady, and she followed, her heart sinking, and heard him give his instructions to the taxi-driver. 'And stop by that place at the end of Arundel Street. Got to buy a couple of presents.'

Presents! she thought bitterly. The best present you could give me would be *not* to stop there. However, she said nothing, only sat silent in the back of the taxi and waited as Wilmot went into the off-licence and came out with a couple of wrapped bottles. He heaved himself in beside her and gave her a look that dared her to say a word.

I can't bear it, she thought, and knew that he would not be in the church tomorrow, and that she would never forgive him for it.

David came. Lucy did not know who had let him know – probably Kitty, or perhaps Alice – but he was there at the church when she arrived with her mother and sisters, and he came forward and took Emily's hand in his for a moment and then walked into the church beside them. Nobody said anything. Kenny was the only man of the immediate family present, and he kept his mother's arm in his, so David fell in quite naturally beside Lucy.

She felt him looking down at her and lifted her eyes to meet his. The last time they had spoken was when she had berated him on the telephone over Geoff and Jilly. She tried to put her feelings into her eyes, and he smiled a little and gave the minutest of nods, and she felt comforted.

'Where's Wilmot?' he murmured, and she grimaced.

'At home. At Mum's. He – wasn't fit to come.' She glanced away. There was no need to hide anything from David, but she felt a great wash of shame. Wilmot had spent the previous evening drinking, and been difficult to wake this morning. If the funeral had been in the afternoon, he might have been able to attend. Perhaps, she thought, recalling how he could be the day after a bender, it was as well that he couldn't. At least he couldn't make an exhibition of himself in the church, or at the graveside. The thought of him doing so made her shudder.

She felt David slip his hand beneath her elbow. It felt strong and warm, the grip solid and reassuring. Oh David, she thought, it feels so right to have you here with me, walking beside me, giving me your comfort and your strength. I know it ought to be Wilmot, but it feels so much better that it's you. It ought always to have been you . . .

Shocked by the thought, she tried to concentrate her mind on the service. The family had followed the coffin as it was borne up the aisle by six undertaker's men, solemn in their black suits. It stood now before them on the bier, closed and silent.

She glanced sideways towards her mother. Emily was standing like a poker, rigidly still, her face like stone. She would not cry, Lucy thought, not here in front of all these people. Emily belonged to the school who saw tears as an imposition on others, grief as something private. She would cry when she was alone, and not even in front of her own family.

Lucy wished that she could be as disciplined, but she knew that the tears were close; she could feel their heat behind her eyelids, the ache of them in her throat. David had dropped his hand from her arm in order to hold his prayer-book, but she felt for it now, slipping her left hand into the crook of his arm and gripping it tightly. She felt his arm tighten in response, holding her hand firmly against his side, and the words of the prayers misted before her eyes. Dad, she thought. Dad. And she looked again at the coffin. Was it all worth it? Was it a good life, in spite of all the hard times?

Wilmot joined them at the graveside.

Thank God, Lucy thought when she saw him coming, that it was all over, the last prayers said, the earth sprinkled on the coffin, the first shovelful heaped on top. Even at a distance, she could see that his steps were wavering and unsteady. He'd either started on his bottle almost as soon as he got out of bed, or he'd been in the pub already. She drew a deep breath, wishing him anywhere but here, and went forward quickly, determined to avoid a scene.

'Wilmot! You've come – are you feeling better, then?' The fiction was that he had arrived from Plymouth the worse for flu. 'You oughtn't to have come out in this cold wind,' she scolded him gently, taking his arm. 'You'll be getting your bronchitis again.'

He stared at her. He certainly looked ill, she thought, with his flushed face and bleary eyes, but would anyone really mistake the signs of drunkenness for influenza? Just don't speak, she begged him silently, just don't draw attention to yourself.

'What are you all coming out for?' he demanded. 'Don't tell me it's all over.'

'Of course it is. Ten o'clock, you remember?' She kept her voice bright. 'You seemed so tired this morning, I didn't have the heart to wake you. And you know you're not well.'

'Not well?' His voice rose to a belligerent shout. 'Whaddoyoumean, not well? I'm as well as I've ever been. I shoulda been here. I shoulda been at the funeral. As senior shon-in –' he stumbled over the words – 'shenior *son-in-law* – I shoulda been *here*.'

Lucy thought so too, but not in his present condition. She glanced around her. People were moving away, gathering around Emily, looking her way and murmuring together. She felt her face burn with shame.

'Wilmot, you shouldn't have come. We'd better go home straight away.'

'*Shouldn't have come?*' His voice rose again. 'Whaddoyoumean, shouldn't have come? I was his shon-in-law, wasn't I? His *only* shon-*son*-in-law.'

'No, John and Bob were his sons-in-law as well.'

Wilmot sneered. 'John and Bob! They'm newcomers. Been in the family five minutes and think they can take over.' He struck himself on the chest. '*I* was the first. Been in the family since – since – when was it, nineteen-thirty, thirty-one?'

'Thirty-one. Wilmot, let's go home.'

'Nineteen-thirty-one,' he declaimed. 'That's over twenty years, that is. That's seniority.'

'Yes, but –' Lucy was beginning to feel desperate. People were staring and she knew that she could not pass this off as flu. And Wilmot was starting to lower his head angrily. If he lost his temper . . .

David was beside them. He took Wilmot's arm in his hand. 'Hallo, Wilmot, old chap. Good to see you again. Look, why don't we make our way home and get the place opened up and ready. I daresay Emily wants the family and a few of the friends to come back for a drink and a sandwich. She'd be glad of your help – as senior son-in-law.'

Wilmot paused and stared at him suspiciously. 'Are you trying to get rid of me? Because if you are—'

'No,' Lucy broke in hurriedly. 'Of course David's not trying to get rid of you. But he's right. Mum needs someone to get home ahead of the rest, and it's our place to do that. And you ought to be out of this cold wind.' What they would do with Wilmot when they got him home, she didn't dare think, but she had to get him away from here, away from the churchyard and all these people. 'Come on. Let's go home and get the kettle on.'

'Kettle? I'd have thought you'd be offering a proper drink.'

'We are. Sherry. And beer for those who want it. But some of the ladies will want a cup of tea, and maybe some of the men as well.' He was allowing her to steer him along the path now, towards the gates that led out on to the road. David, on his other side, kept his hand discreetly under Wilmot's arm and between them they guided him past the crowd and on to the pavement. Lucy paused, feeling suddenly helpless. They couldn't take Wilmot on a bus in this state.

'It's all right.' David seemed able to read every thought in her mind. 'The taxis are waiting. We'll take one of them. Come on, Wilmot, old chap. You'll feel better once you get home. Maybe a lie-down, eh? Before the rest arrive . . .' They got the suddenly heavy body into a taxi and directed it back to the house. Wilmot slumped against them in the back. He muttered something, but Lucy could not catch what it was, and she didn't much care. All she wanted to do, all she longed to do, was get him home and out of sight before the rest arrived.

And that was what they did. It was a struggle, and by the time they'd accomplished it Lucy was hot, breathless and dishevelled. When her mother returned, accompanied by

Kenny and Kitty, with Alice and Eileen and the rest following behind, Wilmot was safe in bed upstairs and already snoring. Heaven knew how much he'd had to drink that morning, Lucy thought, and just at present she didn't care. She was able to tidy her hair, puff a bit of powder on her face and stand in the front room, passing round glasses of sherry or pouring cups of tea, and keep up the pretence that he had flu, and that was all she cared about. Her father's funeral had not been spoiled after all.

But only just, she thought grimly, and not through any efforts on Wilmot's part. She remembered the thought that had gone through her mind when she met him at the station. *If you let me down now, it'll be all over between us.*

He had let her down, and she knew, with ice-cold certainty, that it was all over between them.

Chapter Twenty

After everyone had gone and the clearing-up had been done, Lucy and David slipped out for a walk together. They cut through the streets to Southsea and strolled along the front towards Clarence Pier.

'What will your mother do now, d'you think?' David asked as they looked out over the Solent towards the Isle of Wight. The sky had hazed over with fine cloud and shimmered like a vast dome of mother-of-pearl above their heads. The sea was flat calm, as pale and smooth as grey watered silk. The island seemed to float on the horizon, its silhouette knobbly with trees, the spire of Ryde church tower like a spear pointing to heaven.

'I suppose she'll stay where she is. Kenny's still living there and Kitty comes home when she can. As long as she's got them to look after, she'll be all right. She'll miss Dad, though. They've been together for over forty-five years, David.'

He nodded. 'It's a long time. It must seem as though half of her has been torn away.' His voice was sad and Lucy knew he was thinking of Heather. They had been married for only a few years, yet he still grieved for her. How much worse was it going to be for Emily?

'And what about you?' he asked. 'How are you going to be?'

'Oh, I'll be all right. It's not as if I saw all that much of Dad, after all. I only—'

'I didn't mean that,' he said quietly, and she stopped and looked up at him.

'No. I don't know, David. I don't know how I'm going to be now.'

They walked on. Clarence Pier had been damaged in the war and they struck inland to avoid it, then made their way through Old Portsmouth to the Sallyport, where they had taken Patsy in her wheelchair to see the *Vanguard* come in with the King and Queen and Princesses aboard. How hopeful I was then, Lucy thought, gazing across the narrow neck of the harbour entrance towards Gosport. Wilmot was home and although he was obviously still suffering the after-effects of the war, I really believed he would get better and be the old Wilmot. I really believed we would have a good life together. And now . . .

'I don't know if I can stay any longer with Wilmot,' she said abruptly. 'He's been getting worse and worse, and now . . . Behaving like that at Dad's funeral. I don't think I can ever forgive him that.'

'He was very fond of your father,' David said gently.

'So why get drunk? Why come along late and make a show of himself? Why couldn't he keep off the bottle, just for a few hours, and behave like a decent human being?' Her voice shook. 'It was all I asked of him, David. It's not a lot. If he was going to do that, he ought to have stayed at home in Plymouth. He didn't have to come all this way, just to make an exhibition of himself and show me up and humiliate me.'

'I think Wilmot takes a drink whenever he finds life a bit too difficult to handle,' David said. 'Whenever things get too much for him. It's his way of getting through it. Obviously, he was upset that your father had died, and he needed a drink to help him cope with that. And then the funeral . . . I'm not condoning it, Lucy, I'm just trying to understand it.'

'Well, I can't understand it and I don't want to,' she said bitterly. 'The rest of us didn't have to get drunk. The trouble with Wilmot is that he doesn't remember what it's like to feel sober, and if he doesn't have a drink for a while he thinks he's ill. He doesn't give himself a chance. He's weak, David, that's his trouble, just plain weak.'

'Don't you think he has some justification? After all he's been through?'

Lucy turned and faced him. 'David, he wasn't the only man in a Japanese camp. There were hundreds of them, thousands. Are they all drunks now? I know they had a terrible time, I know they'll never forget it – but they haven't all given way to it. A lot of them are building their lives again. They've put it behind them. Wilmot's just never left. In his mind, he's still there. It's as if he doesn't *want* to leave.'

'That's crazy—' David began, but she interrupted him.

'It's not. It sounds crazy, I know, and it's a crazy thing to want to do, but it's as if he wants to hang on to the – the *sympathy* it got him when he came home. He was fêted. The returning hero. All that. We all made a big fuss of him, we made allowances for him, and he liked it. Mind, I don't blame him for that. After what he'd been through, it would be surprising if he didn't enjoy a bit of pampering, and I was glad to give it to him. We all were. But you can't live like that for ever. That's his trouble – he can't let it go and just be ordinary Wilmot Pengelly again, doing a job of work. So he's using it, trading on it, and because he won't let it go, he still suffers, he dreams about it night after night. And he drinks. And he'll go on drinking until he does let it go.' She paused and added quietly, 'And I don't think he ever will.'

They stood in silence for a while. The sun had begun to sink behind the island. It cast a diffused apricot light through the feathery clouds and touched the small, springing waves with gold. Gulls wheeled and screamed overhead, and one of the Isle of Wight paddle steamers, the *Whippingham*, the one that had been to Dunkirk, churned its way past them into the harbour, making for the railway station jetty.

'So where does that leave you?' David asked. 'Lucy, I hate to think of you living your life like this. You've had almost six years of it now, and I've watched you getting paler and thinner every time I see you. Not that I've seen much of you in all that time,' he added in a lower tone.

'I know. And I've missed you, David.' She hesitated and then said, 'I don't know where it leaves me. I feel I've had almost as much as I can take. I looked at him when he arrived yesterday, and I knew what was going to happen, and I thought – I thought, if you do this to me, Wilmot, it's all over between us. And he has done it.'

'And is it all over?'

She nodded, her eyes on the tall, thin tower of Gosport's Holy Trinity church. 'Yes. I think it is.'

The silence fell again. David's hand felt for hers and he held it in his strong grip. 'What will you do?'

She closed her eyes and leant against his shoulder. 'I don't know. I haven't thought about it. Or maybe I've thought too much.' Her shoulders lifted and dropped again. 'I just don't know what I'll do.'

'The hotel –'

'That's the worst of it,' she said. 'The hotel – Maud and Arthur. They're getting old, it's their home, I can't just abandon them. And then there's Patsy. She could run the place, but she needs help. I can't leave her. It's like a web, David, a web I'm trapped in. Wherever I turn, there's another strand, pulling me back to the centre. And he's in the middle of it all, like a spider.'

'Lucy –'

'I shouldn't have said that,' she said rapidly. 'It sounds awful. He isn't like a spider at all. He's just Wilmot, poor, pathetic Wilmot, who's had a horrible time and can't get over it. And he needs help like the rest of them. I know that. I'm just tired of giving it.' She grimaced. 'The truth is, I'm just not a very good wife.'

'Oh now, you can't say that. You've done all you could.'

'Perhaps,' she said, 'but I'm not doing it any more. Oh, David.' She leant her head against him again and gripped his lapels in her hands. 'All I want to do is come to you,' she said shakily. 'All I want is to walk away from it all – just walk away, without ever looking back – and come to you and stay with you, for the rest of my life.'

He stared down at her bent head, and then he put his arm around her shoulders and held her tightly against him. The sun had dipped below the Island now and the light had turned to a soft, violet dusk. The few people who had been strolling near by had disappeared. David and Lucy were alone.

'You know,' he said quietly into her hair, 'you know that if ever you want to come to me, you must just come. I'll be there. I've always been there for you.'

'I want to come,' she said in a muffled voice. 'I want to come now.'

'Oh, Lucy,' he said, and his voice trembled in his throat. 'Lucy, Lucy, Lucy . . .'

'I know it's wrong. Nobody will want to know us. All our friends . . . But I can't help that. I've had enough, David, I've had enough of it all. I want to come back with you now,' she said rapidly. 'I want to come back to London with you. I don't want to go back to Plymouth with Wilmot – I *won't* go back. I feel – I feel that if I go back now, I'll never get away. Something will happen – something will prevent me. I couldn't bear that, David.' She lifted her head and stared up into his face, her eyes purple in the gathering dusk. 'If I go back now, I'll be caught all over again in the web.'

'Lucy, you're upset, you're overwrought. You're worn out by the last few days – you spent nearly a week sitting with your father, looking after your mother. And now the funeral. And Wilmot. You're in no fit state to make decisions.'

'I'm fitter than I've ever been. I haven't just begun to feel like this, David. I've loved you for years – you know that. Even during the war – even when Heather was still alive. And you love me too. You always did.'

'Yes,' he said, 'I always did. But we both knew it couldn't happen.'

'And now it can,' she said. 'We can make it happen.'

'But not like this. It can't be like this, Lucy, you must see that. You've said it yourself, you can't just abandon Maud and Arthur. And what about Patsy? How could you live with me – with yourself – knowing you'd just walked out on them all?'

'But I've told you,' she said desperately, 'if I go back now, something will happen, something terrible, and I'll have to stay. I know it will. And then I'll never get away.'

By the time they returned to the house, they had talked in the same circle a dozen times, and still nothing had been decided. David urged her a dozen times to take time to think about it, to consider all the consequences before taking an irrevocable step. And a dozen times Lucy repeated that she dared not, that she had a premonition, that if she set foot again through the swing doors of Pengelly's Hotel, she would never be free . . . As they walked slowly back through the darkened streets to the house where she had grown up, she was beginning to tire, though. Her arguments had lost their febrile passion, and David could only hope that a night's sleep would complete the work.

'You know I love you,' he said as they came within sight of the house. 'You know there's nothing I want more than to be with you, but we can't do it at such cost to others. We would never be able to live in peace with ourselves.'

'David, I can't bear it.'

'You can,' he said, holding both her hands in his. 'You can. You're strong, Lucy. That's why you've come so far and done so much. And we *will* be together, I promise you that. We just have to wait a little longer.'

'I think we've waited too long already,' she said sadly, and turned away from him to go indoors.

She had to go back, of course. She knew that already, and knew that her moment of rebellion had been just that: a moment, no more. Going back to London with David, leaving Wilmot to return alone to Plymouth, knowing that Patsy was expecting her to come home, not to mention Maud and Arthur – no, it was impossible. A dream to play with.

'I shall come, all the same,' she said to him as they said goodbye at the railway station. 'As soon as I can make proper arrangements. I know I can't just abandon them all, but this is my life and I've lived it long enough for others.'

'I wonder if we ever have,' he said. 'I wonder if we even know . . . Goodbye Lucy, my dearest dear. Take care of yourself.'

They gazed at each other. The engine humphed impatiently at the end of the platform and a cloud of steam billowed out.

Wilmot had boarded the train first with the luggage and now his face appeared through the swirling mist. He stared at them suspiciously. 'How long are you going to be, Lucy? The train's just about to go.'

'I know. I'm coming.' She did not take her eyes away from David's. She hardly cared what Wilmot thought. He'd know the whole truth before long, anyway. 'Go back and wait for me –'

'I'd have thought you'd had plenty of time to hobnob together, the two of you.' His voice was jealous and he leant out and gripped Lucy's arm. 'Come on. Get aboard.'

'Wilmot, let go –' The whistle blew and the engine let out a trumpeting fanfare. Lucy gave David a despairing glance. 'David –'

'Go on, Lucy.' She was as close as she could come to

refusing to go, and he knew it. He gave her a gentle push. 'I'll see you again soon.'

'Yes. Yes. Soon.' Reluctantly, she climbed aboard and stood looking out through the open window. *'David –'*

'Goodbye, Lucy. Goodbye.' He stood still on the platform, looking at her, his hand thrust into his pocket. He tried to convey his feelings with his eyes. For two pins, he thought, he would have wrenched the door open and dragged her out again.

I love you. He saw her mouth shape the words and nodded them back to her. The wheels began to rattle, the pistons to scrape, and the train slid past the platform. Lucy was receding from him, her eyes wide and desperate. He closed his own eyes and shook his head, and when he opened them again she was almost gone, her face no more than a blur.

'David. I love you . . .' He must have imagined it. He could not possibly have heard her voice over the noise of the engine, but he carried the sound with him as he turned away and walked along the platform to catch his own train, and it rang in his ears all the way back to London.

'I don't like that fellow,' Wilmot said as soon as they were settled on the train. They had a compartment to themselves, and as there was no corridor, there was no fear of interruption until at least Eastleigh. Lucy looked at him in alarm. As far as she knew, he had had nothing to drink that morning, but he had been carrying a bag when they arrived at the station and she knew he had been to the off-licence on the way.

'Don't be silly. David's been a good friend. We've known him for years.'

'You've known him for years. Always in and out of the hotel. Don't think I don't know what's been going on.'

'I've told you before,' Lucy said, her heart beginning to

thump, 'nothing's been going on. David and I have never—'

'So you've said, so you've said.' He sounded offensively bored, as if hearing a lie for the hundredth time that he had never believed in the first place. 'Look, Lucy, I'm not a fool. I can see the way you look at each other. Does it really make any difference whether you've been to bed together or not? You'd like to, that's what matters. And one day, you will.'

Lucy was silent, shocked by his perception. She could not deny the truth of his words. She bit her lip and stared out of the window, knowing that Wilmot was watching her.

'You see?' he said, and he sounded tired and depressed. 'You see?'

Lucy turned swiftly. 'Wilmot –'

'Why don't you stop pretending?' he asked. 'Why don't you stop making out you're the good, loyal little wife – when all the time you're thinking about *him*, wanting to be with him? Why don't you stop being such a hypocrite?'

That stung her. 'Hypocrite? What do you mean? I'm not a hypocrite!'

'You are. Look at you. Lucy Pengelly, the little white saint. Butter wouldn't melt in her mouth. And look what she's got to put up with, saddled with that drunken sot of a husband, never does a hand's turn, no more good to her than a sore arse. That's what people say about you, isn't it? That's what you want them to say.'

'No, of course it isn't! I've never complained –'

'Well, of course you haven't,' he said. 'You're a saint, aren't you, and saints never complain. It's part of being saintly.'

'You're talking a lot of rubbish,' Lucy said coldly.

'I'm not. Just for once, I'm not.' He looked at her, curling his lip in a sneer. 'Saint Lucy. Except that we know different, don't we?'

'I've told you, I've never done anything wrong. I've never been unfaithful to you.'

'Listen,' Wilmot said, 'I may be a drunk but I'm not a fool. I saw the way you looked at him. I've seen the two of you these past few days, slipping away together whenever you've got the chance. I've seen your heads together, plotting and planning. You're going to leave me and go to him, aren't you? Well – aren't you?'

Lucy gasped. It was almost as if he had read her mind. She stared at him, feeling her face whiten as the blood drained away. Her head spun and she felt sick. 'I –'

'Don't try to make excuses,' he said. 'Don't try to cook up some sort of explanation. Just say yes.'

'Wilmot –'

'Just say yes,' he repeated, almost as if it was what he wanted to hear.

Lucy found her voice. It was no more than a husky whisper. 'What – what would you do if I did say yes?'

Wilmot looked at her and she saw his expression shift and knew that it wasn't what he'd wanted to hear. Despite his words, he had wanted her to say no. He wanted her to tell him that she had no intention of leaving.

His eyes dulled, and she knew that it was too late now, too late to do anything about it.

'What would I do?' he repeated flatly. 'I don't know. Chuck myself off a cliff, I should think.'

For the rest of the journey, they hardly spoke. Soon after that, the train had pulled into Eastleigh and several other people had climbed into their compartment. From then on, they were not alone again until they arrived at Plymouth. Somewhere between Dorchester and Bridport Lucy had produced a packet of sandwiches and a Thermos flask of tea, and offered them to Wilmot. He accepted a couple of sandwiches but refused the tea and took a bottle of beer from his own bag. She watched uneasily, hoping that he would not start heavy drinking, but it seemed he had only the one bottle with him.

Lucy nibbled her own sandwich. It was like dust. She stared out of the window, taking no joy in the passing scenery, thinking of Wilmot's words. It wasn't the first time he had threatened suicide, and she had on several occasions been frightened enough to take sharp knives out of the kitchen drawers and conceal them. But gradually she had come to believe that his threats were empty, designed only to draw attention to himself, and there was no real meaning in them. For a long time now, he had said nothing about killing himself.

Now, however, he had started again, and this time she was afraid that he meant it. There was a flatness in his tone that was quite different from the dramatic threats he had made before. It was as if he really didn't care whether he lived or not.

He can't feel like that about me leaving, she thought, feeling cold. He doesn't love me, any more than I love him. He doesn't really want me. Why would he talk like that? He'd be glad to get rid of me, glad to have the place to himself.

Or would he? Without her there, what would happen to Pengelly's? Maud and Arthur wouldn't be able to cope with running it. And she wouldn't dream of leaving Patsy as well – Patsy would come to London with her, she and David had agreed upon that. There would be nobody left who knew how to run the place. Wilmot would have to pull himself together and take charge.

She knew that he wouldn't do that. She knew that he couldn't.

It would be too much for him. If Lucy left Pengelly's the whole place would collapse. The responsibility of the hotel, of his own ageing parents, would crush Wilmot like a rock. He would not be able to bear it, and whatever happened it would be her fault.

By the time the train arrived panting at North Road station and they were gathering their bags together to disembark, Lucy knew that she was still trapped, as surely and as tightly as ever she had been, and there was no escape. She would not be able to leave Pengelly's and go to David.

I knew it would never happen, she thought as she scrambled down from the train and stood dejectedly upon the platform. I knew that if I didn't go from Portsmouth I wouldn't go at all.

And David had known it too. She had seen it in his eyes as he stood on the platform and watched her slide away from him, and as she cried her last words of love into the billowing steam.

Chapter Twenty-one

She couldn't give up that easily.

The hotel wrapped itself around her again like an octopus, its many and various demands like clinging tentacles, so that as fast as she disposed of one, another half-dozen were fastening themselves to her mind. The decorators, the builders, the plumbers, the carpet-fitters . . . The family – Maud, Arthur, Patsy . . . and Wilmot, hitting the bottle harder than ever, all pretence cast aside.

'I just wants a word about the west wall, that damp patch'll have to be seen to . . .'

'Look, the carpet you wanted ain't in yet, but we got another pattern you might like, it's a sort of bright orange with black bits in . . .'

'That new bathroom, it won't do the way you want it, the runout's too level, see, the water won't run away, take half a day to empty. Us'll have to raise the bath, and that means . . .'

'Lucy, have you noticed Arthur's colour lately? I don't like it. He looks proper grey round the gills sometimes, but he won't go to the doctor, I wondered if you'd have a word . . .'

'Why does everything depend on me?' Lucy asked in desperation. She was in the office with Patsy, working on the latest estimate for the redecorating. 'Can't anyone make a decision for themselves? How did they all manage while I was in Portsmouth?'

'They waited till you came back.' Patsy was eighteen

now, and would have been a tall young woman. She took care of herself and kept her long, dark red hair as glossy as a Christmas bell. Her skin had the faint translucency of fine bone china and her eyes were the deep, velvety purple of summer pansies. She was a beautiful girl, Lucy realised suddenly, and wondered why she had never noticed it before. What a shame she was confined to a wheelchair. What man was ever going to want to marry a girl who couldn't walk?

'Well, I'm tired of coping with it all. It's time your father pulled his weight.'

Patsy glanced sideways at her. 'You ought to know by now. Dad's never going to be any help.'

'Patsy! You shouldn't talk like that about your father –'

'Oh, face facts, Mum.' There was no bitterness in the girl's voice, just sadness. 'Dad's just been getting worse and worse, and he's not going to get any better. Not the way things are. He's drinking all the time.' She paused. 'I had to tell him to go away yesterday. He was getting himself in a state – people were looking at him. It's bad for the hotel, I know, but it's worse for him –'

'What do you mean, in a state?' Lucy interrupted. 'What was he doing?'

'Oh, nothing much. Just talking, really. Talking to everyone. Nobody could put their head round the door without him starting on them. It was only the workmen, but what are guests going to think if he does it to them? And he feels so awful afterwards, I know he does.'

Lucy gazed at her. 'Was he drunk?'

'Well, more or less. I mean, he always is, to some extent. He must be, he drinks so much, it's just that he's got used to it so it doesn't show like it would in another person.' Patsy looked at her mother. Her eyes were glimmering with tears. 'Mum, something's got to be done to help him. I can't bear seeing him like that.'

Lucy sighed and ran her fingers through her hair. Kitty

had persuaded her to have it cut short while she was in Portsmouth and it clustered in fiery curls around her face, with only a few silver hairs gleaming among the rich auburn. 'I'll take away all his bottles. He won't be *able* to drink.'

'I don't think that'll stop him. I expect he's got them hidden all over the house.'

'I'll find them. I'll find them all.'

Patsy shook her head. 'He'll just get more, Mum. You can't lock him up. Look –' she shuffled amongst the papers on her desk and produced a sheet of newspaper – 'I was reading this. It's about something called Alcoholics Anonymous. It's a sort of association for people who can't stop drinking.'

'For heaven's sake!' Lucy exclaimed. 'We don't want him joining a *club*!'

'It's not like that. It's to help them stop. It was started in America before the war. People go to meetings every week and they help each other. They have to stop drinking absolutely. Never touch another drop.'

'I can't think of anything better,' Lucy said. 'Or anything more unlikely. Your father's never going to agree to that. He likes his drink. It's just about all he lives for.'

'But it's not doing him any good. I've been reading about it, Mum. It's not just about getting drunk – it'll make him really ill. He already *is* ill. It says here, it's an illness, this not being able to stop drinking. And these people can help. They look after each other.' She laid the paper down and looked at Lucy. 'At least we could *try*. Try to get him to join. If he went to just one meeting – just to *see* . . .'

Lucy twisted her lips together in doubt. 'I can't believe he'll agree, Patsy. But all right, we'll try.' And it just might work, she added to herself, and if he really did give up drinking, perhaps he'd take over the hotel and look after his parents, and then I could go . . . Oh, David, David . . .

*

Wilmot stared at her. He wouldn't even look at the sheet of newspaper at first, and when he did he ripped it into pieces and threw them to the floor. Lucy's heart sank. She hadn't really expected anything different, but now her last shred of hope was destroyed.

'If only you'd just think about it, Wilmot –'

'Think about it? *Think* about it? There's nothing to think about. You're saying I'm a drunk, that's it, isn't it? You've been chucking out hints for months and now you're saying so outright. Just because I like a drop of winter warmer. Look, we had a rum issue every day in the Navy, every bloke over eighteen got it, a proper tot of good Navy rum – stronger than any of this watered-down stuff you get ashore. Would they have issued us that if it had been bad for us? Would they?'

'I don't know why they issued it,' Lucy said. She was half afraid of Wilmot's fury. His temper had grown worse than ever and she dreaded the day when he lost control completely. 'Someone told me it was to kill the germs in bad food when they were at sea for long periods on the old sailing-ships. Or to keep the men under control . . . I don't know. But it can't be good for young boys to be given strong drink, day after day, week in, week out. Of *course* they get used to it, of *course* they can't give it up. And they end up wanting more and more. It stands to reason.'

'Well, we didn't get it, did we? Not us poor buggers who ended up in Japanese prison camp. Not the blokes that slaved and died on the Burma railway. Not the poor sods who spent months in solitary confinement, surviving on a bowl of mouldy rice a day. None of us got rum issue then. We went without for years.'

'Well, you're certainly making up for it now,' Lucy snapped.

Wilmot looked at her. His eyes were red rimmed and bleary, his skin grey, his chin rough and unshaven. She felt disgust, mingled with pity. I shouldn't have said that, she thought. He's right. And he has to have allowance made for the suffering he endured.

'So that's what you think,' he said. 'Never mind what we did, going to sea and fighting for our country. It's all forgotten now, isn't it? Chasing the *Graf Spee* all over the Atlantic till we got her to her knees. We lost men then, if you remember. We were damaged then. But we didn't give up. Off out to the Med, sinking German ships – out to the Far East. Have you got any idea what it was like out there, fighting those Japs? Don't you think *you'd* want to forget it all, Luce?' he said more quietly. 'Don't you think *you'd* want a drink now and then?'

Lucy gazed at him. Pity was uppermost again, disgust merely lingering at the edges. 'Yes,' she said, 'I expect I would. But, Wilmot, don't you think you're drinking too much now? Don't you think it's got the better of you? It's making you ill, you see, and when you can't stop you need help. You'd be so much better if—'

'Can't stop? Who says I can't stop? I can stop any time I want to. *Any* time. Drink's not a problem to me, Luce. It's you that's got the problem.'

'Wilmot, how can you say that? It's not me who can't get up in the morning, who starts on the bottle at breakfast-time, it's not me who can't walk straight by lunchtime or talk without slurring the words. And just as well too, because if we were all like you this hotel wouldn't be where it is now and we'd all be in the gutter.'

'That's right, chuck that at me. It always comes to that, doesn't it? You're the one we all depend on, the one we've all got to thank. And have we got to thank you! On our bended knees, three times a day and facing Mecca. Nothing else will do, will it?' He snorted his derision. 'Oh, stroll on. Saint Lucy! Saint *bloody* Lucy.'

Lucy sighed. It didn't matter how she tried to approach the situation, it always ended like this. And she knew just what would happen next. Wilmot would slam out of the room and go straight upstairs to one of his hidden caches and drink. It was an act of defiance against her. An act, she was beginning to fear, of sheer hatred.

Since returning from Portsmouth, they had been sleeping in separate rooms. Nothing had been said. Lucy had simply removed her belongings from the bedroom and moved into Geoff's room. It was smaller but at least she had it to herself and didn't have to step over the pile of clothes Wilmot scattered around the floor, or sleep with the stink of stale rum and beer in her nostrils.

Nor did she have to endure his sexual attentions, doomed for months now to messy and painful failure.

She bent to pick up the tattered shreds of newspaper he had scattered on the floor. So much for Alcoholics Anonymous. Perhaps they would work for some people, but surely only if you really wanted them to work. There was no point at all in forcing someone to attend who wouldn't even admit they had a problem.

I could walk away from it all, she thought. I could leave him to drink himself to death. He's going to do it anyway, whether I'm here or not. I could tell his mum and dad that we've got to sell the hotel – they could retire on the proceeds and buy themselves a nice bungalow in Newton Ferrers, like they've always wanted – and Patsy and me could go to London. To David. It's what I ought to have done the minute we came back from Pompey.

She couldn't give up that easily.

Now that the idea of selling the hotel had entered her mind, Lucy found herself considering it more and more seriously, convinced that it was the answer for them all.

In the few years since the war, she had almost singlehandedly built it up from a small, inexpensive guest house to a smart hotel, patronised by businessmen who wanted somewhere of class to stay but didn't want to pay Duke of Cornwall prices. Pengelly's, standing a little nearer to the Hoe, met their expectations. Newly refurbished, extended and with a good dining-room where they could entertain their business friends, it quickly acquired a reputation and was now amongst the best-recommended of all Plymouth hotels.

At the same time, it had not lost its family atmosphere. The entrance hall, enlarged and carpeted, had kept a fireplace in which Lucy made sure logs were always burning in winter, or kept bright with a large display of flowers in summer. Two or three small tables with armchairs and a sofa arranged around them invited guests to make themselves comfortable while they waited. And Patsy's bright smile welcomed them as soon as they walked through the swing doors.

Pengelly's would be a good buy. And now that the country was picking up and Plymouth's rebuilding progressing more quickly, people would be looking towards the city for business opportunities. It surely wouldn't be hard to sell.

She began to take more notice of Maud's worries over Arthur.

'What does the doctor say?'

'Tells him he's got to take care of himself. His heart's not strong.'

Lucy looked at her. 'What do you think he ought to do?'

'Do? What can he do? It's age, that's all there is to it.'

'Well, you could think about retiring,' Lucy ventured.

Her mother-in-law stared at her. 'Retire? I thought we already had retired. All I do these days is give you a bit of a hand with the vegetables and that, and Arthur does nothing. Polishes a bit of brass now and then. Nothing more. If that's not being retired, I dunno what is.'

'No, I mean move somewhere more convenient for you. Somewhere without a lot of stairs. A nice little bungalow of your own. Newton Ferrers way, perhaps – you know you've always liked it there.'

'A bungalow? Newton Ferrers? *Are* there any bungalows in Newton Ferrers?'

'I've no idea,' Lucy said, startled. 'It was just that you've always talked about it . . . we could find out. If you think you'd like it. It doesn't have to be there, of course, you could stay in Plymouth. Or Plympton, it's nice there. You can choose what you like. But it could be better for you than being here. It would be quieter.'

'Not be in the hotel any more?' Maud said. Lucy could not tell whether the idea pleased or dismayed her. 'Not be here with the rest of you?'

'Well . . .' It wasn't perhaps the moment to say that she herself was thinking of leaving, leaving both the hotel and Wilmot. Certainly not to say that she wanted to sell the hotel to provide the money for this new bungalow, for Maud and Arthur's retirement and a home of some sort for Wilmot. 'It's just a suggestion,' she said. 'Just something to think about.'

'Well, I don't know,' Maud said, and it was still impossible to say whether she liked the proposal or not. Perhaps she wasn't sure herself. 'I don't know. I'll have to talk to Arthur about it. What does Wilmot say?'

'I haven't actually mentioned it to him,' Lucy confessed. 'I thought it was best for you to think about it before we go any further.'

'Yes, probably just as well,' Maud said, to her relief. 'Well, I'll turn it over in me mind. I suppose it'd help the hotel a bit. Give you a bit more room for guests.'

'Yes, I suppose so.' Lucy hadn't thought of that. She had been looking on it simply as a first step to selling. 'But that's not why – I mean, don't think I'm trying to get rid of you, Mum.'

'No,' Maud said, and smiled at her. 'I don't think that.'

She went out and Lucy sat back in her chair. She felt a little guilty. She had always got on well with her mother-in-law, and they had lived through some difficult times together. They had shared so much. She felt ashamed of her planning now and wished she could have taken Maud into her confidence, but that was impossible. You just did not sit down with your elderly mother-in-law and tell her you were planning not only to break up the family home but to leave her son as well.

The door opened again and Jilly came in. She gave Lucy an uncertain glance.

'Could I talk to you for a minute?'

Lucy hesitated. She hadn't seen much of Jilly since she had come back, hadn't given her much thought. The girl looked peaky, she thought, and rather miserable. Pining for Geoff, probably. Well, there was nothing to be done about that, and she'd have been just as lonely if they'd been allowed to get married before he went away.

'Is it important, Jilly? I've got rather a lot on my mind at the moment.'

'It's about Geoff's dad. He doesn't want me here.' Jilly's eyes filled with tears. 'While you were away – he told me then, he said he couldn't stand me about the place. He said I reminded him too much of – of Geoff – and that made him think about the camp. He said he'd be better if I left – he said you'd all be better . . . Well, I just wanted to know if he'd told you, and what you thought about it, that's all.' The blue eyes were huge. 'Because I think maybe he's right and it would be better if I went away.'

Lucy stared at her. 'Went away? *Wilmot* told you to go away?'

Jilly lifted her shoulders. 'Ask old Mrs Pengelly. She was here when he said it.'

Lucy leant her elbows on the table and lifted her hands to her face. She closed her eyes. I'll walk out now, she said to herself. I'll get up from this table and walk out of this kitchen and out of this hotel and go straight to North Road station and get on a train for London. Just as I am. I won't even bother to put a coat on. I'll telephone David from

274

Paddington and he can come and fetch me and we'll go back to his house and that's where I'll live from then on. I'll never come back again, never, and they can just get on as best they can without me.

'Well,' she said, 'he hasn't said anything to me. He's probably forgotten all about it by now. I wouldn't worry about it any more, if I were you.'

'No, all right.' Jilly half rose and then stood hesitant once more. 'There – there was just one more thing. I think I ought to tell you – I mean, I'm not actually sure, but I think I may be—' She was interrupted by a call from the front hall. She stopped abruptly and they stared at each other. 'That sounded like Patsy!'

'It did.' Lucy was on her feet. 'Oh my God, what's happened now? Don't say Arthur's been taken ill. Or Maud –' She pushed past Jilly and they ran together down the short corridor to the front hall. 'Patsy, what is it? What's happened?'

'Mum,' Patsy said faintly. 'Oh, *Mum* –'

Lucy stopped short. The years reeled away as she took in the scene before her. The boy in his dark blue uniform, the brown sack over his shoulder, the buff envelope in her daughter's hand. The scrap of paper with its letters stuck unevenly across it.

'A telegram,' she said, and wondered at the sudden flood of dread. It wasn't such an uncommon occurrence, after all. Guests frequently sent telegrams to the hotel. Patsy's face, however, bone white, told her that this was no ordinary telegram, and behind her she heard Jilly's gasp and knew that her dread was shared. 'What is it? Patsy, *what is it?*'

'It's Geoff,' Patsy said dully. 'Mum – Jilly – Geoff's missing.' She stared at the telegram again, her lips moving as if she were reading the words silently to herself, as if by reading them once more she could make them say something different. 'Missing in action . . . presumed *dead* . . .'

Chapter Twenty-two

Wilmot took the news worse than anyone else. Predictably, his response was to turn to his only friend in the world: his bottle.

'For heaven's sake,' Lucy said. She was beyond patience with him now. 'Don't you have any willpower at all? Don't you have any self-respect? Don't you think the rest of us are just as upset? *We're* not taking to the bottle, are we? *We're* not drinking ourselves stupid night after night.'

'It's different for you. I'm his father.'

'And I'm his mother. And Patsy's his sister, and your mum and dad are his grandparents, and Jilly –' It was difficult to say what Jilly was. 'Jilly's his fiancée. Or was.'

'A son's special to a man,' Wilmot blustered. 'Ask anyone.' He lifted his bottle and went to pour another glass of rum.

Lucy snatched it away. 'No more special than he is to his mother. Wilmot, I am sick and tired of you taking everything that happens as if it only happens to you. This is mine as well. I brought Geoff up all those years when you were away, I knew him a thousand times better than you did, he was my companion, my right hand –'

'Oh, that's right. Bring it back to that again. I wasn't out in Japan on a bloody picnic, you know. I just happened to be fighting for my country. For you. Or perhaps you'd forgotten that.'

'Of course I haven't forgotten it. I'll never forget it. But it isn't what we're talking about now. It's Geoff we're talking about, Geoff. And he's missing – presumed dead. Wilmot,

Geoff is almost certainly, *dead.*' Her voice rose in a cry for help, for comfort and understanding.

Wilmot turned aside and away from her, and when he replied his tone was filled with his own angry pain. 'I know. I *know.* You don't have to keep on about it. For God's sake – anyone would think you enjoyed repeating it, over and over again. Geoff's dead,' he mimicked her. 'Geoff's dead. Anyone would think you had to keep on saying it just to believe it.'

'I do. I do. I can't believe it if I don't hear the words. I can't take them in. Wilmot,' she raised her tear-stained face towards him, 'we shouldn't be rowing over it. We should be helping each other. Holding each other. Hold me now, Wilmot, please. Just put your arms round me like you used to and hold me close for a few minutes. For God's sake, I just want some comfort, can't you see?'

He stared at her, then, very deliberately, he reached across the table and took back the bottle she had snatched from his grasp. He poured the drink she had denied him and lifted it to his lips in a long swallow.

'That's my comfort, Lucy. The only comfort you can trust.' He put the glass down and looked at it, and his lip curled a little. 'And there's precious little comfort even there now,' he added quietly. 'Precious little comfort to be had anywhere now.' He lifted his eyes towards her. 'It's all my fault. Everything that goes wrong in this family is my fault.'

'Wilmot, don't be silly.'

'Silly. Yes, that's what I am, that's all you think of me, isn't it? Silly. Silly to join the Navy in the first place, silly to go off to war, silly to get sunk and caught by the Japs, silly to come home, silly to let Geoff join the Army – silly, silly, *silly.*' He laughed suddenly and Lucy tried to close her ears against the ugliness of the sound. 'Silly to be born at all.'

'Wilmot –'

'Well, isn't it true?' His voice was truculent. 'Wouldn't it have been better for everyone if I'd never been born?'

Lucy sat very still, then she raised her head and looked at him. She felt bitterly sorry for him, but over-riding her pity was anger, and a sour, gritty disgust.

'You're pathetic,' she said at last. 'That's what you are. It doesn't matter what happens, you've got to take it for yourself, as if you're the only one with a right to feel bad about it. It's got to be you, you, you, all the time. Never mind me, never mind Patsy or your mum and dad, or poor Jilly. You've got to be the centre of attention. And do you know something? I've had enough of it. *Enough.*'

He stood up suddenly, scraping his chair back, and stumbled towards the door. Lucy watched dully. She had done her best. She had tried to give him comfort even when she needed it most herself, she had asked for his help, and nothing had penetrated the barriers he had created about himself. There was nothing left for them now.

Arthur was completely broken. It was as if he had reached the point where he could not have stood any kind of bad news, and this was the worst imaginable. He made no fuss, demanded no attention, simply retreated into himself and seemed to fade away before their eyes.

He didn't even want to listen to the wireless, even when his favourite programmes were on – *Music While You Work* or *Workers' Playtime* during the day, *Ray's A Laugh* or *Take It From Here* in the evenings. The only programme he asked for, plaintively each evening, was *Dick Barton – Special Agent*, and Maud and Lucy had to explain to him over and over again that it wasn't on any more, the new farming serial *The Archers* had taken its place.

'Why did they do that, then?' he asked, his moustache trembling. 'I liked Dick Barton, and Jock and Snowy. They had some good stories. This farming stuff won't last, people aren't interested in that kind of thing.'

'I quite like it myself,' Maud said. 'Dan and Doris and their kids – that young Phil's a caution – and all the village people. It's nice family stories.'

'Bit of action, that's what people want,' Arthur grumbled. '*Geoff* liked Dick Barton.'

Nobody answered. They all knew that Geoff had liked Dick Barton, making sure he was in at a quarter to seven each evening to hear the exciting, galloping music that began it, or listening to the omnibus edition on Saturday mornings while he worked on his motorbike.

Maud, at seventy, was as stalwart as ever. She had been through so much in her lifetime, Lucy thought, that she had either grown hardened to grief or had developed huge inner resources. She made no secret of her distress, but she didn't let it weaken her either. She just got on with living and with looking after them all. She was like a rock in the centre of a sea of grief, letting them all wash up against her and cling for a while. Dimly, Lucy realised how much she had depended on her mother-in-law all these years.

'You've always been here. I don't know what we'd have done without you.'

'Don't talk so silly,' Maud said. 'We just do whatever we've got to do. You've kept us all going. Look what you've done for Pengelly's. We'd never have got the place going like you did after the war. It would still be a little guest house, or we'd have gone bankrupt. You know what things were like.'

'And maybe Geoff would still be alive,' Lucy said, but Maud shook her head.

'That would have happened just the same. You've got to remember God's will. If he wanted Geoff—'

'But *why* should he want him?' Lucy struck the table with her hand. 'Why does it have to be the people *I* love that God wants? Why can't he wait for them to get old, why can't he let them have their lives first? Little Zannah, and now Geoff – and he can't even let Patsy have a proper life, she's got to be hurt. And Wilmot. He says he'd be better off dead and sometimes I think he's right. What sort of a life has he got, for heaven's sake? Why doesn't God take *him*?'

'*Lucy!*'

'I can't help it. I'm fed up with God taking everything that means anything to me. I'm fed up with it!'

She heard a sound behind her and turned in her chair to meet her husband's eyes. They stared at each other and she knew he had heard her words.

'Wilmot –'

'It's all right,' he said. 'It's all right. I know now. I know what you really think.'

'Wilmot, come and sit down. I didn't mean—'

'It's all right,' he repeated, and turned away. Lucy jumped out of her chair and ran to catch him by the arm. 'Let me go.' His voice was dull and flat. 'Let me go.'

'No! You've got to come and sit down. Let me explain.'

'I heard what you said. I know what you meant.' He dragged his arm loose. 'It doesn't matter. Nothing matters any more. Just let me go.'

Lucy fell back, staring at him. He gave her a look of bottomless despair, his eyes like pits, and turned away. They heard his footsteps going down the passage and out of the back door.

'Oh, Mum . . . What do you think he's going to do?'

'Nothing silly,' Maud said, but she sounded shaken and uncertain. 'He wouldn't have the energy. Don't worry, Lucy.'

'He heard what I said. He heard me say why didn't God take him?' She sat down and buried her face in her hands. 'If he does anything, it'll be my fault.'

'He won't do anything. He'll just drink a bit more and forget about it. You know that's what he'll do. It's what he always does.' Maud reached over to touch her hand. 'Lucy, we've got to hold on, we've got to get through this together. We've got to help each other. We can't give up now.'

We can't give up now. Lucy took her hands away from her face and stared at her mother-in-law. She thought of her plans, her idea of selling the hotel, establishing Maud and Arthur in a nice little bungalow, giving Wilmot enough money for a place of his own, and then taking Patsy and herself to London to be with David. And she saw them for what they were.

Dreams. Golden, insubstantial dreams.

She could never do it.

Jilly was inconsolable.

'If only we'd got married before he went,' she sobbed. 'We wanted to be married and you wouldn't let us. I should have been his *wife* . . .'

'It wouldn't have made any difference,' Lucy began helplessly, but Jilly turned on her in a fury.

'Of course it would have made a difference. It would have made a difference to *me*. It would have made a difference to *him*. How can you say it wouldn't have made any difference?'

'I only meant, it wouldn't have made any difference to – to what happened.'

'I know that,' Jilly said with bitter scorn. 'I'm not a *fool*, Mrs Pengelly. But it would have made all the difference in the world to us.'

Lucy was silent. It was difficult for her to accept Jilly's words, for they presented Geoff to her as if in a different world. Not her son any longer, but a grown man, married, with a life of his own. Perhaps that's why I didn't want them to be married, she thought. Because I didn't want him to take that step away from me, the last step a child does take away from its parents. After they're married, you have to take a back seat. They don't have to wait to be twenty-one then, to be independent.

But that's why they *do* have to wait till they're twenty-one. Under that age, they're just too young to take responsibility for their own lives. Until then, parents have to do it for them, it's what parents are for . . .

'It's not fair,' Jilly said bitterly, just as Lucy herself had said years ago. 'Old enough to go to war, old enough to fight for his country – or someone else's country – but not old enough to live his own life. It's not *fair*.'

'Life isn't fair,' Lucy said, as she had herself so painfully learned. 'It's no use expecting it.'

'But you could have made it a bit *more* fair. You could have let us get married.'

Lucy sighed. She felt sorry for the girl, very sorry – but they'd been all through this before. And seeing Jilly's grief wasn't helping her to get over her own. She said, rather tersely, 'Yes, maybe I could, but I didn't, and nothing can change that. We can't turn the clock back and do things differently. And it doesn't help to keep going on and on about it, it really doesn't. We've got to look forward now, Jilly, we've got to start building our lives up again. And you're young. You'll get over it. You'll find someone else—'

'*Oh!*' It was like a shriek. Jilly stared at her, wild eyed. 'You don't understand, do you? You just don't understand. You never will. Oh, what am I going to do, what am I going to *do*?' She lifted her fists to her forehead and clutched at her hair.

Lucy watched her. 'You're hysterical, Jilly. You'd better take yourself out for a walk, or find something to do. It isn't a bit of use giving way like this.'

'Isn't it? Isn't it? Then perhaps you could tell me what would be any use. Oh, it's no use asking. You won't help me. You wouldn't before and you won't now. Oh, Geoff, *Geoff* . . .' She broke into sobs.

Lucy bit her lip. It wasn't helping any of them to let the girl go on like this. Perhaps she'd be better off away from the hotel, away from them all. Out of Plymouth, removed from the house where she had lived so close to Geoff, from

282

the places they'd visited together, she might begin to recover. And she wouldn't be there to remind the rest of them of what might have been.

'Look,' she said gently when Jilly's sobs had subsided a little, 'why don't you go home for a while? A break would do you good. Your mother would be pleased to see you, I'm sure. It would help you to forget.'

'I'll never forget,' Jilly said. 'I don't want to forget.' She wiped her eyes and looked thoughtful. 'Do you want me to go? Do you want to get rid of me? Would you like me to leave altogether?'

'Jilly, it's not that —' Lucy began, and then stopped. Perhaps it would be best, after all, if Jilly left them and found herself another job. Better for Jilly herself. 'I just think we could all do with a break,' she said. 'Go home for a few weeks, Jilly, and then we'll see how we feel.' She touched the girl's arm gently. 'That's all I'm suggesting. Let's give ourselves time to think.'

Jilly looked at her. There was something in the girl's eyes, Lucy thought, a hesitation, as if she had something else to say, but the moment passed and Jilly shrugged and moved away from Lucy's touch.

'All right. If that's what you want.' She sounded tired, defeated. 'I'll send Mum a telegram and I'll go tomorrow.'

Lucy nodded, and turned away. There was work to be done, and enough time had been spent in talking and grieving. In a week, the hotel was to be fully open again, and if Jilly were not to be here a new cook must be found, and more help employed in the kitchen and bedrooms. Life must go on. And at some point, she must find time to write to David and tell him she wasn't coming to London after all.

The thought was like a knife slicing into her heart. This time, she thought, it really must be all over. I just can't bear the pain of seeing him again, talking to him, knowing what we so nearly had, knowing that it will never, never be possible . . .

From today, she must cut David out of her life as surely and irrevocably as Geoff had been cut out. As if he too were dead.

Jilly had left the hotel the day after her talk with Lucy, and the Pengellys didn't expect to see her again. She seemed to have recovered from her hysterics and her face was pale and set as she humped her suitcases downstairs. The family were waiting in the front hall and Patsy had called a taxi which was already parked outside.

'You will come back, won't you?' she said as Jilly came round the desk to hug her. 'You're only going for a holiday.'

'I don't know. It depends on your mum.'

'She'll want you to come back. I know she will.'

Jilly shook her head doubtfully and gave Patsy a kiss. 'I wish you could come and stay with me in Cornwall.'

'I will. I'll come in the summer. But you'll be back here by then.'

'I might be. But if not –'

'I'll see you in the summer,' Patsy promised. 'One way or another, I'll see you then. And I'll come and stay when you have your holidays as well.'

Jilly smiled. 'You've been a good friend, Patsy. I wish we could have been sisters.'

'We are,' Patsy said, suddenly serious. 'We're proper sisters.'

'The taxi's waiting,' Lucy said, and Jilly turned away and went out through the swing doors. At the foot of the steps, she paused and looked back, waiting as Patsy wheeled her chair down the ramp.

Geoff's bedroom window was high above her, an attic window looking out over the rooftops towards the Sound. Lucy slept there now, but to Jilly it was Geoff's room and always would be. She stared up at it, almost imagining that she could see his face there, peeping down, and his hand waving.

Geoff . . .

She turned abruptly and got into the taxi.

The family stood hesitant on the pavement. Arthur glanced from Lucy to Wilmot. 'Well, isn't anyone going to go with the maid? Give her a hand with her bits and bobs?' His moustache quivered. 'A fine send-off, this is, I'll be bound. Pengelly's can do a bit better than this.' He pulled open the door of the car and started to climb in.

'Dad!' Lucy protested. 'You can't –'

'I can. I'm doing it.' He glowered out at her and glared at his son. 'I'm ashamed of you, Wilmot, I'm ashamed of the pair of you. Letting a little maid go off all by herself. Well, her's always been a proper helpful and kindly maid to me, and I'll not let her go like this. *I'll* give her a hand, and I'll see her on her way proper. The rest of you had better get back about your own business. I daresay you've all got jobs to do.'

He slammed the door shut and the taxi started up. Lucy made one more effort to stop him, but she was too late. The car was drawing away from the kerb.

Nobody spoke. Lucy glanced at them, feeling her colour heighten. 'Well, what are you all staring at? I suppose you think I should have gone with her?'

Wilmot shrugged and turned away. He had already lost interest. Maud and Patsy gave each other a swift look. Maud said, ''Tis up to you, maid. 'Tis not for me to say what you should do.'

'Well, I don't mind saying,' Patsy declared. 'Yes, Mum, I do think you should have gone with her. Why not? What quarrel do we have with poor Jilly? All she's done is love our Geoff, and he loved her too. Would he have wanted you to send her away with nobody but Grampy to help her with her bags? Would he have wanted her to be sent away at all?'

'I didn't send her away. It was her own wish.' But Lucy remembered with discomfort that conversation with Jilly. It *had* been Lucy's suggestion. 'It was the best thing for her,' she said pleadingly. 'She needed to get away, to start to forget. She can't live her life grieving for Geoff. She's young –'

'She needed someone to help her,' Patsy said bluntly. 'She needed someone to love her, and not to feel she was being thrown out.' She paused for a moment and said, 'You know she'll never come back, don't you?'

'And if she doesn't, that will be her own decision. She knows there's a job here for her at any time.'

'A job!' Patsy said bitterly. 'When she ought to have been one of the family.'

She turned her chair round and wheeled it back up the ramp. Lucy hurried forwards and pushed from behind. She felt disconcerted and upset. And, uncomfortably, that Patsy was right and she had treated Jilly shabbily.

Writing to David was the hardest thing she had ever done.

We've spent half our lives doing this, she thought, sitting at her desk with a sheet of paper in front of her. Half our lives trying not to love each other, half trying to find a way to be together . . . we were always going to hurt someone. Wilmot, Maud, Arthur, the children . . . All we've ended up doing is hurting ourselves.

Once again, however, there didn't seem to be any choice. She could not leave Wilmot now, with his anxiety over Geoff smothering him in a black cloud of depression. She could not leave Arthur, whose burst of energy when Jilly left had evaporated once more, leaving him like a grey shadow haunting the recesses of the hotel. She could not leave Maud, who had stood by her and offered comfort when she herself had most needed it.

And she knew that even if *she* had done so, Patsy would not leave them. And she could not leave Patsy.

Oh David, David,

I love you so much, and I have to let you go. Since

Geoff went away, everything has been so impossible. I feel I am all that is keeping this family together and if I leave them now, they'll fall apart. I can't do it to them. I can't do it to poor old Arthur, who won't even understand, or Maud who will be so disappointed, or Wilmot who will just drink himself to death. And Patsy — I don't know what Patsy thinks of me these days, but I know that if I walk out now, she'll think even less of me. And she won't come too. She'll stay behind and take on this burden. I can't do that to her, and I can't bear to think of losing her.

She stopped writing. Her eyes were too full of tears and the page was blurred and dissolving under her gaze. She lifted her head, trying to draw the tears back into herself, not wanting to let them fall, but they ran out of her eyes and flowed like a burning river down her icy cheeks.

'I love you so much,' she wrote again, 'but we have to say goodbye. Don't write back to me, David. Don't ever write to me again. I won't have the strength . . .'

She folded the page quickly, before she could change her mind, pushed it into an envelope and addressed it to his home in London. She found a stamp and stuck it on and then got up and walked out of the hotel and down the street to the postbox. The red pillarbox swallowed her letter as if it had not eaten for a week. She stood in front of it, staring at the wide black mouth, desperation welling up inside her. The letter was there, only a foot away from her, and yet it had gone. It was as far away from her as if she had sent it to the moon, and until David received it nobody would know what was inside it.

There was no way in which she could prevent him getting it and opening it and knowing what she had written. By next morning, he would know. By next morning, it would be all over.

Lucy turned and walked back up the street. She passed

Pengelly's without a glance and walked on up to the Hoe. For an hour she paced there on the wide, green expanse overlooking the Sound, where Drake had once played bowls. She leant on the railings and gazed down at the little bathing-pools in the rocks and the big semicircular swimming-pool where she had taught Wilmot to swim so long ago, and she lifted her eyes and looked out across the glittering sea past Drake's Island and the breakwater, to the thin, pencil shape of the Eddystone Lighthouse, sharp as an exclamation mark on the far horizon.

When she came back to the hotel she had, with some determination, put all her previous life behind her, and was ready to start again.

Chapter Twenty-three

Jilly finished the washing-up and dried her hands. She left the dishes piled on the wooden draining-board to dry, and wandered out through the back door into the garden. It was a perfect May morning, with a few late narcissi flowering beneath the gnarled branches of the old apple trees and a flurry of small birds dashing to and fro with beaks filled with tiny, struggling worms and insects. She sank into a battered deckchair and closed her eyes.

Her mother was still indoors, looking after old Mrs Tremaine. David's aunt was over ninety now, almost blind and very frail, though she still had, as the villagers observed, all her marbles. It irritated her profoundly that she could no longer see to read, and one of Jilly's jobs was to spend half an hour or so, at intervals during the day, reading her latest library book aloud. At present, they were working through Dickens, all of whose books old Mrs Tremaine had read years ago but wanted to revisit, and when they'd finished those they were going to start on Anthony Trollope. In between, she liked something lighter, a Regency novel by Georgette Heyer perhaps, or one of Elizabeth Goudge's family stories.

'You read very nicely, dear,' she said as Jilly fell silent. 'Now let's be quiet for a bit. Tell me what you can see, and I'll be able to imagine everything.'

So Jilly would describe the garden; the last lingering flowers of spring, the primroses in the bank, the violets scattering their purple freckles in the grass, the snowy blossom on the apple trees. She talked about the blackbird's nest in the hedge and the scurrying bluetits who were already feeding their first brood in the hole in the stone-filled Cornish bank. She painted a word picture of the pale blue sky, feathered with high white clouds, and when Blackie, the cat, came stalking through the grass she lifted him on to her knee and guided Mrs Tremaine's hand to his furry back.

After that, they sat quietly together and just listened to the sounds: Blackie's purring, the twittering of the bluetits, the alarmed shriek of the blackbird when it noticed the cat, the rustling of the breeze amongst the leaves. Sometimes it was so quiet that Jilly fancied she could hear the whisper of the clouds flying high overhead, and the murmuring of the violets at her feet.

It seemed a very long way here from the horrors of war. Jilly remembered her childhood. She had grown up in the village, only five years old when the war began, but it seemed to have made little difference down here in deepest Cornwall. They had had no air raids, no sirens, no bombs. The blackout hadn't made much difference to villages that had never had streetlights anyway. Even later, when American soldiers had been stationed near by, it hadn't seemed like war, more like a big, cheerful party that went on for months, until suddenly, mysteriously, they all disappeared and the wireless and newspapers had been full of something called D-Day. After that, although the war still dragged on and rationing got worse even here, where people grew their own eggs and vegetables, everyone seemed much more optimistic and it hadn't come as a surprise at all to know that the whole thing was over and the country could look forward to peace again.

Peace. Love and laughter. Buried softly here in this little Eden, Jilly knew that they could have known nothing of the reality of war. Even though some of the young men had gone, never to return, their names now carved on the little stone cross that had been placed outside the church, the village had not really understood what it was like. *She* had not understood; not until she went to Plymouth and saw the destruction there, and looked into the greyness of the people's faces and felt the miasma of weariness and depression that hung over them like an old, encrusted cobweb. They were getting themselves together, the determination that had got them through the war was pushing them on, but she could feel their tiredness, their growing hopelessness as things got worse instead of better, as rationing increased, as they faced the enormous and daunting task of rebuilding the city, their homes, their lives.

It seemed that no sooner had they begun this, than Korea happened, and it all started again. Not the bombing, not the air-raids, but the grinding misery of seeing their young men go off to fight just when they'd been expecting to start living their own lives. The anguish of knowing that some of them would not come back.

Geoff had not come back. Jilly could hardly believe now that he would ever come back. And his name would not appear on any stone cross. He would be forgotten.

David found her there in the old deckchair, her eyes closed, listening as his old aunt liked to listen, to the birds singing and the sighing of the breeze. There was another chair beside her and he dropped into it and stayed quiet, waiting for her to realise he was there. After a bit, she stirred and opened her eyes, and then turned her head.

'Mr Tremaine.' She sat up straight. 'I didn't know you were there.'

'I've been very quiet. I thought you might be asleep.'

'I might have been. I don't know.' She closed her eyes again momentarily. 'Sometimes I think I'd just like to go to sleep and stay asleep for ever.'

'Jilly —'

'It's all right. I don't mean it that way. Just that it's so peaceful, being asleep.' She hesitated. 'And there's always the chance that I might dream about Geoff.'

He gazed at her and reached out his hand.

'It's almost as good as being with him again,' she said. 'It *is* as good, while I'm dreaming it. Dreams are so real, aren't they? And afterwards I've got another memory to think about. To treasure. Even if it's not real, it still seems real to me, and dreams are all I've got now.'

He said, 'It takes a long time before it starts to get better. But it does, you know, in the end.'

'I know. But I haven't got a long time.' Her cornflower eyes looked into his. 'I've got to get better quickly. You see, I'm going to have a baby.'

David leant back in his chair. He didn't let go of Jilly's hand, although it twitched a little in his grasp, as though it wanted to escape. He kept a firm hold of it while he considered her words. It was an important moment, and he didn't want to risk mishandling it.

'Does anyone else know?' he asked at last, and she shook her head.

'I'll have to tell Mum soon. I'm four months gone. She'll notice.' She glanced down at her body, blushing. David realised now that she had changed already, that her breasts had become fuller. Perhaps her waist had begun to thicken too. Changes that wouldn't be noticed if you weren't looking for them, but would now become swiftly more apparent. She had left it late enough to tell anyone, he thought.

'Are you all right? Have you seen a doctor?'

She shook her head. 'I know what's the matter. I'm not *ill*. I haven't even had morning sickness. That's why I didn't think I was expecting at first. I mean, there was just nothing. Except –' She blushed again. 'Well. You know. And I thought that was just because I was upset, with Geoff going away, and – and us not being able to get married.' She glanced away. 'We pretended we were,' she said in a low

292

voice. 'We went away on the bike – we called it our honeymoon. Geoff gave me a ring. We *felt* married.'

'Oh, Jilly,' David said, his voice filled with pity.

'I suppose you're disgusted. You think I'm a slut.'

'I don't. I don't think that at all.'

'No better than I should be. That's what people will say about me.' She laughed without mirth. 'I've never understood that saying. I mean, why should anyone be better than they should be? It don't make sense.'

'Jilly, no one's going to say that about you.'

'Oh, they will,' she said with quiet certainty. 'A lot of them will.'

'Then they're not worth bothering about.'

'They are,' she said. 'People are always worth bothering about. Even the nasty ones.'

David was silent. He felt suddenly that this young girl, who had been deemed not old enough to marry, was possessed of some wisdom. He wondered what advice he could give her, what help. He wondered how he could have the temerity to suppose that he could advise her at all, only minutes after hearing the news, when she had known and lived with it for weeks.

'Have you made any plans?' he asked.

Jilly shrugged. 'What plans can I make? What does a girl like me do? There's homes for unmarried mothers. You go there and have your baby, and then someone comes along and adopts it. That's one thing you can do. Or you can stop at home – if your family don't chuck you out – and have the baby there and keep it. And it grows up with everyone knowing about it. But I don't know about *plans*. It depends on other people, doesn't it? A girl like me can't do much on her own.'

'What do you want to do?'

'Well, I'm not giving it away,' she said in an almost savage tone. 'It's my baby, mine and Geoff's, and nobody else is having it.'

'Well, that's one thing, then. And do you want to stay at home?'

She glanced at him sideways. 'I don't know where is home,' she said simply. 'If Geoff and me had got married, I suppose we'd have stayed in Plymouth. Got ourselves a couple of rooms somewhere or maybe stayed at the hotel. I could have gone on working in the kitchen . . . But they won't want me now, and this is your auntie's house.'

David stared at her. It had not occurred to him that she had, literally, no home. Her mother still owned a small cottage in the village, but it was let to a man who worked on a nearby farm and had a family of four. There was no question of turning him out. He thought of saying that of course this was her home, she must stay here, but it wasn't for him to say any such thing. It was, as Jilly had pointed out, his aunt's house, and an old woman in her nineties might not be at all pleased to find herself sharing her home with a baby.

He felt helpless. But that was nothing, he told himself, to what Jilly must be feeling. Having to absorb this new development, so quickly after losing Geoff . . . The baby was like a time-bomb, ticking away inside her, and although there were another five months before it was actually born, she would have to make her decisions and organise her life well before then. She had hardly any time at all. And the decisions were momentous, affecting not just her and her mother and even his aunt, but her baby too – her baby most of all, he realised suddenly. A new person who wouldn't stay a baby long but would become a toddler, a child, an adult.

He thought of Lucy. She was the child's grandmother. She would help. She had never backed out of a responsibility yet, in all the years he had known her. She had suffered blow after blow and always come back, if not smiling, at least determined not to be beaten.

'You'll tell Mrs Pengelly, of course,' he said, thinking aloud, and was surprised when Jilly drew back, almost snatching her hand away.

'*No!* No, I won't – I can't –' Her voice was edged sharply with distress. 'You mustn't either. Promise me you won't. *Promise.*'

'But why not?' He didn't tell her that he couldn't. Nobody else knew about Lucy's letter. He had carried it around with him for three days and kept reading it, and still he couldn't quite believe what it said.

'Jilly,' he said, 'she ought to know. She has a right to know. It's Geoff's baby.'

'And you know what she'll have to say about *that*,' Jilly said bitterly.

David sighed. She was probably right. Young girls who found themselves 'in trouble' didn't have many friends. Some mothers and fathers supported their daughters, but many turned their backs on them. The picture of the shawl-wrapped figure trudging through the snow with her bundle of shame wasn't so very far from the truth.

'But your mother won't turn you out,' he said. 'She'll help you, I'm sure. And so will I. We'll all sit down together round the table and have a talk about it. You can't manage on your own. You've got to have support.'

Jilly's eyes filled with tears. 'Oh, Mr Tremaine. I don't know what to do –' Her lips trembled and her voice wobbled away into a sob. She put her face in her hands and began to cry.

David laid his hand on her shoulder. It quivered and shook under his palm. He felt deeply sorry for the girl. A few months ago, she had had so much: a young man who loved her, the joy of looking forward to a life together, to a family. Now the young man was missing, probably dead, and she faced the world alone, worse than alone. She had to face the censure of a society that had little compassion for girls in her position, that would stigmatise her and her baby. And the stigma would extend to her mother too, and even as far as Plymouth to the Pengellys.

He wondered if she was right about Lucy. Would she reject the girl her son had loved? There was only one way to find out, but it was a way he of all people could not take.

'Tell your mother,' he said quietly. 'Tell her soon.' He hesitated. 'Unless you'd like me to tell her? I will if you want me to.'

'Oh no,' Jilly said. 'No, I'll do it. I'll do it this evening, after your auntie's gone to bed.' She fumbled in her pocket for a handkerchief, blew her nose and gave a wry smile. 'You'll probably find me packing to go tomorrow.'

'Jilly, don't say that. I'm sure your mother will help you. Look, I'll go in and have a chat with my aunt now, and then I've got to go. I promised to go and see the builder about those repairs to the roof. I'd like to see them done before I go back to London.'

He leant his head back again and closed his eyes, listening to the birdsong and wondering why he had to go back at all. Every time he came down to Cornwall, he felt more reluctant to leave again. Perhaps it was time to think about a permanent move. There was nothing in London for him now, only his job, and he sometimes felt he'd had enough of that. At forty-nine, he was too young to be thinking of retirement, but he could surely find a job in the West. On the *Western Morning News*, perhaps. Or the paper where he'd begun his career, the one his father had edited back before the First World War.

If Lucy had come to him, of course, things would have been very different. He would have had her to work for. A purpose in life. Now, it all seemed rather empty.

He went indoors, where his aunt was now downstairs, having had her morning wash and breakfast in bed, and was sitting in the small sunroom with Blackie on her lap. The sunroom was not too warm at this time of day but sheltered from the breeze, and the air was scented with the flowers

Jilly's mother grew there. His aunt looked as fragrant as the flowers, tiny and dainty in her clean cotton dress with a snowy-white apron, edged with lace, in case she spilled anything, her curly hair like a halo of soft white clouds about her face.

'Is that David?'

'Yes. I'm just going to see the builder about the roof.'

'Little Tommy Pascoe.' David's aunt knew everyone in the village, had known most of them all their lives. Because she had been unable to see them for several years, each had assumed a point at which she remembered them best, mostly as children. 'Are you sure he'll be able to manage it? I wouldn't like him to fall off and hurt himself.'

David smiled. 'Tommy's a good worker. He won't fall.' Pascoe & Son were the biggest building firm in the area and had started to build a new council estate away over near Redruth. 'I'll tell him to look in and say hallo before he starts work.'

'That would be nice. I'd like to have a chat with Tommy again. He used to come here to collect conkers, you know, from the horse-chestnut trees in the drive.' The old lady's faded eyes turned towards him and he felt his usual little spasm of surprise that they couldn't see him. She didn't look blind at all. 'Have you been talking to little Jilly?'

'Yes. She's in the garden, under the apple trees.' He hesitated. 'She looks tired. And it really doesn't seem as if he's coming back.'

'She's had such a sad time,' Margaret Tremaine said. 'So much in love . . . It's the worst time to lose someone. The worst of times and the best of times, as Dickens might have said.'

'How do you mean?' David was always fascinated to hear the workings of his aunt's mind. 'How can it be both?'

'For the same reason. Because they hadn't had time for the first flush of rapture to diminish. The worst of times, because she hadn't had time to discover his faults, and the best because she'll always remember their love as being perfect. She'll never have any regrets to sour the memories.'

David said nothing. He thought Jilly was going to have plenty of regrets. Life was not going to be easy for her. It never was for the girl who was left, literally, holding the baby.

'I think she's going to need quite a lot of help and support,' he said carefully. 'She really did love Geoff, and they badly wanted to be married. She'll always regret that.'

'Oh, I know. And so, I think, will other people. Especially those who prevented it.' The soft eyes were reflective. 'Poor Jean Penfold is already tormenting herself with it. And perhaps Geoffrey's mother is too. Or maybe she hasn't begun to think about that yet. She has her own grief to contend with.'

'Yes, she does.' David thought again of the letter in his pocket. He wanted nothing so badly as to be with Lucy again, helping her bear her sorrow, but she had turned away from him, and he knew that she could not be persuaded to turn back. Their last chance had come, and slipped them by.

And he too was grieving for Geoffrey for he too thought that Geoff must be dead. Nobody seemed to have thought of his sorrow, but in his heart the pain was as sharp and searing as if the boy had been his own son. And for years, he had been very nearly just that. The boy he'd saved from the blitz, the boy he'd given his arm for. The boy he'd walked with on the Hoe and talked to and taught to swim. Lucy's son. His loss, as well as hers, and nobody seemed to realise it.

So deep in thought was he then that he almost missed his aunt's next words. He just caught them, lingering in his ears, the second before they vanished into the spring air, and he jerked his head up and looked at her in astonishment. '*What* did you say?'

'I said, you know Jilly's pregnant.' The old voice was

touched with reproach. 'Really, David, if you can't be bothered to listen to me –'

'I'm sorry. I was listening – I just got distracted for a moment . . . Pregnant?' He echoed the word almost unbelievingly, as if he had no idea that it might be true. 'But how do you know? Did she tell you?'

'David, I'm over ninety years old. I don't have to be told things. I can hear it in her voice.'

'In her *voice*?'

'Of course. When she reads to me. It's a situation that crops up quite frequently in fiction, and whenever Jilly comes to a passage about babies, her voice softens. And if it's a young girl like herself, unmarried but expecting a baby, she has some difficulty in controlling her emotions. It's hardly surprising. Are *you* surprised?'

'That Jilly can't control her voice? Or that she's pregnant?' He shook his head, bemused. 'I don't know . . . She's told me, as it happens. Just now – a few minutes ago. She felt she had to tell someone. She doesn't realise that you know.'

'Well, of course she doesn't. I wouldn't be so foolish as to let her see that I've guessed, not until she was ready to tell me. So it's true . . .' The old lady fell silent for a few minutes. 'Poor child. Poor, *poor* child.'

'I don't think she knows quite what to do,' David said after a moment.

'I don't suppose she does, but at least she'll do nothing silly. Not now she's told someone. That's always the danger period, you see, when a girl hasn't told anyone yet. That's when there's a risk of her doing something foolish.'

'Something foolish' meant either trying to get rid of the baby, by falling downstairs or jumping off a chair, or even by going to some shady backstreet harridan who made a living out of young girls' mistakes; or, worse still, by throwing herself into a river or taking too many aspirins. David shuddered at the thought of either of these measures.

Thank God she had told him, he thought, and hoped his aunt was right that the danger was past.

'I told her she must tell her mother. Then we can have a talk together, the three of us, and decide what's best to be done. She said she'll do it this evening.'

'After I've been safely packed off to bed.' The wrinkled face was amused. 'Do you know, David, one of the most irritating things about getting very old is that you are treated as if you are very young . . . and more often than not, by those who haven't been on this earth more than five minutes! Well, I'll forgive her this time but I'd like to be part of any future discussions. That's if she'll allow it, of course.'

'I don't think she's really in a position to object,' David said with a sigh. 'A young girl like Jilly, in the situation she's in, has very little choice. What can she do if her mother turns her out – if *you* turn her out? She won't be able to find a job, nor a home. A home for unmarried mothers would take her in, but only until after the baby's born. And then she'd have to give it up for adoption. She wouldn't be able to keep it.'

'And does she want to keep it?'

David thought of the intensity of Jilly's voice as she'd said, 'It's my baby. Mine and Geoff's. And nobody else is having it.'

'Yes,' he said, 'she wants to keep it.'

'Then perhaps,' his aunt said, stroking Blackie, 'the situation isn't so very difficult after all.'

Chapter Twenty-four

Wilmot leant over the railings along the road on Plymouth Hoe and stared out over the Sound. It was a fine, sunny morning and the sea reflected the blue of the sky. The waves moved in endless small ripples, as though someone had hammered it all over very gently, and the tiny waves were frosted with white. Across the Hamoaze, the green hills and woods of Mount Edgcombe seemed to float like an island seen in a dream.

He had dreamt of this during all the years he had spent in the Japanese camp. Sometimes the dreams had been waking ones, the vision conjured up deliberately. He had lain on his bed of filthy straw, listening to the whine of mosquitoes and the hums and buzzes of countless other unidentified insects, and tried to transport himself through space and time, to his own country, to the place where he had grown up.

He had pictured the Sound – oddly enough, he'd as often conjured up a memory of it on cold, windy days, with the sea like pewter, as on days like this – and thought of days spent here as a small boy, clambering like a monkey on the rocky cliffs, leaping in and out of the pools, running down to the Barbican early in the morning to cadge some fish from the boats that had just come in . . .

All these ideas and many more had drifted through Wilmot's mind as he had lain in the camp so far away, or gone about the work he and his fellow prisoners were forced to do. If he had not had them to cling to, he would not have survived. And sometimes they had come into his night-time dreams as well, the real dreams over which he had no control, and he would believe himself back at home, walking in through the door to find his family complete – Lucy, Geoff, Patsy, Zannah, his mother and father – and just sitting down to their tea. There was a place laid for him too, and they would all leap up and throw their arms about him, and he would take his place, surrounded by the warmth of their love, and know that from now on everything would be all right . . .

The dreams had been so vivid that he could not believe, when he woke, that they hadn't been true. And as he had lain looking at the bamboo walls of his hut and listening to the shouts of the Japanese guards and the groans and grumbles of the other men, his body and heart flooded with disappointment so bitter that he had not known how to bear it.

He had tried not to dream that dream, but it was no good. Every few weeks it came back to torment him, and even in the dream he began to be aware of the disappointment to come, and he would turn to Lucy as he sat down at the table and say, 'It *is* real this time, isn't it? I really am home . . .' And then he would wake and know the bitter truth and the cruel disappointment yet again.

The years in camp had seemed endless. He did not know how he and the other men had endured them. It could only have been the determination of the body to go on living, the seed of life in mind and heart that was intent on keeping itself alive. Otherwise there were times for all of them when they could have just lain down and died. But dying wasn't as easy as that, even when you were suffering the most dreadful privations. Unless you were ill or weakened or beaten to death, you just kept going, even when you knew you didn't want to, even when you were ready to beg to be put out of this grinding misery.

Nobody begged the Japanese, however. The contempt and loathing they felt for their captors would not allow them to give that satisfaction. They kept their pride, even when it was in tatters like the rags they wrapped around their bodies, even when it seemed shredded beyond repair. They never discarded it utterly and it was probably that which saved many of them in the end.

Wilmot straightened up from the railings and walked slowly down towards the Barbican. All things come to an end, and so the war had ended and with it their incarceration. Those prisoners who survived were sent first to Singapore, where they were fed and treated for their various illnesses, and made fit to go home again. And then the dream had come true at last and he had walked along the ruined street and in through the front door and down the passage to the kitchen.

At the door, he had paused for a second, afraid that it was going to be the same thing all over again – the family sitting round the table, the joyful reunion, the vivid reality of it all that caused him to ask for reassurance that this time it really was true, this time it wasn't a dream, and then the slow, cruel awakening . . . He thought of the day the camp had been liberated, the grinning American soldiers, the medical examinations, the journey to Singapore for more examinations and treatment and learning to eat good food again, the long voyage home . . . You couldn't have all those memories in a dream. It had to be real.

All the same, he had felt sick with apprehension as he pushed the door open and saw Lucy there, alone. And then she jumped up and rushed at him, and after that the reunion was all that he had desired, and this time he did not wake up.

So what had gone wrong?

Wilmot was down by Mayflower Steps now, the jetty from which the *Mayflower* was supposed to have set sail for America with the Pilgrim Fathers. The fishing-boats were all about him, tied to bollards and stanchions, their nets draped over the decks and masts to dry, and their crews putting a few more knots in here and there where something had torn a bigger hole. Lobster pots stood about as well, but the fish had all gone, brought in early that morning and sold on the quays. Lucy herself came down here some mornings to buy fish for the dining-room, and at first Wilmot had come with her to carry the baskets. He'd enjoyed the bustle and the noise, but it was a long time now since he'd come. A long time since he'd had anything much to do with the running of the hotel.

He stopped and sat down on a bollard. Nobody took any notice of him. He rubbed his hand over his face, trying to work out what had happened to the joy of coming home, the happiness he'd looked forward to so much, the love, the laughter that had been so much a part of life before the war had torn them all apart.

There was no doubt it was his fault. He had survived the war but he hadn't been able to survive the peace. He'd lived through the tortures of the camp, but he hadn't been able to live with the memories. Until he came home, he hadn't realised the effect they had had on him. It was like losing your voice with a bad cold; you didn't know it was gone until you tried to talk to someone.

Wilmot had not known that his personality had gone. He had not known that the years had brought about a terrible change.

It hadn't taken long to find out. He had been as surprised as Lucy when he had snapped at her over his grey hair, during those first few moments of their reunion. He'd been as disconcerted over his reaction to her mention of age, but maybe it wasn't so surprising. He'd wanted to come home and find everything just as it had been when he'd gone away, before the war. He'd dreamed of it all being the same. The children, all three of them, grown a bit of course, but essentially the same. Lucy, the girl he had left behind, vibrant with energy, her hair vivid with no trace of white. And it hadn't been the same at all. She'd actually drawn his attention to her grey hairs. She'd stressed that they were both older – reminding him at once of the lost years. And then there'd been the children . . .

Geoff, a fourteen-year-old youth, with a voice that was breaking and gravelly. And Patsy in her wheelchair, bringing tears to his eyes. And no Zannah.

He'd known all this, of course, but it had not seemed real to him until that moment, when his dream was shattered. Not as cruelly as in the camp when he'd woken to that other terrible reality, but cruelly enough, for now he had to face what had been happening to others and what was happening now, and his own situation, which had occupied his mind with such concentration for the past four years, was supposed to take second place.

'I know you've had a dreadful time,' Lucy had said to him, 'but it's over now. You're home again. We've just got to get on with living.'

She'd helped him as much as she could. She'd held him and comforted him in the night, when he woke from his new dreams, the nightmares that took him back to camp as vividly and as cruelly as those camp dreams had brought him home. She'd asked him about the camp, had said she wished she could share the misery so that he could be relieved of some of it. And he'd turned on her then, telling her she couldn't share it, wouldn't want to if she could know only a tenth of what it was like . . . He'd told her he wanted to forget it and she'd said they would never talk about it again, but even that hadn't been right for him. He couldn't leave it alone. He had to keep bringing it up, comparing life at home with life in camp, shrugging their wartime experiences aside because his own had been so much worse.

It was as if the torment would never stop. It went on and on, reaching out to him from the Far East, clawing him back into that endless hell, and nothing would blur the memories, nothing except the bottle.

It was a joy, at first, to taste rum again, to take a long drink of beer. A simple joy, nothing more, which brought a warmth and comfort that he could find nowhere else. Seeking that comfort, he drank more. And more. He was not dependent on it, he told himself, he wasn't what Lucy had started to call an alcoholic. He was just taking the only comfort he could find, and why should he not? Wasn't he entitled to it?

By the time it stopped bringing him comfort, it was too late. He could not manage without it. He tried going without, and felt ill and shaky and disoriented. As soon as he took a sip, he felt better. His body needed it. It was as simple as that, and he was angry when Lucy refused to accept this.

She despised him now. He knew that. The love she had once felt for him had turned first to pity and then to disgust. She looked at him now with loathing and if he tried to touch her she flinched away, as if she felt soiled. Deep in the mists of his fuddled mind, he thought that she blamed him for everything – for Patsy's injury, for Zannah's death, for the war itself. If he hadn't brought her to Plymouth, she could have been evacuated somewhere safe; if he hadn't been in the Navy they could have moved out of the city. If, if, if . . .

It was another form of torture.

And this time, it was a torture that wouldn't end. There was no release from this pain, no going home at the end of it – unless you looked on death as home. Sleep would be enough, Wilmot thought, the chance of a long sleep without dreams . . . but how could you know that was what it would be like? Suppose death was filled with dreams, with nightmares you couldn't wake from? He shuddered and drew back from the thought. Having to dream for eternity of that camp, of the hideous things that went on in it, never able to wake again . . .

He got up abruptly, walking quickly onwards. There was

no escape in the end, he knew that, but it was like being in the camp: you had to keep trying. That spark of life inside you, however tiny, however defeated, would always strive to keep afire. Until in the end it was dowsed for ever.

He turned and walked back along the fish-quays past the fishing-boats and the lobster pots. The pubs were opening now and he thought of going into one. It was a long time since he'd had a drink, but the rum he had taken soon after breakfast had tasted sour, and his stomach had heaved against it. He thought of this new development with fresh despair. It had happened several times lately, and with the comfort of the bottle taken from him, what would he have left?

Nothing, he thought, sinking down on to the bollard he had chosen before. He stared down into the narrow channel of black, scummy water between the quay and the nearest fishing-boat. There would be nothing left at all.

Wilmot sank his head into his hands. He felt the tears seep down through his fingers, hot and stinging. The weight of the world's despair settled like an old man of the sea upon his shoulders, and he knew that he would never be rid of it.

If he could only destroy it now. If he could only take it, this huge growth of misery, and cast it into the bottomless pit where he himself was falling, perhaps then he could rid the rest of the world of its clinging fingers, its grey, slimy tentacles. If it were indeed all his fault, perhaps he could after all mend things. Put right the evil that had come about. If he could take this burden with him into nightmare, perhaps the nightmare itself would be easier to endure.

He stood up. He walked to the edge of the quay. The fishermen had all gone into the pubs to have their midday bite – Cornish pasties, a tankard of beer. There was nobody to see what Wilmot did.

He stepped down on to one of the fishing boats and

crossed its deck to the boat that was moored alongside. He crossed three in this way and finally stood on the far deck, looking down into deep, black water.

It looked almost welcoming, almost comfortable, like a satiny cushion that wrapped itself around the hulls of the gently rocking boats. It seemed to beckon him to come, and he knew that there would be no dreams after all, no nightmares, just endless rest; the oblivion of eternal sleep.

He let himself quite gently down into the water. Years ago, Lucy had taught him to swim, and he had told her that if ever his ship sank he would be thousands of miles from land, so swimming wouldn't be much use. In the end, he was close enough to be able to swim to shore quite easily. But he didn't bother.

Chapter Twenty-five

Nobody blamed Lucy for Wilmot's suicide, but she blamed herself.

'I knew how unhappy he was. I knew he was depressed. I could have done more to help.'

'Look at it this way,' Arthur said. 'He was drinking himself to death anyway. This was just quicker.'

His moustache wobbled. His eyes were red-rimmed, but although Maud had always seemed the stronger of the two until now, it seemed that he was the one who had comfort to give. Pragmatic as ever, he gave Lucy a direct glance from beneath sparse eyebrows and said, 'He wasn't ever going to be happy again, no matter what anyone did. The Japs took all that away from him. He tried, and God knows *you* tried – we all did – but he was broken in that camp and if you ask me, we ought to be thankful he'm at peace at last.'

'But to be so unhappy, to take his own life –'

'And would you rather he'd gone on feeling like that for the rest of his natural span?' Arthur asked with a logic that could not be refuted.

'It wasn't all unhappy,' Lucy said. 'There were times when he was like the old Wilmot. That day when we went to Cawsand. He was happy then, laughing, helping Patsy to swim, racing Geoff . . .' Her voice choked a little. 'And he and Patsy had happy times together.' She turned to her daughter, sitting quietly in her wheelchair. 'You did, didn't you? He did have happy times, with you?'

Patsy reached out a hand and laid it on her mother's. 'Yes, of course he did. And with you too. But he did find

309

life very hard, and I think hearing Geoff was missing was just the last straw. He couldn't bear it any more. He felt so guilty over it. He was sure Geoff was dead – or being tortured. He knew what it was like and he couldn't stop thinking about it. It was just too much.' Gently, she squeezed Lucy's hand. 'It was nothing to do with you.'

'And now,' Arthur said, squaring his thin shoulders, 'we just got to get on with things. Same as we've always done.'

Never had Lucy longed so desperately for David. Never had she so badly needed to feel his arm about her, his quiet strength supporting her. But she had written to David months ago and told him that it was all over between them, and even though she was now technically free, she knew that Wilmot's shadow lay between them still. She could not abandon her grief and go to another man.

She was haunted by memories of him as a young sailor, fresh faced and laughing, ringing the doorbell of her parents' house in Portsmouth, leaning his kitbag on the doorstep. He'd hitch-hiked miles to see her, sometimes only able to stay a few hours before he had to set off back to his ship. She heard his cheeky voice teasing her mother, cracking jokes with her brothers. She heard him speaking in a different tone when they were alone together, telling her he loved her.

I don't think I can bear it, she thought. What went wrong? What happened to him? But she knew the answer to that, and it was a bitter knowledge.

Other memories crowded in. Their wedding day, and Wilmot's face as he turned to watch her walk up the aisle towards him. The train journey down to Devon. Their first night in their own home – only a couple of rented rooms, but theirs, with no one to tell them what to do. The pain of their first parting and the joy of his first homecoming.

A sailor's life is all honeymoons, she'd been told. It was true that the reunions were lovely, but that didn't make up for not having Wilmot there all the time. As time went on, she'd known that she would be happy to give up that special joy just to have him home all the time, to be a proper family. Especially when the children were born.

He'd been going to come out of the Navy, she thought. Another year or two, and if it hadn't been for the war he would have been back in civvy street, and he wouldn't have changed, he'd have been the same happy Wilmot, and he'd still be alive today . . .

At other times, she was angry. How could he have done this to her? How *dared* he just take the easy way out, and leave her with this pain? He was nothing but a coward, she raged. He hadn't been able to take it himself so he'd dropped out, and left his pain to be borne by the people he was supposed to love best. Her anger didn't last long, however. Always, she came back to the torture and the hardships he had endured in the camp, and she knew that she had no right to rebuke him, she had no experience of his pain and could not understand its depths and its immensity.

She could only close her eyes and let her own sorrow wash over her, her sorrow and her regret and her sadness at the waste of yet another life through war.

Patsy was the mainstay of the family now. She felt her own sorrow and grief, but she did not share her mother's guilt. She stayed at her desk and welcomed the guests with her usual smile, and looked only a little paler than usual, with her eyes just a little more shadowed.

'Are you going to let David know?' she asked Lucy, just before Wilmot's funeral. 'And Jilly?'

Lucy looked at her. The emotion drained from her face, leaving it stony. 'Why? I don't expect to see either of them again.'

Patsy was aghast. 'But why not? David was Daddy's friend. He's *your* friend. And Jilly –' Nothing had been said about Jilly returning to the hotel. It just hadn't happened. Patsy missed her sadly and wanted her back.

'Jilly told me that your father took against her in the last few weeks,' Lucy said. 'He didn't want her about. I suppose she reminded him too much of Geoff. So I don't think—'

'But she ought to *know*,' Patsy said. 'We ought to tell her. And David too. He's been part of the family for so long . . . Shall *I* write to them? Would you like me to do that?'

'Oh, do as you like,' Lucy said, turning away. She heard the coldness in her own voice and hated herself for it, but the thought of those two brought fresh pain and she couldn't stand any more pain. 'I don't want to write to them,' she said tightly. 'I don't even want to think about them. But if you want to, you can.'

Patsy did. She wrote to them both, and received letters back. She wondered at David's not writing to her mother, but her surprise was overshadowed by the news that came in Jilly's letter.

She waited until after her father's funeral to impart it to Lucy, when she decided it could wait no longer, and one evening when she and Lucy were alone together she told her about Jilly's baby.

'It's due in November. It must have happened just before Geoff went away.'

Lucy stared at her. Her face was paper white, her eyes huge and almost black. 'A *baby*? Jilly Penfold says she's expecting our Geoff's *baby*?'

'Well, she's not expecting a tortoise,' Patsy said, and apologised at once. 'I'm sorry, Mum, but you look as if – well, as if it's just not possible.'

'It's not,' Lucy said flatly. 'It's not possible. Our Geoff would never have done such a thing. She must have had another boy, she's blaming it on him. The slut!'

'Mum, don't say such things. Of course she's not putting the blame on him. She never had anyone else, she was crazy about Geoff, you know she was. They wanted to get married.'

'Yes, and she blamed me because they didn't. This is her

way of getting back at me. She wants to shame me.' Lucy was beyond reason. The blood had rushed back into her face and she was scarlet now with fury. 'She wants to shame us all, she's just being vindictive. The slut. The hussy. The *trollop.*'

Patsy didn't know what to do. 'Mum, don't talk like that. Jilly's a nice girl, you know she is. She really loved Geoff, and he loved her. They – they were so upset they couldn't get properly married.' She hesitated. 'I think they considered that they *were* married. That time they went off on the bike – I think they took it as their honeymoon.'

'Then they'd no right to. I never heard anything like it. Going off together, pretending they were married. Where did they stay? Tell me that. Nowhere decent, you can take that for granted, no respectable place would have taken in two bits of kids like that and let them share a room. Why, it's disgusting. Disgusting!'

Patsy said nothing. She had never seen her mother so wrought up. It was as if all the sorrow of the past year, all the stress of the years before, had built up like lava in a volcano and was now erupting. She could almost feel the heat of her mother's anger. She knew there was nothing she could do to stem the flow; it would have to burn itself out. If, indeed, it could.

'Anyway, I still don't believe it,' Lucy was saying. 'Geoffrey was properly brought up, he knew right from wrong even if she didn't. He would never have done such a thing, never. I never had any doubts about him, not for a minute.'

'They were in love, Mum,' Patsy said. 'They wanted to be married. And Geoff was going away, they knew they wouldn't see each other again for months, maybe not for two years. They just wanted something to remember.'

'Well, she's certainly got that! But I don't believe it's Geoff's, all the same.'

'Why should she say it is, if it isn't? If it was another boy, she could marry him and give the baby a name. There'd be no point in her saying it was Geoff.'

'Oh, who knows what's going on in that girl's mind?' Lucy said irritably. 'She's in a mess and she's looking for someone to get her out of it, that's all. Obviously the real father won't own up. Perhaps he's already married. She's looking to us to give her a home, that's what she's doing, away from the village so that her friends don't know about her shame. What's she going to do with it, does she say? Give it away for adoption, I suppose. That's how much it matters to her. That's how much Geoff matters.'

'She says she wants to keep it. It's part of her and Geoff.' Patsy held out the letter. 'Read it, Mum. I'm sure she's telling the truth.'

Lucy brushed the letter away. 'Easy to say that now. It'll be a different story when it's born.' Clearly, she was determined to see the worst of the situation and there was nothing that Patsy could say that would change her mind. 'Oh, take it away, do. I've got too many things on my mind to be bothered with a brazen little hussy like that Jilly Penfold.'

Patsy opened her mouth and then closed it again. She turned her wheelchair and took herself out of the living-room, down the passage and into her own bedroom. She sat there for a while, smoothing the letter out on her lap and looking at it, trying to imagine what Jilly must be feeling.

David knew about it, apparently, and so did his aunt and Jilly's mother. They were all standing by her. They hadn't tried to persuade her to give the baby up, and David's aunt had told her there was a home for her in her house for as long as Jilly needed it.

So it wasn't true that she was just looking for somewhere to go, another home, and Patsy felt convinced that she wouldn't change her mind about keeping the baby. Why should she? I wouldn't, Patsy thought, I couldn't ever give up my own baby, and I don't believe Jilly will either.

It'll be my niece, she thought, or my nephew. The only one I'll ever have. She wondered if her mother had thought of it like that, although she knew that Lucy wasn't thinking clearly at all. Too much had happened to her in the past year or so. Too much to be able to take it all in.

Patsy felt as sorry for her mother as she felt for Jilly.

Nothing more was said about Jilly's baby. Maud and Arthur were not told.

'They should know about it,' Patsy said. 'It's Geoff's baby it's their great-grandchild.'

Lucy turned on her. 'Don't call it that! You know I don't believe it. And I told you I didn't want to hear it mentioned in this house again. All this trouble, and you want to bring more. Can't you understand, Patsy, how I feel about it?'

'Yes, I can, but you've got to understand how other people feel too.' Patsy faced her mother bravely. 'It's not just you, you know. It's Jilly as well. She's *having* the baby. And it *is* Geoff's – you know that. How would you have felt if it had happened to you and Dad, if you'd been expecting our Geoff, and Grammy and Grampy had said they didn't want anything to do with you? If Dad had died then? How would you have felt?'

'It didn't happen to me. We didn't give way. We waited. We got decently engaged and then married and we never touched each other that way till our wedding night. And if Jilly had done the same, she wouldn't be in this pickle now.'

'And she and Geoff would never have known what it was like to love each other properly,' Patsy said quietly. 'Geoff would never have known what it was like. He'd have gone to Korea – perhaps to death without ever having made love.'

'*Patsy!* That's *filthy* talk!'

'It's not. It's true. Do you really wish he'd died without ever knowing what it was like?'

'He's not dead! We don't *know* he's dead,' Lucy said

315

fiercely. 'I don't even *think* about that sort of thing. Neither should you. Why, you're only eighteen years old. And in your position –'

'You mean because I'm never going to know either. Because nobody is ever going to want to marry me, because I'm a cripple.'

'Oh, Patsy –'

'It's what you meant, isn't it?' Patsy said, ignoring her mother's outstretched hands. 'I'm stuck in this wheelchair, so no one is ever going to be interested in me. No one will ever love me or marry me and *I won't ever have any children.*'

Lucy gazed at her. Once again, she reached out, but Patsy shrugged away her hands.

'Have you thought what that means? Do you think that because I'm shackled to this chair for the rest of my life, it means that I'm happy about that? Doesn't it ever occur to you that I might want to be loved? That I might want to be married and have my own children? Hasn't it ever occurred to you to think what it must be like for me? It's like being in a prison. Dad was in a prison, and look what it did to him. And *he* got out! I shall never get out.'

'Oh, Patsy. I'm so sorry.'

'Sorry doesn't help,' Patsy told her brutally. 'You've obviously never thought of it, but I've had a lot of time to think about it. I think about what it would be like to have someone who loved me, someone who put me first before anyone else. And I think about the children.' She raised her eyes and looked full into her mother's face. 'I'm never, ever, going to have children, am I? *Am* I?' And, without waiting for the shock to die from Lucy's face, 'That baby Jilly's going to have is Geoff's. You know it is. It's part of our family. It will be my nephew or niece. The only nephew or niece I'll ever have. *And you won't have anything to do with it.*'

She gripped the wheels of her chair and jerked it

restlessly back and forth. 'What right do you have to decide we're not going to have this baby in the family, Mum? What right do you have to make that decision for Grammy and me, and Pompey Grandma and all the rest? What about Geoff? Suppose he comes back and finds out what you've done? And the baby itself. Don't you think the baby has rights as well?' She stared at her mother with eyes that were huge, as black as ebony in her taut white face. 'And how many people have you got left to love that you can throw away this chance?'

In August of that year the Olympic Games were held in Helsinki. The world was once again playing together, although even the Games could not hide the conflict that still raged so bitterly in Korea, nor the threat of the Mau-Mau terror in Kenya, nor the advance of French troops into Vietnam. All over the world there were still clouds, some no bigger than a man's fist, some already grown to looming shadows. Peace had come, and yet it still seemed as far away as ever.

Lucy threw herself into the work of the hotel. This summer was the busiest yet, and all her vision and hard work was paying off in the number of guests coming through the swing doors. She spent all her waking hours in the office with Patsy, or in the kitchen with the new cook, or simply overseeing the work of the rest of the staff. There were five chambermaids now, several waiters in the dining-room, a porter and two girls helping in the kitchen. There was no machine for washing dishes, nor for washing clothes – sheets, pillowcases and towels went to the laundry, as staff was cheaper and more readily available than machinery – but Lucy had invested in two new vacuum cleaners which were used daily on the new fitted carpets.

Pengelly's had earned its reputation in Plymouth. The dining-room was open to non-residents, at lunchtime as well as in the evening, and local businessmen came here

317

with clients, as well as couples who wanted an evening out. Plymouth was coming back to life and needed somewhere sophisticated. Lucy was aiming high.

Maud and Arthur had decided to retire properly at last. The hotel had changed too much for them; it was no longer their home, and it held too many sad memories. Tired, and wanting a rest in different surroundings, they found a tiny cottage in Newton Ferrers, overlooking the river, and moved into it with their own familiar furniture. The cottage had no garden, but there was a tiny paved courtyard at the front and they filled it with old sinks and chamber-pots full of bright flowers, and hung baskets from the low roof, and Arthur made window-boxes for the wide stone sills. There was just room amongst all this riot of colour for the two deckchairs that Lucy gave them for a housewarming present, and they sat there for hours, watching the life of the river and passing the time of day with their new neighbours.

They seemed to be happy at last, Lucy thought with some wonder, away from the city where they had lived all their lives through all the turmoil of two world wars. She wrote to her own mother in Portsmouth and told her about their new contentment, and Emily wrote back to say she was going to live with Alice. 'I'll be better there,' she said. 'I'm fed up with being on my own. Family's what you want round you when you're getting on.'

Family. But my family's dwindling all the time, Lucy thought, and although she still couldn't bear to believe that Geoffrey was dead, somehow his face refused to come to her mind and she could not imagine him ever being at home again. I've only got Patsy left now, she thought sadly.

Patsy said no more about the baby. She knew that it was useless to keep going over the same ground; if the seeds had been sown, they would either sprout or die. She hoped they would sprout, and in the meantime she kept writing to Jilly and looked forward to the baby's birth.

'I'm coming down to see you then,' she wrote. 'I deserve a holiday and I've saved my wages for the fare. I can manage on the train, so long as someone comes to meet me. I want to see you and I want to see the baby!'

'I'm looking forward to seeing you here,' Jilly wrote back. 'Mum and Mrs Tremaine and Mr Tremaine all say you'll be welcome as the flowers in May. There's a lovely little bedroom here, it's going to be the baby's later on and we're painting it yellow, like sunshine, but you'll sleep in it when you come. It looks out over the orchard and the birds sing so loud in the morning it nearly bursts your eardrums. And there are lambs in the fields now, and next-door donkey's had a foal. Come soon, so I can show you it all.'

Patsy read the letter over and over again, imagining the old house set amongst the fields and woods in that mild, leafy part of Cornwall. She thought of the baby lying in its pram beneath the apple trees, the pattern of leaves against a blue sky making a canopy above its head, the music of the birds and the lambs . . . It would be five or six months old before that could happen, of course, because it was due in November, but what pleasure a six-month-old baby would take in watching the hurrying birds and the dancing lambs. I'll go then, she decided, but I'll go sooner anyway. I'll go when it's born, whatever Mum says.

Jilly's baby might not bear the family name, but Patsy, for one, was determined that it would be a true Pengelly.

Chapter Twenty-six

How many people have you got to love that you can throw away this chance?

The question haunted Lucy day and night. To all outward appearances she was her normal efficient self, perhaps rather more brusque than usual, less glad to suffer fools. Who could blame her for that, though, her friends said to each other, when you thought of all she'd been through? The Plymouth community, the businessmen and women, the city council, the bank, looked on her with growing respect and never dreamed of the torment that kept her awake at night.

The only nephew or niece I'll ever have . . . The only grandchild I'll ever have, Lucy thought. Because Patsy was right, she was never going to have children. There would be no more young Pengellys.

This one would not be a Pengelly either, but it would have been if it hadn't been for me, Lucy told herself. If I'd only listened to those two youngsters, so young but so much in love, if I'd only let them get married, we'd be looking forward now to the next generation. I'd be looking forward to being a grandmother.

Doesn't the baby have any rights? Doesn't it have a right to its own family? Suppose Geoff came back and found out what you'd done?

Patsy's voice had been terse and uncompromising. She'd laid it out in black and white, refusing to accept shades of grey. Lucy had seen it in black and white too, but as if in a photographic negative – where Patsy had seen white, she had seen black. And Patsy had seen things Lucy had not even thought of. She had seen the baby as a person, growing up, a person who had not asked to be born in this way, who had done nothing wrong; a person who needed a family, who needed love. The love that Lucy was denying it.

She felt crushed by the weight of her guilt, and began to understand a little of what Wilmot had been feeling in those last few weeks. Guilt, she thought, was a terrible thing. Especially when you could do nothing to put it right. When you must carry it to your grave.

How many people have you got to love that you can throw away this chance?

Chance. The word, echoing in Lucy's mind for the thousandth time, caught for a moment like a cobweb on a nail and hung there, whispering over and over again. *Chance, chance, chance* . . . Had it been thrown away? Or was it still there, drifting in the breeze, waiting to be caught and held . . .

Did she really have to carry this guilt for the rest of her life?

The baby was not yet born. There was time yet. Surely – *surely* there was time.

Patsy had been down to see Jilly in the summer. She said that the girl was blooming, her skin a smooth golden brown, her hair shining. Pregnancy suited her. She hadn't had a moment's sickness, she had no backache or heartburn, and she carried her burden lightly before her. She seemed to live in two cotton smocks, one bright blue, the other as green as beech-leaves, which she alternated, and she wore scuffed sandals on her feet. As far as Patsy could see, she possessed no other clothes.

'She says she doesn't need them. She'll be back to normal in a few months.'

Lucy said nothing. She hadn't been ready then to comment, but she thought of sending Jilly another smock, or perhaps a dress. She could make her a maternity dress in no time. Although her angry pride was slowly dissolving, some of it still lingered in her heart, however, making it impossible to yield completely.

She couldn't forget it, though. She couldn't forget the baby that was coming, the baby that was a part of Geoff, might even look like Geoff. She could remember Geoff so clearly as a baby, his round head almost bald but shaded with a ginger fuzz. The red hair that had come down through the whole family from her own mother. Would this new little member of the family have it too?

Her thoughts brought her up short. *This new member of the family* . . . I've changed, she thought in wonder, touching the words delicately in her mind. I've never thought of it like that before, but it's right. It feels right.

By October, the anger had all gone, leaving only a huge yearning to see her grandchild and to make friends again with the girl her son had loved. Patsy was right, she thought. This was her grandchild, the only grandchild she was ever going to have. There had never been any real doubt of that in her heart, she had just rejected the idea of Geoff and Jilly making love before they were married. But it was natural, wasn't it? Of course he had wanted to love Jilly properly before leaving her for two long years. That was why they'd wanted to be married.

You couldn't stop young love, nor hot blood. It had happened to plenty of young people during the war. Lucy had known some of them, boys and girls she had been at school with, who had 'anticipated marriage' as it was called, and had found themselves 'in trouble'. Some had been lucky enough to get married but others, like Jilly, had found themselves with a baby that had no father. Some of those fathers hadn't even been British. They'd been Polish or Canadian or American. Some had been black.

She thought of Patsy's question: did she really want Geoff to die without ever knowing the pleasure of making love? And she looked into her heart, honestly, without prejudice, and knew that the answer was no. I hope they were happy, she thought. I hope they felt really married, and close. I hope it was good for them, the little that they had.

It was as she thought this, that Lucy knew she must go to Cornwall and see Jilly, the mother of the only grandchild she would ever have.

Bodmin Moor was bleak and treeless, but as the train ran into the lusher part of the county Lucy saw trees that were clothed in gold and brown, glowing like amber against the robin's-egg blue of the sky. From some parts of the track you could see both north and south coasts – the broad sweep of Widemouth Bay, with Bude at its heart to the north, leading down to the rocky inlets of Perranporth and Polzeath; the craggy coves of Mevagissey and the steep cliffs of Minack to the south. The Cornish peninsula narrowed the further west you went, and its character seemed to change with every turn of the track, yet in the centre it could be curiously dull and without feature other than the brown moors and the gaunt fingers of disused mine-workings.

It took two changes on to tiny branch lines before Lucy was able to alight finally at the nearest station to old Mrs Tremaine's house. For the first time, as she stood on the platform holding her small suitcase, she wondered what she would do if David himself were there. It had not occurred to her until this moment that he might be. She felt suddenly nervous. I should have let them know I was coming, she thought. I should have telegraphed ahead. But she hadn't wanted to do that, nor to telephone. She'd wanted to arrive unannounced, so that she could see for herself Jilly's reaction to her, and know what her own was.

The house was about a mile from the station, along a lane bordered on one side by a high, Cornish bank with a hedge on top, and on the other dropping away into a steep, tree-filled valley. Somewhere far below Lucy could hear the rippling of a stream. Some of the trees had begun to turn colour, the sprawling, hand-like leaves of the horse chest-nuts now tawny, the oaks a soft brown, the copper beeches a dramatic splash of deep purple and the common beeches spattered with green and rusty gold like a treasure trove long buried and now come to light. The leaves that had already fallen formed an amber carpet on the floor of the valley, lit by the dappling sunshine that flickered down through the gently shimmering leaves.

It was a warm afternoon. There was only the slightest whisper of a breeze amongst the branches. A few birds flew silently amongst the branches and a squirrel startled Lucy by suddenly running across the lane in front of her and straight up the grey, elephant-leg trunk of the nearest beech where it sat on a branch chattering furiously. It was as auburn as the leaves that sheltered it, with tufts of red hair on the tips of its ears, and Lucy gazed at it enchanted.

The road had begun to descend now and soon she came to a small stone bridge under which ran the little river that had carved this steep, narrow valley. Lucy paused for a moment, resting her case on the low parapet, and looked down into the clear water. A few small fish darted amongst the weeds and she saw a small, long-tailed bird, yellow as a canary, flirting its wings on a rock in the middle of the stream, and then caught her breath as a kingfisher darted away from her, a jewelled flash of red and blue, brilliant as a diamond in the sun.

Slowly, Lucy walked on. No vehicle had passed her since she had left the little railway station, no person had walked along the road. The peace of the narrow lane, the deep woods, the glittering stream, was having a strange effect on her heart. It was as if a tight knot, tied years ago, perhaps as long ago as the beginning of the war when Wilmot had first gone away, was beginning to loosen. I didn't even know it was there, she thought in some surprise, and even laid her hand on her breast as if to feel it.

The stream now ran beside the road, tumbling in a deep, narrow cutting. In spring, there would be primroses along its banks and bluebells carpeting the woods like a glimpse of the distant sea. And the starry snowflake flowers of wild garlic, and the royal glow of purple violets.

I've lived in cities all my life, she thought, and wondered why. Perhaps it was time to make a change. A small hotel somewhere in the country, surrounded by woods and meadows, where people could come to ease the pain in their heart . . . The changing colours of the leaves, the soft rustle of the breeze, the singing of the birds . . .

It wouldn't always be like that, of course. There would be days of rain and wind, cold, dismal days when nobody wanted to set foot outside; days when she would light fires indoors, big log fires with comfortable chairs set around them and lamps on low tables casting a warm, cosy glow . . .

She had arrived at a house. A long, low-roofed house, washed with white, standing back from the road with a garden of flowers before it and a little gate set in the hedge. She stopped, gazing at it a little uncertainly, and then caught a glimpse of the orchard that lay to one side. Hardly an orchard, really, no more than a few apple trees scattered on a rough lawn, but Lucy was more interested in what stood beneath the trees.

A pram. An old pram, high-wheeled, with its shade up and a bit of old net curtain stretched across to keep off cats and birds.

It can't be, Lucy thought, but she had her hand on the gate and it swung open beneath her touch. Scarcely knowing what she was doing, her heart suddenly thumping in her breast, she took a step or two up the path . . . and then another and another, until she was on the rough grass, under the trees, until she was standing beside the pram, looking down in wonder, gazing at a tiny, still-crumpled face, at a round head, almost bald, but just fuzzed over with hair that was already faintly ginger . . .

Geoff. It was Geoff, all over again.

She did not know how long she stood there before she heard a door open and knew that someone was walking across the grass towards her. She turned, still in a haze of wonder, and felt almost no surprise at all to see that it was David. I'm dreaming, she thought, the whole thing is a dream: the walk from the station, the trees and the squirrel and the kingfisher, and now this, a baby that's Geoffrey all over again – and David. It must be a dream.

She watched him cross the grass. Something had happened to him: his one arm was caught up against his chest in a sling. He was thinner than she remembered and looked gaunt, as if he had been ill. Or was just getting older and sadder. But his smile was as warm as ever, and his eyes as tender.

'Lucy.' His voice held the same sense of wonder. 'Lucy, what are you doing here? How did you know?'

'How did I know? Know what?' She glanced at the pram and remembered suddenly. '*Oh!* It wasn't due till November! I hadn't even thought – David, is everything all right? The baby – Jilly – this *is* Jilly's baby, isn't it?' Of course it is, she thought wildly, no other baby could look so much like Geoff. 'David?'

He was laughing. 'Yes, it's Jilly's baby. Your grandson. Born yesterday. The nurse said it was too soon to bring a baby outside, but Jilly insisted, she said this was too good a day to miss. I rather think she was right.' He looked at Lucy. 'We sent you a telegram this morning,' he said. 'I walked down to the village post office and did it myself, but you couldn't possibly have got here so soon.'

'I left early. I – I wanted to see her before the baby came.' Lucy met his eyes steadily. 'I wanted her to know that I was coming to see *her*. To make it all up. I was ashamed, you see. I've been behaving so badly.' Her eyes filled with tears and she gazed at him helplessly. 'Oh David. I don't know what's been the matter with me . . .'

'Lucy, Lucy.' He couldn't touch her. She wondered how he managed, with no hand or arm to use, and felt a sudden spurt of anxiety, but he was still speaking and she couldn't interrupt him to ask. 'Lucy, you've had a horrible time. It's been so hard for you. All these years – and then so much happening, so suddenly. Nobody can blame you for what you've felt.'

'But I've been so unkind,' she wept. 'So unkind to poor Jilly. She'd lost Geoff too, and they wanted so much to be married, and I wouldn't agree . . . And now this poor baby, this lovely little baby . . .'

'I know. I know.' He made an impatient sound. 'God, I wish I could just *hold* you! Put your arms round me, Lucy. Rest against me. It's all right, you won't hurt me . . . Oh, *Lucy* . . .' His voice softened, a whisper so low and deep that it could have been the sighing of the morning breeze. 'If you knew how I've longed for this.'

'I know. I do know. I've longed for it too.' She raised her head from the warmth of his chest and looked up into his eyes. 'I wanted to write to you, but I couldn't. I couldn't make it happen.'

'Sometimes we have to wait for things to happen in their own time. I wanted to write to you, too, but I knew, somehow, that one day you would come.' He glanced down into the pram. 'And what better day could it have been? We couldn't have arranged this, Lucy.'

They stood quietly together under the apple tree. Beside them, the baby snuffled and whispered in his sleep. Lucy breathed in the scent of David's body, savoured the warmth and the strength of him. But he was thin, she thought, and he'd been hurt . . . 'What happened to your arm?'

He laughed. 'A stupid accident. I fell out of one of the

apple trees. I was going back to London the next day, but I had to stay on. I can't do a lot for myself, you see, and my mother insisted. And Mrs Penfold's been a marvel.' He looked at Lucy. 'Jilly, too. I've got to know her pretty well during the past few months and especially this last fortnight. She's a good girl, Lucy.'

'I know. I know she is.'

'What made you come?' he asked after a moment. 'To make it up with her, I know that. But what changed your mind?'

'Patsy. She talked to me like a Dutch uncle.' Lucy smiled ruefully. 'She pointed a great many things out to me, but two or three things especially stuck in my mind. One was that the baby had its own rights, it was part of the family whether I liked it or not, and it wasn't for me to deny it. And another was that this is the only grandchild I'll ever have.' She looked down into the pram and touched a crumpled cheek with one fingertip. 'I've lost so much, David. Zannah, Geoff, Wilmot. You. I can't lose this little one as well.'

He said nothing for a few minutes. They stood close, looking into the pram. Lucy kept her arm around his waist and he stood firm and solid against her body. Then, at last, he spoke and his voice was deep and quiet and sure.

'There are just two things wrong with that, Lucy. One is that you haven't lost me. You never did. I've always been here, waiting. And the other is that this doesn't have to be the only grandchild you'll ever have. There could be others.'

Lucy stared at him. 'Others? I don't understand. Patsy can never –'

'I don't mean Patsy,' he said. 'But you're not too old to have other children, Lucy. If you wanted them. Are you?'

'I suppose not. I'm forty-two. Women do have babies in their forties, but –' She stared at him and he smiled, and his thin face was alight with love.

'Lucy, I'm asking you to marry me. If you could bring yourself to take on an old crock like me, with only one arm and even that one not much use just at present. But everything else is present and in working order.' He grinned suddenly and for a moment she was reminded of Wilmot, the old Wilmot, with his cheeky grin and wicked jokes. And then the memory faded as abruptly as it had come. This was David. *David* . . . 'We can start life again, together. And there can be a new family, if that's what you would like. A new chance for us all.'

A new chance. A new family. A new life. She let the thoughts drift in her mind, circling together like sunbeams in a gleam of light, cutting through the shadows of the past. And to begin it all, this baby that lay beside them, a tiny bridge between the two lives.

Chapter Twenty-seven

The wedding was planned to take place at Christmas. David's injured arm and shoulder would be mended by then – 'I've got to have *one* arm to hold my wife with,' he said with a grin – and their families would have time to prepare. And not only their families. There was a great deal for Lucy to do as well, and David must go back to London and sell his home there, ready to move down to Plymouth.

Lucy seemed to spend half her time travelling down to Cornwall now, and had bought a small car in which to make the journey. Although it was early November, the weather was still mild and they sat in the orchard for hours, discussing their future and making plans.

'Do you want to take on a hotel as well as a wife?' Lucy asked him, a little diffidently. 'It's hard work. I'm on the go from morning till night.'

David considered. 'I want us to do whatever suits us both,' he said. 'I don't believe in unnecessary sacrifices. I don't know a thing about running hotels, but I can still do my own work. I've been asked to do more books, and they can be written anywhere. If you want to keep it going, I don't see why it shouldn't work. But I don't want you slaving from dawn till dusk, and we don't need the money – I can keep us both. What do you think about it?'

'I'm not sure,' she confessed. 'Sometimes – when I come down here to your aunt's cottage, and it's all so peaceful and tranquil – I think that this is all I could possibly want. Somewhere in the country, surrounded by trees and birdsong. But I wonder if I would get bored, with nothing much to do. I've always had such a busy life, David.'

'And don't you think you'll be busy now?' he said, gently teasing her. 'I intend to be a very demanding husband, you know. And there'll be all those children too . . .'

Children. Lucy's heart gave a tiny lurch. She had never told David about the baby she had wanted so badly after Wilmot had come home. She had never dared raise the subject again after the day at Cawsand, and she'd been thankful later that no baby had been conceived. Now, she thought about starting a fresh family, and wondered if it were really possible.

'David . . . do you really want . . . I mean, I'd love to have your baby – your babies – but I'm forty-two, and you're forty-nine. I've got grown-up children . . .' She caught her breath. 'A grown-up daughter, anyway,' she amended sadly. 'And a grandson.'

'So what lucky children they'll be,' he said. 'And what a shame to deprive any of them of each other.'

Lucy laughed. 'David, you're ridiculous! But would you really like us to have children?' She thought of Stevie and caught at his hand. 'Oh, I'm sorry. Of course you would. And I'd like to give them to you. I *want* to give them to you.'

'And I want to give them to you,' he said quietly. 'A family is something to share. And it would change things for us both. We'd have to think very seriously about the hotel, and even about staying in Plymouth. It's still such a mess – there's so much rebuilding yet to do – and I'd like to bring children up in the country. Somewhere like this place, where they can grow up in peaceful surroundings.' He hesitated, then added, 'Perhaps it's not something we should plan anyway. Suppose we just leave it to chance? Or to God's will if you like to think of it that way.'

'Yes,' she said softly, 'yes I think I do.'

They were sitting quietly, hand in hand, when Jilly came

out of the house. Her slender figure had rounded into maturity since baby William's birth, and her face had a new serenity, though there was still a deep sadness in her cornflower eyes. She had just finished feeding the baby, and she laid him in Lucy's lap, where he gazed up at the drifting leaves, golden and tan against the milky blue sky, and blew small, pearly bubbles.

'He really is like his daddy,' Lucy said, looking down at him with tenderness. She touched his silky, auburn hair with one fingertip, scarcely able to believe that she could ever have refused to acknowledge that he was her grandson. He shifted his gaze from the leaves and looked into her face, and her eyes misted. Geoff, she thought, Geoff, where are you? What happened to you, out there in Korea?

Nothing had ever been heard about him. It was eight months since they had heard he was missing, and the presumption of death meant only that his body had not been found. Sometimes men who had been presumed dead did turn up, usually in a prisoner-of-war camp, but it was very rare. As the months went by, nobody really expected to see Geoff again.

Nobody, that is, except Jilly, who refused to lose hope.

'I wish his daddy could see him,' Jilly said, crouching beside the deckchair. 'I mean, I know he will one day, but I wish he could see him *now*. It's such a shame he's missing so much.'

'His own father missed him as a baby,' Lucy said, remembering Wilmot's first long absence, when Geoffrey had been born. 'But at least I could send photographs. I went to the studios twice and he took some lovely portraits of Geoff lying on a rug, and me holding him. And my uncle Jim took some snaps too. We didn't have a camera of our own, of course, not many people did then.'

Jilly didn't have a camera either, but Geoff had had one and left it with her when he went away. She had taken several films of the baby already, but she had no one to send them to.

'I'm putting them all in an album,' she said. 'Geoff'll want to see them when he comes back.'

Lucy sighed. In a way, it was good to see the girl so certain. You could see she wasn't going to forget Geoff, that she'd truly loved him and still did, that if things had been different she would have been a good wife to him and made him happy. But it was cruel, the heartbreak that she must suffer in the end when she was forced to admit that her baby's father was never coming back. And she'd have to face it eventually, Lucy thought. You couldn't go on living on hope for ever, not when it was false hope.

'That's a good idea,' she said gently. 'You'll value it yourself in later years. I often wish I could have had photos of the children when they were little. Especially Zannah.' She sighed. There was only one picture of Zannah, sitting on Wilmot's knee in a studio portrait of the whole family. It had been taken just before he went away the last time.

'It must have been terrible for you, losing your little girl,' Jilly said. 'I can't imagine anything worse than losing your child.'

'There isn't anything worse. And you never really get over it. You just learn to put the feeling away somewhere in your mind. Like an oyster with a pearl, I suppose, except that it never turns into anything beautiful like a pearl, and it always hurts just as much if you take it out again.'

'Perhaps oysters don't think pearls are beautiful,' Jilly said, and Lucy laughed.

'Perhaps not.' She paused for a moment. 'Jilly, what are you going to do? Will you stay here with your mother?'

'I don't know. I've been thinking about it. I'll need to work, to earn money for us both. I wondered . . . I wondered if I could come back to the hotel.'

'The hotel?' Lucy was startled. 'Back to Plymouth? Would you really want to do that, Jilly?' She thought of the conversation she had had with David, their agreement that children would be better brought up in the country, away from the rubble and turmoil of a slowly recovering Plymouth. 'It would be lovely to have you there,' she added quickly, and looked down at the baby again. Having him there in the hotel, growing up under her eyes, a new life, another Geoff . . . 'But you don't have to come back to work. Just live with us, if that's what you want.'

Jilly shook her head. 'No. That wouldn't be right. I couldn't be a burden on you. We've got to earn our living, pay our way.'

'You wouldn't be a burden. It's the least I can do.' Lucy paused again, surprised by the feeling that had welled up inside her. 'Jilly, if it hadn't been for me you wouldn't have to worry about money, about earning a living, you'd have a pension from the Army, you'd have money for the baby. I owe it to you –'

'No. No, you don't owe it to me. It was our choice that we did what we did, Geoff and me. We wanted to be married so we pretended we were. And now it's my responsibility – until Geoff comes back.' She looked at Lucy, and Lucy saw the fear glimmer in the depths of her eyes, the fear that Geoff never would come back. She's beginning to realise it, Lucy thought, she's beginning to realise it and she's afraid to take it in, she's afraid of the awful grief she'd have to bear.

And in the same moment, she realised that there was more than one way in which she could offer support to the girl. Money was not the only thing she had to give.

'You can come to us any time you like,' she said, gently. 'You can come and work, if that's what you want, or you can just come and live with us. We're your family now, Jilly.' She turned to the man at her side, who had remained silent and watchful during all their conversation. 'David and Patsy and me – and you and William. That's right, isn't it, David?'

He nodded, and she felt an overwhelming gratitude, for they had not discussed this, hadn't taken Jilly's plans into account when making their own, and she knew that they might yet be called upon to make sacrifices. But did that matter, when they had all they wanted anyway? Almost all, she amended, thinking with a pang of her lost son. Even so, they could afford to be generous.

And if Jilly were right, and Geoff did come back . . . well, then there would be nothing more to ask, nothing in the whole of the world.

After that last mild weekend in early November, winter came crashing upon them. Back in London, David wrote that he was having some difficulty in selling the house he had bought. At the same time, he was packing up his belongings – not many, since he had lost almost everything he had owned in the house that had been bombed, and had gathered only a few sticks of furniture since. His arm was still troubling him a little, so progress was slow, but he was determined to be ready for their wedding, a week before Christmas.

Lucy was in the hotel, still trying to decide what to do about Jilly. She wanted to help the girl, and she longed to have her little grandson with her, but she dared not hold out hopes for a future that might never be realised. Suppose she and David decided after all to sell the hotel – what would Jilly do then? And what about Patsy? She couldn't be abandoned. There was so much to consider.

In the end, she asked Patsy for her own opinion and, as usual, Patsy came up with her own brand of pragmatic commonsense.

'I don't know why you worry so much about things, Mum. It's simple. You and David go and live in the country and let me and Jilly run the hotel.'

Lucy stared at her. 'What?'

'We're perfectly capable of it,' Patsy said patiently. 'I do all the accounts as it is, and Jilly knows about the housekeeping side and the cooking. We'd make a good team. And you could go off and live your own life. It's about time you did, after all.'

'But the hotel's been my life,' Lucy said, bemused.

'Then it's time it wasn't. Look, Mum, you've built it up from an ordinary little guest house to what it is now. You've done a wonderful job. But you never really intended to run a hotel, did you – not when you first married Dad?'

'Well, no, not really. I was going to be an ordinary naval wife, bringing up a family – that's all I really wanted. And then when he left the Navy I suppose he'd have found some other job and I'd have gone with him, wherever that was. But the war changed all that, and afterwards the opportunities were there –'

'And you took them. And now you've got another opportunity to live your life whichever way you want. You're getting married again. You can start fresh. A *new* life – not the remains of the old one.' Patsy leaned forwards and gripped Lucy's hand. 'It's a chance for you, Mum – and it's a chance for me too.'

'For *you*?'

'Yes. Don't you see – I don't want to be dependent on you all my life, just because I'm in a wheelchair. If I could walk, I'd be earning my own living, making my own life.' Her voice grew lower. 'I'd be getting married, having my own children. Well, maybe I can't do those things, but I can still earn my living. I'm doing that now, aren't I?'

'Yes. Yes, you are. But –'

'No buts, Mum. I could run this place. All I need is a pair of legs – and that'd be no problem if Jilly could be here. She could run all the practical side with one hand tied behind her back.'

'But she's so young,' Lucy said helplessly. 'And she's got a baby.'

'I don't think anyone's young these days,' Patsy said. 'We

all had to grow up fast during the war. And women grew up faster than anyone else.' She looked at her mother and said seriously, 'Think about it, Mum. I'd love to run this hotel myself, and I'd like Jilly to help me. It's a chance for all of us.'

Put simply, like that, it seemed the obvious solution. Yet Lucy could not quite bring herself to accept it. She thought about it, wrote to David and, when he came to Plymouth again, discussed it with him endlessly.

'Patsy's so keen, I can hardly bear to refuse her, but I just can't believe they could manage. There's such a lot to managing a hotel and Jilly's hardly more than a child. And she's got her own baby to look after. I don't know what to do, David.'

'You don't have to do anything,' he said. 'You can leave things just as they are. Or you can invite Jilly to Plymouth and let her work with you and Patsy. Let them take a lot of the work off your shoulders, and see how they manage. And just wait.'

'Wait? What for?'

'Something will happen,' he said, smiling at her. 'Something always does. Life doesn't stand still, Lucy, my darling. Something will happen, one day, to show you what to do, and I have a feeling it will be something good.'

Lucy looked at him and saw the darkness in his eyes, the love and the tenderness that shone in their depths. A baby, she thought, with a quickening of her heart. Our baby. Yes, that would tell me what to do.

Preparations for the wedding went ahead. The hotel needed some redecoration – with new paints and wallpapers coming on to the market almost daily, Lucy wanted to give the foyer a smart new look. Most of her family were coming from Portsmouth and she wanted to make a good impression.

'I need a good costume as well,' she said to Patsy. 'I

thought perhaps something in blue. It's always been my colour.'

'Yes.' Patsy looked at her mother. Her hair, once the flaming bronze of autumn leaves, had softened to a warm, burnished copper, with just a few silver hairs like streaks of sunshine. Her figure was as slender as ever, and she still bore herself tall and proud. Her skin, translucent as bone china, glowed with her new happiness; she looked as if a lamp had been lit somewhere within.

'You'll look beautiful in blue,' Patsy said. 'A good strong blue, not too light but not dark either. A sort of delphinium colour.'

They went shopping for it together, Lucy pushing Patsy's wheelchair into the big new Dingle's and Spooner's stores, where they could reach every department by lift. They wandered for hours, gazing at the new products that were coming into the shops now, looking at glassware and china as well as clothes, and by the time they emerged Lucy was dazed.

'I can't believe I've spent so much money on myself.'

'It'll be well worth it. You look lovely in that suit.' They had found a costume in exactly the shade of blue that suited Lucy best, a delphinium just as Patsy had suggested. It brought out the deep violet of her eyes, and deepened the auburn tone of her hair. They had found a small confection of a hat that matched it, and Lucy had picked black patent shoes and bag. And Patsy had not been forgotten. For her, there was a warm winter dress in gold and deep brown, with a full skirt that would drape sumptuously across her legs in her chair.

'You'll be my bridesmaid,' Lucy said, pushing the chair back along the newly built Royal Parade, so different from the old streets of Plymouth. 'You'll follow me up the aisle.'

'We'll have to think who's going to push me, then,' Patsy remarked, and then giggled. 'A fine pair David and I are going to look – him with one arm and me with no legs! People will think you're starting a nursing home.'

'Patsy! What a thing to say.' But Lucy laughed too. Then her face grew sad. 'Who do you think I should have to give me away? There's only Grampy, or my brother Kenny. If Geoff had been here . . .'

They moved along the wide pavement in silence, each thinking of Geoff. It was over eight months now since he had been posted *missing, presumed dead*, and there had been no further news. His personal belongings would be returned soon, and they all knew there was little hope of his turning up. Only Jilly clung fiercely to her belief that he was still alive somewhere, and nobody had the heart to try to persuade her otherwise. She would accept it in her own time, and you couldn't hurry such sadness along.

'Patsy, sometimes I feel so guilty,' Lucy said suddenly. 'Being so happy, planning to get married again, when we don't even know what happened to him. It seems so callous, so *cold.*'

'I know.' One of the nice things about Patsy was that she never told you not to be silly, or that you were worrying unnecessarily. 'It's all happened so quickly, hasn't it? Geoff going away, and then the bad news. Jilly and the baby. And then you and David. I'm not surprised it makes you feel strange, it makes me positively dizzy at times. But I don't think you need to feel guilty, Mum. Geoff would have been thrilled about you and David. You know how much he always thought of him.'

'Yes.' He looked on him like a father, Lucy thought, more than he ever looked on Wilmot. Poor Wilmot. How different it would have been for him if there had been no war. He would have grown into a fine man, even-tempered and good-humoured.

'If Geoff does come back,' Patsy went on quietly, 'he'll be glad to see you and David married.'

'I know. I know he would. But – oh, Patsy –' Lucy's

voice broke – 'do you realise, he wouldn't even know his
father's dead? We'd have to tell him all that. It's almost too
awful to think about.'

A cloud drifted across the sun. The brightness of the day
seemed suddenly dimmed, and the clothes they had bought
no longer exciting. Lucy pushed Patsy's chair the rest of the
way home in silence, glad that her daughter could not see
her face. At last they came to Lockyer Street and she paused
at the foot of the ramp.

'I am doing the right thing, aren't I, Patsy? It seems so
soon after Geoff – and your father . . .'

Patsy turned her head to look up into her mother's face.
Her lips were smiling but her voice was grave as she said,
'Of course you're doing the right thing, Mum. You've
loved David for a long time. You deserve your happiness.
And no one would begrudge you that for an instant.' She
paused. 'Life has to go on, you know, and there's no law to
say you can't be happy more than once.'

As she spoke, the sun came out again from behind its
cloud and shone down on her, illuminating her smile and
gleaming on her bright, coppery hair. Lucy gazed at her,
wondering why it was that this daughter, who had been so
badly treated by life, had so much wisdom in her heart. And
then she smiled back.

'Let's go indoors,' she said, 'and try on these gorgeous
clothes again.'

Everything was arranged. The repainting and papering was
complete, and the hotel looked bright and inviting once
more. Lucy's new costume hung in her wardrobe and she
opened the door a dozen times a day to gaze at it. She felt
like a young bride again, and even more so when David took
her into the best jeweller's shop in Plymouth and bought
her an engagement ring.

'David! I hadn't even thought about it.'

'I had, though.' He slipped the sparkling diamond on to

340

her finger and kissed her lips. 'We're only going to do this once,' he said, 'and I want to do it all properly. My darling Lucy.'

'Oh, David.' Her lips trembled under his. It can't be happening like this, she thought, dazed, we're two middle-aged people, we can't be feeling as if we were just eighteen . . . But that was exactly how she did feel. The love and happiness bubbled up inside her, as it had over twenty years ago, and it felt just the same. Perhaps it always did.

They bought a wedding-ring too, but David kept this and she suspected that he looked at it as often as she looked at her diamond. She wished there were something she could give him, and eventually settled on a new watch. He tried it on and she admired it before taking it away again.

'You can have it the day before the wedding, so that you can wear it then.'

The day was close now. All the arrangements were made for the family in Portsmouth to come by train, and Jilly was back at the hotel and taking over the cooking once more. No more had been said about her and Patsy managing the hotel, but Lucy knew that the idea had not gone away, and she found herself considering it more and more seriously.

She took Jilly shopping as well, and they bought a blue dress, a shade or two lighter than Lucy's, which set off her dark hair and exactly matched her cornflower eyes. 'You can walk behind me up the aisle,' she said. 'I want you and Patsy both there. You're a daughter to me now.'

On the last afternoon, she closed the door of the hotel behind her and walked up to the Hoe alone. David was staying in a neighbouring hotel – it was unlucky, Maud had said firmly, for the groom to see the bride on the night before the wedding – and Lucy glanced about her cautiously as she walked up the street, afraid that he too might be walking on the Hoe. But there were few people about on this cold, murky December day, and she pushed her hands deep into her coat pockets and stepped out briskly, feeling the sting of icy air on her cheeks.

How much had happened since she had first come here, she mused, leaning over the rails to look at the little rock pools and the big half-moon swimming-bath. Young and eagerly in love, it had seemed that nothing could mar the happiness she and Wilmot had shared. For a moment, she felt sad again, but then she reminded herself of Patsy's words. Life had to go on – and there was no law to say you couldn't be happy more than once. Whatever Wilmot had suffered, it was over now and he was at peace. Lucy's task was to go on living, to go forward and to enjoy the happiness she had been granted anew.

She gazed down at the pools. The big pool was closed for the winter and empty, ready to receive its annual spring-clean. The others were filled with green sea-water. In summer they were alive with boys and young men, showing off their swimming and diving prowess. Geoff himself had learned to swim down there. Now, they too were deserted.

Lucy felt the tears sting her eyes and for a moment she seemed to see the figures of her husband and son diving into the pools, racing each other, laughing and teasing . . . And then the vision faded and she knew that the cries she heard were those of seagulls, and the figures she saw were nothing but spray. The boy and the man had gone for ever.

Goodbye, Wilmot my dear, she thought, and then she turned away and began to walk back along the wide expanse of the Hoe.

It was fast growing dark. Only a few hurrying figures were visible now in the chilly dusk. She passed them without a glance, and then one in particular caught her eye. There was something familiar about the gait, something about the build and the set of the shoulders that she knew. Something she had always known.

Lucy stopped and stood rigidly still. Her heart felt as if it had ceased to beat.

'No,' she whispered. 'No, it can't be . . .' Her mind went back, almost frantically, to the vision she had thought she saw down there on the rocks a moment or two before. The boy and the man, lost and gone for ever. And yet here they were before her, the two merged into one striding figure, one man who approached and then saw her and hesitated, just as she was hesitating, and then came on faster, finally breaking into a run and calling her name.

'Mum! *Mum!*'

'Geoff . . .' Lucy breathed, and her hands fluttered to her throat. 'Oh, *Geoff* . . .'

There was barely time to tell all, and they went to bed at last exhausted by the telling. It was almost too much for Geoffrey to take in. His father dead – his own son born – his mother on the verge of marriage . . . He shook his head, bemused, and didn't know whether to laugh or cry.

They needed to know his story too. How he had been captured and sent to a prisoner of war camp, had escaped almost as soon as he had arrived, and spent months hiding in the bleak Korean countryside before stumbling into a friendly village where he was cared for until he could be handed over to the Americans. He had been repatriated immediately, with no time to let his family know. It was clear that it would take weeks, perhaps months, to tell them, and perhaps they would never know it all.

'The good thing is, I've been invalided out of the Army,' he said, holding Jilly's hands tightly. 'Or will be, soon. I'll be staying at home. So I can take over here, Mum, if you want a rest.'

'Take over?' Lucy blinked. Once again, events were running away with her. She looked at him, suddenly afraid, wondering if he would have the same problems as his father. The pattern was frighteningly similar.

However, when everyone else had gone to bed, she crept into Patsy's room to see if there was anything her daughter needed, and Patsy dispelled her fears. 'It's a wonderful idea, Mum. Geoff knows what it is to run a hotel, and Jilly will be a marvellous help. And I'm happy to carry on doing what I've been doing. It's the answer to everything.'

'Is it? I hope so, Patsy – but I wonder. Your father never got over what happened to him. Suppose Geoff –'

'Geoff's different,' Patsy said firmly. 'He wasn't kept prisoner for years and beaten and tortured. He never lost control of his life – he kept it. He escaped and survived. He came back. And besides –' she grinned wickedly '– he's your son too, don't forget. He's just as bloody obstinate!'

'*Patsy*.' But Lucy was relieved by her daughter's words and she went to bed feeling comforted. Perhaps, after all, everything was turning out for the best. And the main thing was that Geoff was home again, safe and sound, and there would be another wedding in the family, just as soon as it could be arranged.

It was only as she drifted off to sleep that she realised that nobody had told David that Geoff was home.

After the chilly dampness of the day before, it came as a surprise to find the sun shining next morning. The sky was clear, the pale, milky blue of winter, and the air fresh and crisp. Everything seemed to be washed clean, and when Lucy looked out of her window towards Dartmoor she could see the tiny hilltop church of Brentor in the distance, like a finger pointing hopefully towards the sky.

The wedding was to be at eleven. There was good time to serve breakfast to all the family and guests, and then everyone vanished to their rooms to get ready, while the hotel staff rushed to prepare the dining-room so that they too could attend the service.

Flowers weren't easy to come by in December, but there were early daffodils from the Scilly Isles to brighten the dining-room, and hot-house roses for Lucy and the girls to carry. By some miracle, Geoff's uniform had been cleaned and pressed overnight and, when the cars arrived to take them all to church, he took his place beside his mother and they were the last to leave the hotel.

'I'm so glad you arrived when you did,' Lucy said, taking his hand. 'I did so much want you to be here, to give me away . . . Are you sure you don't mind, about me and David?'

'It's been a lot to take in,' he admitted, and she was instantly anxious.

'Should we have waited? Should we have postponed it?'

'*No.*' He squeezed her fingers. 'Don't jump at me, Mum! I was going to say, it's been a lot to take in – hearing about Dad, and seeing William. It'll take me a while to get used to it all. But as for you marrying David – no, that seems absolutely right. After all, he was always part of the family, wasn't he?'

'Yes,' Lucy said. 'Always.'

The taxi drew up outside the church. Inside, they could hear the notes of the organ. They walked into the porch and were met by Jilly, pushing Patsy in her wheelchair, and the priest who came forward smiling.

'Mr Tremaine's here and waiting as anxiously as a young bridegroom,' he murmured, and gave Lucy a broad smile. 'You look very, very nice, Mrs Pengelly.'

Mrs Pengelly. It was the last time she would be called that. When she walked through this door again, she would be Mrs Tremaine, married to the man she loved, and looking forward all over again to a life of new hope.

Geoff stepped beside her and she rested her arm in his and turned to smile at him. David still doesn't know, she thought. He still doesn't know that the boy he treated as a son, the boy whose life he once saved, has been brought back to us. And then the organ began its joyous pealing and they moved forward together, into the body of the church and up the aisle.

David stood before the altar. As the notes of the organ

changed, he turned towards them. He saw Geoff, and Lucy recognised the amazement, the incredulity and, finally, the sheer joy that illuminated his face. And then she could see nothing through her tears except the blaze of heartfelt love in his eyes, as he held out his hand towards her. And she knew that she could, at last, walk with confidence into the world of love and laughter.